The Lessons *of* Time

Giuseppe Ferrone

ISBN: 978-0-646-84004-8

First published in Australia in 2022 by Thorpe-Bowker Australia.

The Lessons of Time.

Cover design by Ross MacLennan of www.bookcoveraustralia.com

Typesetting by allinonebookdesign.com.au

The author can be contacted at giuseppeferrone@outlook.com

A catalogue record for this book is available from the National Library of Australia.

Author: Ferrone, Giuseppe, 1959-,

Genre: Fiction.

About the Author

Giuseppe Ferrone is a high school history teacher in Perth, Australia, with degrees in history, business, and education. He is passionate about the important lessons we can learn from the past – which inspired him to write this novel.

The author has also written two other books; both are historical non-fiction: *The History of Molise & Abruzzo Italy* published in 2020 and *Big History* published in 2021.

To get a more immersive experience from this book, readers are encouraged to listen to each song in between the chapters whil reading the lyrics.

The author welcomes your feedback by email at: giuseppeferrone@outlook.com

He has dedicated this book to his grandson, Luca.

Imagine

Imagine there's no heaven
It's easy if you try
No hell below us
Above us only sky
Imagine all the people
Living for today

Imagine there's no countries
It isn't hard to do
Nothing to kill or die for
And no religion too
Imagine all the people
Living life in peace

You may say I'm a dreamer
But I'm not the only one
I hope someday you'll join us
And the world will be as one

Imagine no possessions
I wonder if you can
No need for greed or hunger
A brotherhood of man
Imagine all the people
Sharing all the world

You may say I'm a dreamer
But I'm not the only one
I hope someday you'll join us
And the world will live as one

John Lennon (1971)

Contents

1	Prologue	9
2	Otto	21
3	Philip II of Macedonia	35
4	Julius Caesar	73
5	Charlemagne	111
6	Pope Urban II	153
7	Christopher Columbus	201
8	Otto von Bismarck	237
9	Franz Ferdinand	271
10	Vladimir Lenin	295
11	Adolf Hitler	335
12	Robert Oppenheimer	355
13	John F. Kennedy	401
14	Osama bin Laden	453

Prologue

My name is Luca Evangelista. As a high school history teacher I have often been fascinated by alternative history and the legitimacy of the butterfly effect. If events from the past are altered, how do these changes impact the future course of history? I am reminded of the following quotation from the 1990 book "Good Omens," by Terry Pratchett and Neil Gaiman:

> It used to be thought that the events that changed the world were things like big bombs, maniac politicians, huge earthquakes, or vast population movements, but it has now been realized that this is a very old-fashioned view held by people totally out of touch with modern thought. The things that change the world, according to Chaos theory, are the tiny things. A butterfly flaps its wings in the Amazonian jungle, and subsequently a storm ravages half of Europe."

Benjamin Franklin provides a poetic perspective in his interpretation of a proverb that has been around since the 14th century in English, and the 13th century in German, long before the concept of the butterfly effect was developed:

> for want of a nail the shoe was lost,
> for want of a shoe the horse was lost,
> for want of a horse the rider was lost,
> for want of a rider the battle was lost,
> for want of a battle the kingdom was lost,
> and all for the want of a horseshoe nail."

The lack of one horseshoe nail could be inconsequential, or it could indirectly cause a defeat in a war, resulting in the downfall of a kingdom.

There is no way to predict which outcome will occur.

The 19th century French mathematician and physicist Jules Henri Poincare had this to say about what we now refer to as the butterfly effect:

> A very small cause which escapes our notice determines a considerable effect that we cannot fail to see, and then we say the effect is due to chance. If we knew exactly the laws of nature and the situation of the universe at the initial moment, we could predict exactly the situation of that same universe at a succeeding moment. But even if it were the case that the natural laws had no longer any secret for us, we could still only know the initial situation approximately. If that enabled us to predict the succeeding situation with the same approximation, that is all we require, and we should say that the phenomenon had been predicted, that it is governed by laws. But it is not always so; it may happen that small differences in the initial conditions produce very great ones in the final phenomena. A small error in the former will produce an enormous error in the latter. Prediction becomes impossible, and we have the fortuitous phenomenon.

One of my favourite short stories I read as a teenager was Ray Bradbury's classic science fiction work, *A Sound of Thunder* which when published in 1952, predated the Chaos theory and the butterfly effect. Set in 2055, it tells the story of a man named Eckels who travels back in time 65 million years ago to shoot a dinosaur. Warned not to deviate from the tour guide's plan, Eckels (along with his guide and the guide's assistant) heads off to attempt to kill a Tyrannosaurus Rex that was going to soon die anyway from a falling tree landing on it. Eckels panics at the sight of the creature and steps off his given path treading on a butterfly in the process, leaving his guide to kill the T-Rex.

The guide is enraged and orders Eckels to remove the bullets from the dead dinosaur before they return to 2055. Upon arrival, he finds out that by stepping off the path, he killed the butterfly and changed the future. Eckels is confused to find that the world has changed. Language is altered, and an evil dictator is now in charge. A confused Eckels notices a crushed butterfly stuck to the sole of his boot, and realises that in stepping off the path, he killed the insect and changed the future.

Bradbury writes:

> Eckels felt himself fall into a chair. He fumbled crazily at the thick slime on his boots. He held up a clod of dirt, trembling, 'No, it cannot be. Not a little thing like that. No!' Embedded in the mud, glistening green and gold and black, was a butterfly, very beautiful and very dead. 'Not a little thing like that! Not a butterfly!' cried Eckels. It fell to the floor, an exquisite thing, a small thing that could upset balances and knock down a line of small dominoes and then big dominoes and then gigantic dominoes, all down the years across Time. Eckels' mind whirled. It couldn't change things. Killing one butterfly couldn't be that important! Could it?

Bradbury envisioned the passage of time as fragile and liable to be disturbed by minor changes. In the decades since the publication of *A Sound of Thunder*, physicists have examined its accuracy. Without the ability of time travel, there is no way of knowing how plausible the story is, beyond the use of predictive modelling. Bradbury's work raises the whole question of what time actually is, and whether it is predetermined by external causes, or can be changed by choice and free will.

Physicists refer to the Arrow of Time, the non-reversible progression of entropy or disorder. As time moves forward, matter becomes more and more chaotic, and does not spontaneously return to its original state. If you break an egg, it remains broken and cannot spontaneously re-form, for example. The Arrow of Time gives us a sense of the past, present, and future. The term was first used by the astronomer and physicist Arthur Eddington in 1927, who explained it as follows:

> Let us draw an arrow arbitrarily. If as we follow the arrow we find more and more of the random element in the state of the world, then the arrow is pointing towards the future; if the random element decreases, the arrow points towards the past. That is the only distinction known to physics. This follows at once if our fundamental contention is admitted that the introduction of randomness is the only thing which cannot be undone.

In short, the passage of time as we perceive it does exist, conditional to the existence of entropy. As long as entropy is non-reversible, time can be said to exist. The closest thing we have to a true measurement of time is a measurement of entropy. If the progression of time is nothing but a journey towards chaos, it makes sense for small changes to affect the future by amplifying chaos.

We do not yet know if entropy creates time, or is a by-product of it. Subsequently, we do not know if changing the past will change the future. Would stepping on a butterfly shift the path of entropy? Did Eckels move off the path because of his own free will, or was that event already predetermined? Was the dystopian totalitarian future that he returned to always meant to be? These interconnected concepts; entropy, the butterfly effect, Chaos theory, determinism, free will, and time travel; have captured many imaginations since their discoveries. Films ranging from "It's a Wonderful Life" to "Donnie Darko" to the "The Butterfly Effect," and more recently "Inception" and "Interstellar," have explored these complexities of cause and effect. We like to think we can predict the future and exercise a degree of control over powerful systems such as the weather and the economy. Yet the butterfly effect shows that we cannot.

The systems around us are chaotic and entropic, prone to sudden change. For some kinds of systems, we can try to create favourable starting conditions, and we can be mindful of the kinds of catalysts that might act on those conditions; but that's as far as our human power extends. If we think that we can identify every catalyst, and control and predict outcomes, we are only setting ourselves up to fail.

In one of Stephen King's great novels, *11/22/63*, a young man named Jake discovers a portal in the pantry of a diner, which leads back to 1958. After a few visits and some experiments, Jake deduces that altering history is possible. However long he stays in the past, only two minutes go by in the present. He decides to live in the past until 1963, so he can prevent the assassination of President John F. Kennedy, believing that this change will greatly benefit humanity.

After years of stalking Lee Harvey Oswald, Jake manages to prevent him from shooting Kennedy. Upon returning to the present, he expects to find the world improved as a result. Instead, the opposite has happened. Earthquakes occur everywhere, his old home is in ruins, and nuclear war has destroyed much of the world. As King said: "*Not good to fool with Father Time.*" In addition to being a masterful work of speculative fiction, *11/22/63* is a classic example of how everything in the world is interconnected.

Although the concept of the butterfly effect has long been debated, the identification of it as a distinct effect is credited to Edward Lorenz (1917-2008). Lorenz was a meteorologist and mathematician who successfully combined the two disciplines to create chaos theory. During the 1950s, Lorenz searched for a means of predicting the weather, as he found linear models to be ineffective. In an experiment to model a weather prediction, he entered the initial conditions as 0.506, instead of 0.506127. The result was surprising: a somewhat different prediction. From this, he deduced that the weather must turn on a whim and a dime.

A tiny change in the initial conditions had enormous long-term implications. By 1963, he had formulated his ideas enough to publish an award-winning paper titled: "Deterministic Non-Periodic Flow." In this paper, Lorenz states that weather prediction models are inaccurate because knowing the precise starting conditions is impossible, and a tiny change can throw off the results. To make this concept understandable to non-scientific audiences, Lorenz began to use the butterfly analogy. In speeches and interviews, he explained that a butterfly has the potential to create tiny changes which, while not creating a typhoon, could alter its trajectory. A flapping wing represents the miniscule changes in atmospheric pressure, and these changes compound as a model progresses. Given that small, nearly imperceptible changes can have massive implications in complex systems, Lorenz concluded that attempts to predict the weather were impossible.

The butterfly effect is humbling to us humans. It is a model that exposes the flaws in other models. It shows our understanding of science, and the scientific method, to be less accurate than we assume, as we have no means of making accurate predictions, due to the exponential growth of errors. Before the ground-breaking work of Lorenz, people assumed that an approximate idea of initial conditions would lead to an approximate prediction of the outcome.

In his book, *Chaos: Making a New Science*, James Gleick writes:

> The models would churn through complicated, somewhat arbitrary webs of equations, meant to turn measurements of initial conditions into a simulation of future trends. The programmers hoped the results were not too grossly distorted by the many unavoidable simplifying assumptions. If a model did anything too bizarre, the programmers would revise the equations to bring the output back in line with expectation. Models proved dismally blind to what the future would bring, but many people who should have known better, acted as though they believed the results." One philosopher declared: "The basic idea of Western science is that you don't have to take into account the falling of a leaf on some planet in another galaxy, when you're trying to account for the motion of a billiard ball on a pool table on Earth.

At the cutting edge of cosmology, is the theory of a multiverse. Advances in astrophysics over the past 30 years have led cosmologists to the mind-expanding conclusion that the universe we inhabit is just one of many in existence – perhaps an infinite number. If this theory is right, then the billions of galaxies and trillions of stars in our known universe, are but a tiny fraction of an incomprehensibly vast array, that is known as the multiverse.

As the MIT physicist Max Tegmark wrote in his 2014 book, Our Mathematical Universe:

> Our entire universe may be just one element, one atom, as it were, in an infinite ensemble; a cosmic archipelago.

If a multiverse exists, Tegmark argues it includes

> ... parallel universes where you never get a parking ticket, where you won a million-dollar lottery, where you have a different name, where Germany won World War II, where dinosaurs still roam the Earth, and where Earth never formed in the first place.

One of the theories behind a multiverse is the idea that the universe expanded at a mind-boggling speed in the fraction of a second after the Big Bang. During this period of inflation, there were quantum fluctuations which caused separate bubble universes to pop into existence, and themselves start inflating and blowing bubbles. Russian physicist Andrei Linde came up with this concept, which suggests an infinity of universes no longer in any causal connection with one another – so, in other words, they are free to develop in different ways – including differing laws of physics.

Cosmic space is big – perhaps infinitely so. Travel far enough and some theories suggest you would meet your cosmic twin – a copy of you, living in a copy of our world, but in a different part of the multiverse. String theory, predicts a randomly large number of universes, all with slightly different physical parameters. The most interesting, is the quantum multiverse theory. Physicist Hugh Everett came up with this idea; which is predicted by his "many worlds" interpretation of quantum physics. Everett's theory is that quantum effects cause the universe to constantly split. It could mean that decisions we make in this version of Earth within this universe, have direct implications for other versions of ourselves and Earths, living in parallel universes – creating a butterfly effect.

Why am I sharing all of this with you? Well, because all of these concepts dramatically entered my world when I encountered the beings from the Vega star system. My life as a humble high school history teacher was turned on its head and changed forever. Here is my story, starting with that fateful morning in my classroom!

Across the Universe

Words are flowing out like endless rain into a paper cup
They slither wildly as they slip away across the universe
Pools of sorrow, waves of joy are drifting through my opened mind
Possessing and caressing me

Jai guru deva, om
Nothing's gonna change my world
Nothing's gonna change my world
Nothing's gonna change my world
Nothing's gonna change my world

Images of broken light which dance before me like a million eyes
They call me on and on across the universe
Thoughts meander like a restless wind inside a letterbox
They tumble blindly as they make their way across the universe

Jai guru deva, om
Nothing's gonna change my world
Nothing's gonna change my world
Nothing's gonna change my world
Nothing's gonna change my world

Sounds of laughter shades of life are ringing
Through my open ears inciting and inviting me
Limitless undying love which shines around me like a million suns
It calls me on and on across the universe

Jai guru deva, om
Nothing's gonna change my world
Nothing's gonna change my world
Nothing's gonna change my world
Nothing's gonna change my world
Jai guru deva

Jai guru deva
Jai guru deva
Jai guru deva
Jai guru deva
Jai guru deva

The Beatles
John Lennon and Paul McCartney (1968)

2

Otto

Perth, Australia, February 2022

'THE ONLY TIME ANYBODY HEARD ADOLF HITLER CRY WAS when he placed the cyanide capsule between the teeth of his dog Blondie and snapped his mouth shut, killing his beloved German shepherd almost instantly, just before he and Eva Braun then proceeded to commit suicide.'

'Why did he kill his dog, Mr Evangelista?' James nervously asked from the front row of the classroom.

I looked directly at James, he was a highly intelligent and sensitive young man, who I thought was understanding for the first time, the depth of human depravity, and the extent to which one individual can influence the course of history in such a profoundly negative way. I drew a deep breath.

'He wanted to make absolutely certain the cyanide capsule would do the job, James. In fact, he still wasn't satisfied, so when the time came to end their lives, as well as biting on the capsule, Hitler also shot himself in the right temple with his hand revolver, while at the same time Eva took her cyanide.'

'Why did Hitler commit suicide?' I heard Ella ask from the desk directly behind James.

I felt bad about having to separate Ella and James, right at the beginning of the school year. It was common knowledge in the school that they were in a relationship. I could relate to how they felt being separated. But it was for their own good. I had met my ex-wife in high school. We hooked up in Year 10 at the age of 15, just like these kids did, last year. Were James and Ella destined to become husband and wife too?

'From deep down in the bunker, in the centre of Berlin, 30 metres underground, Hitler could hear the Russian tanks rolling in and machine gunfire getting louder and louder, closer and closer. As delusional as he was, he finally realized the war was lost. He blamed everybody other than himself right up to his last breath. He wasn't about to be captured alive and paraded around humiliatingly by the Russians like a circus animal. Hitler knew what was in store for him if the Russians got their hands on him. Mussolini had been captured by Italian partisans only days earlier, while trying to make an escape out of Italy with German assistance. When they captured him, they shot and killed him and his mistress Clara Petacci, and then strung their lifeless bodies upside down in a Milan square for the whole world to see. Hitler wasn't about to suffer the same fate.'

'What happened in those last few hours in the bunker sir?' asked Chris, James' best friend and Ella's twin brother.

'On the morning of 30th April 1945, Hitler met with his generals in one last-ditch desperate attempt to muster some kind of resistance to the Allied advance. With a sprawling map of Berlin and surrounding areas laid out on a conference table, he barked orders about non-existent troop movements. It was clear to his generals that he had become totally delusional. After repeated attempts to remind the Fuhrer that these forces had already been defeated, Hitler unleashed his final ferocious outburst, blaming his incompetent generals for Germany's defeat. He was distraught and emotionally spent. The war had been lost. At lunchtime he sat down with Eva for his last meal, a simple dish of pasta and tomato sauce; then what Eva had dreamed about for over 15 years finally came to fruition; they got married! Champagne and cake was shared amongst the loyal entourage before the couple shut themselves away in their room and committed the final act. Hitler had instructed his adjunct to take their lifeless bodies to the surface, smother them with kerosene, and burn the bodies to the point of charred remains. He didn't want the Russians to recognize the bodies when they arrived later that afternoon.'

I glanced at the clock, the lesson had only fifteen minutes left in it. This gave me enough time to talk about the end of the fighting in the Pacific which of course ultimately brought about the end of World War Two. I knew the discussions were going to centre around the reasons the United States dropped the two atomic bombs. Sure enough, when I opened up the class for questions, James shot his hand up.

'Sir, do you think it was necessary for the USA to drop those two atomic bombs?'

'President Truman was a good and moral man. He was traumatized by that decision. In his autobiography he rationalized it by stating the Japanese had made it very clear they were not going to surrender, but instead every man, woman and child was going to defend the homeland to the bitter end. Truman realized for the USA to conventionally win the war, a massive land invasion of Japan was required. This would involve literally millions of allied forces and the end result would have been a bloodbath, with millions of military and civilian lives lost, and the war being prolonged for a number of years. The alternative he reasoned, was to drop one atomic bomb on a smaller Japanese city, and show them the awesome destructive power of this nuclear weapon, forcing them to unconditionally surrender. Although hundreds of thousands of lives were lost, this was far less than the millions that would die from a full scale invasion, and the war could be ended quickly. After the Hiroshima bomb was dropped on 6th August 1945, they didn't surrender! So three days later a second bomb was dropped on Nagasaki, and then the emperor was forced to unconditionally surrender, ending the War.'

'And the end result is we now have a world terrorized by nuclear weapons,' shouted Bradley from the back row.

'Yes Bradley, that's true. Once we unleash a technological Jeannie, we can't put it back in the bottle. This is one of the big fallacies of the human condition. Science and technology has brought humanity many wonderful things, but the downside is our relentless thirst for discovery, invention, conquest, power, and wealth accumulation has also directly led to the global problems we face today; not just nuclear weapons, but also global warming, overpopulation, pandemics, and resource depletion, to name a few more.'

'I wish I could go back in time and undo the Industrial Revolution and the development of nuclear weapons,' said James, in a voice laced with quivering emotion.

I didn't know why at the time, but that heartfelt statement hit me like a ton of bricks! Was it the sincerity of James that garnered my deep guttural reaction, or was it something I felt instinctively from what was about to unfold at the end of the lesson?

I was looking forward to the end of the lesson. I had the next period free and was planning to reply to numerous emails from parents and the school administration, while enjoying a cappuccino from the school's recently acquired automatic coffee machine. I also made a mental note not to forget to book a nice restaurant to celebrate Isabella's thirtieth birthday. Nobody believed our relationship would last. We were like chalk and cheese. Different backgrounds. Different life experiences. The emotional and physical abuse she suffered as a young girl, wasn't her fault. Yet she had demonstrated enormous courage and dignity to escape her struggles, strengthen her will, and pursue her dream of becoming a theatrical actor and soul-jazz singer. I was incredibly proud of her. Her experience had left a permanent scar on her though. She had great difficultly letting go and trusting a man.

She shuddered every time I told her I was her protector and guardian angel; but I was. I was determined she wasn't ever going to suffer any more. I owed it to her to put on a big celebration for her milestone birthday. So in addition to the romantic dinner I was about to organise in the only revolving restaurant in town, thirty-three floors up, with a breathtaking view of the wider metropolis; I was also in the process of arranging a function for about thirty of our closest family and friends. I knew she was going to jump up and down about me making such a fuss over her; but it was the least I could do. The fact of the matter was I didn't rescue her; she rescued me.

As I was sitting at my desk, a man whom I had never seen before walked into my classroom.

'Can I help you with anything?'

'Luca Evangelista, you are a gifted teacher. If there were more of your type in this world, there wouldn't be the dire problems facing this planet now.'

'Excuse me, who are you?'

'I am your benefactor. I have been observing you for some time. You are the chosen one. I searched this planet long and hard. I found you.'

'I don't understand. Do you have a child at this school? I can direct you to the school administration building if you like.'

'All of you on this planet are my children. I have been watching the development of your civilization for a long time from afar. It took all of my powers of persuasion to have Earth included in our Program.'

'What Program? What is your name? Who are you? Do I need to go and call for assistance?'

'You can call me Otto. I like that name.'

'How can I help you Otto? What did you mean by the Program?'

Otto came to the front of the classroom and sat on the desk closest to my table. He closed his eyes. Suddenly the room was in total pitch darkness. His eyes lit up brilliantly, laser-like, temporarily blinding me; and an image appeared on the whiteboard. It was surreal. His eyes were flickering rapidly, as if processing huge amounts of data in nanoseconds. I saw horror! Cities destroyed and underwater. Masses of people starving. Waves of displaced refugees. Piles of dead bodies being dumped into open pits. Wasted tracts of barren agricultural land. Dead animal carcasses. Nuclear missiles launching from mountainous locations and submarines. Horrific blinding mushroom clouds. I was stunned. I could see all of these images were coming directly from his thoughts. His face was cold, hard, and stone-like, totally devoid of any emotion.

'What is this Otto? Who are you?!'

'This is the fate of your planet if we don't intervene.'

'What do you mean by intervene?'

'I am not from your world. I am from another world. A planet within what you call the Vega star system, 25 light years from Earth.'

I was absolutely flabbergasted!

'Do you expect me to believe this?'

Even as I said that, I had seen enough to understand this 'man' was not from our world. It wasn't only the unbelievable technological prowess I witnessed, but also an aura of wisdom, serenity, and self-assurance about him, the likes of which I had never seen from any human being.

'A tactical nuclear war between China and the United States over Taiwan in 2024. Mass starvation, the total submersion of cities underwater, and a refugee exodus on a massive scale; as a direct result of global warming, by 2045. A Third World War in 2053; and a global totalitarian government emerging from the survivors and ashes. Do you want me to go on?'

'No,' I said softly, feeling defeated. 'Please don't go on.'

'I am here as your benefactor, to help reverse these horrific events, and I have selected you to change the course of your world's history.'

'Sure sure……How do you expect me to do that?'

'We are much more advanced than you are. For many Earth centuries we have been using our Program to help civilizations like yours, those that have gone off the rails and reached a point of no return, to change their past and avert disaster. The turning point for us was when we developed the ability to travel across interstellar space faster than the speed of light, with wormhole technology. We can use this technology to hone in on any civilization within a 1,000 light-years radius of our planet. You will be surprised how many civilizations there are within 1,000 light years of our Vega star system. Earth is number 142 in our Program.'

'Why me Otto, why me?'

'You consider yourself to be a global citizen and really care about this planet. You are a passionate humanist, quick witted, and courageous. You have a deep understanding of the historical events that you will be seeking to undo.'

'Hang on my friend, what do you mean "seeking to undo"?'

'As I said, I have been studying your planet and its history for some time. It was my decision to select Earth for the Program, but I came up with fierce opposition from Thero.'

'Who the hell is Thero?'

'Thero is a member of our Ruling Council and has something against your planet. He doesn't want it to be salvaged. He wants your Earth to suffer its current fate of destruction. Thero has travelled widely to many other worlds. I believe he worked closely with an alien civilization that visited your Earth and assisted the Egyptians.'

'The Egyptians?!'

'Yes. Thero and the alien civilization planted the seeds of a great empire within ancient Egypt fully expecting those seeds of wisdom would position the Earth to flourish and avoid the major problems it finds itself in now.'

'So how did you manage to get the Earth into your Program then, Otto?'

'I persuaded the majority of our Ruling Council members that the

Earth was worth saving. I showed them that human beings, although complex, and capable of great evil and destruction, are also emotional creatures equally capable of love, empathy, and creativity. This combination is uncommon amongst the civilizations we have visited. Thero did not accept the decision and fled to the other planet. I shall call it Planet X. I fear he may try and stop you.'

'Stop me? Stop me from doing what?'

'From travelling back into your historical time of course, and changing a number of major events which I have identified,' replied Otto somewhat surprised.

'What events?'

'There's 12 of them. If you change them all, the forces of universal time, space, matter, and energy, will create a ripple effect which will alter the future of your planet to one of perpetual peace, creative intellectual flourishment, and harmony. Each event is independent of the others. So by changing any one of these historical events, we will not be changing any of the other subsequent events. That's why each event has to be visited and changed separately. The butterfly effect and Chaos theory developed by you humans do not quite apply in the manner in which you understand them. We have highly sophisticated computer simulations which were able to pinpoint the 12 events that need to be changed. The changes to the 12 historical events will alter the fabric of future time to get the result we want for your planet. Each time travel mission will be to another version of your Earth. You see Luca, we live in a multiverse. By changing each of these 12 events, you will be setting the course of your version of planet Earth, towards a much better future'

'What are these 12 events, and how on Earth do you expect me to change them?'

'Let's take one question at a time. The 12 events are; first, to stop the assassination of Phillip II of Macedonia on 21st October 336 BCE; second, to stop the assassination of Julius Caesar on 15th March 44 BCE; third, to stop Charlemagne becoming Holy Roman Emperor on 25th December 800 CE; fourth, to stop Pope Urban II launching the Crusades on 27th November 1095; fifth, to stop Christopher Columbus from discovering the New World in 1492; sixth, to stop the

European imperial powers from carving up Africa in 1885; seventh, to stop the assassination of Franz Ferdinand on 28th June 1914; eighth, to prevent Joseph Stalin from succeeding Vladimir Lenin as the Ruler of the Soviet Union in April 1922, securing the position for Leon Trotsky instead; ninth, to prevent the rise of Adolf Hitler to Chancellor of Germany on 30th January 1933, by making sure he is admitted into the Vienna Academy of Fine Arts in 1908; tenth, to delay the development of the first atomic bomb by at least three years, in the Manhattan Project, in October 1941; eleventh, to stop the assassination of President John F. Kennedy on 22nd November 1963; and finally, to prevent the September 11, 2001 attack on the United States.'

'Oh My God! Are you for real man!?'

'I am deadly serious Luca Evangelista.'

'How am I expected to do this, Otto?'

'I have secured the use of a wormhole that is programmed to take you back in time, for up to a 3-day window before each of these critical events. You will be given the name of a specific person to contact, and you will arrive at a location very close to where that person lives. Don't ask me why, it will take me forever to explain this to you, and in any event you won't be capable of comprehending it, but that person will be expecting you. He or she will know exactly what you are planning to do and will help you achieve it. In all 12 instances, the nominated person will have access to the historical figure or event you will be seeking to influence. I will return you back to the present time and fully debrief you on what you have achieved, when you have successfully completed each mission; and then prepare you for your next mission. While you are back in time, it is absolutely imperative that you do not kill any person, either directly or indirectly. If you do, you will set the future course of the Earth on to another totally unpredictable path, one which may be even worse than the fate of your planet now. Do you understand all of this, Luca?'

As he was telling me all this, my heartbeat was racing and my adrenaline pumping with a combination of fear and excitement. I had often dreamt of travelling back in time and changing the course of history for the better. My favourite dream was travelling back to Dallas Texas on the 22nd November 1963 at midday, and racing up to the Texas

School Book Depository Building to firstly see if Lee Harvey Oswald was the assassin of JFK, and if he was, to stop him from carrying out his dire act. Good God! This was now one of the 12 missions Otto had given me! My instincts were to implicitly trust this 'man', and go ahead with his plan, regardless of the consequences. But, could I trust him? Was he telling me the truth? Did he have some other ulterior motive? I needed more time to think about this unbelievable situation he was presenting to me.

'I understand Otto, I understand. What about language barriers, suitable clothing, resources; and what will happen if I die?!'

'Language barriers, suitable clothing, and resources will be taken care of by me, and your contact person. I will also ensure you safely get back to the present, each time. But it will be your responsibility to stay alive,' said Otto, matter-of-factly.

Quite randomly, the Bee Gees classic *Stayin' Alive* was ringing through my head! 'I must stay alive. I must stay alive. I must stay alive,' I kept repeating to myself.

'Will I be able to let my partner Isabella know?'

'I was expecting this question Luca. I know you can trust her. She won't tell anybody about me and your mission. I have already come into her dreams and spoken with her. She is expecting you to tell her. Isabella will be important for your state of mind. You will need to be able to emotionally process the events you are about to encounter with somebody you totally trust and love. That person is Isabella. In my world, we haven't evolved to experience the emotion of love in the way you humans do. The ability to love unconditionally fascinates me the most about your people. But Luca, that shall be a subject for us to discuss on another day. You have an important mission to prepare for.'

'Otto, I'm not sure I can do this. I don't think I am your man. I need to think about this carefully and sleep on it.'

The fact that Otto let me sleep on it, and didn't threaten me in any way, leaving my classroom peacefully, went a long way towards alleviating my concerns about whether this "man" was sincere.

That night, I visited Isabella. She told me Otto had appeared in her dreams over three consecutive nights, telling her he would be approaching me with a mission that had the potential to change the future of our world for the better. At first, she was highly sceptical. But after his third "visit" she was convinced it was all real.

Suffice to say, I had a sleepless night, tossing and turning; equally excited and fearful of what I was about to embark on. I knew instinctively, I could not possibly turn Otto down.

Human Touch

You and me we were the pretenders
We let it all slip away
In the end what you don't surrender
Well the world just strips away

Girl ain't no kindness in the face of strangers
Ain't gonna find no miracles here
Well you can wait on your blessings darlin'
But I got a deal for you right here

I ain't lookin' for prayers or pity
I ain't comin' round searching for a crutch
I just want someone to talk to
And a little of that human touch
Just a little of that human touch

Ain't no mercy on the streets of this town
Ain't no bread from heavenly skies
Ain't nobody drawin' wine from this blood
It's just you and me tonight

Tell me in a world without pity
Do you think what I'm askin's too much?
I just want something to hold on to
And a little of that human touch
Just a little of that human touch

Oh girl that feeling of safety you prize
Well it comes with a hard hard price
You can't shut off the risk and pain
Without losin' the love that remains
We're all riders on this train

So you been broken and you been hurt
Show me somebody who ain't
Yeah I know I ain't nobody's bargain
But hell a little touchup
And a little paint

You might need somethin' to hold on to
When all the answers they don't amount to much
Somebody that you can just talk to
And a little of that human touch

Baby in a world without pity
Do you think what I'm askin's too much?
I just want to feel you in my arms
And share a little of that human touch

Bruce Springsteen (1992)

3

Philip II of Macedonia

Aigei, Macedonia, October 336 BCE

'Sir, I don't understand why you are taking extended leave all of a sudden.'

'I am working on a major history project, James. I will look forward to telling you and the rest of the class all about it, when I finish.'

I could tell from the expressions on their faces they weren't buying my reason. James in particular, looked quite saddened and despondent about the prospect of not having me as his history teacher for the next six months.

'Anyhow class, this is the last lesson I'm going to be having with you for a while, so let's make the most of it!'

The rest of the class time was occupied with a vigorous discussion about the reasons for the Cold War. We spoke about the ideological gulf between American capitalism and Soviet communism, and how the seeds of this great struggle had been sown with the Russian Revolution of 1917; and then the carving up of Europe and Germany, and the Berlin Crisis, in the immediate aftermath of World War Two. I wish I could let these kids know I was going to be immersed in the monumental Russian power struggle between Joseph Stalin and Leon Trotsky to take over from Vladimir Lenin, but of course Otto had sworn me to secrecy! In fact, he said if any other person from the present, other than Isabella, was to find out about my "mission," the wormhole would immediately vaporize and my quest to give the world a better future, come to a grinding halt!

I spent the evening before my first mission with Isabella.

'I am proud of you, baby. I don't know how Otto found you. I know you well, Luca. Nobody is better equipped, physically, emotionally, and intellectually, to take on this time travel, as I know you are. It's almost like all of your life you have been preparing for Otto's visit, honey.'

I knew Isabella's words were heartfelt. I could also see fear in her eyes. Fear of the unknown. Fear she wasn't going to see me again. That night, we held each other tight while sharing our hopes, fears, and aspirations throughout the evening. All of our combined life experiences interconnected into one. It was during that night, I realised just how deeply in love I was with her.

While she was laying asleep beside me, I remembered one of our most romantic experiences. The nights we had dinner on the balcony of a 650 years old Benedictine monastery, converted into a hotel, overlooking the old town of Sorrento and the Mediterranean, in Italy. The hotel had a large balcony, surrounded by wrought iron railing covered in multi-coloured flowers. This is where guests would sit for breakfast, lunch, and dinner. The views were spectacular. Directly in front of the balcony was the Mediterranean. All manner of luxurious boats and cruise ships would sail by. Often we could see people enjoying themselves on the decks, while the sound of music filled the air. In the background in front of us, loomed Mount Vesuvius, looking docile and harmless, but of course, ready for a major eruption any time, creating an eerie feeling of danger. To the immediate right of the balcony, we could look down at the old medieval town of Sorrento. From the marina, there was a constant flow of boats moving to and from the magical island of Capri. Further in the distance, also to the right of the balcony, was the Bay of Naples, and the urban sprawl of this great cosmopolitan city. To the left of the balcony, for as far as the eye could see, were limestone cliffs, with pockets of sandy beaches nestled within small coves.

There was an elevator embedded within the rocky cliff alongside our hotel which would take guests down to a secluded cove with a white sandy beach. Isabella and I whistled away countless hours laying under "Cinzano" and "Aperol Spritz" umbrellas, in multi-coloured deck chairs on the beach, enjoying cocktails from the hotel's beach bar, while watching the cruise ships glide by. In between cocktails we would swim in the sparkling blue-green Mediterranean. It was the best seven days we had shared as a couple. At night, we would have dinner on the balcony, seated at a candle-lit table while a tenor accompanied by a guitarist and accordionist sang some of the most romantic Italian songs. Whilst enjoying our sumptuous seafood and pasta dinner, we would watch brightly lit cruise ships pass us by, again, hearing the joyful sounds of laughter and music. Then we would finish off the evening by retiring to our room and making passionate love. It was during this trip to Italy, when I realised Isabella was going to be my life partner.

Otto had instructed me to thoroughly research each of the 12 historical events before undertaking each journey back in time. I needed to understand as best I could from all of the available primary historical sources, the personalities, feuds, loves, hatreds, jealousies, ambitions, and political intrigues of the key characters. So that's what I did, starting with the world of King Philip II of Macedonia.

Philip II was born in Pella, the capital city of ancient Macedonia, in 382 BCE, and ruled the Macedonian kingdom from 359 to 336 BCE. He was the youngest son of King Amyntas III and Eurydice. After the death of Amyntas III, there was a decline in the political and economic stability of Macedonia as his successors and brothers, Alexander II and Perdiccas III stumbled in their respective rule of the kingdom.

This instability was triggered by external attacks from the nearby Thracians, Illyrians, and Greeks. The Thracians occupied parts of eastern Macedonia, and the Illyrians were threatening the kingdom from beyond north- western Macedonia. Thebes, the strongest military power in the region at that time, often interfered in the affairs of Macedonia, while the Greek colonies in Chalcidice presented obstacles to the economic prosperity of Macedonia.

According to the Greek historian Diodorus Siculus, while the Thebans held him hostage between 368 and 365 BCE, Philip demonstrated a very keen interest in studying their military strategies, techniques, and weapons. He was particularly interested in understanding the fighting style of the elite Theban Sacred Band, which was to be of great benefit to him in later years when he would lead his own armies into battles.

After Philip was released from Thebes, at the request of his brother, King Perdiccas III, he started to implement his reforms within the Macedonian army. Unfortunately, before he had completed this exercise, his brother tragically died. While leading the army against the Illyrians in north-western Macedonia, Perdiccas III was fatally wounded and died in battle. The Macedonian army also suffered a humiliating defeat, losing most of its 4,000 soldiers. After this victory, the Illyrians conquered and occupied north-western Macedonia, becoming a clear and present danger to the very survival of the Macedonian kingdom.

Philip became the King of Macedonia in 359 BCE. His kingdom was on the brink of outright collapse, and neighbouring kingdoms were hovering like vultures, poised to attack. In addition to these external threats, Philip also had to deal with internal turmoil. There were noble contenders, often encouraged by foreign rivals, who coveted the throne. In spite of this tremendous pressure, the 21 years old Philip began to demonstrate his formidable strengths as a ruler, military strategist, and diplomat.

Shortly after taking control of the kingdom, he bribed the Thracian king with gifts and convinced him to execute a Macedonian rival, who was in hiding in the Thracian court. Philip also defeated in battle, another rival for his throne who was supported by the Athenians. Skilfully though, in order not to upset the Athenians he reached an agreement to handover the territory of Amphipolis to them. Within a year of taking the throne, Philip had brilliantly eliminated all of the immediate political rivals threatening his power, and firmly established himself as king.

But the job had not been completed. Not by a longshot. He was determined to regain the territory lost in north-western Macedonia, so in 358 BCE Philip put his improved and reorganized army to the test and fought the Illyrians face to face in a fierce battle. With great confidence the Macedonians prevailed over the legendary Illyrians, who fled in panic leaving 7,000 dead on the battlefield. North-western Macedonia was now free, including Lyncestia, the birthplace of Philip's mother.

Philip was acutely aware that with a relatively small army of 10,000 he could not adequately defend his kingdom, so he created a pool of new recruits by convincing the chiefs of numerous smaller nearby principalities to join him, offering those that did, prestigious positions within his court.

Now that his north-western frontier was secure, Philip turned his attention to the east, with the intention of taking control of the Struma basin north of Chalcidice. The presence of his army there raised great alarm within nearby Greek colonies, particularly Amphipolis, which panicked and complained to the Athenians. But Athens had its own problems at the time and was powerless to stop Philip. After failing to secure a peaceful alliance, Philip amassed a large army and attacked and retook control of Amphipolis; but this time gave them a degree of independence under Macedonian supervision.

In the same year of 357 BCE, in spite of Athenian opposition, Philip's army also conquered the city of Potidaea in Chalcidice, and then turning northward, grabbed control of Pydna, a Greek colony on the Macedonian coast. Over the next couple of years his army also added the Athenian-allied city of Methone, where unfortunately Philip lost an eye after being struck by an arrow. Following this battle, the army advanced eastward into Thracian territory and conquered the town of Crenides, later to be renamed Philippi. In the process, the Macedonians took over lucrative gold mines which added significant wealth to the kingdom. The eastern frontier was now also secured.

With his army reorganized into an efficient fighting machine, full of confidence and equipped with the very best weapons of the time, Philip turned his attention south. First he ventured into Thessaly where he won a quick victory, and by 352 BCE was in tight control of a region extending as far south as the pass of Thermopylae. The subsequent peace agreement he brokered with the Thessalians required that Philip marry a local noble woman, Nicesipolis, who bore him a daughter whom he named Thessalonika, in honour of his victory over Thessaly. At this point, the Macedonians were literally at the northern gates of Greek city-states, which were heavily defended by a combination of powerful Athenian, Spartan, and Achaean armies.

Now that his southern frontier was secure, Philip returned to Macedonia to take care of domestic affairs. In 348 BCE, he mobilized his army to the Chalcidice peninsula, and rid the area of Greek influence, commencing with the city of Olynthus; the most prominent city for the northern Greeks and a symbol of Greek power and influence. Philip occupied the city and sold its entire population into slavery; something the Greeks regularly did, but not the Macedonians.

After Olynthus, the Macedonian army occupied 31 other Chalcidician cities and towns, redistributing the land to Macedonian citizens. One of the cities sacked was Stageira, the birthplace of Aristotle. The entire Chalcidice peninsula was now Macedonian.

A turning point in the rule of Philip also occurred in 348 BCE when the Macedonian army intervened on behalf of Thessaly, to free the Greek city-state of Delphi from a rebellion. Delphi was a highly revered religious and spiritual centre whose neutrality was preserved by the Amphictyonic League, an ancient and largely religious association of central Greek city-states. In coming to the assistance of Thessaly, Philip had to tread carefully so as not to upset the Athenians and the Thebans who opposed each other, but also had vested interests in Delphi.

Already having an alliance with Thebes, Philip proposed to the Athenians that they assist him in removing the rebels from Delphi. Highly suspicious of Philip's motives, the Athenians declined his overture. Demonstrating his patience and diplomatic skills though, Philip kept the dialogue alive with Athens, and ultimately convinced a group of older noble Athenians that he wished no harm, but instead wanted the Delphi matter resolved peacefully. To demonstrate his goodwill, he gave the Athenians his word that Macedonia had no intention of occupying the resource-rich region of Attica, located to the immediate north of Athens.

The Athenians, including his most outspoken enemy Demosthenes, accepted Philip's promise. The Thebans on the other hand, were upset with Philip drawing himself so close to their archrival, Athens. Philip negotiated himself out of this tight situation by seeking the authority of the Amphictyonic League to remove the rebel group from the Council, and appoint himself as a member, to which they agreed.

So, in a masterstroke of sheer diplomatic brilliance, Philip avoided what had been an almost certain war with Athens; ended the rebellion at Delphi; saved the Amphictyonic League from dissolution; averted a confrontation with Thebes; made an alliance with Athens; and positioned himself as a voting member of the League. In the process, Philip's prestige within the Greek city-states of the region was significantly enhanced.

Nevertheless, in spite of Philip's achievements, the great Athenian orator Demosthenes continued to see the Macedonian king as a threat to the Greek city-states. In 351 BCE he delivered the first of his Philippics, a series of speeches between 351 and 349 in which he denounced Philip and warned the Greeks about the Macedonian threat to their independence and liberty. His most famous oration was the third Philippic in which he described Philip as being.... "not only not Greek, nor related to the Greeks, but not even a barbarian from any place that can be named with honors, but a pestilent knave from Macedonia, whence it was never possible to buy a decent slave." In spite of this heavy criticism from the respected Demosthenes, the peace agreement between Athens and Macedonia remained intact for the time being.

During 345 BCE he lead his army into further battles against the Illyrians, Dardanians, and the Thracians, as well as putting down a series of rebellions; including one in 344 BCE coming from the Thessalians. In 342 BCE Philip conquered Epirus and replaced King Arybbas with his young brother-in-law Alexander. Philip astutely had a growing sense that war with Athens was imminent so he proceeded to negotiate alliances with a number of Greek city-states not friendly to the Athenians.

By 340 BCE heavy pressure was placed on the peace agreement after it was established Athens had sponsored anti-Macedonian uprisings in the northern Aegean region of Greece. In retaliation, Philip captured the Athenian grain fleet; and as a result, under the leadership of Demosthenes, Athens and Thebes jointly declared war on Macedonia. Over the next two years, under the leadership of the Athenians and Thebans, a number of other southern Greek city-states joined the alliance, amassing a great army to invade Macedonia.

On 2nd August 338 BCE, the two opposing armies met face to face in the Cephisus river valley close to the village of Chaeronea on the road to Thebes. On the northern side stood Philip's army of 30,000 infantry and 2,000 cavalry, the largest Macedonian army ever assembled. One of the commanding generals was Philip's 18 years old son, Alexander, who was in charge of the cavalry. On the southern side, stood the united Athenians, Thebans, and the Achaeans with 35,000 infantry and 2,000 cavalry, the largest army ever assembled since the Persian invasion. Both armies were closely matched. During the battle, the Macedonian right flank was penetrated and began to retreat.

Seeing this, a Greek general gave orders to continue to push on and drive Philip's army all the way back to Macedonia. As the Macedonians retreated, the Greek flanks broke ranks and began their pursuit. Not realizing they had been tricked, the Greeks found themselves encircled by the Macedonians, and were proceeded to be slaughtered by Alexander's cavalry. When the battle had ended, the majority of the Greek army, including the elite Theban Sacred Band, lay dead in the fields of Chaeronea. Out of respect for the Theban Sacred Band, who upheld their tradition and fought to the last man, Philip erected a statue of a lion to commemorate their sacrifice and bravery. Many ancient historians consider the Battle of Chaeronea as depicting the end of classical Greek civilization.

Following his victory at the Battle of Chaeronea, Philip consolidated his conquests by placing military garrisons in the Greek city-states of Thebes, Chalcis, Ambracia, Corinth, and the Peloponnesus. He then arranged for representatives of the majority of Greek city-states, including Athens, to a peace conference at Corinth where he literally made peace with each and every one of them. Sparta was a prominent absence at the conference. This did not trouble Philip because he didn't consider them to be a threat to him. Philip then organized the Greek city-states into an alliance which was known as the League of Corinth.

After securing peace with the Greek city-states, Philip then turned his attention towards the other remaining major threat, the Persians. After discussing this threat, the League appointed Philip as the commander-in-chief of the combined military forces. Some Greek military officers were upset with this decision, and absconded to the Persian side to be employed as mercenaries willing to fight against the Macedonian-Greeks. These Greek commanders were able to persuade a combined force of 50,000 Greek soldiers to also join the Persian army as mercenaries, according to the Roman historian Quintus Curtius Rufus. After the Corinth conference, Philip returned home to prepare for the upcoming military expedition into Persia.

Let's now turn to Philip's personal life and his numerous marriages. It has been said that if ever there was a big weakness he had, it was "marrying for love." The woman in question was Cleopatra-Eurydice, a young Macedonian noble girl whom he married in 337 BCE. Blind-sided by his love for the young Cleopatra, Philip failed to realise that his seventh marriage to her would lead to an acrimonious breakup with his sixth wife Olympias, and estrangement from his son Alexander. Olympias was a very proud woman and fiercely protective of her son Alexander.

Philip's marriage to a young Macedonian made Olympias feel neglected and significantly weakened within the power hierarchy of Philip's court. She also saw the marriage as a threat to the legitimacy of her son Alexander being heir to the Macedonian throne. Olympias' worst fears were realized when young Cleopatra bore Philip a son, Caranus, in 336 BCE. During the Spring of that same year, in preparation for the Persian offensive, Philip decided to send an advanced force of 10,000 soldiers to be jointly commanded by his two most accomplished generals, Attalus and Parmenion.

Meanwhile Philip was preparing for a big celebration at his palace in Aegae; the marriage of his daughter by Olympias, also named Cleopatra, to Prince Alexander of Epirus, who happened to be the brother of Olympias. A lavish festival was planned with much entertainment and games. Philip had invited many guests from all over his kingdom. He also of course invited his sixth wife Olympias, who even though she was the mother of the bride Cleopatra, and the sister of the groom Alexander, initially did not want to attend until Philip met with her and reassured her she would be most welcome. The wedding was a grand affair that spanned over two days. The first day of entertainment and activities concluded without incident, but disaster struck on the second day.

According to the historical sources, during a procession in the theatre at Aegae, while standing between his son Alexander (the bride Cleopatra's natural brother), and his new son-in-law Alexander, a member of the royal bodyguard and a lover, named Pausanius, stabbed and killed Philip when he thrust a Celtic dagger into his chest. Pausanius ran to escape towards some waiting horses, but tripped over a vine and fell down. His pursuers caught up with him and speared him to death with a javelin. This is how the surviving sources describe the assassination of King Philip II of Macedonia.

The man often described as one of the greatest kings of Europe, who liberated Macedonia from foreign occupation and then proceeded to conquer much of Greece, now lay dead in his own palace, killed by his lover and one of his seven bodyguards. After his death, he was succeeded by his son Alexander, who would go on to conquer much of the known world at the time and assume the title of Alexander the Great.

As I read the above notes I wondered how close to the truth these events actually were. I also wondered how I was going to solve the biggest mystery of all; who was behind the assassination of Philip, and why did they (or he) do it? Finding the answers to these questions was going to be the heart of my first time-travel mission, into ancient Macedonia and to the court of King Philip II. It seemed to me there were a number of plausible scenarios behind the assassination.

The first one of course, involves Pausanius acting entirely on his own, killing Philip because he was rejected as his lover, and also subjected to the most horrific sexual and violent abuse instigated by Attalus, a close adviser and general to the king; and Philip did nothing about it. The second scenario involves Philip's sixth wife Olympias conspiring with (or without) her son Alexander to arrange for Pausanius to murder Philip because after his seventh marriage to the young beautiful Macedonian noble girl, Cleopatra-Eurydice, she (or they) was (or were) fearful Philip would anoint his son Caranus from Cleopatra, as his heir to the throne, thereby displacing Alexander. A third scenario involves King Darius III of Persia through his network of spies, convincing Pausanius to kill Philip and then giving him safe exile in Persia.

As we have seen, Philip had already commenced preparations for an invasion of Persia. Philip's generals, Attalus and Parmenion, were already in Persia leading an expeditionary force of 10,000 Macedonian soldiers at the time of Philip's death. They were critical of Philip's planned invasion of Persia and did not consider Alexander as a legitimate heir to the throne because his mother Olympias was not of

Macedonian blood, unlike the young Caranus. They may have been recruited by Darius as part of the plot to execute Philip first and then Alexander later; after which they would take control as regents for the young king Caranus.

Yet another similar scenario involves a rival noble Macedonian family, who believed they had legitimate claims to the throne, being behind the plot to kill Philip, and then later Alexander. Aeropus was the patriarch of this family, and two of his sons Heromenes and Arrhabaeus were members of Philip's royal court, and were also sympathetic to the plight of Pausanius. The plan could have involved this family then taking control of the monarchy. There didn't appear to be any credible scenario involving the Athenians being a part of a plot to kill Philip, although of course, this could not be entirely ruled out.

It was early morning on 19th October 336 BCE. I had arrived in the Macedonian city of Aigei, not far from Philip's spectacular hilltop palace. I was waiting for Philip's eldest son and Alexander's half-brother, Arrhidaeus, who lived with his father in the palace. His mother was Philinna, from the Thessalian capital city of Larissa, and he had been named after his great-grandfather general Arrhidaeus. Otto had chosen Alexander's half-brother because he was friendly with both his father and brother, and was a man of impeccable character, not considered a political rival or a legitimate heir to the throne; yet he possessed excellent inside knowledge of the rivalries and intrigues within the royal court, and wished no harm upon his father or brother.

Arrhidaeus, like his half-brother Alexander, had been tutored by the renowned Greek philosopher Aristotle, and was a mentor to his younger brother, even though within the court Arrhidaeus was believed to have a learning disability and an inferior intellect. Otto told me although he had an autistic spectrum disorder, he possessed a photographic memory and a talent for mental arithmetic.

As I stood disorientated by the side of the main road leading to the palace, and taking in the surroundings, I heard footsteps from behind me.

'You must be Luca Evengelista?'

'Yes, and I believe you are Arrhidaeus?'

'Come, follow me.'

We walked into a field. The sun was just rising, radiating onto the mountains in the background. After a few minutes, we sat together on a bench, under a large fig tree.

'This is where I often come to get peace and quiet from all the crazy people surrounding my father. Now, listen carefully. I am aware of why you are here. Otto has fully briefed me. You will be known to everybody as Luca, a visitor from the city of Larissa where my mother was born, and a close friend of mine. Do you understand?'

'Yes, of course.'

'You have a very big responsibility on your shoulders, Luca. Of course, I know my father is destined to die on the morning of the 21st, and there's absolutely nothing I can do about it. If I try to change the course of history in any way, it will not prevent the death of my father. The only person who can prevent that death of course, is you. Even if I so much as speak to anybody about a plot to kill my father, it will seal his fate and history will remain unchanged forever.'

'I am aware the wedding celebrations for the marriage of your half-sister Cleopatra to her uncle, prince Alexander of Epirus, will commence tomorrow.'

'Yes, and what a lavish affair it is going to be Luca! My father has been personally involved in all of the preparations at his palace. He has invited hundreds of noble guests from within the kingdom and from allied kingdoms throughout the Greek world. There will even be emissaries from the Italian city-states, Egypt, and Carthage attending. It will be two days of non-stop feasting, music, games, religious ceremonies, and entertainment. My father knows you are visiting me. I have a room adjoining mine prepared for you in the palace. Come, let's go.'

I wondered whether Philip had also invited the Samnites – an Italian tribal group based in the Apennine mountains who had been in Italy well before the Latin Romans, and who were my ancestors on my mother's side of the family.

As we walked up the hill, the spectacular palace loomed, dominating the landscape. The royal complex was strategically located, enclosed by two rivers and surrounded by the Piera mountains. Within the foothills of the mountains in the valley, I could see the city of Aigei sprawled below me. The name "Aigei" is derived from the ancient Greek word *aiga* (goat) and means "the land with many goats." The city's economy was based on animal husbandry. A forest full of game and plenty of wood was used by the king as political leverage when exercising his foreign policy; but also the rivers close-by, that were used for the transportation of wood and as a rich source of fish, added to the city's wealth and economic prosperity.

I could see in the background that the city was surrounded by fortified walls to keep enemies out. At the beginning of the reign of Philip the city walls had been strengthened, and reconstructed with a new wall surrounding the slope where the city-centre laid. City walls also surrounded the two hills to the south of the palace, where the acropolis was located. The walls were 3 metres thick and were reinforced with watch-towers.

Up to a certain height the fortification was constructed in stone with facades of porous cornerstones, a material transported from the Vermion mountain quarries, about 10 kilometres away; while higher up the walls, the material used was unbaked mud-bricks. A grand ornate gate was constructed at the eastern end of the walls, and a smaller one at the walls' north-western corner.

The palace was getting closer now. It was more than three times the size of the Parthenon in Athens. Impressively laid out across the front entrance, I counted 30 huge marble columns on the façade. I could see it had two levels. It was designed for Philip by the renowned architect Pytheos, and covered an area of 12,500 square metres. The palace was not designed to be just the king's private residence even though he, his family, friends and closest advisers lived there; but instead it was built for the benefit of the people of the Macedonian kingdom, with a large banquet and entertainment hall in the centre which could accommodate up to 1,000 people. Flanking the front entrance there were seating benches for up to 500 people, and surrounding the palace, the beautifully manicured gardens and grounds could accommodate a further 3,500 people. It was very much a symbol of Macedonian power for the people!

As we entered the palace there was a peristyle open courtyard with an elaborate giant fountain, a lavish pond full of exotic fish in the centre, and immaculate marble statues of 12 of the most sacred gods surrounding the pond. This was the heart of the palace and operated as an agora; a meeting place for the public, for social, political, spiritual, trade, artistic, and cultural activities. I could see a hive of activity in the agora, as the many slaves and servants were preparing the courtyard for the wedding celebrations.

'Father, come and meet my dear friend Luca,' shouted Arrhidaeus, his voice echoing around the courtyard.

Philip was at the far end, he turned and came towards us, with two men, one on either side, accompanying him. He was taller and more muscular than I imagined. I could clearly see the black patch covering his right eye.

'Luca, welcome to my palace,' he bellowed as he wrapped his arms around me and embraced me so tight that I felt like a rag doll with the stuffing taken out of it.

'Thank you. It is an honour to be in your presence.'

'Let me introduce you to my two dearest and closest friends and bodyguards, Leonnatus and Perdiccas.'

They both nodded at me without muttering a word. Of course, I knew quite a bit about them from my research.

'You must be feeling tired. Show him to his room, Arrhidaeus.'

With that, my first encounter with the mighty king Philip of Macedonia ended, as he swiftly turned around, with military precision, and made his way back to the other side of the courtyard, bodyguards in tow, closely tagging him.

'Come Luca, I have prepared your room for you.'

We proceeded across the courtyard into an open foyer with a marble staircase to the right. In the centre of the foyer was an imposing, 10 metre-high, statue of Zeus. As I began to follow Arrhidaeus up the winding staircase, I could see a grand entrance at the opposite end of the foyer. The doors were open. I caught a glimpse of a magnificent long table stretching across the huge banquet hall.

'My father usually has seven bodyguards, Leonnatus and Perdiccas are his two most loyal. He has to make do with six for the time being, because after Pausanius was removed, he wasn't replaced,' Arrhidaeus pointed out to me, turning around and looking me directly in the eyes as we were climbing towards the end of the staircase.

He clearly knew I was aware of why Pausanius had been removed, but once we reached the end of the stairs, I couldn't resist.

'Why was Pausanius removed?'

'My friend Luca, that is a leading question. I don't think the surviving sources from your time got the whole story right. Let me fill some of the gaps in your knowledge for you.'

By now, we had entered a lavishly appointed but small bedroom, with a large window giving a spectacular view of the fields and mountains in the background.

'I'm sure you will be comfortable here. The upper level of the palace contains the living quarters and consists of over 50 rooms. The far eastern end is cordoned off for my father's living quarters. He has his own secure staircase. The remainder comprises rooms similar to this for everybody else. Now, you asked me about Pausanius.'

There was a couch in the room. I sat down as Arrhidaeus opened a cabinet and took out a large ceramic jug. He poured red wine into two goblets and handed me one, while sitting alongside me.

'Okay, here's the thing with Pausanius. He was my father's lover, but became jealous when my father suddenly jilted him and replaced him with a younger lover, also called Pausanius; let's call him Pausanius 2 and the original Pausanius 1. When number 1 found out, he confronted my father here in the palace, and there was an almighty frenzy of screaming and shouting. To make things worse, my father was drunk and with number 2 when the confrontation happened, so you can imagine the scene. Number 1 was banished from the palace and stripped of his bodyguard role. He taunted and stalked number 2 so much, that he took his own life. Now as it turned out, number 2 was related to Attalus, a powerful noble, close adviser to my father, and his most decorated general; whose family had been dishonoured, so he wanted revenge.'

I was sipping the wine while listening with intense interest.

'This wine is really good. Better than most wine I drink in the 21st century.'

Although I had made a fleeting reference to the 21st century, Otto had made it very clear to me, and I presume to Arrhidaeus as well, that there could never be any discussion about the 21st century, otherwise the mission would be abolished and the wormhole vaporized.

'Nothing but the best for my father. It comes from his own personal winery estate at the foot of the nearby mountains. Now let me continue, because you will see how the actual story deviates somewhat from your understanding of the history.'

'That's the thing with ancient history,' I interjected. 'The further back in history we go, the less complete and reliable the surviving sources are.'

'Attlaus took his revenge by inviting Pausanius-1 to dinner, getting him drunk, then along with his three bodyguards, subjected the jilted lover to the most humiliating and degrading sexual and physical abuse. When Pausanius complained to my father, he was helpless to punish Attalus, as he was about to send him to Asia Minor to establish a bridgehead for his planned invasion of Persia. At the time, my father was also preparing to marry Attalus' niece, the young and beautiful Cleopatra-Eurydice whom he had fallen madly in love with. Sensing a full scale scandal looming, my father then approached Pausanius and offered him a position in the administration of his royal court, not his old job back as a bodyguard. This upset Attalus greatly, but my father was caught between a rock and a hard place. He wasn't going to let this sordid saga damage his reputation. So what did Pausanius do? He seduced my father's then fiance and Attalus' niece, the young Cleopatra! My father only found out about it when I happened to overhear the clandestine lovers planning a late night rendezvous. From what I overheard, they were clearly having a passionate intimate relationship. In hindsight, this was a brilliant act of revenge by Pausanius; humiliating and offending his two most hated enemies, my father king Philip, and Attalus.'

'Oh my God! No historian from my time considered this possibility! Yes, it was a very creative act of revenge! So, what is your father going to do about it?'

'My father plans to arrange for his bodyguards to imprison and then ultimately kill Pausanius, after his daughter's wedding. As far as I am aware, I am the only person he has told this to.'

'Okay. What we don't know at this stage is if Pausanius is acting alone, or whether he has conspired with others, in planning to kill your father. If he has conspired with others, from the research I've done, it is my firm belief, that more than likely the conspiracy involves either your father's ex-wife Olympias, or king Darius of Persia,' I said as I finished the wine.

'Get some rest now Luca.'

After Arrhidaeus left the room, I lay on the bed and closed my eyes, contemplating what lay ahead. I knew it wasn't my job to seek out any conspirators, but if I could uncover a plot in the short time I was here, it would be a bonus. My mission was to simply prevent the assassination from happening. To achieve this, I had to deny Pausanius the opportunity of sticking the dagger into Philip. I fell asleep pondering the thought of how best to achieve this.

After a couple of hours, I was awoken by a knock on the door.

'Luca, are you awake? I have some important information I want to share with you,' said Arrihdaeus.

'Yes, please come in.'

'I have the address of Pausanius. I think you should follow him. I have it on good authority that he is home alone now. He does not know you, so you should be able to keep an eye on him without him realizing it.'

An hour later, I was sitting in an inn sipping wine, about 50 metres away from the simple mudbrick residence of Pausanius, on the opposite side of the road. It was one of many similar houses lining the road. From my vantage point, I had a clear view of the front entrance to his home. I figured if he was involved in a conspiracy of some sort, he would surely be meeting with his partners in crime at some stage in the final days before the fateful deed was carried out.

As I sat there and waited, I thought of the upcoming wedding. I was looking forward to seeing first-hand how the ancient Macedonian nobility enjoyed themselves. My wedding had been a lavish affair. Being of Italian background, no expense was spared. We married as 20 year olds. It had cost my poor parents a fortune.

Being humble working class people, I knew they had to borrow their half share. We had 330 people celebrating at one of the inner city five-star hotels, at $300 a head. Sure everybody enjoyed themselves, but I felt bad our parents had spent so much money. This money could have been used to give us a heads-up in life, such as a useful deposit on a home. Instead, we started our married life renting a one-bedroom apartment. Right from the word go our marriage was on the rocks. It turned out we didn't really share much in common.

We had hooked up in high school as 15 year olds, with great plans for our future together. Our parents weren't happy. Too young they thought. No opportunity to experience life. Too intense and serious, but they eventually relented to our matrimonial wishes. Anyhow, none of this helped our cause. We wanted kids early but it wasn't to be. After 10 years together, we finally threw in the towel. That was 5 years ago. Things might have been different if we had children, I couldn't help pondering.

Suddenly, I saw Pausanius leave his house. In addition to his simple white toga, his face was partially covered by a hood. It had to be him because he lived alone. I followed him from a safe distance on the opposite side of the road, while he walked briskly with long strides. He kept stopping and looking nervously around as if to make sure nobody was following him. Luckily there were a number of people on my side of the road because it was lined with various food stalls and artisan shops. He was heading to what seemed like the noble neighbourhood of the city. All of a sudden the mudbrick houses became larger marble-stone villas with high walls and elaborate gardens. After about 15 minutes, I saw him enter one of the villas. This villa had its front gate open unlike the others.

I noticed the gate remained open after he entered, so after waiting what seemed like an eternity but in reality was probably no more than five minutes, I made my way to the front gate. Looking inside, I saw nobody, but as I crept in, I could hear voices in the background coming from the garden area to the right of the villa entrance. There were many trees and shrubs in the garden so I was able to venture forward, hiding from tree to tree. All of a sudden I saw Pausanius seated on a bench overlooking an elaborate pond with fountains. Seated alongside him was an elegant woman dressed in luxurious purple silk. As I got to a closer tree behind them, I could just hear their conversation.

'That bastard must pay for what he has done to me and my son,' she said.

'Philip and his entourage will be entering the sacred theatre on the morning of the second day of the wedding ceremony at sunrise. We will strike then,' replied Pausanius.

'He is going to be heavily guarded. How are you going to deliver the fatal blow?'

'As invited officials of his royal court, we will have unrestricted access. Trust me, Philip is not going to leave that theatre alive. If for whatever reason I fail, Heromenes will be there to ensure your wishes are carried out, my queen.'

'With Philip out of the way, the only other obstacle to my son taking the throne is Attalus. I will persuade my son to deal with him when he is king. My son Alexander must not know anything about what we are planning. Do you understand? Remind Heromenes to remain silent too. There will be two horses ready for the escape.'

'I want Philip, and that filthy swine Attalus, to suffer for what they did to me", said Pausanius, seething with hatred-filled anger.

My mind was racing at a million miles an hour. My goodness! This was a conspiracy to kill Philip and replace him with Alexander. Olympias was the mastermind! She needed to ensure Philip's young pure Macedonian son Caranus, was dealt with as well, otherwise the young child would become king and Attalus would become his regent and gain full control of the kingdom. Well she dealt with him alright. She killed Caranus and his sister Europa, as well as driving their young mother Cleopatra-Eurydice to suicide. I felt eerily comfortable with the knowledge Alexander the Great knew nothing of the conspiracy.

I promptly left and made my way back to the palace.

'What did you find out?,' asked Arrhidaeus with great interest.

We were seated on a sofa in. his study within his living quarters. Again, he gave me some of that excellent red wine from his father's estate.

'Well, the mastermind is Olympias, no doubt about that, but Alexander is not involved. She has managed to persuade Pausanius and Heromenes to carry out the awful deed. That solves the mystery of why there were two horses waiting for the assassins to escape.'

'This changes everything Luca. How are you going to stop two assassins from killing my father?'

'I'm not. We are going to stop this together.'

I could see Arrhidaeus was startled by my suggestion and had a tortured look on his face. Otto had made it clear to me I could seek the assistance of his nominated contact persons to change the course of historical events as long as they followed the golden rule, and were not directly responsible for the death of anybody.

'Yes my friend, of course I will assist you. My brother Alexander is hosting a dinner tonight at his villa in the fields outside of the city. His mother Olympias will be there along with some of his closest friends. He has invited me, and asked me to bring you along. Luca, you will of course need to conduct yourself in a cordial and friendly manner when you encounter Olympias. She must not suspect anything. By the way, she treats me like shit, so don't be surprised if she starts trying to humiliate me. I think she is still obsessed with the idea that I may somehow takeover from my father rather than her son. Well that's clearly not going to happen. My father and I have discussed this, and I have told him in no uncertain words, I don't want to be king. No way.'

'Of course,' I replied in a soft voice, contemplating the surreal evening that was about to unfold.

Alexander was born in 356 BCE at Pella in Macedonia. At age 12, he showed impressive courage when he tamed the wild horse Bucephalus, a black stallion with a ferocious demeanour. The horse remained with Alexander when he conquered Persia and beyond. From age 13 to 16 he was tutored by the great Greek philosopher Aristotle, who inspired him with a lifelong interest in philosophy, literature, medicine, and the natural sciences. He also developed an open, progressive, and critical mind under the guidance of Aristotle. While left in command of the remaining Macedonian armed forces in 340 during Philip's military campaigns, Alexander defeated the Thracian peoples called the Maedi.

As we have seen, two years later he commanded the left wing at the Battle of Chaeronea, in which Philip defeated the allied Greek states. During this battle Alexander displayed great personal courage when he led the attack which broke up the Sacred Band of Thebes, an elite military unit consisting of 150 pairs of lovers. In 337 Philip divorced Olympias, and, after an argument at a feast held to celebrate his father's new marriage to the young noble Macedonian, Cleopatra-Eurydice,

Alexander and his mother fled to Epirus. Shortly afterwards, Philip requested his son return to the kingdom, upon which father and son were reconciled. Since Philip's marriage to the young pure Macedonian noble Cleopatra-Eurydice though, Alexander's position as heir to the throne was in jeopardy. This really angered Olympias.

Arrhidaeus and I made our way to Alexander's villa across the fields on a moonlit night. There was a gentle breeze swaying across the crops and olive trees. As we approached the villa I was struck by its grandeur, sitting there on higher ground, overlooking the surrounding terrain.

'My father spared no expense in building this villa for Alexander soon after my brother defeated the Thracians,' said Arrhidaeus as we approached the entrance.

'Brother! Welcome! Come in,' said Alexander with genuine excitement.

'This is my dear friend Luca.'

'Luca! It is my pleasure to meet you! Come in and let me introduce you to my guests.'

I was immediately struck by Alexander's genuine charming warmth. He certainly had an aura of charisma about him. Tall and strong with long fair hair down to his shoulders, he was in excellent shape. Just like his father, he greeted me with a tight bear-hug. As we walked into the dining room, I could see the others were all seated.

'Everybody, this is Luca. Let me introduce you.'

As he introduced each person, they stood up, acknowledged me, and then sat down again.

'Olympias, my mother. My dearest friends, Heromenes, Leonnatus, Perdiccas, Thessalus, and Ptolemy.'

Olympias was seated at one end of the table, and Alexander proceeded to his seat at the opposite end. On either side of Alexander were two empty seats for us.

'Come, sit down. I am so happy you will be joining us for my sister's wedding celebrations beginning tomorrow,' said Alexander jovially.

The table had been set with an abundance of assorted hot and cold meats, cheese, vegetables, fruits, and nuts. There were two large ceramic jugs of wine. Two servants entered the room and proceeded to pour wine into each of our silver goblets.

'I hear you and Arrhidaeus are childhood friends,' said Olympias.

'Yes. We met at school and have remained in contact on and off since.'

'My brother is a man of few words and never told me about you,' said Alexander with a mischievous grin directed at his brother.

As the evening progressed, I noticed Olympias was drinking heavily and was particularly affectionate with Heromenes; the amorous couple were making regular eye contact and touching each other while drinking and engaging in animated conversation.

About halfway through the evening, Olympias unleashed her pent up fury.

'My ex-husband is a scoundrel. He is a compulsive womanizer and lover of young men. He has taunted me ever since he married the slut, Cleopatra. I know what he's up to. He wants his infant son from her to take the crown away from Alexander and I. That bastard will never succeed. My son Alexander is the legitimate heir to the throne, and he always will be!'

'Mother, please refrain from speaking with such hatred towards my father,' shouted Alexander, clearly annoyed.

'On the night my marriage was consummated, I dreamt that a bolt of lightning came into my womb, and a great fire was kindled. The gods had brought to me, my son Alexander. I remember the next morning Philip told me that he had inserted the royal seal into my womb, in the form of a lion.'

'Enough mother, enough!'

Seeing the look of distress on Alexander's face, the eminent tragic actor and very close friend of Alexander, Thessalus, rose to his feet and proposed a toast.

'May the gods always watch over the courageous young lion Alexander, legitimate heir to the Macedonian throne.'

Immediately, everybody except a clearly annoyed Alexander, rose to their feet, raising their goblets.

'Here, here! To Alexander!'

'My dear friend Thessalus, that wasn't necessary. I am looking forward to seeing your performance in my father's theatre at sunrise on the second day of my sister's wedding,' said Alexander in a calm manner.

As the dinner wore on, I briefly observed those in attendance, thinking about how history had remembered them. Of course Alexander himself was destined to become one of the greatest military strategists and conqueror of Asia. Olympias, would be remembered as the mother of Alexander, enduring a stormy marriage to Philip, extremely ruthless and fiercely ambitious for her son, and a likely conspirator in the assassination of Philip.

Arrhidaeus, a minor player remembered only as Alexander's half-brother with a learning disability, who went on to become king of Macedonia after Alexander's death, ironically enough. Leonnatus, one of the king's bodyguards who killed Pausanius with a javelin, after he stabbed Philip. Perdiccas, also one of the king's bodyguards, and brother in law of Attalus, who gave chase to Pausanius, after the assassination. Thessalus, one of Alexander's closest friends and an accomplished actor. Ptolemy, close friend of Alexander and possible illegitimate son of Philip, due to the king having had a relationship with his mother Arsinoe.

Ptolemy, of course, after the death of Alexander went on to take control of Egypt, creating the Ptolemaic dynasty, the last ruler of which was the famous queen Cleopatra, lover and seducer of first Julius Caesar and then Marc Antony. I had a particular soft spot for him because he also created the great library of Alexandria, which unfortunately was burnt down by Caesar's army. And then finally, amongst the guests at this dinner party was Heromenes; a man pretty much forgotten by history, even though as it was now turning out, he was a co-conspirator in the assassination of Philip, and from what I was clearly seeing that evening, a lover of Olympias.

'Are Heromenes and Olympias lovers?' I asked Arrhidaeus, as we made our way back to the palace across the fields.

'It's an open secret that my father takes great delight in ridiculing Heromenes. Heromenes is obsessively infatuated with Olympias and will literally do anything for her. That's why it doesn't surprise me at all to know he is in on the plot to kill my father. I despise the man, and am feeling comforted in the knowledge I am going to stop him from committing the ghastly deed.'

'Why do you despise him so much?'

'I have only had one great love in my life. Her name was Dora. One day about six months ago, on my way to the markets I saw my love kissing Heromenes in a nearby inn. It was a passionate kiss, forged in my mind forever. Without giving her any explanation, I ended the relationship and stopped seeing her. I was utterly heartbroken.'

The next day was full of joyous celebration at the palace. Cleopatra, the daughter of Philip and Olympias was marrying her uncle Alexander, Olympias' brother and the king of Epirus. This marriage was arranged by Philip to enable him to form a political alliance with the Greek kingdom of Epirus. Alexander had been brought to the court of Philip in 350 BCE for his protection from family members seeking to kill him, so they could eliminate him as a potential rival to the throne of Epirus. Philip's actions put a stop to that.

In 342 Philip was instrumental in making Alexander king of Epirus, after dethroning Alexander's uncle Arybbas. In 334, two years after marrying Cleopatra, at the request of the Greek colony of Taras, Alexander crossed the Adriatic into Italy to aid them in battle against the Italic Samnite tribes, defeating them in 332, and making a peace treaty with the Romans. This particularly sparked my interest, because, as I have mentioned previously, the Samnites originated from Molise, the region of central Italy in the Apennine mountains, in which my parents were born.

After the death of her husband in battle in 331, Cleopatra ruled as queen of Epirus. After the death of her brother, Alexander the Great, a number of the conquerors' closest friends and generals, including Leonnatus and Perdiccas, attempted to marry Cleopatra in order to enhance their own power and prestige. She rejected them. In 308 though, she accepted a marriage proposal from Ptolemy, as we have seen, a close friend and general of Alexander the Great, and ruler of Egypt; but before it occurred she was captured by Antigonus, the King of Sardis, and yet another general in Alexander's conquering army, who after spurning his requests to marry her, and believing she had become too powerful and influential, arranged for her to be executed in that same year.

The palace had been transformed. It was going to be a lavish festival with much entertainment and games. Philip had invited various guests from all over his kingdom and beyond to take part in all of the celebratory activities, and witness the marriage of his beloved daughter. He also invited Olympias, the mother of the bride and the sister of the groom. At first she was apprehensive, but after being assured that Philip would welcome her, she accepted the invitation.

True to his word, Philip was courteous and made up with her on the morning of the first day of the wedding celebrations. On the first day, most of the celebrations were held in the great banquet hall of the palace. As I stood near the entrance I could see hundreds of nobles from throughout the Macedonian-Greek world and beyond enjoying an incredible assortment of the most delicious food and wine, brought to the palace from all corners of the kingdom, prepared and served by an army of servants who were in constant discrete motion from the kitchens to the hall.

Meanwhile, outside the palace building in the gardens were over 3,000 regular Macedonian citizens enjoying food, wine, and continuous entertainment by musicians, dancers, actors, jesters, athletes, and poets. The morning had started at sunrise in Philip's private temple in the presence of the high priests, with the bridal couple sacrificing a cow to the gods, immersing themselves in its blood, as an offering of good fortune in their marriage.

Arrhidaeus remained by my side for most of the day, offering a running commentary on who the various nobles were, where they were from, and the family, political, or diplomatic ties they had with Philip. He also introduced me to many of the guests, and filled me with much thrilling gossip. It was interesting to see three groups forming within the great hall; one surrounding Philip, another surrounding his son Alexander, and another surrounding Olympias.

This said it all for me. The political factions within the Macedonian court were laid out in that hall for anyone to clearly see. I kept a watchful eye on Pausanius and Heromenes throughout the day; at no stage did I see them make any contact with each other, nor with Olympias. Clearly, they had gone to extraordinary lengths to avoid each other, and therefore any suspicion.

Everybody was asked to leave the great hall in the middle of the afternoon, to enable the servants to prepare the hall for a lavish banquet, and set up the stage for evening performances by the very best musicians and actors in the Macedonian and Greek worlds. Three very large elaborately decorated marquees were set up within the gardens of the palace, in a heavily guarded area cordoned off from the regular citizens. Again, like clockwork, the three political factions congregated within their respective marquees. Arrhidaeus and I, like many other invited guests, floated between the Philip and Alexander crowds. Tellingly, there was a smaller group in the Olympias marquee, many of whom were Greek nobility, who virtually all remained in that location.

Then at sunset, with much fanfare, all of the invited guests made their way back into the great hall and were allocated seats at one of the four long banquet tables. I could see that Philip had gone to great lengths to seat everybody in a manner that was the most politically and diplomatically advantageous to him. I had never seen such an abundance and variety of food laid out on the tables. There were richly coloured exotic fruits as well as the usual variety of hot and cold meats, vegetables, seafood, and an assortment of olives, cheeses, breads, and nuts; and much free flowing wine.

The entertainment was just spectacular! Young male and female dancers in colourful costumes were meandering throughout the hall and in between the tables, to the sound of orchestral music rich in strings, flutes, and percussion. What I remember the most was the constant beating of drums in perfect unison with the young exotic dancers.

The bride and groom had their own table smack-bang in the centre of the great hall, and were receiving much attention from the performers. When the dancers and musicians were finished, the second act was a theatrical performance the likes of which I have never seen before. It was clearly a dramatic Greek tragedy being performed by over thirty actors in elaborate costumes on the big stage; and low and behold, the star of the performance was none other than Alexander the Great's close friend, Thessalus, who 'died' in the most tragic circumstances at the end of the production.

Philip was clearly having the time of his life. He was a loud, boisterous, and jovial man. As I watched him so happy, chatting away with a constant stream of guests coming to him at the head of the royal table, I had three overriding thoughts flooding my mind. Firstly, what a great negotiator and diplomat he was, for that was exactly what he was actively engaging in, throughout his daughter's wedding! Secondly, if I had not been sent from the future to intervene, this was going to be his last night alive.

My final thoughts were more elaborate. I don't know why, but I kept thinking about the historical sources which recounted Philip's own marriage to his seventh wife Cleopatra-Eurydice, the young Macedonia noble. During the first evening of celebrations, the bride's uncle, general Attalus, had insulted Alexander the Great by praying to the gods that his niece would produce a legitimate heir to the throne. Alexander was so offended that he threw a wine goblet at Attalus while shouting out: 'What do you take me for, a bastard?!' Philip then stood up, drew his sword and charged towards his son, but collapsed onto the floor in a drunken stupor. Alexander was then heard to say: 'This is the man who wants to go from Europe to Asia, but cannot cross the room from one table to the next.' Soon after, Alexander and his mother were exiled from the kingdom.

Later that evening, even though the festivities continued into the night and into the next day, Arrhidaeus and I were able to disappear upstairs for an hour or so, to put in place a detailed plan of action. We sat on the couch in his room, wine goblets in hand.

'I believe my father will not be escorted by any of his bodyguards when he enters the theatre tomorrow morning. He now considers himself to be invincible, protected by the gods, so doesn't want mere mortals guarding him.'

'Well that decision cost him his life, the first time around. Arrhidaeus, I have been thinking long and hard about how we will prevent the assassination from happening. We must stop Pausanius and Heromenes from entering the theatre. They are still in the palace downstairs as we speak. Is there a servant in this palace whom you particularly trust?'

Arrhidaeus paused, thinking carefully. 'Yes. Stefanos is very loyal to me. He will do whatever I instruct him.'

'Is he downstairs now?'

'Yes. What are you thinking, Luca?'

'Okay. My plan is for Stefanos to approach Pausanius and let him know there is a messenger outside the entrance to the palace who has important information to pass on to him. He will be on tender hooks so out of sheer curiosity and nervous anxiety, will go outside. When he does, you and I will be waiting for him. We will ambush him. I will strike him with a blow to the back of the upper neck. I am trained in martial arts to the highest level, having done it since I was literally 6 years old. So I know precisely where to strike him to render him unconscious but not risking killing him. We will then tie his hands and feet, gag him, and carry him to one of the small storage buildings near the main lake in the palace gardens. This area is a fair distance from the palace entrance, dark and secluded, so nobody will see us. Then we will do exactly the same with Heromenes, straight after dealing with Pausanius.'

'Simple and brilliant,' said Arrhidaeus, duly impressed.

Arrhidaeus was such an honourable man. I could see why Philip and Alexander were so fond of him. His mother Philinna was a Thessalian dancer who Philip had seduced. His learning difficulties ruled him out as a rival to his half-brother for the throne. To further his power and political influence in Persia, Philip had wanted Arrhidaeus to marry the daughter of the Persian satrap of Caria, Pixodarus; even though the satrap had offered his daughter to Alexander, and Philip declined. Upon hearing his father was now offering his half-brother in marriage instead, Alexander became angry, fearing such a union might produce a possible heir who would rival his claim to the throne, so it didn't proceed.

The historical sources mention Olympias may have been responsible for Arrhidaeus' learning difficulties, by drugging him with harmful poison, in an attempt to eliminate him as a potential rival to her son for the throne; but there is no proof of this. I wouldn't put it past her though, having witnessed her ruthless ambition firsthand. When Philip died, Alexander took his half-brother with him on his military campaigns into Persia and Asia, to protect him from being used as a pawn, or from possible assassination by rival noble families. After Alexander died in 323 BCE, the Macedonian army in Asia proclaimed Arrhidaeus as king, taking the name Philip III of Macedonia. However, he was just a figurehead, with the real power being held by general Perdiccas.

When Alexander died, an immediate conflict arose between Perdiccas, the commander of the cavalry; and Meleager, the commander of the phalanx army. Perdiccas did not want Arrhidaeus to become king, but instead wanted to wait and see whether the pregnant Persian wife of Alexander, Roxana, was expecting a baby boy. If so, he believed the infant should become king, and Perdiccas, his regent. On the other hand, Meleager wanted Arrhidaeus, as the closest living relative of Alexander, to become king.

After the murder of Meleager under highly suspicious circumstances, a compromise was agreed by Perdiccas. Arrhidaeus would become king and assume the name Philip III; but Roxana's infant son would assume the name Alexander IV and become co-sovereign; with Perdiccas acting as the regent for the infant. This resulted in Philip Arrhidaeus becoming a token king, and the real grip on power well and truly being in the hands of Perdiccas.

Shortly after becoming king, Cynane, the daughter of Philip II, travelled to Asia to offer Arrhidaues her daughter Eurydice as a wife. Fearing this as a threat to his hold on power, Perdiccas sent his brother Alcetas to Macedonia in an attempt to kill Cynane. When Alexander's troops in Asia heard of this plot, they reacted with such indignity and shock that they insisted the marriage go ahead. After the marriage, the influence of Perdiccas was eclipsed by Eurydice, who held major sway over her husband king Philip Arrhidaues III. Eurydice's chance to put her newfound power into action came when the first war of the Diadochi sealed the fate of Perdiccas, creating a new settlement at Triparadisus in Syria in 320 BCE.

The wars of the Diadochi were a series of conflicts that were fought between the surviving generals (Diadochi) of Alexander the Great, to gain territory and power as a result of disputes over the rule of his empire. The wars occurred between 322 and 281 BCE. Eurydice moved swiftly to orchestrate the removal of the first nominated regent, Peithon, representing Roxana and Alexander's infant son (Alexander IV); but was powerless to block the too-powerful, Antipater, who was made new regent. Philip Arrhidaeus and his wife Eurydice were forced to follow Antipater to Macedonia.

Antipater died of natural causes in the following year, nominating as his successor-regent not his son Cassander, but a friend of his, Polyperchon. Cassander's refusal to accept his father's decision sparked the second war of the Diadochi, in which Eurydice once again saw a chance to free Philip Arrhidaeus from the control of the regent. An opportunity presented itself in 317 BCE, when Cassander expelled Polyperchon from Macedonia. Eurydice immediately allied herself with Cassander and persuaded her husband to nominate him as the new regent. Cassander reciprocated by leaving Eurydice in full control of the kingdom of Macedonia when he left on a military campaign in Greece.

All this succeeded in doing, was creating an extremely volatile situation, when in the same year of 317, Polyperchon and Olympias (yes, Alexander the Great's still-alive scheming mother!), allied themselves with the Greek king of Epirus, Aeacides, when he invaded Macedonia. Overwhelmed by this invasion, Philip Arrhidaeus and Eurydice had no choice but to escape, only to be captured at Amphipolis and thrown into prison. It soon became clear that Philip Arrhidaeus was too dangerous and influential to be kept alive, because many enemies of Olympias saw him as a useful tool who could be used against her; so as a result, Olympias, the mother of Alexander the Great, had him executed on 25th December 317 BCE, while his wife Eurydice was forced to commit suicide.

In the following year, when Cassander reconquered Macedonia and avenged Philip Arrhidaeus' death, he interred the bodies of Philip Arrhidaeus and Eurydice in a royal ceremony held at the palace in Aegae, and held funeral games in their honour. Olympias died in the following year, 316, a sad, lonely, and bitter elderly woman.

We waited outside the palace in complete silence in the darkness as the servant Stefanos delivered the message to Pausanius to come outside. Suddenly Pausanius appeared. As we had arranged, Arrhidaeus walked towards him as a distraction while I crept behind him and delivered a precise blow to the back of his upper neck with the open palm of my hand. He immediately fell to the ground. We quickly gagged and tied him. He was frantically gyrating to try and prevent us subduing him. This was to no avail. Soon we had him firmly under control and proceeded to carry him to one of the small storage buildings in the palace gardens. We repeated exactly the same process with Heromenes, except this time, we took him into one of the adjoining storage buildings. There were five of them in total. They were both securely tied down, and weren't going anywhere. Exhausted, we then called it a night. Tomorrow was going to be an eventful day.

On the morning of 21st October 336 BCE, I arose half an hour before sunrise, quickly dressed and met Arrhidaeus downstairs just as the sun was about to rise. The entourage was already gathered around Philip. I could hear the steady rhythm of drums. All of the invited guests were seated in the theatre and were being entertained by a troop of acrobats and dancers. The gathering in the theatre was the climax of the marriage festival. It started with a procession involving the carrying of marble statues of the 12 Olympian gods, followed by a bigger bronze statue of King Philip II.

A large number of foreign dignitaries from neighbouring Greek city-states and alliances as well as the Macedonian nobility were gathered in the theatre. Once the statues were in place, just as Arrhidaeus had predicted, Philip entered alone, supposedly to show that he did not need his bodyguards around him to stay safe among his own people.

I had been advised earlier that Philip intended to enter with the two Alexanders (his son and son-in-law), but changed his mind at the last minute, sending them ahead of him. From where I was seated in the front row alongside Arrhidaeus, I had close and unrestricted access to the king and his entourage. As Philip moved to the centre of the stage to acknowledge the cheers of the crowd, I caught a glimpse of one of the king's bodyguards, Attalos, who was seated four seats to my right. Having delivered a brief speech thanking everybody for attending, and wishing his daughter and son in law the blessings of the gods; Philip was now making his way in my direction to his nearby seat, in between the two Alexanders.

As he was walking unaccompanied, I saw Attalos jump out of his seat in an agitated state and race towards Philip. I darted out of my seat instinctively and projected myself forward in a thrusting dive toward Attalos just as he was about to insert a dagger into Philip. The crowd was horrified. I heard screams and gasps. Everything happened in split seconds.

The next thing I knew, I had toppled Attalos to the ground literally at the feet of Philip, and firmly wrapped my hands around the would-be assassin's neck. He still had the knife in his hand and was about to dig it into my chest, when I grabbed his right wrist, and with all of the force I could muster pushed the knife away from me. Then, in an instant he instead plunged the knife into his stomach. Bleeding profusely, he lay there, losing consciousness right in front of my eyes, as the bodyguards immediately whisked a startled Philip out of the theatre and towards the sanctuary of his palace. Luckily for me, the knife did not damage any of his vital organs, and Attalos survived.

'You saved my life Luca. How can I ever repay you?'

I was in Philip's quarters with Arrhidaeus. He had asked everybody else to leave the room.

'My king, I did nothing more than what you would have done for me.'

'Of all the people who would want to kill me, I would never have imagined Attalos.'

'It was a conspiracy father', said Arrhidaeus, himself still in a state of shock. He went on, 'last night we subdued the two other assassins, Pausanius and Heromenes. They are still bound and gagged in your palace gardens as we speak.'

'They are scum! Heromenes' father Aeropus put them up to this!! He has coveted my crown for a long time. He thinks his family bloodline is more noble and of purer Macedonian blood than mine, and despises me! How did you know of this attempt on my life?'

I had to respond to this question very carefully and diplomatically, conscious of Otto's instructions not to reveal any information which may destabilise the wormhole. I certainly needed to leave Olympias out of it. I was relieved he hadn't accused her. I couldn't share the whole truth with Philip.

'I overheard Pausanius and Heromenes late last night in the palace gardens, thinking they were alone. As soon as I grasped the horrid deed they were planning, I let your son know. That's when we swung into action and took them both out of the equation. We had no idea Attalos was also involved.'

Hours later, I was back in the 21st century about to be debriefed by Otto. We met at a piano bar, close to where I lived. I could see Otto was very nervous when he arrived. He clearly wasn't accustomed to noisy public venues.

'Do you have music and entertainment in your world, Otto?'

'No. We don't have what you call, music. Our main form of entertainment comes from virtual reality holograms. We can recreate any thought, any period in our history, or any scenery. I know your civilization is at the cusp of developing this technology too. We have had it for centuries, so have perfected it to the point that many of our citizens choose to remain in their virtual worlds, rather than experience the reality of their lives.'

'Well, that's interesting to know.'

'You did well Luca. The mission was a success. In that multiverse, Philip goes on to live another twenty years before his son Alexander takes over and rules for another twenty years. During that period, father and son establish Macedonia as the greatest empire of the ancient world; not only controlling the majority of the Greek city-states including Athens and Sparta; but also the Persian empire, and much of the Italian peninsula. After conquering Persia, Philip and Alexander turned their formidable army onto the Roman Republic, allying themselves with the Samnites, and defeating the Romans in a series of battles. After Italy, their forces conquered Carthage in north Africa. The end result was a formidable empire that lasted until the death of Alexander the Great; when it then imploded due to its sheer size, corrupt rulers, and invading barbarian tribes. But all of this has set the butterfly effect on the right path, Luca.

As instantly as Otto appeared, he had vanished. I knew it wouldn't be long before he re-emerged to brief me on my second mission – to stop the assassination of Julius Caesar. I needed to see my mother before embarking on that next mission. She was the matriarch of my family. The glue that held it together. In her early seventies, every Sunday night she arranged a family dinner at her place. In addition to her, also attending this weekly family event were my three older brothers, their partners, and children. I envied my brothers. They each had two kids. I had four nephews and two nieces.

My Mum would get up at sunrise on Sunday morning to prepare her hand made pasta, alternating between ravioli, gnocchi, cannelloni, and my absolute favourite, her lasagne. During the dinner, my eldest brother would play my father's favourite Dean Martin and Frank

Sinatra songs. We were all engaged in animated conversations. If you've seen a group of Italians together, it seems like they are talking over each other, even quarrelling, when in fact everybody is listening intently and with great respect! It's just that we've mastered the art of engaging in multiple conversations at the same time, and finishing each other's sentences.

While I was relaxing on my sofa, enjoying my favourite Montepulciano red wine, with the television news flickering in the background, my mind wandered back to my childhood, and happy memories of the family making our home made tomato sauce. My father and uncle would go to the same farm each year, and pick the very best tomatoes.

Then over a weekend we would make the tomato sauce; washing the tomatoes, cleaning the empty beer bottles, boiling the tomatoes in a large stainless steel pot, adding spices, extracting the sauce by hand, then filling and sealing each bottle. The tomato sauce was based on a family recipe going back over 300 years from the Molise region of central Italy where my parents were born. It is in the Apennine mountains of Molise, where the ancient Samnite tribes that fought against Rome, originated.

With my eyes closed, and in a totally relaxed state, I imagined the delicious taste of my Mum's home-made ravioli, cannelloni, or lasagne, dripping in our tasty fresh tomato sauce, often accompanied by her meatballs, made with a mixture of pork and beef, and the size of tennis balls. It wasn't only tomato sauce we made, but also dried sausages, and red wine. Such wonderful memories flooding into my mind. I missed my father so much. He was too young to die in the tragic way he did.

Mad World

All around me are familiar faces
Worn out places, worn out faces
Bright and early for the daily races
Going nowhere, going nowhere

Their tears are filling up their glasses
No expression, no expression
Hide my head, I wanna drown my sorrow
No tomorrow, no tomorrow

And I find it kind of funny
I find it kind of sad
The dreams in which I'm dying
Are the best I've ever had
I find it hard to tell you
I find it hard to take
When people run in circles it's a very, very
Mad world, mad world

Children waiting for the day they feel good
Happy birthday, happy birthday
And I feel that every child should
Sit and listen, sit and listen

Went to school and I was very nervous
No one knew me, no one knew me
Hello, teacher! Tell me, what's my lesson?
Look right through me, look right through me

And I find it kind of funny
I find it kind of sad
The dreams in which I'm dying
Are the best I've ever had

I find it hard to tell you
I find it hard to take
When people run in circles it's a very, very
Mad world, mad world

Enlarging your world
Mad world

Roland Orzabal – Tears for Fears (1982)

4

Julius Caesar

Rome, Italy, March 44 BCE

When Otto told me the name of my contact in Rome, I was very excited, but also apprehensive. So much has been written in the history books about this man, much of it complimentary, even more not so complimentary. This person was in the eye of the storm which was to climax with the assassination of Julius Caesar. He fought alongside Caesar in the eight-year campaign for the conquest of Gaul. He was a cousin of Caesar. Feared by the noble patricians and admired by the plebeians.

Although a brilliant general, he was a compulsive womaniser and gambler, heavy drinker, and always short of money. Many considered him to be the first true celebrity, in the modern-day sense of that word. He was an impulsive, highly emotional, and very aggressive man, with a short temper, one minute friendly and charismatic, and the next minute, prone to outbursts and full of rage. I began to wonder why Otto had chosen this man. Did he trust him enough?

I arrived in the centre of the Roman Forum on the 13th March in the year 44 BCE. It was a well-planned rectangular-shaped area, situated on low-lying land between the Palatine Hill and Capitoline Hill. The Forum was the nerve-centre of important religious, political, legal, economic, and social activities in the Roman Republic. The Forum was a hive of activity. It was just after midday. The news announcer was on his podium, crying out the events of the day while people walked past him, going about their everyday lives, apparently oblivious to his presence, but no doubt listening in. What immediately struck me were the buildings. They were magnificent, covered in marble with imposing columns, glistening in the reflection of the bright sunlight, and towering over the Forum.

I recognised the Senate, under repair, one of the largest buildings in the Forum, alongside the even larger administration and treasury building. Also nearby were the public baths. People from all social rankings were coming in and out of this temple of relaxation, and socialising. It seems the sources were correct when they referred to the baths allowing, slaves, plebeians, equestrians, and patricians to all access the hot pools, spas, and steam at the same time.

What also grabbed my attention was the clear distinctions within the social and power hierarchy based on what people were wearing and doing. There were wealthy and powerful patricians, dressed in multi-coloured silk togas, purple and red being the most prominent, in no particular hurry, engaging in animated conversation. They were few and far between and were mostly congregated outside what I immediately recognised to be the Temple of Jupiter, the most important temple in ancient Rome, located on the Capitoline Hill. It was surrounded by the Area Capitolina, a precinct consisting of shrines, altars, statues, and monuments.

The majority of people were plebeians, wearing drab dirt-covered white togas. There were merchants, couriers, artisans, farmers, carpenters, shop-keepers, fruit and vegetable sellers, butchers, barbers, bakers, tax collectors, priests, prostitutes, soldiers; all of whom seemed to be in a hurry. Where were they going? I could also see slaves clearly engaging in the most mundane manual tasks, such as street-sweepers, servants, and labourers.

Mixed in with this diversity of people were horses with carts, and stray dogs. The Forum was a rich mixture of diverse sounds, ranging from multiple conversations, echoing shouting, screaming, bouts of laughter, the newsreader, carts moving along the numerous narrow roads branching out from the Forum, and the barking of dogs.

My rendezvous point was right in front of the newsreader. His booming voice could be heard echoing around the Forum as he was informing the gathering crowd about the upcoming gladiatorial games, preparations for the Parthian military campaign, religious festivals with free food and wine to celebrate particular gods, and grain shipments arriving from Egypt. As I was standing in the bright midday sunlight amongst the relatively small and confined crowd intently listening to the newsreader, there was a tap on my shoulders, and I instinctively swung my head around.

'You must be Marc Antony?'

'The one and only. Come Luca, let's get away from this noisy babble.'

With that, we walked across the Forum and up the Palatine Hill, passing one luxurious villa after another. Marc Antony walked quickly, with confident strides which I imagined must be the hallmark of great generals, as I meekly followed behind him. He was constantly being greeted by passers-by. Antony pleasantly responded and addressed each of them by name. He was definitely a celebrity. These villas were owned by the elite patricians of Rome, including many serving as senators.

After walking for around fifteen minutes, with the crowds thinning, we arrived at a fairly humble non-descript villa on a side street off the main boulevard coming from the Forum, and entered. As I walked in I saw two slaves enter the small reception court-yard, one, a beautiful young lady with jet-black glossy long flowing hair, whispered to Antony; while the other, an older thin bald man, brought in an ornately decorated ceramic jug of wine.

'Welcome to my little slice of paradise,' said Antony beaming with pride. 'I had a bigger villa on the boulevard, but had to sell it to pay off my gambling debts. Make yourself comfortable, while I fix you a wine.'

He sat on a reclining couch opposite me, as we sipped our wine. He was a strikingly handsome, muscular man, with curly black hair, piercing brown eyes, and clearly charismatic. I had read so much about the great Marc Antony, and now here he was, the man himself, my helper in Rome. I was feeling speechless. This must be how fans of celebrities feel when they meet their idols, I thought. Marc Antony definitely had that effect on me. He was at the centre of so many events in late Roman Republican history that I couldn't help but be overwhelmed by his presence.

Did the surviving sources get the character and intentions of Marc Antony right? Did the sources get the assassination of Julius Caesar right? These were some of the fascinating questions I was hoping to get definitive answers to. I was feeling apprehensive sure, but the excitement of this mission was really hitting me as I sat there in his presence.

'Do you know, when Otto came into my dreams, and then appeared in real life, telling me about the fate of Caesar, I was shocked. I'm still finding it difficult to believe that my dear friend and great leader is going to be killed in the Senate house the day after tomorrow! Otto told me although there were many conspirators, the leaders were Brutus and Cassius! My initial guttural reaction was to literally go out and break their necks with my bear hands. Believe me Luca, I still want to kill those despicable creatures. But Otto made it very clear to me that if I so much as even let anybody know about the assassination, let alone harm anybody, then history will never be changed, Caesar will definitely die, and your future world will end in disaster.'

'I must admit, Antony, I was very surprised when Otto told me you were my contact here in Rome. You are very close to Caesar, related to him, and have fought many battles alongside him. I understand the rage you feel, and admire you deeply for containing it.'

'It's not going to be easy to contain it, Luca. But I'm glad you are here, and that together we can stop this despicable deed from occurring. I will need you to check my impulses to kill those bastards, though.'

'Antony, we can assume that by now, the conspirators have formulated their plot, and are just laying low, biding their time until the Ides of March. This gives us time to discuss and implement my plan to stop it.'

'What plan do you have in mind, Luca?'

'I want you to introduce me to Marcus Tullius Cicero.'

'Why do you want to meet that little turd? He's not involved in the conspiracy is he? I will kill him if he is!!'

'Antony, I am concerned you will have a brain-snap for a few seconds and kill somebody, thus undoing our chance to stop the assassination. Please promise me now, that there will be no violent outbursts while I am here for the next couple of days?'

Antony looked directly at me, full of rage, but I could see in his eyes, he clearly understood the gravity of the situation. I felt certain there would be no violence from him, even though he didn't respond to my question.

'Is Cicero involved?' Antony repeated.

'I don't know. The surviving sources indicate he wasn't aware of the conspiracy, even though he approved of the assassination after the event, claiming that Cassius and Brutus had carried out a noble act, and saved the Republic from a tyrant.'

'Caesar, a tyrant? He is a man of the people. He is disgusted with the indecent corrupt behaviour of the senators and rich landowners. Caesar has worked tirelessly to give the people of Rome a better quality of life. He is no tyrant.'

'Why do you want to meet Cicero?' Antony again asked.

'Because Cicero is a very influential senator. His opinion holds sway with a majority of the senate. We need to persuade him to cancel the senate meeting on the Ides of March, in two days. He has grave reservations about Caesar, and believes he is setting himself up to become King of Rome. As you know Antony, Caesar is due to leave Rome for the East three days after the Ides to lead an army to conquer Parthia, and retrieve the standard confiscated by them when they defeated Crassus' army nine years ago and brutally executed him by pouring molten gold down his throat. You in fact will be leading the Roman army out of Rome alongside Caesar, will you not?'

'Well yes. Yes I am. But you are assuming Caesar will still be alive, Luca.'

'He will be. We are going to make sure of that. I will need your help. You have many connections in this city.'

'Yes I do. But Cicero is not one of them.'

'I am well aware of Cicero's hatred of you. He thinks you are unworthy of holding a position of responsibility in the Republic, such as tribune of the plebs. He fears you Antony. He sees you as a tyrant-in-the-making as much as Caesar. We need to capitalize on his fear of you, to convince him to cancel the senate meeting.'

'Well, we can attend Cicero's villa tomorrow morning, on the pretext I have some urgent tribune business I wish to discuss with him. I can introduce you as a personal friend of mine from northern Italy who is a fellow lawyer and an admirer of Cicero. How does that sound?'

'That's fine. How much influence do you have in the plebeian assembly?'

'Luca, as Caesar's representative, I have enormous power over all of the other tribunes in the assembly, all of whom are great admirers of Caesar. Cicero knows I have the assembly in the palm of my hand.'

'I thought that was the case. Now correct me if I'm wrong, but the plebeian assembly has the power to veto decisions made by the senate. Does it not?'

'Yes, of course it does.'

'Does that include decisions to call a meeting of the senate when there is a conflict with the interests of the assembly and the Republic?'

'What do you mean?' said Antony, looking very puzzled.

'I believe the plebeian assembly has the power to veto the senate meeting on the Ides, because it will interfere with yours and Caesar's planning of the Parthian military campaign. In other words, Caesar is going to be preoccupied on that day and will not be able to attend the senate. The Parthian campaign is of great importance to the Republic, and it is on this basis that you are going to persuade Cicero tomorrow to not go ahead with the senate meeting. As a duly appointed Dictator, it will be ludicrous if the meeting goes ahead without Caesar's presence. In fact, Antony, the senate appointed him Dictator in order to safeguard the interests of the Republic, did it not?'

'Well technically yes. In reality they appointed him Dictator because they were shit scared of him and his army, and wanted to curry favour by staying in his good books.'

'I have considered whether Caesar can exercise his emergency powers as Dictator and cancel the senate meeting himself, but if he does that, he will be playing right into the hands of the conspirators who believe he is behaving like a tyrannical king. So the plebeian assembly is the best avenue; and you hold the power over the tribunes in that assembly. What do you think of my plan, Antony?'

'Excellent. I will relish the opportunity to put that whining delicate loud-mouthed pansy in his place, along with his band of power-hungry empty-headed corrupt senators!'

That evening, I was laying on a comfortable bed in Antony's villa. He requested I stay with him, and his servants prepared a room for me. I began to recount in my mind, the achievements of Mark Antony, according to the surviving sources.

Marcus Antonius was born in Rome in 83 BCE. He was the son of a praetor (military commander) and grandson of a respected consul, both of whom shared his name. As a young cavalry officer he was deployed in the East, where he was part of an army led by general Pompey that won major victories in Palestine and Egypt. In 54 he went to Gaul to join his mother's cousin, Julius Caesar as a general. In 49 he was elected a tribune of the plebeian assembly and served as a staunch defender of Caesar against his rivals in the senate. During Caesar's first yearlong dictatorship, Antony was his second in command.

By 48 he was in Greece with Caesar in the Battle of Pharsalus. A year later, Antony's violent expulsion from the senate by the anti-Caesar faction gave Julius Caesar and his legions a big motivation to cross the Rubicon River in northern Italy and trigger the Republican Civil War in 47 between those loyal to Caesar and those loyal to Pompey. Caesar prevailed. After his defeat Pompey fled to Egypt where he was brutally executed. When Caesar assumed his fifth and final consulship in 44, Antony was his co-consul. He still continued to hold his tribune position. During the feast of Lupercal, Antony offered Caesar a crown to wear on three separate occasions, with Caesar refusing to wear it each time.

We don't know if this was a set-up in order for Caesar to dramatically demonstrate to the people he was not a tyrant and had no interest in becoming king, or if not, then we don't know Antony's motives for doing this. As the Ides of March approached, Antony had become aware of rumours of a plot against Caesar but was unable to warn him in time. After the death of Caesar, he did everything he could to protect his friend's legacy from the senators who had conspired against him. He took charge of Caesar's Will and during the funeral delivered a passionate eulogy for the stricken leader, igniting the rage of the common people against Caesar's assassins.

In his eulogy, Antony spectacularly persuaded the audience to withdraw its support of Brutus, who he said, was a cold-blooded murderer and not a defender of the Republic as he claimed, and to condemn him as a traitor. With tears streaming down his face, Antony engaged in dramatic rhetoric to stir the crowd to revolt against the conspirators. In fact, after the funeral, a mob of angry citizens attempted to storm the villas of Brutus, Cassius, and many of the other conspiring senators, forcing the conspirators to flee Rome, their lives in grave danger.

It came as a profound shock to Marc Antony when he found out Caesar had bequeathed his enormous wealth, reputation, and name to his posthumously adopted son Octavian. Antony was deeply humiliated and enraged. He had expected Caesar to anoint him as heir. Antony was very reluctant to hand over Caesar's legacy to a seventeen years-old boy, whom he considered unworthy of stepping into the shoes of the great conqueror. As a result, Antony moved to the north of Italy and put together an army of loyal troops to take on Octavian, who had won favour with Caesar's soldiers. In 43 the two armies first clashed. Outnumbered, Antony's army was driven back in two battles at Mutina and Forum Gallorum, but Antony had impressed Octavian so much as a military leader, that Octavian formed an alliance with him.

Along with their less-known rival Lepidus, who had been a close friend of Caesar, Octavian and Antony formed the Second Triumvirate, splitting the provinces of Rome between them. Octavian would remain in Rome and rule the West; Antony the East; and Lepidus Africa. Within a year, Antony led a triumvirate army and defeated Caesar's assassins, Brutus and Cassius, in the Battle of Phillipi in Greece, eliminating the two remaining leaders of the Republican cause in a battle that firmly established Antony's reputation as a formidable general.

In 41 BCE Antony began a passionate romantic affair with the Egyptian queen Cleopatra, who had been Caesar's lover in the last years of his life. Cleopatra was a descendant of Alexander the Great's close friend general Ptolemy, whom I had met, and who assumed the rule of Egypt after Alexander's death. Cleopatra and Antony had twins, Alexander Helios and Cleopatra Selene; but Antony was forced to return to Rome to deal with the aftermath of his wife and brother-in-law's failed rebellion against Octavian. The senate pushed for some kind of reconciliation between the triumvirs, forcing the recently widowed Antony to marry Octavian's sister, Octavia, in 40. In 37, after the triumvirate was renewed, Antony returned to Cleopatra and fathered a son, Ptolemy Philadelphus.

The lovers became more open in their relationship, participating in deification ceremonies where they took the roles of the Greco-Egyptian gods Dionysus-Osiris and Venus-Isis. In a provocative manner, they also paraded their three children, and Caesarion (Cleopatra's son by Julius Caesar) in costumes as legitimate royal heirs, flaunting the Roman law's refusal to acknowledge marriage with outsiders. Politically, Antony grew more and more interconnected with, and dependent on, the Egyptian kingdom, having turned to Cleopatra for help following his failed military campaign against the Parthians in 36.

Meanwhile, Octavian grew in power, eliminating Lepidus from the triumvirate on the pretext of a rebellion. In 32 Antony divorced Octavia. In retaliation, Octavian declared war, not on Antony, but on Cleopatra and Egypt. Soon after, a series of battles occurred in western Greece, where Antony and Cleopatra had superior numbers, but lost a number of decisive battles to the brilliant naval attacks of Octavian's general (and childhood friend) general Agrippa. After their combined forces were defeated in the Battle of Actium, on 2nd September 31 BCE, Antony and Cleopatra's remaining ships made a desperate getaway back to Egypt, hotly pursued by Agrippa and Octavian. As Octavian entered the exotic Egyptian capital Alexandria, Antony and Cleopatra made a pact to commit suicide. After thinking his lover had already committed the act, on the 1st of August 30 BCE Antony stabbed himself with a sword, dressed in his full Roman ceremonial military uniform, and was brought to die in the arms of a hysterical Cleopatra.

Octavian managed to capture Cleopatra and intended to bring her and her children back to Rome, but she was able to kill herself with a poisonous snakebite. After Antony's death, all of his Roman honours were revoked by the senate, and his statues were removed. Antony's major rival in the senate, Cicero, decreed that nobody in the dead general's family should ever bear the name Marc Antony again. Octavian had now become Emperor in all but name. Three years later in January 27 BCE he was granted the honorific name Augustus Caesar, and ruled Rome as its first Imperial Emperor for the next four decades, until he died in August 14 CE.

'The senator will see you now,' whispered a servant as we waited in a spacious well-furnished room adjoining Cicero's office.

His villa was luxurious. I knew that Cicero had expensive tastes. He came from a wealthy land-owning family; but in spite of this, they were not patricians, and he was proud of being a self-made man, rising all the way to the top, serving as Consul of Rome. Not only was he a brilliant orator and lawyer, aggressively defending the interests of the Republic, and pursuing corrupt officials, no matter how powerful and well connected they were; but he was also a distinguished philosopher and prolific writer. Much of Cicero's correspondence survived, helping future generations gain an in-depth understanding of the late Republic period of Rome. I often quoted Cicero in my ancient history classes.

'For what do I owe the honour of your visit, Antony?'

Cicero was sitting behind a very large white marble desk. It was piled up with scrolls. He was signing a number of documents, a servant standing alongside him. The servant grabbed the signed documents and left the room, staring at Antony. We were seated on a low couch, a couple of metres away from the desk, clearly designed in an intimidating manner to give the impression we were looking up to the great orator. As soon as we walked in, it was clear there was a frosty tension and animosity between them.

'My friend Luca is a lawyer and great admirer of yours. Don't know why,' Antony said with a cheeky grin.

Cicero ignored Antony, making me feel welcome with a smile.

'We cannot conduct the senate meeting tomorrow,' snapped Antony bluntly, startling the clearly annoyed Cicero.

'There is important business to discuss and resolve in the senate. Why can't we hold the meeting?'

'Because Caesar and I have much planning to attend to in preparation for the Parthian campaign. You know we must depart Rome on the 18th, three days after the Ides.'

'This senate meeting was scheduled over a month ago. It must go ahead. As Consul and Dictator, Caesar must attend.'

The tension in the room was extreme.

'Now you listen to me very carefully. Caesar and I have the power to destroy you and your wretched followers. Do you hear me. We have played your game for long enough. Caesar is a man of the people. He has no time for your snot-faced patrician meetings! There is much planning he and I need to complete. We will not be attending the senate on the Ides. Do you understand?'

'Miss that meeting at your peril,' Cicero calmly responded.

Antony's rage was unleashed. He rose from the couch, walked

towards Cicero, came around to his side and grabbed his right hand.

'This is your weapon. You use this hand to attack my reputation and that of my good friend and man of the people, Caesar,' he said as he exerted an enormous squeezing force on his right hand, and pushed it backwards towards Cicero's right shoulder.

Cicero was grimacing with pain and looking directly into Antony's eyes. For what seemed like an eternity they maintained menacing eye contact. Then suddenly Antony let go of his hand.

'I am a tribune of the plebeian assembly! I again, demand the senate meeting tomorrow be cancelled!'

And with that, Antony proceeded to leave the room, motioning me to follow him.

Marcus Tullius Cicero was born in 106 BCE in the city of Arpinum in Latium. He was the son of a wealthy but non-patrician land-owning family who arranged for Cicero to be educated in Rome and Greece. In 89 he completed military service under Pompeius Strabo (the father of general Pompey) and made his first appearance in the courts as a defence lawyer in 81. In 79 he brilliantly defended Sextus Roscius against a fabricated charge of parricide (murdering his father), which established his reputation as a renowned lawyer and orator.

In 75 he commenced his public service career in the Republic as a quaestor (an elected position involving financial administration) in western Sicily. In his capacity of praetor, a judicial position of great power at this time, he made his first important political speech in 66, when, arguing against Quintus Lutatius Catalus and leading conservative Optimates in the senate, he spoke in favour of conferring on Pompey, command of the military campaign against Mithradates VI, king of Pontus, in north-eastern Anatolia (modern-day Turkey). His relationship with Pompey, whose hatred of Marcus Licinius Crassus he shared, was to be the focal point of his career in politics. In 63 he was elected Consul, ironically with the backing of the Optimates in the senate who feared the revolutionary ideas of his hostile rival, Catiline.

In one of his earliest consular speeches, he opposed the agrarian bill of Servilius Rullus, protecting the interests of the extremely wealthy land-owning absent Pompey; but his primary concern was to investigate and make public the treasonous intentions of Catiline, who after being defeated in the consular elections of 64, tried again in the elections of 63, over which Cicero presided, wearing armour beneath his toga for his own protection. Catiline suffered a humiliating loss, and out of revenge, planned to carry out an armed uprising in Italy, and an arson attack in Rome.

Cicero had difficulty in persuading the senate of the danger posed by Catiline, but a "last decree" proclaiming martial law was passed on 22nd October 63. On November 8th, after surviving an attempt on his life, Cicero delivered his first speech fiercely against Catiline in the senate, resulting in Catiline fleeing Rome that night. Evidence incriminating Catiline and his conspirators was secured by Cicero; and after a senatorial debate, in which Cato the Younger insisted on Catiline's execution, against the will of Julius Caesar; Cicero overrode Caesar and ordered the execution of Catiline and his conspirators.

When announcing their death to a large crowd with the single word "vixerunt" ("they are dead"), Cicero received a tremendous ovation from plebeians and patricians alike, which inspired his subsequent appeal in politics to "concordia ordinum" ("concord between the classes"). He was hailed as the "father of his country" and gained a great reputation as the defender of the Roman Republic. He was now at the pinnacle of his career.

At the end of 60 BCE, Cicero declined Caesar's invitation to join the First Triumvirate; a political alliance between Caesar, Crassus, and Pompey. Cicero considered this alliance to be unconstitutional and not in the interests of his beloved Republic. He also rejected an offer from Caesar in 59 to take a position on his staff in Gaul. In 58, when Publius Clodius became Consul, Cicero's life was in danger because he had given evidence against the Consul during a trial for profanity and corruption in 61. After Pompey refused to protect him, Cicero had no choice other than to flee Rome.

Publius Clodius then used his power to convince the senate to declare Cicero as an exile and enemy of the Republic. Cicero first went to Thessalonica in Macedonia, and then to Illyricum in Greece. In 57, thanks to the influence of Pompey and the tribune Titus Annius Milo, he was recalled to Rome on 4th August. Cicero landed at Brundisium Italy on that day and was greeted with great enthusiasm during his voyage back to Rome, which took a month. During the winter of 57-56 Cicero tried unsuccessfully to sever the strong political link between Pompey and Caesar. Pompey ignored Cicero's advice and renewed his triumvirate alliance with Caesar and Crassus at Luca in April 56.

Under heavy pressure from Pompey, Cicero then agreed to align himself with the "big three" in the senate, and committed himself to this loyalty, in writing. In 52 he was delighted when Milo killed Clodius but failed miserably in his legal defence of Milo. In 51 Cicero was persuaded to leave Rome to govern the province of Cilicia, in southern Anatolia, for a year. The province had been expecting a Parthian invasion, but it never happened, although Cicero did capture some brigands on Mount Amanus.

This feat resulted in the senate granting him a "supplicatio" which was a period of public thanksgiving. Cicero was disappointed by this. He had hoped for a full-on triumph, a processional return through the streets of Rome. There was widespread acknowledgment that he had governed Cilicia competently and with great integrity, unlike many corrupt governors of provinces during the years of the Republic.

By the time Cicero returned to Rome, Pompey and Caesar were fierce rivals for complete power. He was on the outskirts of Rome when Caesar crossed the Rubicon River and invaded Italy in January 49. Cicero met Pompey outside the walls of Rome on 17th January and accepted a commission to supervise the recruiting of soldiers in Campania. With Caesar's army close to Rome, Cicero decided not to leave Rome with Pompey and a group of anti-Caesar senators including Cato, on 17th March.

In a meeting with Caesar in Rome on 28th March, Cicero demonstrated great integrity and courage when he stated his intention to propose in the senate that Caesar should not pursue the war against Pompey any further. Cicero disapproved of Caesar's dictatorship, even though he realised that in the succession of battles which continued until 45, he would have been one of the first victims of Caesar's enemies, had they triumphed.

According to the surviving sources, Cicero was not involved in the conspiracy to assassinate Julius Caesar on 15th March, 44. Two days after the murder of Caesar he spoke in the senate in favour of a general amnesty to the conspirators. He then returned to his philosophical writing and visited his son, who was studying in Athens. At the end of August, he returned to Rome and delivered his 14 Philippic orations which condemned Marc Antony, imitating the great speeches of the Greek Demosthenes against what he perceived to be the tyrannical rule of Philip II of Macedonia. Cicero delivered the first of these speeches in the senate on 2nd September 44, and the last on 21st April 43; signifying his prominent re-entry into Roman politics.

His policy was to make every possible political use of Caesar's adopted son Octavian (the future Emperor Augustus), whose intelligence and maturity beyond his years, he severely underestimated. He sought to drive the senate to declare war on Marc Antony, who had taken control of events immediately after Caesar's death, and was now pursuing one of the assassins in Cisalpine Gaul. No sources have survived to show how Octavian managed to deceive Cicero in the intervening period between the defeat of Antony in Cisalpine Gaul in April, and Octavian's march on Rome to secure the consulship in August.

It was in May that Octavian learned of Cicero's ill-timed remark that "the young man should be given praise, distinctions, and then be disposed of." The Second Triumvirate comprising Octavian, Antony, and Lepidus was formed at the end of October; and Cicero was soon earmarked for execution, particularly at the urging of Antony. He was captured and killed near his country villa on the outskirts of Rome on 7th December 43 BCE. At the request of Marc Antony, his head and hands were displayed on the "rostra," the speakers' platform at the Forum in the centre of Rome.

It was now approaching midday. Antony and I were heading for an inn just outside the Forum to have lunch.

'Ah. This is my favourite place. The wine is sublime and the food is delicious.'

As soon as we walked in, it was obvious Antony was a celebrity. The chatter came to a grinding halt. There must have been over fifty people in the place. They were clearly not patricians, but everyday working people.

'Carry on!' said Antony in a commanding voice, as we sat at a table in the back corner of the rustic room.

An obese middle aged man approached us. He clearly was the owner of the place. Antony rattled off an order of roast meat, vegetables, an assortment of fruit and cheese, and an abundance of wine.

'Only the best for you, Antony. Please let Caesar know how grateful we the people are for being liberated and given hope for the future,' the owner said, beaming with genuine enthusiasm.

Antony did not say a word. Instead he motioned for the man to leave us, which he duly did. We were seated away from the others, and with the noise of their chatter echoing in the room, we could talk with discretion.

'I am going to protect Caesar, watch him like a hawk, be with him all of the time tomorrow, and not let anybody near him.'

Antony was clearly distressed as he spoke.

'Antony, it won't be as easy as that. We cannot alert Caesar to the threat on his life. He can't be suspicious in any way. Otherwise as you well know, history will just not change and neither will the future. Our focus needs to be on stopping the actual assassination. My fear is, even if Caesar doesn't attend the senate tomorrow, they will get to him in some other way either tomorrow, or in the next couple of days before he departs Rome. If Caesar can survive tomorrow, then we must persuade him to march out of Rome on the following day the 16th, and not the 18th as planned; and commence his Parthian campaign, with you by his side, and the great Roman army behind you both.'

'I know Caesar is very keen to get on with the Parthian campaign. He also detests senate meetings. I believe with the help of his other two key generals, I can convince him to not attend the senate tomorrow, and depart on the 16th. Caesar has invited me to dinner at his villa tonight. His good friends, and his two other closest generals, Decimus and Lepidus will be there. So all three of us will be with him to try and convince him to depart Rome earlier. I will go and visit Decimus and Lepidus this afternoon while you rest in my villa, and give them advance notice of our intentions. Caesar often invites people at short notice, so we can expect others may be there tonight as well. I want you to come along with me, Luca.'

I knew that many of the surviving sources mentioned Caesar's good friend Decimus as one of the key conspirators, but I did not consider it appropriate to mention this to Antony for two reasons; firstly, Otto clearly had not told him, and secondly, not all of the sources identified Decimus as a ringleader. I knew Antony respected him as much as Caesar; so it remained for us to see if he was involved.

'That's fine. I will look forward to meeting Caesar. Antony, the surviving sources mention that on the eve of the assassination, a number of the key conspirators met at the villa of Brutus. So I wonder if they will in fact be gathered there tonight. We need to plant somebody there tonight, listening in. If we can identify all of the key conspirators, then we should be able to keep Caesar safe tomorrow.'

'And how do you propose we do that, Luca?'

'If you could choose one man whom you trust with your life, a man who is fearless, not widely known, and has the ability to break into a villa unnoticed, find a safe hiding place, and listen to the conversations, who would that man be?'

'Appius is my man. He is my most trusted slave. My fixer. He is very capable of pulling this off, and very discrete. Appius is prepared to die for me, so if he is caught by the conspirators, he will immediately commit suicide. That's how loyal he is to me. I used him once to break into a patrician senator's villa, and take some gold he had hidden, to repay debts this swine owed to me. Appius did the job perfectly, completely unnoticed.'

'No suicides please Antony. Remember Otto's rules. If anybody dies in connection with our efforts to change the course of history, the wormhole will vaporize and all of our efforts will amount to zero!'

'Can you explain what a wormhole actually is, Luca?'

I ignored Antony's question. I was about to meet the great conqueror Julius Caesar, himself. A larger than life figure who for the better or worse, had stamped his authority not just on Rome, but on human history. As I rested alone in Antony's villa later that afternoon, goblet of undiluted wine and a bowl of olives in hand, I reflected upon his influence and the events of the assassination, as recorded in the surviving sources.

Julius Caesar had returned to Rome in triumph after conquering

Gaul for eight years, and was hailed as a hero. During his time as a Roman general, his army of legions killed almost two million people, and enslaved hundreds of thousands, in over fifty decisive battles. Although he was loved by the citizens of Rome, he caused great concern in the Roman senate, especially amongst the old elitist patrician Optimates. The man who was soon to be hailed as Dictator for life transferred his skills as a military commander into the political skills of leading the Republic. Demonstrating that he truly loved the people of Rome, he implemented a number of significant and necessary reforms which improved the lives of the ordinary plebeian people.

Always loyal to his army, one of his first decisions was to offer prime farming land in Italy to his experienced army veterans. Next, he gave grain to the urban poor and planned to move these same poor people to the newly acquired colonies in Anatolia (modern-day Turkey), Greece, and North Africa. He limited the terms of the provincial governors to ensure they didn't become too entrenched in power, enriching themselves from corrupt activities; and increased the size of the Senate to include many loyal followers.

Caesar created a new calendar which is still in use today, and provided both gladiatorial games and feasts to celebrate the gods, as a form of entertainment for the common people. Before becoming Consul and Dictator, the city of Rome had suffered much violence and corruption, and was affected by high unemployment. Caesar not only provided jobs through public works projects, but also cleaned up the dangerous city streets, ridding them of the roaming gangs. He was a man of learning, building the first public library.

While these reforms made him popular among the common people, they brought panic and deep resentment to his enemies, many of whom were from wealthy patrician families. To these powerful men, their beloved Republic no longer existed, especially after Caesar was named Dictator for life in February 44 BCE, a completely unconstitutional act. These patricians believed they no longer had a voice, as Rome was rapidly coming under the control of a person whom they believed was a power-hungry would-be tyrant.

Caesar's often display of extreme arrogance and vanity (he was very self-conscious about his balding head, for example) offended many in the senate. This arrogance became evident after Caesar's triumphant return to Rome following his defeat of rival Roman commander Gnaeus Pompey in Spain. He rode into the city adorned in regal garments and a laurel crown, something many people saw as unnecessary. Other wars he fought in had been against foreigners, but his victory in Spain resulted in the deaths and torture of many citizen soldiers of Rome, to the great resentment of traditional Republicans. One tribune, Pontus Aquila even refused to rise as Caesar passed in the triumphant parade, something that angered the conquering hero.

Despite the hostile feelings of some, numerous honours were given to him; he was awarded the titles of liberator and imperator; his birthday was made a public holiday; his birth month, Quinctilus, was renamed in his honour to Julius (July); he was also named the father of his country, as well as a Consul for ten years. In all processions an ivory tower of Caesar was to be carried alongside the statues of the Roman gods, and all of this was done without Caesar objecting. This arrogance became increasingly more evident as time passed; for example, he sat attired in the purple regalia of the ancient Roman kings on a specially built golden chair while attending the senate, often refusing to rise out of respect, to any member who approached him.

He also constructed a massive private palace on Quirinal Hill; this was his residence which I would be visiting with Antony in the evening. Even those who knew him best came to believe he was losing his judgment and sense of what was best for the people. His friends believed this was due to him being overworked, tired, and troubled by his bouts of epilepsy. Although those around him suffered from his arrogance, others believed the conquering hero was becoming more of a divine figure than a ruler, which was in stark contrast to many traditional Roman beliefs.

Amongst his friends and enemies, there was a growing sense of animosity, questioning why the senate allowed what appeared to them as blasphemy. Did Caesar actually believe he deserved to be praised and revered like a god? To many he appeared to be more of a king than a ruling representative of the people; someone who was no longer answerable to the senate and the people. This heightened sense of self-worth was best demonstrated during the annual February Festival of Lupercalia, when Marc Antony attempted to place a laurel wreath on Caesar's head while he was adorned in the usual purple robe, and seated in the Forum on his golden throne. But Caesar pushed the laurel wreath away, refusing the gesture, affirming that only Jupiter was the king of the Romans. Unfortunately, not everyone considered him to be sincere in his refusal. Many even believed he set-up the entire event with Antony to gauge how the people would react to the prospect of him becoming king.

The time had come to save the Republic from this would-be king, and so a conspiracy was hatched. Who would dare plan to kill the Dictator for life of the Roman Republic, knowing if they failed, they would be branded as traitors and executed? Well, there were sixty of them involved in the conspiracy! There were the usual old enemies of Caesar – friends and supporters of Pompey who were seeking revenge, high office, and profit. Next, there were those who many believed were friends of Caesar, people who, while being rewarded for their loyalty, disliked many of his policies, especially his hesitancy to overthrow the old conservative patrician-Optimates power structure. They also disapproved of his peace-making attempts with the supporters of Pompey. Finally, there were the idealists, those who respected the Republic and its ancient traditions, led by Brutus. Individually, although their reasons were diverse, they collectively believed the salvation of the Roman Republic depended on the death of Julius Caesar.

The four leading men of the conspiracy according to the surviving sources, were an unusual mix of both friends and enemies. The first two men although friends of Caesar, believed they had not been rewarded substantially enough for their loyal service to Caesar; Gaius Trebonius served as a praetor and Consul and had fought with Caesar in Spain; Decimus Junius was governor of Gaul, a close friend, confidant of Caesar, and a key commander in the victorious army against the Gauls.

The next two conspirators were clearly not friends of Caesar; Gaius Cassius who had served with both Crassus and Pompey as a naval commander, and who some believed conceived of the assassination plot; and the highly regarded Republican Marcus Brutus, whose family ties went back to the founding of the Republic in 509 BCE, served under Pompey, and who was the brother-in-law of Cassius. Brutus was the son of Caesar's mistress Servilia. Some consider Brutus was actually Caesar's son, but there is no proof of this. Brutus was married to Portia, the daughter of the great orator and senator, Cato the Younger.

Cato was a strong supporter of Pompey and outspoken critic of Caesar, who committed suicide in 46 BCE while in North Africa. He had refused to surrender to Caesar after the conqueror's victory at Thapus. After Cato's death, both Cicero and Brutus wrote eulogies in praise of the great Roman. To Cicero, Cato represented the pinnacle of Roman stoic virtue, a statement that angered Caesar. Despite all of this, Caesar continued to have faith in Brutus, forgave him, and supported him for a position as a praetor, which was a stepping stone to becoming Consul.

There were other key conspirators such as Publius Casca, who would strike the first blow against Caesar; Gaius Casca, his brother, who supposedly struck the final blow into the dictator's ribs; and Lucius Cimber, governor of Bithynia, who signalled the start of the frenzied attack. To these men power had to be taken away from Caesar, at any cost, and returned to what they believed was its rightful place, in the Roman senate.

Brutus believed there was widespread support for Caesar's assassination. The conspirators met together secretly, in small groups to avoid suspicion. Luckily for the conspirators, Caesar had dismissed his Spanish bodyguard in October of 45 BCE, believing that he was invincible and nobody would dare to harm him. The conspirators realised the attack had to be carried out decisively and soon, because Caesar was planning to lead his formidable army on a three-year (minimum) military campaign against the Parthians, and was due to leave on 18th March.

But where and when should they strike? Should they attack when Caesar rode on the Appian Way, the major road that cut through the centre of Italy? Could they attack while he was walking home on the Via Sacra? Or could they attack while he attended a gladiatorial event? After considerable debate, the final decision was made to strike during a session of the senate at the Theater of Pompey, on 15th March 44, the Ides of March. Meetings were being held there because the Roman Senate House was under repair. The attackers decided they would strike with daggers, which could easily be concealed within their senatorial togas.

There were a number of omens which all seemed to suggest Caesar should not attend that senate meeting. Firstly, Caesar's horses grazing on the outskirts of Rome were seen to be weeping. Secondly, a bird flew into the Theater of Pompey with a piece of laurel, but was quickly devoured by a larger bird. Thirdly, on the night before the Ides, Caesar's wife Calpurnia had a dream of him bleeding to death in her arms. Finally, a soothsayer named Spurinna warned him to beware of danger, to occur on or before the Ides of March. Caesar was not a superstitious man and although hesitant, ultimately ignored the omens.

The historian Suetonius wrote:

> These warnings, and a touch of ill-health, made him hesitate for some time whether to go ahead with his plans or whether to postpone the meeting.

On the day of his death, Caesar was feeling sick, and as Suetonius said, had second thoughts about attending the meeting of the senate, but one of the conspirators and his good friend Decimus arrived at his home and urged him to not disappoint those waiting for him.

That morning, a large crowd accompanied Caesar on his way to the senate. Just as he entered the theater a man named Artemidorus tried to warn him of imminent danger by thrusting a small scroll into his hand. This scroll contained information about the conspiracy, but Caesar never had a chance to read it. The dictator entered and sat on his throne. Marc Antony, who had accompanied Caesar, was conveniently distracted outside the entrance to the theater by Trebonius, as planned. There were two hundred senators in attendance that day, along with ten tribunes.

Cimber approached the unsuspecting Caesar and handed him a petition on behalf of his exiled brother; Caesar of course, did not rise to greet him. Cimber grabbed at Caesar's toga and pulled it back. Caesar reportedly said: "Why this violence?" Casca dealt the first blow with his dagger; Caesar immediately tried to defend himself by raising his hands to cover his face. The remaining conspirators surrounded the shocked and distressed Caesar; Cassius struck him in the face, and another in the ribs. Brutus delivered the final blow. Caesar collapsed and died at the feet of a prominent statue of his old enemy Pompey. There had been a total of 23 stabbings.

Suetonius described the attack:

> ...at that moment one of the Casca brothers slipped behind and with a sweep of his dagger stabbed him just below the throat. Caesar grasped Casca's arm and ran it through with a stylus; he was leaping away when another dagger caught him in the breast.

The remaining senators ran from the theater. Afterwards, Rome was in a state of utter chaos and confusion.

Suetonius wrote that there were some who disliked Caesar who wanted to seize the slain leader's corpse and throw it into the Tiber River, confiscate his property, and revoke his laws and decrees; however, Marc Antony maintained a cool head and put a stop to any such plans. While the conspiracy had all the makings of a great plan, little attempt was made to prepare for the aftermath. After committing the murder, the conspirators made their way to the Capitoline Hill and the Temple of Jupiter. Brutus spoke from a platform at the foot of the hill, trying desperately in vain to calm the crowd. Meanwhile, a group of slaves carried Caesar's body through the streets of Rome to his home; people were weeping as it passed.

The funeral procession on 20th March was a public spectacle. A pyre had been built on the Field of Mars near the family tomb; however, Caesar' body was quickly seized by locals and taken to the Forum where it was burned on a much simpler pyre. The ashes were returned to the Field of Mars and his family tomb; and the city continued to mourn throughout the evening. Interestingly, in his *The Twelve Caesars* Suetonius wrote that Caesar may have been aware of the plot to kill him, and because of continuing ill-health knowingly exposed himself to the attack.

> Almost all authorities, at any rate, believe that he welcomed the manner of his death...he loathed the prospect of a lingering end – he wanted a sudden one.

Brutus believed the death of Caesar would bring a return of the old Roman Republican traditions; instead the city was in a state of shock, there was utter chaos, and the people became increasingly hostile. On 17th March the senate agreed to a compromise, under heavy pressure from Marc Antony; while the laws of Caesar would remain in place, there would be an amnesty for all of the conspirators. Unfortunately, peace was impossible to maintain, and the conspirators had no choice other than to flee Rome. Ultimately they were hunted down by Antony and Octavian, and killed.

Suetonius ended his chapter on Caesar as follows:

> All were condemned to death… and all met in different ways – some in shipwreck, some in battle, some using the very daggers with which they had treacherously murdered Caesar to take their own lives.

Meanwhile in Rome, the young Octavian, the adopted son and heir of Caesar, received not only his war chest, but also the support of the army. A final conflict between Marc Antony (with the help of Cleopatra) and Octavian, would see the demise and suicide of Antony and his Egyptian lover, and would bring Octavian to power as Augustus, the first Emperor of the Roman Empire.

'Who have you brought with you, Antony?' said Caesar, as we were escorted into the dining room of his lavish palace by two servants.

'This is my good friend Luca. He is a lawyer based in the north of Italy. We have known each other since childhood and he's visiting me in Rome for a few days. I give you my word he can be trusted.'

'You know your word is solid gold with me. Welcome Luca. Make yourselves comfortable.'

Caesar then proceeded to introduce me to Decimus and Lepidus, who were seated on either side of the great conqueror, in the ornately appointed dining room that adjoined a large atrium with a spectacular pond surrounded by exotic lush green leafy plants. In the middle of the pond was a large statue of Jupiter in the form of a fountain. Antony was wrong on this occasion, it seemed Caesar hadn't invited anybody else. We took our seats opposite the three distinguished military commanders. There was a large map of Parthia and the adjoining kingdoms on the table, surrounded by ample food and wine. I was dazzled with the realisation I was in the company of the four greatest generals of Rome at that time of the late Republic; the high command of the Roman legions.

Caesar stood up and began to outline his plans for the campaign.

'We have mobilized sixteen legions, comprising 60,000 soldiers and 10,000 cavalry. In addition, we have thousands of auxiliary cavalry and light armed infantry. Six of the legions have already been sent to Macedonia to train, along with a large consignment of heavily-guarded gold, to finance our expedition. The remaining ten legions are waiting and ready on the outskirts of Rome and currently scheduled to march with us three days after the Ides. This military venture is going to take us a minimum of three years to complete; but I think it's going to be more like five or six years. We will commence with an attack on the kingdom of Dacia, and topple King Burebista, who has been threatening the northern border of our Macedonian province. After Dacia we will then travel into Armenia to commence our invasion of Parthia. Once we conquer and subdue Parthia, our forces will move on through the Caucasus and attack the kingdom of Scythia. Then I want us to swing around and finish off another big job undone, the conquest of Germania in the north.'

Antony then rose to speak.

'Caesar, your plan is brilliant. Just like the critics who said we would never conquer Gaul, we now have the same senatorial spineless cowards rubbishing our plans for Parthia and beyond. Led by Cicero, they have been trying to lobby you to yet again postpone the Parthian invasion, using the excuse you need to concentrate on resolving domestic political problems. Let's shut these bastards up once and for all. Let's not attend the senate meeting tomorrow, and instead make urgent arrangements to prepare our legions to depart Rome the day after tomorrow, two days earlier than planned?'

'Here here! I have often wondered why you give these shitheads the time of day. You are the supreme ruler of Rome, Caesar. You and only you know what's best. I agree with Antony. Let's snub them. We don't need to attend the senate. That time can be better spent preparing to leave Rome earlier,' said Lepidus, with strong conviction.

'Now, now, boys, hold on,' said Decimus as he jumped up from his chair. 'By snubbing the senate we will be playing directly into Cicero's camp, who are constantly accusing you of behaving like a king!'

I was surprised how nervous Decimus was when he spoke. Why wouldn't he want to snub the senate and leave Rome earlier? Was he one of the conspirators? Or was he genuine about not wanting his friend Caesar to play into the hands of the senate?

Marc Antony stood up. He was clearly annoyed with Decimus.

'Cicero and his henchmen have been actively spreading rumours that the reason Caesar wants to invade Parthia is because it has been prophesised by the Gods that only a Roman king can defeat Parthia! We must put a stop to this, once and for all. You must exercise your full power Caesar! Show them who is really in charge by snubbing the senate tomorrow and leaving Rome with our great army the day after! I have looked into it. The legions are fully prepared to depart two days earlier than scheduled!'

Caesar had been seated expressionless, in silent contemplation, right hand pinching and rubbing against his chin. Antony knew this meant the great conqueror was in a state of deep reflection, listening carefully to every word being spoken. After a number of minutes of silence, Caesar lifted himself from his chair.

'I have been unsettled over the last few days. A number of prominent senators have been urging me to attend the senate meeting tomorrow; Cicero and Brutus in particular, have bordered on pressuring me. I have been in regular contact with the legions camped outside the city. They are restless. They constantly ask me why we haven't marched yet? They don't like the petty politics being played out by the senate. Last night I had a vivid dream. I dreamt we conquered the Parthians. I dreamt we conquered the Germanic tribes. I dreamt of a greatly expanded Roman Empire! I dreamt of returning after years at war, with my loyal men behind me; and infused with enough power, energy, prestige, and the blessing of Jupiter, to fully implement my unfinished pact with the people, without any interference from the senate again. I dreamt of becoming the First Emperor of Rome. Guiding Rome to even greater glory! When I awoke this morning, my mind was crystal clear about what I must do. I have decided not to attend the senate meeting tomorrow. I have also decided we will march out of Rome at sunrise, the day after tomorrow. We will spend the entire day tomorrow in final preparations for our assault on Parthia.'

'Hail Caesar!' shouted Antony.

Lepidus and Decimus responded, 'Hail Caesar!'

I couldn't help observe Lepidus was much more enthusiastic than Decimus about Caesar's decision. I was worried Decimus was part of the conspiracy, and would inform the others of the monumental decision made by Caesar tonight. But then in any event, it was going to be common knowledge when Caesar did not attend the senate meeting tomorrow.

I was also conscious that as we were having dinner with Caesar, Antony's slave-fixer, Appius, was undertaking his extremely dangerous clandestine mission to infiltrate the meeting of conspiratorial senators at the villa of Brutus. Antony and I had a nervous wait ahead of us. It had been agreed Appius would meet us later in the evening at the villa of Antony, and debrief us of the events that transpired. A lot hinged on Appius, if I was to succeed in my mission to prevent the assassination of Julius Caesar.

I could see Caesar was absolutely determined to not attend the senate meeting, and even more determined to leave Rome with his formidable army, the day after. The die for the changing of history had been cast.

After a few hours of eating, drinking, story-telling, and laughter; including an animated conversation about the best way to die, in which Caesar stated he preferred a sudden death on the battlefield; I was breathless when all of a sudden Queen Cleopatra of Egypt made a brief appearance with Caesar's son Caesarion!

She had been staying in Rome with Caesar. The surviving sources state she was trying to convince Caesar to anoint their son as the heir to the great conqueror. Of course, we know this was to no avail because in his Will, Caesar nominated his great-nephew Octavian as his rightful heir. Antony and I left, leaving the three great generals to linger longer. I was still suspicious about Decimus, but decided not to mention my suspicion to Antony. I didn't have to!

'Do you know what Luca? I think Decimus may be a part of the conspiracy to kill Caesar. He wasn't his usual self. He was nervous. He was determined to persuade Caesar to attend the senate meeting.'

I was surprised to hear Antony's suspicions. We were walking through the dark and deserted streets of Rome, back to Antony's villa. I decided to keep my concerns about Decimus to myself.

'Isn't Decimus a long-standing friend of Caesar?'

'Well yes. They have been close friends for many years. What promises did those vile creatures make, to convince him to turn against his close friend?' muttered Antony angrily.

Once we arrived at Antony's villa. We waited. And waited. And waited. Hours passed, it was well into the early hours of the morning, and there was no sign of Appius. The longer we waited, the more convinced we became that Appius had failed and was probably executed. That thought alarmed me! If Appius was dead, the wormhole would vaporize, and we would not be able to prevent the assassination of Julius Caesar.

Then, just as we were resigned to the fact Appius had failed, he burst into the villa, covered in bloodied gashes, his toga heavily soiled and torn, panting uncontrollably out of breath, and in a state of panic. Two of Antony's servants immediately attended to him, cleansing his wounds. He didn't appear to have any life-threatening or serious injuries. After a couple of undiluted wines, he was more relaxed and ready to talk.

'I arrived at the villa of Brutus late in the afternoon, as the sun was setting. I had been watching the villa for a few hours before. I knew Brutus and Portia weren't home yet. I monitored the comings and goings of the slave servants. Then I saw an opportunity to enter. When I did, I quickly determined the safest place was for me to hide in the roof. I knew the villa was of a type with a low hanging ceiling with just enough space between the panels for somebody slim like me to hide in between. So I made my way onto the roof and into the ceiling of the main dining room, and lay perfectly silent for a number of hours. Fortunately, I was able to find a spot which gave me a good view of the room underneath me. I could see the dining room had been set by the servants for eight people. Then, people started entering the room. First it was Brutus and Portia. Soon after, the room was also occupied by six senators: Gaius Cassius, Lucius Cimber, Gaius Trebonius, Publius Casca, Pontius Aquila, and Quintus Ligarius.'

'Well, well, well, what a bunch of wretched bastards!!' shouted a clearly distressed Antony.

'Continue Appius,' I said.

'I couldn't believe what I was hearing. They were planning the timing and logistics of killing Julius Caesar in the senate tomorrow. Lucius Cimber will distract Caesar by requesting his brother's banishment order be repealed, allowing the assassins enough time to surround Caesar. It was agreed Publius Casca will inflict the first blow with his dagger. Gaius Trebonius has been given the job of luring you, my master Antony, away from the entrance of the Theater of Pompey, so Caesar enters unprotected.'

'Jupiter!! Please give me the strength to kill these scums of the earth with my bare hands!!' shouted Antony.

I motioned Appius to briefly stop, while Antony calmed down.

'Go on Appius.'

'It was becoming clear that Cassius had persuaded Brutus to join the conspiracy. Cassius wants revenge for the defeat of Pompey. He says Caesar should be killed boldly but not brutally and viciously, so that the conspirators can be perceived by the people as liberators and not murderers. Cassius had recruited his brother-in-law Brutus, by passionately arguing Brutus must be involved because his family honour is at stake, since it was his ancestor, also named Brutus, who played a key role in the banishment of the last king of Rome, Lucius Tarquinius Superbus, and the creation of the Republic. There are many others involved, but no other names were mentioned.'

'I can't believe it!' screamed Antony.

He was literally trembling with rage, but I could see he knew the stakes were high, and again, we waited a few minutes until Antony calmed down. Appius continued.

'And then as if I wasn't shocked enough, the biggest shock of the night came next. I couldn't believe my eyes!'

'What happened Appius?' I urgently asked.

'Marcus Tullius Cicero appeared!'

'Oh My God!' I shouted in a complete state of shock.

'He was heavily disguised. But once he removed the hood and fake hair, it was him alright. Cicero is the mastermind of this assassination. He planned it all. It was he who recruited Cassius to convince Brutus. It was he who decided it must happen in the senate tomorrow. He rambled on for half an hour reminding the conspirators that they were about to carry out a great and honourable deed tomorrow. They were going to kill a tyrant. They were going to save the Republic from a descent into tyranny and anarchy. He reminded them that history will forever remember them as liberators and heroes. He also said the majority of the people of Rome would support the conspirators and rejoice in the removal of a tyrant. He must have repeated ten times, the importance of his name having nothing to do with the planning of the conspiracy and the carrying out of the assassination. He would not be carrying a dagger under his toga tomorrow. He promised though, that after the deed, he would give his full support to the conspirators and ensure the senate completely pardoned them. My master Antony, they then proceeded to discuss whether you should be killed too. All of them except Brutus wanted to kill you. Cicero in particular argued strongly that you needed to die along with Caesar, otherwise the Republic would be in grave danger of you replacing Caesar as a tyrant. Brutus was absolutely determined and steadfast that you should not be killed, master Antony. Brutus said he wanted the public to see him as a heroic liberator of the Republic, through the killing of the tyrant Caesar, just like his famous ancestor was involved in ridding Rome of its last king. Killing anybody else would muddy this legacy, he argued passionately. Brutus then said, if they decided to kill Antony, he would not take part in the assassination of Caesar. After more discussion, they agreed not to harm you master. They also agreed Brutus would strike the final blow.'

'How did you get injured Appius?' I asked.

'Everything was going fine until the ceiling collapsed under my weight! I fell straight onto the table. You should have seen the looks on their faces! All hell broke loose. I frantically tried to escape. They attacked me. Casca had me in a headlock. Cassius had a dagger and struck me a number of times. I don't know how, but I managed to break free from their clutches and ran for my life. They of course, dared not chase me in the streets. They recognised me. They know you sent me master Antony.'

With that, the plot to kill Caesar was unveiled. Antony and I remained in the room; by now it was close to sunrise on the Ides of March.

'We must warn Caesar! They could strike him at any time! Even as we speak.'

'Antony, you know we cannot alert Caesar in any way, shape or form. His palace is a fortress in any event. Heavily secured and guarded. Nobody will harm him there. We need to see Caesar shortly after he rises. He is known to start his day at sunrise. Lepidus and Decimus need to come with us. We will convince Caesar to accompany us to the legion barracks outside of Rome. The four of you can then prepare them for departure. Caesar will be safe there.'

'Luca, I am concerned Decimus may be one of the conspirators.'

'We have no reason to incriminate him, Antony. Sure, he wasn't comfortable with Caesar deciding not to attend the senate, but he did explain his reason. Let's keep a very close eye on him, but give him the benefit of the doubt. Remember, he is a close and loyal friend of Caesar.'

'Leave him to me. I will make sure his movements are closely monitored by a couple of my most trusted men.'

I couldn't help sensing there was a bitter rivalry between Antony and Decimus for Caesar's favour and attention. I began wondering, was it Antony and Cicero, for different motives, who were responsible for planting the seeds which resulted in some of the ancient historians asserting the involvement of Decimus in the assassination? My gut-instinct was telling me Decimus was not a conspirator. Unlike Cassius and Brutus, Decimus always fought for Caesar, never against him, and was part of Caesar's inner circle of his most trusted advisers, along with Antony and Lepidus.

In his mid-twenties Decimus joined Caesar's forces that were fighting in Gaul. He won an important naval battle off Brittany and served with Caesar in the siege at Alesia, which sealed Rome's ultimate victory over the Gauls. When Caesar's enemies in the senate tried to strip Caesar of his power and Caesar fought back, triggering a civil war with Pompey, Decimus sided with Caesar. Once again, Decimus won a victory at sea, this time on Gaul's Mediterranean coast.

A grateful Caesar named Decimus acting Governor of Gaul, while Caesar went off to challenge his enemies elsewhere. After more than four years of hard fighting, Caesar returned to Rome in 45 BCE, with Decimus by his side. This to me, demonstrated Decimus had great loyalty to Caesar and that we were justified in giving him the benefit of the doubt.

'Antony, is there any way the legions can leave Rome this afternoon, rather than tomorrow morning. The more we close the window of opportunity, the less likely they will get to Caesar.'

'Yes it can be done. I was thinking exactly the same, Luca. I'm sure I can convince Caesar.'

Antony arranged for his servants to inform Lepidus and Decimus to meet at Caesar's palatial villa for an urgent meeting in one hour. We then made our way to Caesar's place.

'Didn't you get enough of me last night, boys?' chuckled Caesar as we entered his study.

'I have been reviewing our plans for the Parthian campaign, Caesar. There is no reason why we can't leave Rome with the legions this afternoon,' said Antony.

'Why the haste?'

'The soldiers are very restless, as you know. They are unnerved with the politics and vicious rumours circulating in Rome.'

'You mean the crazy rumours about a plot to kill me? My wife Calpurnia awoke me in the early hours of this morning begging me not to go to the senate today. She dreamt I was covered in blood-soaked stab wounds, and lay dying in her arms. The reason I'm not going to the senate is not because I fear for my life. I'm not going because I have come to the same conclusion as you Antony. We have much more urgent business to attend to. We will leave Rome this afternoon, and cleanse ourselves of the political stench of this city for years.'

A servant walked into the room and advised Caesar that Lepidus and Decimus had arrived.

'Show them in,' instructed Caesar.

'Perfect timing boys. We will be leaving Rome with the legions, in the middle of this afternoon.'

Lepidus and Decimus weren't surprised. I sensed they were prepared for what Caesar had told them. The professional military commanders swung into action mode.

Within an hour of the meeting, we were at the legions barracks on the outskirts of Rome. Caesar and his three commanding generals were in full military regalia, impressively directing the troops and engaging in a series of meetings in their respective marquees. I remained with Antony. Caesar seemed comfortable with my presence. The legions were excited about their earlier departure, and were clearly highly motivated and intensely loyal to the four commanders.

It was clearly evident Caesar possessed an abundance of charisma and empathised with his soldiers. Then, by mid-afternoon, I watched in awe, as the formidable army of legions marched on their great quest to further significantly expand the territories of Rome. I waited for over an hour, until the last of the soldiers disappeared over the horizon from view. Caesar was safely away from Rome now. He was doing what he loved the most, leading his legions into conquest. He was surrounded by his three most loyal friends and commanders; Antony, Lepidus, and Decimus. I still had a lingering doubt about the motives of Decimus. But there wasn't much I could do about it now. I knew Antony would keep a close eye on him. I had succeeded in my mission. I had prevented the assassination of Julius Caesar in Rome, on the Ides of March. I was ready to return home.

Otto expressed a rare faint smile when he appeared at the piano bar. The pianist was playing Billy Joel's classic 1973 hit, "Piano Man" as we settled down at a table in the back corner of the bar; me with a gin and tonic, Otto with his customary glass of water.

'You are rewarding my confidence in you in spades, Luca. That's the second successful mission under your belt now. Congratulations.'

'I wouldn't get too excited yet. I've got ten more to go, and they seem to be getting more and more challenging.'

'Well, in that universe, you will be pleased to learn Julius Caesar succeeded in conquering not only Parthia and many of the surrounding eastern kingdoms, but the Germanic kingdoms as well, virtually doubling the size of Roman-controlled territory. He returned to Rome after six years, and became the first Emperor of Rome. He ruled successfully in consultation with the senate, for eleven years. Upon his death, from natural causes, his great-nephew and heir, Octavian, became the second Emperor of Rome, assuming the name, Augustus. Your friend Marc Antony died in battle during the Parthian campaign. A distraught Caesar gave him a glorious funeral with full military honours. Your gut-feeling was right; Decimus played no part in the conspiracy to assassinate Caesar. It was Cicero who damaged his reputation by spreading the malicious rumour that Decimus had betrayed his good friend Caesar. Cicero did this because he feared Decimus would gain the loyalty of the assassinated Caesar's legions, and go on to become a tyrant himself.'

After Otto's usual vanishing act, I walked the fifteen minutes to my home, in the still of the night, thinking about my next mission, to stop the Frankish King Charlemagne from becoming Holy Roman Emperor in 800 CE. I was physically and emotionally exhausted. As soon as I arrived home, I collapsed onto my bed fully clothed, and slept like a log for twelve hours.

Time Machine

I'ma gonna build myself a time machine
On particle physics and the power steam
It runs on diesel oil and Donnie Darko daydreams
Packed a pair of socks and a hunting rifle
Change of underwear and some snacks of trifle
Scared of going back you know how I'm forgetful

To go back and to see the way things really used to be
Not the way we remember them at all

Packed up, sat in my DeLorean
Like some kind of amateur historian
I'll visit the Renaissance and the Romans, the Victorians
Drinking in Deadwood in the 1880s
Rock and roll and drive thrus in the 1950s
Trying not to change things so the plot lines don't get shitty

To go back and to see the way things really used to be
Not the way we remember them
To go back and to see the way things really used to be
Not the way we remember them at all

'Cause I can't recall, you tell it to me false
What if everything were to change completely
If you just saw a replay of the crucial scenes
From the passenger window of a time machine

In truth the real reason that I built this here machine
Was just to travel back a couple of years
To when we first met before the fights and tears
To a time when you and I first got together
Simple days and simple words like "forever"
Dripped off our tongues, come on you must remember

To go back and to see the way things really used to be
Before life quietly dismembers
All the best things about you and I before the doubts
Drowned out all of the mirth and mercy
Come on baby please you must remember

Please remember

Frank Turner (2013)

5

Charlemagne

Rome, Italy, December 800 CE

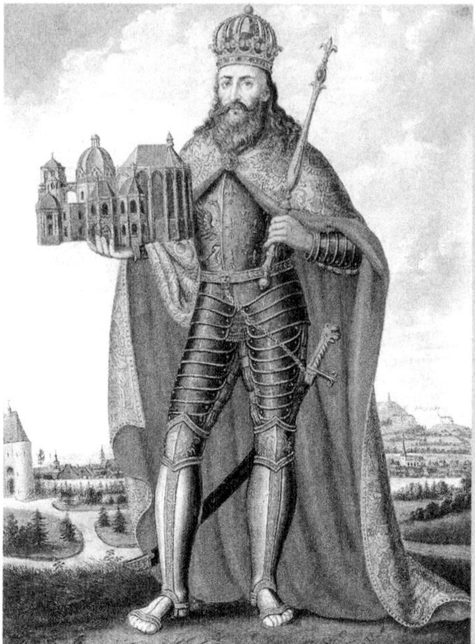

I arrived in Rome at around midday on 23rd December 800 CE. Looming in front of me was Saint Peter's Basilica. This was the original cathedral and adjoining papal palace and apartments that stood from the 4th to the 16th centuries, where the new St. Peter's Basilica was then erected, which stands to this modern day in Vatican City. Construction of the original basilica, which was built over the historical site of the Circus of Nero, began in 318 CE during the reign of the first Christian Roman emperor, Constantine I, and took around forty years to complete.

Over the next twelve centuries, the basilica-cathedral gradually gained importance, eventually becoming a major place of pilgrimage in Rome for true-believers. Papal coronations were held at this basilica; including that of the current Pope Leo III, and his predecessor, Adrian I. In 846, the Muslim Saracens sacked and damaged the basilica. The raiders seemed to have known about Rome's extraordinary treasures. It was an easy target at the time because the basilica was outside the Aurelian Walls, surrounding and defending Rome. When it was sacked, it was filled to overflowing with rich liturgical vessels, many made of solid gold; an assortment of jewels; and housed many of the priceless relics of saints, assembled by the Church to that time.

As a result, the Saracen raiders destroyed Saint Peter's tomb, and pillaged the holy shrine. By the 15th century the basilica was falling into ruin. Discussions on restoring parts of the structure commenced after the return of Pope Julius II from Avignon. Two people involved in the reconstruction were the Renaissance architects Leon Battista Alberti, and Bernardo Rossellino, who improved the apse (a semi-circular vaulted area for the cathedral choir) and partially added a multi-storey benediction loggia to the atrium façade, on which renovations continued intermittently until the new basilica was begun.

Alberti pronounced the basilica to be a structural abomination, saying: "I have noticed the basilica of St. Peter's in Rome a crass feature; an extremely long and high wall has been constructed over a continuous series of openings, with no curves to give it strength, and no buttresses to lend it support. The whole stretch of wall has been pierced by too many openings and built too high. As a result, the continual force of the wind has already displaced the wall more than six feet from the vertical; I have no doubt that eventually some slight movement will make it collapse."

The design of the cathedral was in a typical basilica form; with the plan and elevation resembling those of the Roman basilicas and audience halls, such as the Basilica Ulpia in Trajan's Forum, and Constantine's own Aula Palatina at Trier; rather than the design of any Greco-Roman temple, such as the Pantheon in the centre of Rome. Constantine went to great pains to build the basilica on the site of Saint Peter's grave, and this influenced the layout of the building, which was erected on the sloped Vatican Hill, on the west bank of the Tiber River.

The basilica was built outside the boundaries of the ancient city, and the façade could be approached from the city of Rome to the east. The exterior, unlike earlier pagan temples, was not lavishly decorated. Since the crucifixion and burial of Saint Peter in 64 CE, the site was thought to be the location of the tomb of Saint Peter, where there had stood a shrine. With its increasing prestige, the basilica-cathedral became richly decorated with statues, furnishings, and elaborate chandeliers; and side tombs and altars were continuously added.

The structure was filled with the tombs and bodies of saints and popes. Bones continued to be found as late as February 1544 CE. The majority of these tombs were destroyed during the sixteenth and seventeenth centuries demolition of the Old St. Peter's Basilica. The remainder were transferred to the New St. Peter's Basilica, which stands on the site of the original basilica.

As I admired the original basilica, I recalled from my research that the cathedral was capable of accommodating up to 4,000 worshippers. It consisted of five aisles, a wide central nave (principal aisle) and two smaller aisles to each side, which were divided by 21 marble columns taken from earlier pagan buildings. It was over 350 feet long, built in the shape of a Latin cross, and had a gabled roof which was timbered on the interior, standing at over 100 feet at the centre. An atrium, known as the "Garden of Paradise" stood at the entrance, and had five doors which led to the body of the cathedral. The altar of this original St. Peter's Basilica used several Solomonic columns. According to tradition, the emperor Constantine took these columns from the Temple of

Solomon and gave them to the Church; however, the columns were more than likely taken from an Eastern Orthodox church.

I was meeting with one of Charlemagne's closest advisers, Alcuin of York, outside the walls, near the main entrance of the basilica. As I waited, I observed a constant movement of church officials in and out of the basilica. Then I saw a distinguished looking man approaching me, he was finely dressed, and looking confident he locked his eyes onto mine, smiling gently.

'Luca Evangelista, it is my great pleasure to meet you. I know you've just arrived and haven't been waiting long. Otto has told me much about you. As a man of learning, the biggest problem I am going to have while we are together over the next few days is resisting the temptation to ask you a thousand questions about your world in the 21st century! It gives me enormous joy though to just know that humanity will still be around then!'

'Alcuin of York, believe me, the pleasure is all mine. I don't believe history has given you the recognition you deserve. Obviously, I cannot go into detail. You are a man of enormous influence. I respect you very much for using your influence wisely, and for the betterment of humanity.'

'Why thank you Luca. I wasn't expecting that! I am lucky to be a close friend and adviser to the most powerful man in the world; and he actually respects and listens to my advice. It's an awesome sense of responsibility. Yet, between you and I Luca, I have an equal dose of fear of Charlemagne, for as great a man he is, he also has an enormous capacity for violence and revenge. This is the tightrope I navigate every day; yet I find it most exhilarating.'

'I know Otto has shared with you the reason I am here. Charlemagne is going to be crowned as the Holy Roman Emperor of Europe, by Pope Leo III on Christmas day, the day after tomorrow. Some of the surviving sources tell me that this is to come as an unexpected surprise to Charlemagne and to yourself.'

'When Otto told me, it was a complete surprise to me! I'm not sure if your surviving sources have got it right when they say it was a complete surprise to Charlemagne, though.'

'You think he knows he's going to be crowned Holy Roman Emperor on Christmas day?'

'I honestly don't know. We've been here in Rome a number of weeks now, and he has met privately with the Pope on two occasions. It is very unusual for Charlemagne to meet with great men of power on his own, without me by his side; so even before the arrival of Otto, I was already suspicious about what they were discussing privately, but I must say, I never imagined it would be the planning of a coronation. It may not have been. Hence why I'm not sure if Charlemagne is in on this plan with Pope Leo.'

'I am here to stop the coronation from happening. We need to convince Charlemagne that it is not in his interest to give the Roman Catholic Church that much power; for make no mistake, by crowning Charlemagne as Holy Roman Emperor, as intoxicating as that grant of power may be; it is in fact demonstrating to the world that the Pope possesses the ultimate power, not the kings.'

'I agree with you, Luca. Pope Leo III is setting a trap for Charlemagne. We must convince him of this.'

We made our way into the Basilica of Saint Peter, which was walled off and heavily secured. On either side of the great cathedral stood two other lavish buildings; the Papal palace, to the north; and the residential apartments for Cardinals and envoys, to the south. Alcuin took me to the two-level residential apartments, where servants directed me to a bedroom upstairs. Although I was feeling excited by this mission, I knew the next few days were going to be full of adrenaline-rushing dramatic events, so I lay on the bed, closed my eyes, and collected my thoughts on the life of my helper and protector in this world, Alcuin of York.

The scholar Alcuin of York, is one of our best sources for eighth century Europe. He was educated in the cathedral school at York, England, and became a monk and teacher there. He was a deacon of York when, in 781 CE, he was returning from a visit to Rome and met Charlemagne, king of the Franks, at Parma in northern Italy.

Charlemagne immediately recognised in Alcuin, a highly intelligent and loyal scholar, and political adviser who could help him to achieve a renaissance of learning; reform the Church; and also guide him on the intrigues, dramas, and politics of Europe at that time. At the king's invitation, Alcuin joined the royal court in 781, and became one of

Charlemagne's closest advisers on religious, political, and educational matters. Alcuin was made head of the palace school at Charlemagne's principal palace in Aachen (now in Germany).

This school was attended by members of the royal court, and the sons of noble families. He also established a great library there. Alcuin also revised the church liturgy (worship rituals); and along with another great scholar, Theodulf of Orleans, he was responsible for an intellectual movement within the Carolingian empire in which many schools of learning were attached to monasteries and cathedrals, and Latin was restored as the principal language of the Church and nobility. In 796, Alcuin became abbot of Saint Martin's monastery at Tours (now in France), where he also established a school and library.

Alcuin was a superb strategist, teacher, and scholar. He had the ability to guide others through what he saw as "golden whirlpools of spiritual meaning," and to inspire them to rise to even greater intellectual heights. He wrote educational manuals, poetry, and copied classical texts from the Greek and Roman worlds; and above all, he was a prolific writer of letters. At Charlemagne's court he acted virtually as an English Ambassador; providing a direct link with the English royal court, exchanging information and ideas on a regular basis, not just with secular and religious leaders, but also with personal friends, many of whom were scholars and philosophers.

His correspondence was clearly appreciated, for it was collected and distributed to centres of learning across Europe, such as in Salzburg, as early as 798. Many of his letters were passionate critiques of society at that time, reflecting not only his views on Church reform, but also political, social, educational, and philosophical issues. A missionary friend was recommended to be a "preacher of piety, not exactor of tithes," for guiding people how to live a good moral life, rather than taking taxes for the benefit of the Church.

In a letter to the monks of Jarrow and Monkwearmouth in Northumbria England, he encouraged them to:

> Consider the splendour of your churches, the beauty of your buildings, your way of life according to the Rule. Let the boys be present with praises of the heavenly king, and not be digging foxes out of holes or

> following the fleeting courses of hares. He who does not learn when he is young, does not teach when he is old."

Alcuin was also a very pragmatic man of action. For example, he knew that the oil needed for church services was scarce in England, so he arranged for olive oil sourced from the Frankish kingdom to be distributed amongst the Northumbrian bishops. His distress and horror at the Viking attack on the monasteries at Lindisfarne in 793 was very evident in his letters both to the Bishop of Lindisfarne, and the king of Northumbria.

In his letter to the bishop, he said:

> When I was with you, the closeness of your love would give me great joy. In contrast, now that I am away from you, the distress of your suffering fills me daily with deep grief, when heathens desecrated God's sanctuaries, and poured the blood of saints within the compass of the altar, destroyed the house of our hope, trampled the bodies of saints in God's temple like animal dung in the street.

Alcuin saw the Viking onslaught as divine retribution for the lapse in the moral standards of the Northumbrian people, much as he might have interpreted an epidemic of disease as punishment for human sin.

Worse was to happen to his homeland, however; and Alcuin might have had difficulty in explaining the rampaging Viking activities throughout Europe of the ninth and tenth centuries in terms of God's punishment for sinful behaviour. In another letter to the Bishop of Lindisfarne, Alcuin proclaims: "What security is there for the churches of Britain if St. Cuthbert with so great a throng of saints will not defend his own? Either this is the beginning of greater grief or the sins of those who live there have brought it upon themselves."

One of Alcuin's poems celebrates York and its splendid library, where he spent so many happy years; and he lists many of the authors whose works were on its shelves: classical Latin writers such as Virgil, Cicero, and Lucan. The cathedral library at York became even more famous throughout Europe after Alcuin's time, only to be utterly destroyed by Danish Vikings in an attack in 866. Fortunately, Alcuin's writings have not been lost to humanity, and they remain a key source which give us a unique insight into one of the most traumatic periods of European history.

'Luca, are you awake?'

I must have been in a deep sleep because it took Alcuin a few minutes to awaken me.

'I would like you to come along with me to a lecture I am giving in the papal hall about Charlemagne's achievements; and his revolutionary reforms in politics, administration, education, and in the improvement of society. There will be a number of influential cardinals and nobles in attendance.'

'Sure, I would love to come,' I said, as I rubbed my eyes trying to eliminate my drowsiness, surprised I had slept for three hours. I was clearly more fatigued than I realised. Maybe it was the cumulative effects of time travel wearing me down. I never asked Otto if there were side effects when humans travel back in time in the worm hole. I made a mental note to ask him that question.

'I had no intention of delivering this lecture until Otto came into my life. The purpose of the lecture is going to be to assert the supreme control that Charlemagne has over the Church. Although the delivery of my message is going to be subtle; by the end of my presentation those cardinals and nobles will be left in no doubt who really has the power!'

'Does Charlemagne know you are delivering this message?'

'No. He is aware I am giving a lecture, but as always, leaves it entirely up to me as to what I actually talk about. Although I have no doubt he will approve, once we let him know what Pope Leo and his power-hungry cronies are really up to!'

We only had a short walk from the residential apartments to the magnificent hall within the pope's palace. When we arrived there were already a number of cardinals in their "blood-red" outfits mingling with elegantly dressed men, clearly representing some of the most powerful and influential noble families in Rome at the time. The room filled quickly. As Alcuin was circulating around the elegant hall, jam packed with paintings and sculptures documenting the progress of the world from ancient times, and mingling with Rome's elite, I discreetly sat in the back corner, literally out of sight.

I decided to keep myself relatively anonymous in this mission, because the politics, infighting, and intrigues, were very intense at this time, and I didn't want to in any way jeopardize the success of my mission, by raising any unnecessary suspicions about who I was, and my purpose in Rome. There was a lot of pressure within the higher echelons of the Church for Leo to assert his power over kings, and it was a number of cardinals and powerful families in this room who were driving this pressure. Alcuin calmly walked to the podium at the opposite end of the hall to where I was sitting, and proceeded to commence his lecture, as everybody sat quietly.

'Your eminences and gentlemen, my king has delivered much good to his realm and to the Church. Let me summarise his achievements so far. In 771 Charlemagne became king of the Franks and immediately embarked on a quest to unite all Germanic peoples into one kingdom, and to convert all of his subjects to Christianity. As a skilled and brilliant military strategist, he has devoted much of his reign engaged in warfare in order to accomplish his goals. Soon after becoming king, he conquered the Lombards, the Avars, and the Bavarians, in successive order. As you are all aware, he has been waging a decades-long series of battles against the pagan-worshipping Saxons, rightfully earning his reputation for efficient ruthlessness. In 782, at the Battle of Verden, Charlemagne demonstrated his sheer power and devotion to the Lord, when he ordered the execution of over 4,500 Saxons who refused to disown their pagan gods and convert to Christianity. This dramatic act, convinced the remaining conquered Saxons to convert to the faith of our Lord. He then declared that anybody who didn't get baptized and follow all of the other ways of the Church, would be put to death. In his single-minded mission as defender of Christianity, need I remind you that Charlemagne has given money and land to the Church, and has made a solemn oath to protect your holy father, the Pope. Charlemagne has reformed the Church, political governance, and the management of finances; streamlined and strengthened the military, and improved the living standards of the common people. He has elevated the pursuit of education, and promoted a flourishing scholarly intellectual awakening. He has given prominence to the liberal arts, using his court as a benchmark, ordering that his children and grandchildren be well educated, and has even pursued studies himself. Our great king has established a new monetary standard, the "livre caroliniienne," which is based on one pound of pure silver; as well as a universal system of accounting for income and expenses which has been applied throughout his realm, thus strengthening commerce and trade. As many of you honoured princes of Christ and noble gentlemen are clearly aware, Charlemagne has expanded the reform program of the Church; including strengthening the Church's internal power structure, advancing the skill and moral quality of the clergy, standardizing liturgical practices, improving on the basic tenets of the faith, and rooting out all forms of paganism and corruption. When it comes to political governance, he has tightened the central control of all provinces within his realm, streamlined the bureaucracy, made all representatives of the king fully accountable, and implemented a literacy program to improve their skill levels. Under the watchful eye of our great King Charlemagne, there has been an expansion of literature, writing, the arts, architecture, jurisprudence, and scriptural studies. Our leader has also initiated a concerted effort to copy and preserve classical texts mainly from the Greek and Roman worlds, working closely with the many monasteries scattered throughout his realm. He has promoted the concept of applying practical and rational ideas and solutions to resolving social problems and conflicts, using the common language of Latin amongst the learned; and a common writing style that enables easy communication across his realm. Part of Charlemagne's success as a warrior, defender of the Lord's faith, able administrator, and strong ruler, can be traced to his admiration and strong commitment to learning and education. His vast conquests have brought him into contact with a diversity of cultures and different ideas coming from Moorish Spain, Anglo-Saxon England the place of my birth, and Lombard Italy. Our king has greatly increased the number of monastic schools and scriptoria (centres for book-copying) throughout the realm. In addition to myself, Charlemagne has assembled an esteemed ensemble of valuable advisers, those of whom are still alive are here in Rome; including the Visigoth, Theodulf; the Lombard, Paulinus of

Aquileia; and Angilbert, Einhard, and Waldo of Reichenau, all Franks. We honour those who have been taken by our Lord, including Paul the Deacon, Peter of Pisa, and Angilram. Our majesty has played an important role in determining the economic destiny of his realm. Pursuing his father's reforms, Charlemagne abolished the monetary system based on the gold sou, and he and the Anglo-Saxon King Offa of Mercia took up the system set in place by his father, Pepin. There are strong pragmatic reasons for his abandonment of a gold standard, notably an acute shortage of gold itself. The gold shortage is a direct consequence of the conclusion of peace with Byzantium, which has resulted in the ceding of Venice and Sicily to the East, and the loss of their trade routes to Africa. The resulting standardization has harmonized and unified the complex array of currencies into a single currency, thus simplifying trade and commerce. As I have stated, Charlemagne has done this by establishing a new monetary standard, the "livre carolinienne" which is based upon a pound of silver – a unit of both money and weight – and is worth 20 sous or 240 deniers. Our great king has looked after the interests of the common people by directly controlling the prices of staple foods and commodities to ensure they are affordable for everybody. Unlike his father Pepin, and uncle Carloman, Charlemagne has expanded the reform program of the Church. His reforms have focused on the strengthening of the internal power structures of the Church as I have stated, to the advantage of our Pope and all the eminences present today; advancing the skill and moral quality of the clergy right down to the parish- village level; and standardizing liturgical practices. I do not need to remind you all that our great king's authority now extends over the entire Church, its people, and possessions. Charlemagne can discipline clerics, take control of ecclesiastical property, and define orthodox doctrine. The territory controlled by our king is the largest since the Roman Empire itself. Charlemagne exercises the "bannum," the supreme right to rule and command over all of his territories. He also has supreme jurisdiction in judicial matters; makes all laws and legislation; leads the army; and protects the Church and the poor. Since 780, Charlemagne has reformed the local system of administering justice and has created the "scabini," professional experts on law. Every count and governor in the realm has the help of seven of these "scabini" who are supposed to know every national law so that all men can be fairly judged according to it. Judges are banned from taking bribes and are supposed to use sworn inquests to establish facts. Our majestic king does not take lightly any abuses of the judicial system. On the political governance side of things, the kingdom is subdivided into three separate areas to make administration easier. These areas, Austrasia, Neustria, and Burgandy, are the inner core of the vast kingdom, and are supervised directly by the "missatica" system and the noble household directly accountable to our king. Outside these three inner core areas, is the "regna" where administration rests upon the counts. Beyond these areas are the "marcher" areas which are ruled by powerful governors hand-picked by our king because they are too far away for his direct regular influence. These marcher lordships are present in Brittany, Bavaria, Spain, and Avaria. In addition to these, Charlemagne has also created two sub-kingdoms in Aquitaine and Italy, ruled by his sons Louis and Pepin respectively. While our king has overall authority in these wider regions, they are ruled fairly autonomously, with their own chancery and minting facilities. Every year our Charlemagne holds the "Placticum Generalis" an annual meeting of nobles, administrators, counts, governors, cardinals, and lords, held at a place nominated by the king. This annual meeting is called for three reasons: to gather the Frankish forces to go on military campaign; to discuss political and ecclesiastical matters affecting the kingdom and legislate for them; and to make judgements on matters of law. All of the important men in the kingdom must attend the meeting, because it is a critical way for Charlemagne to make his will and ideas known. Now finally, let me turn to the tragic events that afflicted our holy father Pope Leo III. We know that Leo is not a member of the nobility. So therefore, on the day he was elected pope, on 27th December 795, he angered the nobility by sending the keys of Rome to Charlemagne, indicating that he recognised our great king as the true protector of Rome. Many Roman aristocrats resented placing Rome under the protection of a non-Roman. Prompted by what we now know to be jealousy, ambition, and the belief that only somebody from the nobility should hold the office of Pope, a number of relatives of the former Pope Adrian I, including his nephew, formed a plot to render Leo unfit to hold his office. On the occasion of the procession of the Greater Litanies, held on the 25th April 799, when our holy father the Pope was making his way towards the Flaminian Gate, he was suddenly viciously attacked by a gang of armed men. After he was brutally knocked to the ground, a vile attempt was made by these thugs to rip out his tongue, and tear out his eyes, so as to disable him from performing his holy duties. Thank God, he was rescued by two of Charlemagne's "missi dominici" (diplomatic representatives), who were able to subdue the attackers, using considerable force. Leo's life was clearly in danger so he fled Rome, heading north, where he was sheltered by Duke Winiges of Spoleto. After recuperating, Leo then headed under tight guard, across the Alps to Paderborn, where Charlemagne, who was camped during a military campaign, received him with the highest respect and honour. We know that Pope Leo was accused of adultery and perjury by his enemies. Charlemagne ordered the accusers to come to Paderborn so he could personally hold court and make a judgment on the veracity of the accusations, but they didn't turn up. Our great king then had Leo securely escorted back to Rome. As you are well aware, Charlemagne and his entourage, including my good self, arrived in Rome last month, with the primary intention of holding a judicial council with the accusers and Leo, in order to ascertain the truth. On the 1st December, the council was held, and representatives from both sides submitted their arguments to Charlemagne and myself. I have been authorised by my great king Charlemagne to now advise you that this morning, Pope Leo III took an "oath of purgation" in writing, swearing in the presence of our great king and the Lord, that he was innocent of all charges. Charlemagne accepted the oath of the holy father, and has hereby decreed that all of the accusers must be permanently exiled from Rome.'

There was an audible gasp from the audience. I couldn't believe what I was hearing! I knew that a number of noble relatives of the former Pope Adrian I were in the audience, along with numerous cardinals who maintained their loyalty to Adrian. It dawned upon me that some of the people in this audience were going to be exiled from Rome.

They had been brilliantly ambushed by Charlemagne and Alcuin. Clearly, the "oath of purgation" given by the Pope this morning, and referred to in the surviving sources of history, had been carried out in absolute secret. The true reason for this "lecture" was kept highly confidential by Alcuin; even from me! I understood why he needed to keep this under absolute wraps. It was a brilliant move orchestrated by Alcuin, on behalf of Charlemagne, on two fronts.

Firstly, there was a seriously veiled threat in this speech directed at Pope Leo and his followers, to not overstep their ambition for power, for the real power lay in the hands of Charlemagne; and the great king was not going to tolerate anybody, not even the Pope, encroaching on his tight hold on power. And secondly of course, this enormous raw power was on show here and now, right in front of my eyes, with the exiling from Rome of all accusers, who were the enemies of Leo, and therefore also the enemies of Charlemagne. The extent to which Charlemagne was willing to follow through on his commitment to act as the protector of popes, was just put on display. This "lecture" given by his loyal adviser Alcuin, showcased in no uncertain terms, who really held the absolute power; and it wasn't Leo, or any future Pope for that matter; it was Charlemagne!

As Alcuin was completing his lecture, a distinguished looking "church official" came towards me. I was puzzled by this man. He was the only high member of the clergy in the hall not dressed in the cardinal red. He was in full black attire.

'Luca Evangelista, I know why you're here. I have been closely watching every step you have taken; in Philip's Macedonia; in Caesar's Rome; and now in Charlemagne's world. At first, I decided just to watch you, and not intervene, expecting you would stumble along the way, as all frail humans ultimately do. I'm here now Luca. You are not going to succeed with this mission. Otto will not succeed in rehabilitating the pre-determined future of your planet.'

Just as I was about to muster-up a response, the mysterious man walked away, vanishing into the crowd of dignitaries, who were mainly gathered in a number of small groups in the centre of the hall, clearly shocked by the "lecture" they had just witnessed.

'Come Luca, we must go now. I have well and truly set the cat amongst the pigeons.'

And so with literally everybody in that room fixing enraged

stares on us, I followed Alcuin out of the papal hall and back to the apartments.

As I lay on my bed, I gathered my thoughts. Who was this mysterious visitor in black? He knew about my previous missions. He knew Otto. It had to be Thero from the Vega star system, who was hell-bent on stopping my time travel mission from succeeding. Otto had warned me about him; and now here he was. I had to keep one step ahead of him. All of a sudden it dawned on me, that from now on, my job was going to be much more difficult and dangerous, with Thero as an extra obstacle to contend with.

That evening, Alcuin had arranged for Charlemagne's closest advisers to meet with him and myself in a secluded Benedictine monastery, in the small town of Mentana, on the outskirts of Rome. This particular monastery had been chosen because abbot padre Caselli and his monks were faithfully devoted to the great king, and so it was highly unlikely word of the meeting would get back to Pope Leo and his collaborators. Charlemagne was on a hunting trip and was staying overnight at a Papal retreat with a number of cardinals loyal to him. He was due back in Rome tomorrow afternoon.

The daily life of a Medieval monk revolved around the hours, which were divided into eight cycles of daily devotional prayer. The day started at 5am with the lauds, an early morning service of silent solitary divine prayer. In between the other seven prayer services, the monks engaged in a variety of duties including; washing and cooking; tending to the herb and vegetable gardens; producing wine, ale, and honey; providing medical care to the community; helping the poor; educating boys from noble families; providing hospitality to pilgrims; and the hand-copying of classical manuscripts.

When we arrived, abbot Caselli, and his prior, Adolfo, took us on a tour of the monastery. In the centre of the complex of buildings was a cruciform, or cross-shaped church. At the west end of the church was the narthex, a covered porch in front of the main west doors. We entered the main doors into the nave (main aisle) of the church, which formed the bulk of the church, and reached from the west end to the choir area at the east end. The north and south ends both contained altars. Caselli told us that two classes of monks lived in the monastery.

The first were lay monks, who were secular members, and were not bound by the strict monastic rules of prayer. The lay monks did the day to day tasks needed to run the monastery. The other monks were the monastic or choir monks. These monks devoted their time to prayer and learning. The lay brothers worshipped at the west end of the nave, while the monastic monks worshipped at the east end. A screen known as the pulpitum, separated the choir from the nave. Additional altars were located in the transepts as well as the high altar. These altars were founded by wealthy nobles who wanted prayers said to a favourite saint, or for prayers to be recited for themselves and their families.

We then proceeded to the cloister, a rectangular covered walkway built around a central garden. The cloisters were used by the monks for exercise, study, and movement under cover between the different buildings in the monastery. The cloisters were located on the south side of the church, where it was naturally sunnier and warmer. At the east end of the cloister leading to the nave was the processional doorway, which was used by the monks as they moved to and from the church on important religious processions. The two storey buildings on the east side of the cloister were an extension of the southern transept. These buildings were used by the choir monks, and the religious leaders of the church. The upper floor was mainly used as a dormitory for the monks. Access to the upper floor from the church was via the night stairs.

Using the night stairs, the monks could walk directly from their sleeping quarters into the church in the early hours of the morning, to recite prayers. On the ground floor of the east range accessible only from the south transept was the sacristy which was used to store the church valuables when they were not in use. In the sacristy there was also a passage which led from the cloister to the cemetery, where all of the past monks belonging to this monastery, were buried. Alongside the sacristy and accessible from the cloister was the library, where we would be meeting.

An important factor when building this, and every other monastery, was the availability of fresh flowing water. Water of course, was needed for drinking, irrigating plants, and also to flush away waste. The monks had built extensive water ducts to channel the water to where it was required within the monastery complex. In the centre of the east cloister wall was the chapter-house. This is where the abbot, prior, and leading monks, met to discuss the daily running of the monastery. The chapter-house had rich decorations, both inside and on the doorway leading to it. This reflected the importance of the room to the Benedictine church and its members.

The roof of the chapter-house was securely vaulted. Around the edge of the room was a series of stone benches on which the members would sit. The chapter was held every day after morrow mass and started with several readings from the Old Testament. The west range of the monastery was run by the secular members. Entrance to the monastery complex was through the west range, and this is where all visitors, including us, were greeted, and where guest rooms were provided. A monk known as the cellarer worked in this area, and he was responsible for ensuring the monastery was supplied with all necessary provisions. The cellarer would visit the surrounding local towns and buy supplies. He would offer a fair price for goods, especially to those that really needed the money.

The lower floors to the west range is where the supplies were stored in barns. The kitchen was one of the rooms located on the south side of the cloister. Adjoining the kitchen was a large room called the refectory, where the monks dined. Also on the south side was a warming room, one of the few rooms in the monastery where there was a continuous fire; highly sought after in the winter months. The refectory was much like a large hall in a castle where banquets were held. The tables were arranged along the side walls, and at the far end was a raised area where the abbot, prior, and other more senior members of the monastery, and visiting dignitaries would sit to dine. Scriptural readings would be performed by one of the monks while the food was consumed.

All monks were required to wash their hands before entering the refectory. The refectory could accommodate all of the over 150 monks in one sitting. Not far from the refectory was a simple infirmary (hospital) where sick monks or travellers could be tended to. A large amount of bread was required to feed not only the monks but also the poor within this town community. The bakehouse was located close to the refectory. Fish was a key part of the diet of the monks. To ensure a good supply of fresh fish, artificial fishponds and hatcheries were constructed near the vegetable garden. Like all monasteries, there was a garden devoted to the cultivation of herbs. They were important not just for adding as ingredients for food, but also as medicines for healing the sick.

The monks had a good understanding of what properties each herb had, and how to apply them. This knowledge had been accumulated by the Benedictine Order over many years. The green area inside the cloisters was used for this purpose. Surrounding the cloisters was an extensive fruit and vegetable garden, olive trees, and grape vines. Near the main entrance to the monastery was a large two-storey gatehouse. The archway through the gatehouse was wide enough for a horse and cart or carriage to pass through, which is exactly how we got inside. There was also a separate archway for people to come and go on foot. Adjoining the archways was a small room for the porter, who controlled which people could enter the monastery complex.

Attending the dinner meeting in addition to myself and Alcuin, were Charlemagne's close advisers and confidante's; Theodulf, Paulinus, Angilbert, Einhard, and Waldo. As we sat in the beautifully appointed library, adorned with spectacular religious tapestries on the walls, enjoying the monastery's red wine, and an assortment of cheeses and olives, with freshly baked bread, Alcuin introduced me to the others.

I had done my research on each of them, so knew their backgrounds well. Theodulf was a writer, poet, and the Bishop of Orleans during the reign of Charlemagne and his son, Louis the Pious. He was a key member of the Carolingian Renaissance, and an important figure during the many reforms of the Church under Charlemagne, working closely with Alcuin. He went on to establish a number of public schools outside of the monastic areas he oversaw, following through on that idea which had impressed him so much during a trip to Rome in 786.

Paulinus acquired a thorough education in Latin culture, both in pagan Roman and Christian classics. He also possessed a deep knowledge of law and jurisprudence, assisting Charlemagne greatly in judicial matters, throughout the kingdom. In 794, he took a leading role in the Frankish national council at Frankfurt, where Adoptionism was condemned. Adoptionism was an early Christian non-trinitarian theological doctrine, which stated that Jesus was adopted as the Son of God at his baptism, and his resurrection. He authored a book against this heresy, which was widely read throughout the realm. In 796, Paulinus accompanied Charlemagne's son Pepin, on his military campaign against the nearby hostile Avars.

Angilbert was a noble Frankish poet who was educated under Alcuin, and served Charlemagne as a secretary, diplomat, as well as being his son-in-law after marrying the king's daughter, Bertha. Angilbert's Latin poems reveal he was a cultured man of the world, enjoying the closest friendship of Charlemagne and his family. He was given the nickname "Homer" because he wrote extensive poetry, and was the author of an epic describing the daily life of the palace, and the meeting in Rome between Charlemagne and Leo. He was venerated as a saint, and is still honoured on the day of his death, 18th February.

Einhard was a Frankish scholar and courtier, and a dedicated servant of Charlemagne, and his son Louis the Pious. His main work was a biography of Charlemagne, the "Vita Karoli Magni", which was a comprehensive account of the great king's life and accomplishments, and one of the most precious literary bequests of the early Middle Ages.

Finally, there was Waldo, a Carolingian abbot and bishop who belonged to a noble Frankish family. From 786 until 806 he was Abbot of Reichenau Abbey, where he established an outstanding library and school. Charlemagne made him Bishop of Pavia and Basle in 791. In 805 the great king gave him the honour of Bishop of the Saint-Denis Cathedral in Paris; a position which entrusted great power on him within the Church hierarchy.

As we sat enjoying our wine and food, Alcuin rose to speak.

'I have something of the utmost secrecy to share with you. Our great king is going to be ambushed in the basilica during the Christmas day mass. The holy father, Pope Leo III is going to place a crown upon Charlemagne's head and proclaim him as the Holy Roman Emperor of Europe. A number of prominent nobles and his closest cardinals have advised him to carry out this deed. The coronation is designed to show the world that the Church and its Pope hold supreme power over earthly kings, including our great Charlemagne.'

'Is it such a bad thing for our king to become a Holy Roman Emperor?' interjected Einhard.

'I can see what Alcuin is saying. It's not good', said Angilbert.

'This is a raw grab at supreme power, by Pope Leo III, and it must be stopped!' said Paulinus, with a sense of urgency.

'Does Charlemagne know of the holy father's intentions?' asked Theodulf.

'I don't believe he does, but I cannot be sure. As you are all aware, since we arrived in Rome, Charlemagne has had two private meetings with Pope Leo III. We don't know what they discussed because nobody else was in attendance, and our great king has chosen not to tell us, saying only, it was Church business,' replied Alcuin.

I rose to speak.

'Honoured gentlemen, we have a delicate dilemma here. The obvious solution is for us to let the king know about the Pope's plans. The problem with doing that though is firstly, he will want to know how we discovered the plot; and secondly, if he is aware of the coronation plans, and has colluded with the Pope, he is likely to react aggressively to our intervention. We are gambling on whether he knows or not. If on the other hand, he is totally unaware of the Pope's intentions, and disapproves of them, it may not be easy for him to prevent the coronation without offending the Pope; which may have grave repercussions for himself, us, and his realm.'

'Luca is right. We do have a dilemma. Luca and I have an audience with Pope Leo III tomorrow morning to discuss a number of matters including our great king's proclamation of the Pope's innocence on all charges brought against him; the banishment of the accusers from Rome; and plans for the Christmas day mass', explained Alcuin.

Alcuin had caught me by surprise. I had no idea he had arranged to meet the Pope, and that I was coming along too. I felt certain he would explain it all to me later.

'Tomorrow morning, I am going to try and extract some more information from the Pope, regarding his intentions for the Christmas Day mass,' continued Alcuin.

After the conclusion of our discussions, Alcuin invited abbot Caselli, and prior Adolfo, to join us for a formal dinner which comprised all produce from the monastery; including the roast pork, a large variety of fruit and vegetables, an assortment of cheeses, olives, bread, and of course, the excellent red wine. During dinner, abbot Caselli gave us a brief history of the founding of the Benedictine Order.

Traditionally, 529 CE is considered to be the year in which Saint Benedict founded his first monastery at Monte Cassino, southeast of Rome. He died and was buried there in around 547. Some decades later, the monastery was destroyed and not rebuilt for a long time. Benedict developed a set of Rules, which govern the behaviour of monks, and the organisation of Benedictine monasteries. In 594 Pope Gregory praised Benedict's Rules and the man himself, increasing the popularity and reputation of the Benedictine Order within the Church. In the late 6th and during the 7th centuries, further monasteries were set up within Italy, France, Spain, England, and Ireland.

Throughout the Carolingian empire, particularly under the active encouragement of Charlemagne, hundreds of monasteries throughout Europe came under the Benedictine Order. The monasteries became important centres not only of of religious life, but also of political administration, economic development, and of theological and secular learning. Books were written and copied in the "scriptoria" (writing rooms) of monasteries, ancient texts were preserved, and abbey schools trained and educated the clergy and the ruling elite. The monks dedicated themselves mainly to liturgical prayer. The monasteries owned farms, and sometimes entire villages, whose peasants sustained the monks with part of their produce.

The papacy also started to protect many of the monasteries from the influence and interference of nobles and local bishops. The accumulated wealth and social prominence of the monasteries also attracted criticism, and as a result, a number of reform movements tried to steer the Order back to a simpler, austere, and a more-humble way of life, in accordance with the teachings of Saint Benedict. This was certainly the case in the monastery where we were having our dinner.

The following morning, the day before Christmas, I was up at the break of sunlight, awoken by the majestic chanting of a choir coming from the basilica cathedral. I found out they were monks from all over Italy, rehearsing for the Christmas mass to be held at midday tomorrow, in the presence of Pope Leo III and his majesty Charlemagne.

After having a light breakfast of scrambled eggs, bread, and cheese, in the apartment refectory, during which Alcuin explained he wanted me to accompany him to meet the Pope because he trusted my judgment; Alcuin and I walked the short distance to the papal palace for our meeting with Leo. The basilica, palace, and apartments were interconnected by an elegant network of covered archways, surrounding the large rectangular cloister of lawn, ponds, fountains, and numerous sculptures of popes and saints, in the centre of the complex.

To the north of the cloister stood the magnificent church basilica, to the south the grand entrance, to the west the papal palace, and to the east the apartments in which I was residing. The entire complex was surrounded by high walls. As we waited in the papal palace, I pondered the life and achievements of Pope Leo III.

Leo was born in 750, the son of humble peasants, Atyuppius and Elizabeth. Unlike many of the cardinals and those who entered the papal household, he was not a member of the nobility. In fact, his family lived a modest life in southern Italy. He was made a cardinal of Santa Susanna by Pope Adrian I, and was also given the role of chief treasurer in the papal palace.

Leo was a cardinal when he was elected to succeed Pope Adrian I on 26th December, 795. Unlike Adrian, who had tried to maintain strict independence in the growing dispute between East and West by balancing the Byzantine emperor against Charlemagne; Leo immediately sided with Charlemagne by recognizing him as the patron of the Church and the Romans; sending him the keys of the confession of Saint Peter, and the standard of the city of Rome; and requesting that Charlemagne send a permanent diplomatic envoy to be stationed in the papal palace.

In return, Charlemagne was very grateful and sent letters of congratulations, and a great part of the treasure which he had seized after his conquest of the Avars shortly before Leo's papal coronation. Charlemagne's gift enabled Leo to become a substantial benefactor to the churches and charitable institutions of Rome, gaining him many allies. As we have seen, on 25th April, 799, during a religious procession in Rome, Leo was physically attacked by assailants incited by Adrian's supporters, who accused him of misconduct, and whose ultimate plan was to blind Leo and remove his tongue, thus disqualifying him from the papacy.

Leo fled across the Alps to his benefactor and protector, Charlemagne, at Paderborn. Exactly what was negotiated by them there, is not known from the surviving sources, but Leo was safely escorted back to Rome and resumed his duties under the heavy protection of Charlemagne's allies. Confusion in Rome continued however, and that's why Charlemagne and his closest advisers went there in November of 800, to restore order in the Church, which was greatly disturbed.

On 23rd December, in the presence of Charlemagne and Alcuin, Leo solemnly purged himself of the charges against him, to the complete satisfaction of Charlemagne. The surviving historical sources then go on to record that two days later, on Christmas day, at a large gathering in St. Peter's Basilica, ostensibly for the consecration of Charlemagne's son, Louis the Pious as king, Leo suddenly crowned Charlemagne Holy Roman Emperor. By carrying out this act, Leo obliterated his earlier humiliation and established the legal precedent that only the Pope could confer the imperial crown. More importantly, Leo made his position as Pope secure by becoming the immediate beneficiary of the coronation, itself an illegal and revolutionary proceeding.

According to Charlemagne's biographer Einhard, Charlemagne had no knowledge he was going to be crowned emperor, and if he had been informed, would have refused the imperial crown. Meanwhile, the Eastern imperial throne in the Byzantine capital of Constantinople was controversially held by a woman, Irene of Athens. The coronation of Charlemagne greatly offended the Byzantines, who had seen themselves to be the rightful heirs of the Roman Empire, and the defenders of Rome; but Empress Irene, like many of her predecessors since Justinian I, was too weak to offer protection to the city of Rome.

Leo's motive to create a new Western Roman Empire alongside the Eastern Byzantine one proved to be ineffectual, because the Byzantines regarded Charlemagne as an illegitimate usurper. Leo's act, which clearly had been planned in advance, also carried wider connotations because it drove a deeper wedge between East and West, causing an intense rivalry that persisted until the 13th century. By allying the papacy with the Western Roman Empire, it meant Charlemagne and his successors became ever more deeply involved in the religious, liturgical, and spiritual affairs of the papacy and the Catholic Church.

Although the relations between Pope and Emperor were relatively amiable, Charlemagne controlled imperial administration and Church reform. Yet in 809, when approached by Charlemagne's theologians for a ruling, Leo confirmed his strict dogmatic interpretation of the "Filioque" clause, which was the doctrine that the Holy Spirit originates from both the Father and the Son. This clause had been introduced into the Nicene Creed; but, because the clause had always been rejected by the Eastern Byzantine Church, Leo, in the interest of maintaining peace with the Greeks, urged that the creed should not be chanted in public masses.

After Charlemagne's death in 814, the hatred of the Roman nobility against Leo reasserted itself. In response, Leo had some of the conspirators executed, and submitted an account of his action to Charlemagne's son, Louis, who had succeeded his father. Leo died soon afterward, in 816, after a reign of over 20 years. The surviving sources do not record the cause of his death. There is little doubt that Charlemagne saw himself as superior to the Pope, since without his protection, the Pope would not survive. On the other hand, since there was no automatic right of succession in Frankish law, the Church's blessing was understood as a necessary, sacramental seal of succession. It was this power struggle between Pope and King, which I was endeavouring to untangle, by ensuring Charlemagne would not be crowned Holy Roman Emperor by Pope Leo III.

After what seemed like an eternal wait, the papal guards escorted us into Leo's office. It was huge, and decorated with lavish paintings, sculptures, manuscripts, and what I recognized to be an enormous plush rug from the orient. A large crystal chandelier dominated the centre of the room. Two of the walls had floor-to-ceiling cabinets with bookshelves full of manuscripts. Although Leo was sitting behind a gigantic oak desk when we walked in, he immediately got up and motioned us to sit on one of his two hand crafted sofas embroidered with tapestry, while he made himself comfortable on the other. He also motioned the three officials present to leave the room.

'Alcuin, my good friend, welcome to you. And this must be your friend Luca?'

'Yes, your eminency. Luca and I studied together in York. He is on a tour of Italy.'

'Welcome to Rome, Luca. My cardinals have told me about your lecture yesterday, Alcuin. When they told me you directly threatened the power structure and role of the Church, I thought, that could not possibly have been your intention. I needed to hear directly from you, what that speech was all about. I owe a deep debt of gratitude to you, Alcuin. I know you played an instrumental role in convincing our majesty Charlemagne of my innocence of all the charges laid against me by my sinister spiteful accusers. Thank you. I trust arrangements are being made as we speak, for the conspirators to be banished from Rome forever.'

'Yes, your eminence. I can assure you they will all be evicted from Rome by midnight tonight. Now, there is a huge favour you can do for me.'

I could see Leo was visibly annoyed Alcuin had ignored his statement about the purpose of the speech he gave to the cardinals and nobles yesterday. It took him a little while to respond.

'Anything Alcuin. Anything. Just ask.'

'Is it your intention to crown Charlemagne, Holy Roman Emperor, during the mass tomorrow?'

The jovial expression on Leo's face, suddenly changed to one of stony shock. All the colour was immediately drained from his large cheeks. His eyes were firmly fixed onto Alcuin's, and he wasn't blinking. This lasted for over a minute, but it seemed like an eternity. I noticed his right hand was uncontrollably shaking.

'Is this what your speech was about? Did Charlemagne put you up to this? Did he send you here to get himself crowned as an Emperor? He could have discussed this directly with me, you know?'

'No, your eminence. I have not discussed this matter at all with my king.'

'Well then, why in the good Lord's name do you think I would want to crown the king as Holy Roman Emperor? I have never heard anything more outrageous!'

Leo was now visibly angry, and his whole body was trembling with what appeared to be pent-up rage. I could see Alcuin was very calm and measured, closely observing all of Leo's bodily and emotional reactions. I was impressed.

'Your eminence, I had a vivid dream last night. This was no ordinary dream. It was one of probably only half a dozen that I have had in my entire life, where the messenger is the archangel Michael. Each of the other dreams have come to fruition. So when Michael came to my dreams last night and told me of your intentions, I had absolutely no reason to doubt him.'

Wow! I thought, this man was brilliant. How could Leo argue with that!

Leo was clearly surprised by what Alcuin had just said. After all, it was the archangel Michael who inspired the Roman Emperor Constantine to convert to Christianity, and gained the reputation as the warrior saint. In the 4th century, Saint Basil the Great's writings placed Saint Michael over all the angels. He was given the title "archangel" because he heralded, and took priority over, the other angels. In the 6th century, the view of Michael as a healer prevailed in Rome, after a plague struck the city, and the sick slept in the church of the Castel Saint Angelo waiting for his salvation.

The church was later dedicated to him, for saving Rome. In the 6th century, the growth of devotions to Michael in the Western Church was expressed by numerous feasts dedicated to him. In Roman Catholic teachings, the archangel Michael had four main roles; the leader of the Army of God; the angel of death, carrying the souls of all the deceased to heaven; the weigher of souls in his perfectly balanced scale; and finally, the special patron of the Chosen People in the Old Testament, and guardian of the Church. Alcuin knew that Leo could not possibly contest his vision of Michael. It was also a brilliant way of putting the question directly to Leo without incriminating any person, including Charlemagne himself. It was incredible to see Leo deflate and capitulate in front of our very eyes.

Alcuin seemed very satisfied with the unenviable position he had placed Leo in. Surprisingly, Leo abruptly ended the meeting, not saying another word. Instead he motioned us out of his office, and arranged with his guards for us to be escorted out of the papal palace. This in itself was mystifying. What was Leo thinking? Was he going to go ahead with the coronation tomorrow now that he knew we were aware of his plans? And the biggest question of all still remained unanswered; did Charlemagne know about the coronation plans?

Charlemagne was having a banquet at his Rome residence in the evening with his closest advisers. Alcuin asked him if I could attend, and he said it was fine. Clearly Alcuin enjoyed enormous respect from the great king. It was clear that tonight, we were going to somehow establish whether Charlemagne was aware of the Pope's coronation intentions; and led by the brilliant Alcuin, devise a scheme to avoid this fateful event occurring; if that's what Charlemagne wanted, of course. It was going to be a fascinating evening, and I was looking forward to it. Apart from the high drama about to unfold, I was of course, looking forward to meeting the great king himself, in person. Another notch to my string of fascinating historical characters that I was getting the privilege of meeting on this great quest to change the future of our planet.

I had the afternoon free to do whatever I wished. I decided to visit the Papal Library, which housed the largest collection of ancient and early medieval manuscripts in Europe, at that time; this library was to be the forerunner to the Vatican Library, which exists to this day as one of the greatest libraries of modern times.

The library was housed within the Papal Palace complex. I wasn't surprised to see it was a magnificent building with a very high ceiling, jam-packed not only with manuscripts, but also priceless works of art and sculpture from throughout Europe and Asia Minor. The librarians were all highly educated monks who were hand-chosen by the Pope from all over Europe. Being a librarian in the Papal Library was a very prestigious position. I was given a personal librarian, who escorted me to a large desk, which I had to myself. His job was to find me whatever manuscripts I wanted to see. I have always enjoyed the scholarly ambience of libraries.

As a teenager in high school, whereas most of my friends spent morning recess and lunch playing basketball, soccer or cricket, I would make my way into the school library where I was safe, and could create my own world simply by the choice of books I read. Although sociable and comfortable in the presence of people, I have always enjoyed the solace of my own company, and books have always been my gateway into a myriad of other worlds and minds; much like this time-travel gig I was currently engaged in.

More medieval books survive from the Middle Ages than any other artistic medium. Scholars refer to the hand-made books of the Middle Ages as manuscripts. Books that contain artistic decoration are called illuminated manuscripts. Manuscripts that survive from the European Middle Ages are generally of a religious nature, reflecting the canon, doctrine and practices of Christianity, though there are also Jewish and Muslim books, and other types of books that survive from the period as well. A medieval manuscript is a codex, meaning a book made of pages bound between two boards. Ancient scribes wrote on scrolls that were stored in boxes.

These ancient scrolls from mainly the Greek and Roman worlds only survive in occasional fragments, because a scroll is especially vulnerable to physical degradation. The pages of codices, on the other hand, are protected by their covers, and have a much greater chance for survival. As a result, medieval codex books have survived in greater numbers than ancient scrolls. The original manuscripts of the Bible, the works of Aristotle, Plato, Cicero, Caesar, and other ancient writers do not survive. They are known today because medieval scribes, including Benedictine monks, diligently copied them.

Recording and disseminating information is quick and easy today, but in the Middle Ages this process was slow and laborious. Monastery libraries housed most books, and all books were copied by hand, usually by monks. This process of copying and disseminating scrolls and manuscripts was essential to the preservation of human knowledge. Some monks travelled to distant monasteries to view and copy books to bring back to their own monastery's library. Fires destroyed many medieval libraries and the books they housed. Because of this and other accidents of history, not all texts survived the Middle Ages.

Books were essential to the practice of Christianity. Medieval Christian missionaries such as St. Benedict of Nursia, and St. Augustine of Cantebury, brought books with them as they travelled from place to place preaching and establishing new churches. The Gospel Book of

St. Augustine survives today in the Parker Library of Corpus Christi College, at Cambridge University. It contains the text of the gospels – Matthew, Mark, Luke, and John, of the New Testament – an essential work for teaching potential converts about the life of Christ. A series of images illustrating the life of Christ prefaces the text, and each book of the gospels begins with a hand-drawn illustration detailing the events unique to that gospel, though some of these are now lost.

The illuminate manuscripts are among the oldest manuscripts in existence. The illustration of books was functional as well as decorative. Illuminated initials and painted miniatures marked the beginnings of important sections in the text and allowed readers to navigate the book. Prefatory image cycles prepared the mind of the reader to engage with the text. Some illustrations elaborated doctrines, recorded events, or simply told stories. In illuminate manuscripts, words and images worked together to inform the medieval reader, and occasionally these readers left their own mark. These books were highly interactive.

Nearly all medieval manuscripts provided ample space in the margins for readers' notes and comments. Given that in the early Middle Ages few people were literate outside of the Church, the books were usually commissioned individually by those who could read, such as wealthy patrons or fellow religious orders. The notes in the spaces would allow the owner to add a prayer or comment which would personalise the book for them. They could also expand on the writing or highlight a passage in a similar way.

The monk-scribes often did leave their own comments in the margins of manuscripts, and often a section at the end detailing who they were, which religious order they belonged to, and what it was like writing the book. In the early Middle Ages, the manuscripts were made out of animal hides, which were cheaper and more durable than papyrus. At this time, paper had not yet been brought over from the Islamic world. Of course, Latin was the language of manuscripts, because it was the language of scholars and of the Church. There were so many languages in Europe, scholars needed a common language in which to communicate at a higher level.

I asked the librarian to send me a number of prominent manuscripts, one after the other, which I savoured and thoroughly enjoyed, because they were all literary masterpieces in their own right. Firstly, there was the "Regula Sancti Benedicti" ("The Rule of St Benedict"). This was the original manuscript of the Rule of Saint Benedict of Nursia, which he wrote to establish the "blueprint" for how Benedictine monasteries should operate, and how the monks should behave and conduct their lives.

Secondly, there was the Gospel of Saint Cuthbert, an early 8th century pocket gospel book, written in Latin. Its finely decorated leather binding was one of the first. The essentially undecorated text contained the Gospel of John, written in a script regarded as a model of elegant simplicity. The book takes its name from Saint Cuthbert of Lindisfarne, in north-east England. The librarian told me the book had been gifted to the Papal Library by Alcuin.

Thirdly, there was an original manuscript of the Islamic Quran. The whole text was produced by five scribes in Hijazi script. It was beautifully illustrated in rich and striking colours.

Next, I examined a beautiful manuscript of the original Christian bible, the Old Testament. What was striking about this version was how many illustrations it contained. The book was clearly designed for illiterate people to follow the main story, just by viewing the illustrations.

Following from that, I viewed a series of manuscripts from ancient Greek and Roman times; including the poetry of Gallus, Vergil, and Ovid; historical treatises from Herodotus and Livy; and the entire works of Plato. I was reassured to know, that under the stewardship of Charlemagne, monks around Europe were translating into manuscripts the original works of Valerius Flaccus, Julius Caesar, Marcus Cicero, Quintilian, Tacitus, Macrobius, Ovid, Ausonius, Petronius, Horace, Suetonius, Lucretius, Frontinus, Martial, and Juvenal.

I pondered how influential Charlemagne had been in preserving so many classical texts. There are a series of volumes called the *Codices Latini Antiquiores* which have survived into the modern world, containing descriptions of all known Latin manuscripts, Christian and Classical, made up until the year 800 CE, the year in which I was now visiting. I passed the entire afternoon in complete ecstasy, immersed in these great classical works of literature.

We gathered at Charlemagne's Rome residence just after sunset on what was Christmas Eve. In addition to Alcuin and myself, his close advisers who had all attended the dinner at the monastery library the previous evening were also there. On the way to the dinner, Alcuin told me he had met with Charlemagne that afternoon, as soon as he returned to Rome from his hunting trip, and told Charlemagne of the Pope's intentions to crown him as a Holy Roman Emperor at the Christmas Day mass tomorrow.

According to Alcuin, Charlemagne was shocked and angry. He demanded to know how Alcuin knew of this. Quite brilliantly, Alcuin repeated to Charlemagne exactly what he had told Pope Leo III; that the archangel Michael had come to him in a dream and declared the coronation was to occur. During the sumptuous banquet dinner, catered for by an army of servants, Charlemagne outlined to us, a stunning and dramatic plan for tomorrow's mass. A plan that I'm certain none of us present would have contemplated beyond our wildest dreams.

During the Christmas Day mass, Charlemagne was going to pre-empt Leo, by declaring himself to be the new Pope of the Church. He was going to justify this incredible act by claiming that he alone was God's representative on Earth, and therefore had a legitimate claim to become the Holy Father of the Church. He was also going to claim that Leo, although exonerated of all the charges laid against him, remained with a tarnished reputation not worthy of a Pope.

Furthermore, Charlemagne was going to use his immense power to decree that all future Frankish Kings, starting with his heir and son, Louis, would automatically assume the title of Pope. With the exception of Alcuin, who expressed unconditional support and agreement with Charlemagne's bold plan; the other advisers expressed reservations on ecclesiastical Church-traditional grounds. The reservations were futile to Charlemagne. He asked all of us present to swear an oath of total loyalty to himself and his plan, including me! We all obliged. That was it. There was no further discussion. Charlemagne was to crown himself as the Pope, tomorrow. I thought long and hard. Is this what Otto wanted? Was this going to change the future of our Earth for the better?

I was confident it was going to be viewed positively by Otto for two reasons. Firstly, I will have succeeded in stopping the coronation of Charlemagne as Holy Roman Emperor; and secondly, by starting a precedent where Frankish kings automatically became Popes, I knew from my knowledge of history, this was going to greatly diminish the power of the Catholic Church, and ultimately with the demise of the Frankish kings, lead to the demise of the Popes themselves.

Christmas day started with a breakfast at the papal apartments attended by Alcuin and the other advisers. We then relaxed by playing a card game similar to modern day poker. I then went for a solitary walk in the basilica gardens to clear my mind. At fifteen minutes before midday, we made our way the short distance to the basilica cathedral. The mass was due to start at midday.

When we arrived, the basilica was full. We were escorted to our reserved seats towards the front of the church near the majestic grand altar. A choir of 100 monks, all dressed in black, in the upstairs gallery, were chanting hauntingly beautiful choruses while we all waited for the stars of the "show" to arrive. And then it happened. Pope Leo III entered first. Directly behind him was Charlemagne. And behind him was a procession of regally-attired cardinals in a sea of red.

The Pope and Charlemagne were both dressed in their full imperial regalia. The entire front rows of the basilica were reserved for the cardinals. The Pope and King were seated alongside each other in front of the altar, facing the audience. The Pope then proceeded to conduct the liturgical Latin mass. I was fluent in Latin, which held me in good stead. The formalities of the mass were completed in around thirty minutes. Then suddenly, Charlemagne arose to speak, and motioned for Leo to remain seated. He proceeded to the high altar so that everybody present in the cathedral, including Leo, who had turned his seat around, were facing towards him.

'Your holy eminence, cardinal princes of the Church, noble dignitaries, and others, I hereby speak on behalf of our Lord the holy Father, and Jesus Christ, the son of God. I came to this great city to preserve the honour of the papacy. I came to this city with the total power vested in me by Jesus and his father God. I came to this city as the protector of the Church. With the strength and blessing given to me by Jesus the son, and God the holy Father, I hereby proclaim myself to be the Pope. Leo, you are immediately relinquished of all your papal powers and duties. They shall now vest in me, effective herewith. Furthermore, the position of Pope shall automatically vest in my heirs, upon assuming the throne of the Frankish Kingdom, starting with my honourable son Louis, and then to his future heirs.'

There were loud gasps of shock echoing throughout the cathedral. Leo was mortified and remained motionless, not saying a single word. A number of the cardinals and nobles in the front rows were visibly distressed and angry.

'Hush!' screamed Charlemagne.

'How dare you denigrate me and the holy father and his son, with your disgraceful display of disloyalty!'

Charlemagne was livid. The noise ground to a halt immediately. Not a single sound could be heard. The choir was not singing. There was deadly silence as Charlemagne continued.

'I shall take the title of Pope Charlemagne I. All of the positions of cardinals shall be vacated effective immediately. I shall then appoint all of the cardinals over the next few days. All of the property of the Church shall come under my direct control. I alone shall decide the fate of the Church and its teachings.'

Charlemagne then proceeded to walk down the main aisle and take congratulations from many of the cardinals and nobles in the forward rows. I was in the third row to the right of the main aisle. The great King-Pope was nearby me in the main aisle. Suddenly, I heard an almighty scream as a man jumped from the upper choir balcony and landed directly on Charlemagne. All hell broke loose as this man dressed in a black clerical gown produced a knife and began to attack the King-Pope. I was certain it was Thero!! I raced toward the main aisle and violently pushed Charlemagne to the ground just as Thero was about to thrust a dagger into the great king's chest. There was panic and commotion throughout the cathedral. Thero and I were engaged in a vicious fight to the death.

He repeatedly tried to stab me, while sitting on top of me. I managed to break free by punching him in the face. I instinctively kicked the knife out of his right hand. It went hurtling to the ground. I had to muster all of my martial-arts expertise to subdue Thero. At one point in our violent scuffle, he was screaming at me: 'You can't stop me! You can't stop me!' After a number of hits to his head, he was dazed. It was at this point that he broke my grip on him and just raced out of the basilica, aggressively pushing bystanders out of the way. A number of Charlemagne's guards, who were stationed outside the cathedral, raced after him. But it was to no avail. He had escaped.

Shortly after the assassination attempt, Charlemagne and Alcuin met with me in the Papal Palace.

'You saved my life today Luca Evangelista. I do not know much about you, but as a trusted friend of Alcuin, you are now a lifelong friend of mine. I will forever be grateful for your supreme act of bravery today. Luca, will you please do me the honour of kneeling before me?'

'Yes, your great eminence.'

With that, Charlemagne produced his ceremonial sword and proceeded to tap me on the right shoulder with it.

'Luca Evangelista, by the powers vested in me by Jesus and the holy Father, I hereby admit you to the Order of the Paladin Knights.'

'I am truly honoured, your eminent majesty.'

The Paladin Knights were thought to be romantic works of literary fiction, like King Arthur, passed down from the Renaissance. But now I knew otherwise. They were Charlemagne's closest military advisers; totally loyal to the great king, and prepared to give up their lives for his kingdom. Other Paladin Knights included Alcuin himself; Roland, the nephew of Charlemagne; Rinaldo of Montalban, Roland's cousin; Namo, the duke of Bavaria; Salomon, the king of Brittany; Astolpho, an English duke; Fierabras, the son of the king of Spain, who was a Muslim, but eventually converted to Christianity and fought for Charlemagne; Turpin, an archbishop; and Ogier, a Danish prince.

They were originally knights or counts of the palace, and were attached to Charlemagne personally instead of being the lord of some estate; and they held various important positions within the kingdom. I knew of the importance of Alcuin. I also found out for example, that Roland's role was to defend the kingdom's border with Brittany.

That afternoon, Charlemagne placed the former Pope Leo under arrest, as well as over 200 people loyal to Leo, including cardinals, bishops, papal officers, and influential nobles. They were all packed into the dungeon cells of the Castel San Angelo not far from the basilica. According to Alcuin, he was going to remove them from Rome, once he was satisfied the great city was free of unrest, and secured; and take them all to a compound in northern Italy, where they were to be executed. Suffice to say, he appointed 30 cardinals, all of whom were very loyal to him, and created a new position of Cardinal-Regent. This person would be the leader of the Church, and fully responsible for maintaining control and harmony, and of course, implementing all of the "reforms" Charlemagne was to introduce. By the end of Christmas day, I was back in the 21st century, ready to be debriefed by Otto.

It was a Friday evening and the piano bar was full of younger professionals and office workers letting their hair down after the end of another working week; the Billy Joel impersonator was playing a pretty good rendition of "Uptown Girl". I secured a small round table in a back corner of the bar, a gin and tonic in hand, and observed how carefree everybody was, seemingly oblivious to the great problems and challenges facing the planet, and the dire fate of Earth. Why didn't the majority of this generation appear to care about the fate of future generations, including their own children and grandchildren? These kids didn't protest and march in university campuses! I knew the answer to my question. Earlier generations had created a "monster" by unleashing climate change, nuclear weapons, globalisation, inequality, terrorism, overpopulation, religious conflict, and all of the other global problems we now faced. These kids were resentful of this, but also had a great sense of entitlement. At exactly 7pm as planned, Otto appeared, in his customary all black.

'Why do you and Thero always wear black?'

'Where we come from, we long discarded any sense of fashion and the use of colours in clothing. To us, clothing serves a strictly functional purpose and is not an extension of a person's personality. A lot of it is to do with the political structure of our society and civilization. The closest description of our system of governance, using your ideologies, would be communism. But its compassionate communism literally as envisaged by your Karl Marx, where everybody is treated and respected equally, and there is no extreme wealth and poverty; instead the wealth and resources are shared amongst all citizens.

The pursuit of knowledge and ideas for the improvement of the individual and society as a whole, is the primary goal in our world.

This was the catalyst behind the rapid advancement in our technology when our governance system was first introduced for the entire planet. Make no mistake, we went through the inevitable cycles of other political ideologies, including various forms of harsh totalitarianism, soft democracy; and the conflict they created, before we got to what we now have and enjoy. So everybody is happy to dress in black, Luca.'

'Okay, that's why Thero was in black.'

'Yes. I warned you about Thero. Let me clarify what he can and cannot do. He has no superhuman powers by the way. He is in the form of a human. He cannot kill anybody except the key person whom you are seeking to influence, but only if that person is in your presence. So for example, in the world you just came from, Charlemagne was literally the only person Thero could have killed, and of course, he certainly tried to. He can only remain in a particular time period, when you are there. So he cannot arrive earlier and cannot leave later. He also can communicate with, and in any way seek to influence, any person, when he travels back in time. Having failed to stop you so far, he is going to become increasingly determined, hostile, and desperate. You must always be wary of, and alert to, him.'

'I will be better prepared for Thero. I wasn't sure how you would react to Charlemagne turning the tables on Leo, and crowning himself Pope!'

'Well that definitely took me by surprise as much as it did you and the others, Luca. What he did, really clipped the wings of the political, imperial, and power, aspirations of the Catholic Church. By appointing himself as Pope, Charlemagne set in motion a series of events that dramatically reduced the power and influence of the Catholic Church not just in Europe, but around the world. Christianity lost its influence to such an extent that by the 20th century, only a few hundred thousand people worldwide kept the religion alive, mainly in underground movements. In that universe, it also paved the way for an earlier and greater acceleration of humanism and science, which resulted in an explosive exponential expansion of technology, placing that version of the Earth, two centuries ahead of your version. For example, by the early 21st century, that Earth was engaged in interstellar exploration. You must remember Luca, even though we are talking about alternative Earth's in multiple universes, whenever you travel back in time and change history, there is a profound ripple effect on the fabric of space and time which is altering the future of your Earth. This creates a significant butterfly effect. Charlemagne significantly reducing the power of the Catholic Church was a big one. Your next mission, to prevent the Crusades from occurring is also going to profoundly affect the future of your planet, if you succeed.'

Whilst back in the 21st century for a week, I took the opportunity to call in on my family and my closest friends. As far as they were concerned, I had taken a sabbatical from teaching to further my education by studying various online short courses; and also to continue working on my book. They knew I had a love of learning and writing, so it wasn't a difficult stretch to convince them I would undertake this. My Mum was still in mourning from the tragic and sudden loss of my Dad.

He was a fit and healthy man in his seventies when he was struck by a van on that fateful day just over six months ago. Since retiring five years earlier from his humble position as a cleaner in a public hospital, he led a well-structured life. Every morning at around 8am he would go to the local shopping centre to buy whatever provisions my Mum wanted, mainly so she could cook her delicious Italian traditional dinners every night. She was accustomed to Dad controlling all the finances and doing the shopping. This was probably the biggest thing she had to get used to after he passed.

Anyhow, after doing the shopping, Dad would then take public transport to see more of the city and extended suburbs of Perth, Western Australia, where we all lived. He would for example often take the train for the 20 kilometre trip to the port city of Fremantle, or the 70 kilometre trip to the southern coastal resort town of Mandurah. Sometimes on a hot day he would take two buses to Scarborough beach, the best in Perth, just to wade into the ocean and feel the Indian Ocean breeze on his face. Three days a week, he would make his way to his beloved Italian Club at around 11am to catch up with his friends, while playing cards and enjoying some Italian dried sausages and wine.

It was while he was on his way to the Italian Club that his life came to an abrupt and sudden end. On that particular morning it had been raining. After completing his morning shopping which also included visits to the bank and pharmacy, he arrived home, spoke with my Mum briefly, and made his way to the Club by catching a bus. Even though it was only a fifteen- minute walk to the Club he caught the bus that day because of the inclement wet weather. When he got off the bus, only two bus stops away from where he boarded, he proceeded to cross the road but didn't see a van approaching.

Although the driver was within the 60kph speed limit, the van struck him with such force that he rolled over the bonnet and landed on the side of the road where it met the kerb. Six witnesses saw him sit up for a few moments. His right arm, which took the bulk of the impact was badly broken. Dad was seen to be holding his arm and grimacing with pain. The driver was an eighteen-years old tradesman on his way to a job; who was very distraught and badly shaken after the accident. Within minutes the ambulance arrived to take my still-conscious Dad to the hospital, which was only ten minutes away. While in the ambulance he lost consciousness. As soon as the ambulance arrived in the emergency department he was immediately treated by trauma surgeons.

Meanwhile, I had been on school holidays and was at my local favourite café working on my book, when my brother called. He told me to rush to the hospital immediately because Dad had been in a serious accident. Within fifteen minutes I arrived at the emergency department. My brothers and Mum were nowhere to be seen. Then after a few minutes of high anxiety, one of the emergency surgeons directed me to a bare room, with just chairs. My Mum and two of my brothers were already in there. My eldest brother was on a family holiday in the south west. I dreaded what was going to come next.

The surgeon advised us they had done everything possible to try and save him, but my Dad had died a few minutes earlier from massive internal bleeding. We were all in a complete state of shock. My Mum was hysterical, and inconsolable with grief. They had been married for well over fifty years. Before leaving the hospital the four of us got to see my Dad, laying on a bed in another bare room, in eternal peaceful sleep, with a blanket covering him up to his chest. I gently kissed Dad on the forehead and bid him goodbye with all of my love. The surgeon reassured us Dad had died peacefully and with no pain because they had tranquilized him. My Dad was fit and healthy. Why didn't he see the van approaching?

This question has racked my brain ever since. If only Dad had stayed home on that fateful morning for five minutes longer, he wouldn't have ventured to meet his fateful destiny. Literally five minutes after he left home, my uncle and auntie, came for a spontaneous visit. If they had arrived only five minutes earlier, Dad would have stayed home. I fell asleep that night with beautiful happy memories of my Dad teaching me to play soccer in the park opposite where we lived, when I was a young boy.

‘39

In the year of ’39, assembled here the volunteers
In the days when lands were few
Here the ship sailed out into the blue and sunny morn
The sweetest sight ever seen

And the night followed day
And the story tellers say
That the score brave souls inside
For many a lonely day sailed across the milky seas
Ne’er looked back, never feared, never cried

Don’t you hear my call though you’re many years away
Don’t you hear me calling you
Write your letters in the sand
For the day I take your hand
In the land that our grandchildren knew

In the year of ’39 came a ship in from the blue
The volunteers came home that day
And they bring good news of a world so newly born
Though their hearts so heavily weigh
For the Earth is old and grey, little darling, we’ll away
But my love, this cannot be
Oh, so many years have gone though I’m older but a year
Your mother’s eyes, from your eyes, cry to me

Don’t you hear my call though you’re many years away?
Don’t you hear me calling you?
Write your letters in the sand for the day I take your hand
In the land that our grandchildren knew

Don't you hear my call though you're many years away?
Don't you hear me calling you?
All your letters in the sand cannot heal me like your hand
For my life
Still ahead
Pity me

Queen – Brian May (1976)

6

Pope Urban II

Clermont, France, November 1095 CE

I HAD DONE MORE PREPARATION THAN USUAL FOR MY NEXT MISSION; one in which I was about to get immersed in the complex and murky medieval world of the Crusades; particularly the launching of the First Crusade by Pope Urban II in a speech he gave in the open air, in the French city of Clermont, on 27th November 1095. I was about to embark in the morning. That previous evening, I reflected carefully on my research; including the connection between the medieval Christian Crusades and the current 21st century extreme Muslim Terrorism afflicting the US-led capitalist world; culminating in the attack on the United States on September 11, 2001. An event I would be seeking to undo in my final mission. I wanted to get into the head of Urban, and understand as best I could, his motives for launching the Crusades.

"A grave report has come from the lands around Jerusalem, that a race absolutely alien to God has invaded the land of the Christians. They have either razed the churches of God to the ground or enslaved them to their own rites. They cut open the navels of those whom they choose to torment, drag them around and flog them before killing them as they lie on the ground with all their entrails out. What can I say of the appalling violation of women? On whom does the task lie of avenging this, if not on you? Take the road to the Holy Sepulchre, rescue that land and rule over it yourselves; for that land, as scripture says, floweth with milk and honey. Take this road for the remission of your sins, assured of the unfading glory of the kingdom of heaven." When Pope Urban spoke these words, apparently everyone present shouted: "Deus vult! Deus vult!" This translates to: "God wills it! God wills it!"

In this vivid and exaggerated language, as reported by an eye-witness, Robert of Rheims, Pope Urban II launched the First Crusade.

Four years later, in 1099, after having endured a journey of extreme hardship, the self-proclaimed "Knights of Christ" arrived at Jerusalem. On 15th July, 1099, the crusaders stormed the walls and put its Muslim defenders to the sword to reclaim Christ's city from Islam. While nearly 950 years later Christian-Muslim relations are still under severe strain, it is ironic that the Crusades were primarily intended to solve problems brewing within western Europe at the time. As the head of the Catholic Church, Urban was responsible for the spiritual wellbeing of everybody in Latin Christendom.

Yet Europe was engulfed by violence, lawlessness, and anarchy, primarily as a result of the diminished power of the secular Holy Roman Emperor, Henry IV of Germany, who had been excommunicated by the Church because he had challenged papal authority. Henry was no Charlemagne! In Urban's mind, the root cause of the anarchy and chaos was a deep fracturing of faith; and he was determined to restore peace and stability. If this was to be achieved, spiritual faith would have to be astutely blended with savvy political tactics; and Urban believed he had the ability to pull this off. It was Urban's genius that he conceived of a plan that offered benefits to the pope and to all of his flock. Perhaps he achieved this partly because of his family background. He was from the region of Champagne in northern France, and was a man of honourable noble blood.

The combination of his high-born ancestry, and a successful career in the Church gave him a direct insight into the ambitions, hopes, and fears, of the knightly classes, and this goes a long way to explaining why crusading satisfied the aspirations of so many. Urban astutely linked several ingredients familiar to medieval society; such as pilgrimage, and the idea of a holy war against the enemies of God, with an unprecedented offer of salvation; a powerful combination virtually guaranteed to enthuse the warriors of western Europe.

To persuade people in any historical age to leave their homes and loved ones, and to venture into the unknown, it is necessary to convince them the endeavour is going to be worth their while. As many conflicts in the past have revealed, propaganda can play a vital role in stirring the masses, in any build up towards a war. In modern times it has largely been common nationalism which has been the glue uniting peoples with the smart use of propaganda; back then, it was the common religion of Christianity. Pope Urban II's address at Clermont used highly passionate and inflammatory language and images to provoke moral outrage from his audience.

The Muslims were described in language that emphasised their "otherness" and their barbarity towards innocent Christians. In reality, while it was true that pilgrims were occasionally mistreated, it was also the case that there had been no systematic persecution of Christians by Muslims in the Holy Land, for decades. Yet Urban's impassioned rhetoric demanded a response from the knights of Europe. He called for vengeance, a concept that was second nature to knights accustomed to correcting an injustice through the use of brute force, supported by the weight of the moral might of God. By referring to authorities on Church law, such as Saints Augustine and Benedict, Urban and his circle of close advisers constructed a case whereby violence could, in certain circumstances, be seen as morally justified.

This of course required a just cause, usually in the form of a reaction to the aggression of a demonised "other," in this case the alleged atrocities committed by the Muslims. Proper authority was needed to proclaim a war. Also, the response had to be proportionate but not excessive, in order to maintain its moral value. To these "just war" principles, crusading added the taking of a vow and an association with pilgrimage. So because it was judged to be morally positive, the crusade became an act of penance that merited a spiritual reward. Earlier attempts to restrict the violence that plagued eleventh-century Europe included the Peace of God movement in which the Church forbade fighting for a specific period under the threat of ecclesiastical penalties.

At Clermont however, Urban urged the knights of Europe to cease all of their private conflicts and wars, and to begin a battle worthy of their noble status; to fight for God was to serve the ultimate Lord; and to win forgiveness for their wicked lives was a prize immeasurably greater than any earthly riches could offer. There is no doubt these violent knightly warriors had committed many acts not in accordance with the will of God and teachings of Christianity; and it was here where Urban offered them a chance to atone themselves and avoid a terrible fate. Virtually every church in Christian Europe had a sculpture or fresco of hell; savage devils gouging out the eyes of screaming sinners; or sinners skinned or tortured with spears and pitchforks; and impaled humans roasted for eternity.

The message from the Church was terrifyingly simple; there was no avoiding the consequences of sin; a knight therefore, needed an escape route from the fires of Satan. These same frescoes also showed heaven as a place of peace, tranquillity, and everlasting security. The making of pilgrimages and giving of indulgences (donations) to monasteries could only go so far to avoid hell, but Pope Urban II brilliantly presented what one contemporary described as "a new way to attain salvation."

Urban judged correctly that the crusade would be a sufficiently arduous and life-threatening experience to deserve the redemption of all past sins, and the remission of all penance. In effect, by going on God's crusade, the knights and their army of Christians, would have all of their sins wiped clean. As far as the knights were concerned, the best aspect of all this was that they could continue their lust for fighting, only now their energies would be directed towards the enemies of God, rather than to their fellow Christians.

Those who wished to take part in the crusade had to make a public statement of their commitment in the form of a sacred vow, and being marked up with the sign of the cross. Often amidst highly emotional scenes, enthusiastic recruits would surge forward and demand to have a cloth pinned to their shoulder, desperate to bear the symbol that represented Christ's sacrifice, and their own imitation of his suffering. Preachers adopted the words of Christ himself: "If any man will come after me, let him deny himself, and take up his cross and follow me." If a crusader deserted his vows, then he deserved damnation into hell.

According to Urban's command: "He should forever be regarded as an outlaw, unless he came to his senses and undertook to complete whatever of his obligation was left undone." An additional benefit of the crusade was the bringing of huge numbers of people under the direct control of the Church, even though it was temporary. We can clearly see Urban had found a way to enhance the standing of the papacy while offering something attractive to his true believers.

The call to free the Holy Sepulchre in Jerusalem, and the Orthodox Christians of the East, was shaped in a familiar form; namely a pilgrimage. This was a fundamental feature of medieval life; the concept of turning to a saint for help was an everyday experience, and people sought the assistance of these heavenly beings in their health, harvests, fertility, protection, and the forgiveness for their sins. The presence of a saint was symbolised by relics, parts of a saint's body, or objects associated with his or her life, that were believed to retain their holy power, and to offer a conduit to divine help.

The veneration (giving gratitude) of relics often required a journey to be undertaken; and some saints became associated with particular causes. Saint Leonard of Noblat, for example, was the patron saint of prisoners. People in captivity prayed to him, and when their imprisonment ended, they would make a pilgrimage to the town of Noblat in central France and, as a show of gratitude, would place their prison chains onto the church altar.

While many pilgrimages were simple processions or visits to local churches, longer journeys to important shrines, such as that of Saint James of Santiago de Compostela in north western Spain, grew in popularity during the eleventh century. This was a pilgrimage which I myself completed a number of years ago. The ultimate pilgrimage destination was the Holy Land; the place where Christ lived and died. Because He had ascended to heaven, there was no body to venerate, and so the focus was on places touched by His presence and His death, most particularly His tomb, the Holy Sepulchre in Jerusalem.

The regaining control of the Holy Land, and particularly this site, became the principal goal of the First Crusade. For the crusaders, a journey there deserved the greatest reward; the remission of all their sins. This was integral to the hearts and minds of medieval men; and the notion of regaining Christ's land for Christianity lay at the core of Urban's appeal.

Even though the papacy advanced spiritual motives as the prime reason for the crusade, it is clear that more worldly power-wealth-political factors also played a big role. Robert of Rheims's account of Urban's speech, written around 1106, highlights these other motives, when he claimed the pope spoke of a land of milk and honey, an alluring prospect for people burdened by poor harvests, and in search of a change from the drudgery of village life. While the desire to liberate the city of Christ had to take absolute priority, otherwise God would not favour the expedition, some crusaders would need to remain in the Levant to hold and secure the territory.

There was very little point in taking control of Jerusalem, if everyone then proceeded to return home. So really, the First Crusade was as much a war of Christian colonisation and plundering wealth accumulation, as well as a Christian liberation of the Holy Land from the Muslims. For those prepared to take a chance, the possibility of a new life was beckoning. However, as it turned out, while huge numbers were willing to become crusaders, relatively few chose to remain in the East. If the hope of plunder and riches helped to draw people towards this great adventure, the acquisition and retention of wealth proved much harder to actually achieve.

It was an external event that triggered Urban's desire to restore the spiritual wellbeing of western Europe. In March 1095, envoys arrived representing Emperor Alexius of Constantinople, to appeal for help against the Muslims of Asia Minor. Alexius ruled the Byzantine Empire, the successor to the ancient Roman Empire, and had, until recent years, controlled territories that stretched across Asia Minor to Antioch in northern Syria, as well as modern-day Greece, Bulgaria, and Albania.

By 1095, much of Asia Minor had been lost to Muslim invaders, although ongoing troubles within the Muslim world gave him an opportunity to fight back. For many years Alexius had sent requests to western Europe for groups of well-armed knights to help his cause, and there was by then, a strong tradition of western mercenaries serving in the Byzantine imperial army. In 1095 however, Alexius understandably, failed to anticipate that Pope Urban II would use this opportunity to make a far wider appeal to the people of Latin Christendom, and launch a crusade. Pope Urban himself had a clear agenda when it came to Alexius.

In 1054, disputes over religious doctrinal matters, and also the relative authority of the pope, compared to the patriarch of Constantinople, had created a schism (or split) between the Catholics in the West, and the Orthodox Church in the East; a situation which still exists in the 21st century. In spite of this split, the two groups maintained cordial contact, and Urban saw his crusade as an opportunity to forge stronger relations; although from his perspective, the Roman Catholic Church was the senior partner because the Catholics were the people offering to help their Orthodox brothers from the clutches of the Muslims. In fact, Urban cast himself in the role of a "father" to his "son" the Byzantine emperor, and saw Rome as a "mother" to Constantinople.

Urban and his closest advisers considered how best to broadcast the appeal of the crusade. In an era before the advent of mass communication it was of vital importance to make as big a visual impact as possible. This meant the staging of numerous public ceremonies, culminating in the Council of Clermont, which was particularly well publicised with invitations sent to churchmen across France, Spain, Italy, England, and parts of Germany. Urban chose Clermont for its central location.

The meeting attracted thirteen archbishops, eighty bishops and cardinals, and over ninety abbots. For a fortnight, the pope laid down a legislative program for the spiritual recovery of Christendom. On the pinnacle day of the Council, Urban unveiled the centrepiece of his agenda – the launching of a crusade. Urban knew that his own personal presence was critical, and with this in mind, he embarked on a significant tour that took him hundreds of kilometres northward to Le Mans and Angers, and then down to Bordeaux, Toulouse, and Montpelier in the south. This was no spontaneous trip, but instead was intricately planned to gain the maximum impact.

The arrival of such a powerful figure was bound to excite attention, and Urban did his utmost to exploit this. Time and again, for example, at Saint-Gilles, Le Puy, Chaise-Dieu, Limoges, Tours, and Poitiers, the pope would appear on the feast day of the local saint, or else he would consecrate a new building, or attend an important festival. In other words, he was careful to choose an opportunity that allowed him to address the biggest crowds possible. The arrival of the papal entourage was a magnificent sight to behold.

The wealth and splendour of Pope Urban II and his court was clearly evident as he arrived at a new place, wearing his conical white cap with a circlet of gold and gems around the base. It was not just through his personal appearances that Urban recruited crusaders. The audience at Clermont carried the call back to their homes and, even though the response to his speech had been rapturous, the pope had little sense of the extraordinary zeal with which his words would be taken up. News of the papal expedition surged across Europe, and saturated the Latin West with crusading fervour.

I arrived in Clermont, France on the morning of 25th November, 1095. The man I was meeting with would be waiting for me outside the entrance of the Guilhem Castle, built by the Giulhem family, lords of Clermont, in the late 11th century, about ten years before the period I had just entered into. The castle was a magnificent stone structure, perched high up on Puech Castel Hill, overlooking the town of Clermont, and the surrounding fertile countryside, which was full of small farms and vineyards. It had a rampart fortification facing the valley which was built of stone, and was flanked by seven semi-circular towers.

The castle was built on the site of an ancient fortress, erected by the Visigoths in the 5th century. The strategic site permitted control of the Herault valley, the town of Clermont, and the main road to Bedarieux. I could see the castle in the distance, and made my way towards it. When I arrived, sure enough, there was a well-built, tall man waiting outside the entrance. He saw me approaching and walked towards me with a beaming smile.

'Luca Evangelista, I am Bohemond. It is my pleasure to meet you. Come, there is an inn down in the valley, where we can enjoy some fine ale.'

It was a bright sunny day, but bitterly cold. As we ventured down the hill, my face was struck by a chill of wind which continued until we got to the valley. The inn was large. On one wall was a procession of what appeared to be stuffed heads of bears and deer; clearly the result of numerous hunting expeditions. The entire inn was decorated with papal flags and Church paraphernalia, to celebrate the visit of the pope and other high ranking Church officials from all over Europe, for the Council meetings.

There were around a hundred men in the large room, in three groups, chatting and laughing loudly, while enjoying ale. When we walked in, many of them acknowledged Bohemond with a degree of respect, and then continued their banter. We went straight to the bar counter, where an attractive woman in her twenties served us two large silver cups of ale. She seemed to know Bohemond well, so it wasn't surprising there was strong sexual chemistry between them. So this is how the knights flirted in medieval times! We then made our way to a small table near the opposite wall to the stuffed game.

'I wrote a whole chapter about your father in my book,' I confidently stated to Bohemond, as we sat down.

Bohemond was clearly taken aback by my comment. He was an exceptionally handsome man, with long wavy blonde hair down to his shoulders, and piercing bright blue eyes. His complexion was immaculate, which I found to be unusual, considering he was a knight who had already fought in numerous battles. His muscular build clearly demonstrated he regularly exerted his body. His Viking ancestry was obvious.

'Oh really? So my father is still remembered in the 21st century?'

'Not just your father, you are too. My book was a comprehensive history of what we call the Molise-Abruzzo region of central Italy, where my parents came from. It started from the ancient Samnites, who were in Italy centuries before the Romans. Incredibly, even in the 21st century, there wasn't a single history book exclusively devoted to that little-known region of my parents' birth. So I wrote the book. I had to devote a chapter to your father, Robert Guiscard, because as you know, he was instrumental in creating a kingdom in southern Italy, which is at its peak today, in your world, as we speak. Your father was a great Norman knight and conqueror, Bohemond.'

'Yes he was Luca. I still miss him deeply. He's been dead for ten years now. As a child, I idolised him. He was my role model for the correct behaviour a knight of our Lord should display. I couldn't have achieved what I have, without the inspiration and guidance my father gave me. I am a proud Norman; and I am here in Clermont representing the interests of my family. As you are no doubt aware, my uncle Roger, now rules over southern Italy and Sicily.'

'Oh yes, I am well aware of the power and influence of your uncle. Now tell me Bohemond, what are your ambitions?'

'I come from an honourable family ancestry, with a tradition of conquests going right back not only to Normandy, but even further to the Vikings. I want to conquer and control territory for myself. I'm sure you know that William, the conqueror of England, is a close relative.'

'Yes, I know. I thought you harboured such an intense ambition Bohemond. I think your opportunity to achieve conquest of new lands has arrived.'

'What do you mean, Luca?'

'Pope Urban II is going to make a big and profound announcement at the end of this Council Conference, here in Clermont.'

'Yes, I have been hearing strong rumours amongst my fellow knights that his holiness has some kind of spiritual pilgrimage to the Holy Land, in mind, and that he will be calling for volunteers amongst the knights of Europe, to provide security for the pilgrimage. That's why he has invited the most esteemed counts and knights here. Perhaps he wishes to broker some kind of truce or understanding with the Muslim hoards who now control the Holy Land, including Christ's city of Jerusalem?'

'It's much more complicated than that, Bohemond. The pope is going to announce a massive military expedition with the objective of removing the Muslims from the Holy Land, and ensuring that Christians regain control of Jerusalem.'

'You mean a full scale war?'

'Yes Bohemond, except he is going to call it a crusade. All Christians who participate will be absolved of all their sins.'

'Holy mother of Christ! A religious war against the Muslim hoards!

'I am here to stop the pope from announcing the crusade. I cannot go into detail of course, you know Otto's strict instructions; but suffice to say, the crusades set off a long and arduous chain of events in human history which involve an ongoing and at times vicious struggle between Christianity and Islam, that continues well into the 21st century!'

'I see Luca. What role do you expect me to play to stop this crusade from happening?'

'Well it's not just one crusade. The First Crusade triggers six more. It becomes seven crusades over two centuries. Do you see how big this Jeannie will become if we allow it to be unleashed here in Clermont?'

'Jeannie?'

'Never mind, Bohemond, it's a saying from the future. Now, to answer your question. You are very influential amongst the knights of Europe. Many of the most powerful knights have been summoned here to Clermont for this Council. I want you to convince these knights not to go ahead with the crusade, and instead to lead them on a military expedition as mercenaries to assist the Byzantine Emperor Alexius, and to protect Constantinople and the remainder of his empire, which is in clear and present danger of being attacked by the Seljuk Muslims. You see Bohemond, Pope Urban is going to use the excuse of helping Alexius, as the justification for his crusade. But all it is for him, is a naked grab for power. Urban wants to take control of the Byzantines with the objective of eliminating the schism, and uniting the Orthodox Christians under the banner of Papal Roman Catholic domination.'

'If I manage to persuade the knights to go against the wishes of Urban, and follow me instead, what will be in it for me and them, Luca? Do you realise the enormous power the Church has? People will be terrified to undermine the pope.'

'Okay, let's get down to the finer details. Let's start with the other most powerful knights, also gathered here in Clermont. Other than you, Bohemond of Taranto, there are; Godfrey, count of Bouillon; Raymond IV, count of Toulouse; Robert Curthose, count of Normandy; Robert II, count of Flanders; and Hugh, count of Vermandois.'

'You have done your research very thoroughly, Luca.'

'Bohemond, if we can convince these other five knights to reject Urban's crusade, and instead support your military expedition to Byzantine, then trust me; if you play your strategic cards right, there will be an abundance of land and resources, for all of you to conquer.'

'That's all very well and good, but how are we going to persuade these esteemed knights to go against the wishes of our holy father, the pope?'

'Our host, William Guilhem has arranged for the legitimate pope, Clement III, to arrive at Clermont, on the morning of the 27th. Until he announces this to us, we must pretend we have no idea of this event about to occur. As you no doubt are aware, Guibert, the archbishop of Ravenna, was elected pope in 1080, and consecrated as Pope Clement III in Rome, in March 1084. He commands a significant following in

Rome and throughout Christendom Europe. He was elected in direct opposition to the illegitimate Pope Gregory VII, who was the leader of the movement in the Church which opposed the traditional claim of European monarchs to control high level Church appointments. This tradition goes back to the great Charlemagne, whom I had the honour of meeting. So Gregory put himself in direct opposition to the supporters of imperial monarchical rights, led by the Holy Roman Emperor. This led to the conflict known as the Investiture Controversy. Pope Gregory went too far when he excommunicated the Holy Roman Emperor, Henry IV, and supported a rival claimant as emperor. So, in 1080, the pro-imperial Synod of Brixen pronounced that Gregory was deposed, and replaced as pope by Guibert, who became Pope Clement III. He has reigned as the legitimate pope in opposition to the "anti-imperial" line of popes, starting with Gregory VII, then Victor III, and now of course, Urban II.'

We made our way back to the Guilhem Castle, where I was staying. All six of the prominent knights brought to Clermont, were staying in the castle as well, as guests of lord William Guilhem. During the course of the eleventh to the thirteenth centuries the lord counts controlled most of the lands in the county of Champagne, in which Clermont was located. In three particular areas the lord counts left a clear imprint on the region: its feudal aristocracy, its villages and towns, and its international fairs.

The lord counts and their barons routinely granted fiefs of modest rents or small parcels of land to knights, in return for loyalty and military service. The large scale feudalisation of land starting from the mid-eleventh century resulted in the extension of extra-familial rights and restrictions over much property. At this time, marriages, inheritances, sales of property, and donations were attended to orally with pledges backed up by a handshake. There were no written agreements in place. It wasn't until the thirteenth century that sealed letters were widely used to formalise these arrangements. So I appreciated how giving one's word was considered to be a bond of good faith from one party to another. This is certainly how the knights of this time conducted their affairs between each other, and with the nobility.

I was given a comfortable room in the upper level residential quarters of the castle. As I lay on the bed, feeling quite exhausted, I reflected upon the life of my helper in this world, Bohemond. Although his baptised name was Mark, almost all contemporary documents refer to him as "Bohemond", a childhood nickname that his father assigned to him in reference to a legendary giant. Bohemond's father was Robert Guiscard, the Norman founder of the Duchy of Apulia and Calabria. In 1058, Robert divorced Bohemond's mother, the Norman, Alberada, and married a Lombard princess, in order to strengthen his power base in southern Italy. This divorce was to Bohemond's detriment, because it deprived him of his paternal inheritance; even though he was the oldest son of Robert.

Although Bohemond was viewed as an illegitimate bastard in the eyes of the Church, his father Robert still treated him as an equal, especially when it came to military ventures. Under Robert's mentorship, Bohemond cultivated the strategic skills that would be essential in his conquests of land in Italy, Sicily, the Balkans, and Anatolia. Bohemond seized control of the Italian cities of Taranto and Bari from his half-brother, Roger Borsa, and sought further conquests in Byzantine territories of southern Italy, in a series of invasions that, although unsuccessful, greatly annoyed the Byzantine imperial family. Bohemond would develop a complex relationship with the powerful Byzantine Emperor Alexios Komnenos.

The interactions between the two men were documented in "The Alexiad" which was written by Alexios' daughter Anna Komneme. She was not the biggest fan of Bohemond, and often presented him in a negative manner. Anna was both attracted and repelled by this brash, arrogant, charismatic Norman. In her book she described him as blonde, clean-shaven, and very tall, but beautifully proportioned. "A certain charm hung about this man" she wrote, "but was partly marred by a general air of the horrible." It was not just international enemies that Bohemond had to deal with, as there was also a succession battle between himself and his half-brother Roger Borsa, for control over their father's land.

On top of all of this, Bohemond and his uncle Roger I of Sicily were asked to lead the First Crusade, by Pope Urban II. After leading an army in the First Crusade in 1096, Bohemond ventured to Constantinople, where he made the difficult decision to pay homage to Emperor Alexios, in order to strengthen his own political and power ambitions; and also joined with the other crusader armies. In spite of his reputation as an enemy of the Byzantines, he soon reached agreement with Emperor Alexius, and swore an oath of allegiance to him.

But this only aggravated the rivalry between Bohemond and count Raymond of Saint-Gilles for the position of supreme leader of the crusade. Although charming when necessary, Bohemond was ambitious, aggressive, and capable of duplicity when it served his ends. He became one of the expedition's most influential leaders, and in particular played an important role in the Siege of Antioch (1097-1098). The city ultimately fell to the crusaders as a result of a betrayal orchestrated by him. After contentious political tactics, Bohemond was able to gain sole control over Antioch, where he remained, as the other crusaders proceeded to march on to Jerusalem. At the Siege of Antioch in the spring of 1098, Bohemond was successful in breaching the city's walls.

Once in command, he took the title of prince of Antioch, thus ignoring his promise of 1097 to give the fortress city to the Emperor. Bohemond did not however, stay in his principality of Antioch for long. In 1100, Turkish forces captured him, and he remained their prisoner until 1103. Soon after his release, when fellow Norman knights paid the ransom, Bohemond departed for Europe to solicit support for a crusade against the Byzantine Empire, in response to Byzantine attempts to regain control of Antioch. Supported by an army of loyal followers, Bohemond launched an invasion of Byzantine territory in 1107, but soon suffered a crushing defeat. He lived his remaining years in southern Italy. His son, Bohemond II, by Constance, the daughter of King Philip I of France, succeeded him as Prince of Antioch.

Bohemond appears in all of the major works of literature relating to the First Crusade. He is particularly prominent in the "Gesta Francorum" and in narratives derived from it; including Baldric of Bourgueil's "Historia Ierosolimitana", the source for much of the Siege of Antioch. Some scholars have suggested that Bohemond himself was responsible for the creation and dissemination of the early favourable accounts of his deeds; but this theory is controversial.

Similarly, since the establishment of a poetic tradition recounting the First Crusade, the so-called "Canso d'Antioca" seems to have emerged around the same time as the second-generation prose narratives. Many scholars, impressed by Bohemond's prominence in the surviving literature, have proposed that his tour of Europe inspired the beginnings of this tradition. In contrast, the Bohemond of the parallel Old French poetic tradition, the "Chanson d'Antioche" cuts a less impressive figure.

Bohemond had arranged for all five of the other knights as well as lord William Guilhem of Clermont, to meet with he and I in the dining hall of the of the Guilhem Castle for dinner that evening. An enormous sumptuous banquet had been arranged by the lord. Two boars had been roasted on a pit and were placed at each end and of the long rectangular table which spanned the centre of the hall. Then a team of servants placed a mixture of fruits, vegetables, cheeses, olives, and condiments on the table, with ample canisters of wine and ale. Bohemond proceeded to introduce me to each of these distinguished knights; each of whom I had meticulously researched, knowing full well I would be immersed within their world.

Godfrey of Bouillon was born in 1060 to count Eustace II of Boulogne, and his wife Ida, who was the daughter of duke Godfrey II of Lower Lorraine. His elder brother Eustace III, inherited Boulogne and the family's estate in England. In 1076 his maternal uncle named Godfrey as the heir to the duchy of Lower Lorraine, the county of Verdun, the Marquisate of Antwerp, and the territories of Stenay and Bouillon.

But the Holy Roman Emperor Henry IV delayed confirming the grant of Lower Lorraine, and Godfrey only won the duchy back in 1089, as a reward for fighting for Henry. In 1096, Godfrey joined the First Crusade with Eustace and his younger brother, Baldwin. His motivations are unclear; he had never shown any notable devotion to the Church, and in the Investiture Controversy he had supported the German emperor against the pope. The terms of the mortgage agreements he drew up in preparation for going to the Holy Land suggest that Godfrey had no intention of staying there. But he managed to raise considerable funds, and a formidable army; becoming one of the most prominent leaders of the First Crusade.

Upon his arrival at Constantinople, Godfrey immediately clashed with Emperor Alexius over the oath the emperor wanted the crusaders to take, which included the provision that any recovered lands that once had been part of the Byzantine Empire, were to be restored to the emperor. Though Godfrey clearly had not planned to settle in the Holy Land, he balked at this oath. Tensions grew so strained that they came to violence; but ultimately Godfrey took the oath, even though he harboured serious reservations and much resentment. That resentment seems to have grown stronger when Alexius surprised the crusaders by taking possession of Nicaea, after they besieged it; robbing them of the opportunity to plunder the city for spoils. In their progress through the Holy Land, some of the crusaders took a detour to find allies and supplies, ending up establishing a settlement in Edessa.

Godfrey acquired Tilbesar, a prosperous region that would make it possible for him to supply his troops more easily, and help him increase the number of his followers. Tilbesar, like many of the other areas acquired by the crusaders at this time, had once been Byzantine territory; but neither Godfrey nor any of the other conquering knights offered to return any of these lands to the Emperor Alexius. After the crusaders captured Jerusalem, fellow Crusade leader, Raymond of Toulouse, refused to become king of the city, so Godfrey agreed to become the ruler; but he would not take the title of king. He was instead called "Advocatus Sancti Sepulchri" (Protector of the Holy Sepulchre). Shortly thereafter, Godfrey and his fellow crusaders defeated and turned back an army of attacking Egyptians.

With Jerusalem secured, at least for the time being, most of the crusaders decided to return home. Godfrey now lacked support and guidance in governing Jerusalem; and the arrival of the papal legate Daimbert, archbishop of Pisa, further complicated matters. Daimbert, who soon after became the patriarch of Jerusalem, believed the city and the entire Holy Land should be governed by the Catholic Church and therefore come under the direct control of the pope. Against his better judgment, but realising he had no alternative, Godfrey became Daimbert's vassal. This would make Jerusalem the subject of an ongoing power struggle for many years to come. However, Godfrey was to play not further part in this matter because he died suddenly on 18th July 1100.

Raymond of Toulouse was born in Toulouse, France in 1041. Upon becoming a count, he began to reassemble his ancestral lands, which had been lost to other families. After thirty years he built up a significant power base in southern France, where he controlled 13 counties. This made him more powerful than the king. A devout Christian, Raymond was a staunch supporter of the papal reform that Pope Gregory VII had initiated, and that Urban II continued. So I knew Raymond was going to be the most difficult man around this dining table to convince to reject Urban's crusade and follow our plan instead. He is believed to have fought in the Reconquista in Spain, and may have gone on a pilgrimage to Jerusalem. When Pope Urban made his call for a crusade, Raymond was the first leader to take up the cross.

Already well over 50 years old, and considered elderly, the count left the lands he had so carefully consolidated, in the hands of his son, and committed to go on a perilous journey to the Holy Land along with his wife. In the Holy Land, Raymond proved to be one of the most effective leaders of the First Crusade. He helped capture Antioch, then led the troops onward to Jerusalem, where he participated in a successful siege, yet refused to become king of the vanquished city. He lost an eye in battle. Later, Raymond captured Tripoli, and built near the city, the castle of Mont Pelerin. He died there in February 1105.

Robert Curthose was the eldest son of William the Conqueror, the first Norman King of England, and Matilda of Flanders. His nickname, Curthose, which derives from the Norman French "Courtheuse" was acquired when his father teased him as a child for having short legs. Robert was born in 1054. In his youth, he was reported to be courageous and skilful in military exercises. He was however, also apparently prone to laziness and weakness of character, which annoyed nobles; and which the King of France exploited to stir discard with his father William.

Robert was not satisfied with the share of power allotted to him, and was often at odds with his father, and his younger brothers, William and Henry. In 1096, Robert embarked for the Holy Land on the First Crusade. To raise money for the crusade he mortgaged his duchy to his brother William for the sum of 10,000 marks. William the Conqueror died in 1097. On his deathbed he summoned his younger sons, William and Henry. Robert Curthose was on Crusade and so could not attend. England was bequeathed to William's second surviving and favourite son, William Rufus, and despite his bitter differences with Robert Curthose, William the Conqueror left Normandy to Robert. To Henry, the youngest son, later destined to inherit all of his dominions, he left just 5,000 silver pounds. Robert fought at Dorylaeum in 1097, and was present at the capture of Jerusalem in 1099. His courageous leadership contributed to the victory at Ascalon in 1099.

When William II was killed in a hunting accident in the New Forest on 2nd August 1100, Robert was on his return journey from the First Crusade. As a result of his absence, his younger brother Henry was able to seize the crown. Upon his return, Robert claimed the crown of England; believing he was the rightful heir. In 1101, he crossed the Channel with an army and landed at Portsmouth in July. Henry I had expected him at Pevensey, where he had assembled a formidable army. Robert headed towards London but was intercepted by Henry at Alton in Hampshire.

Robert was persuaded to renounce his claim to the throne of England, in return for a pension of 3,000 marks per annum, and the abandonment of any claim by Henry, to Normandy. This wasn't to last for long though. In 1105 Henry I invaded Normandy, and in 1106 met Robert's army at the Battle of Tinchebray. Henry prevailed, and claimed Normandy as a possession of the English crown. Robert was captured in the aftermath of the battle, and imprisoned in Devizes Castle for twenty years before being moved to Cardiff, where he learned Welsh and wrote poetry. In 1134, Robert died at Cardiff Castle, in his early eighties.

Robert II, count of Flanders, was born in 1065. He was the eldest son of Robert I of Flanders and Gertrude of Saxony. From 1085 to 1091, Robert II was regent of the county while his father was on a pilgrimage to the Holy Land. After becoming a count in 1093, Robert joined the First Crusade. He made his wife, Clementia of Burgundy, regent in Flanders, and assembled an army for the crusade. After reaching Constantinople, the crusaders were obliged to swear an oath of loyalty to the Byzantine Emperor Alexius I Komnenus, and promise to return to the Byzantine Empire any land they might capture. Robert

II, whose father had already served Alexius during his pilgrimage in the 1080s, had no problem swearing his oath; but some of the other leaders did, which resulted in some delay in leaving the city for the Holy Land.

Robert II then participated in the Siege of Nicaea, after which the army was split into two groups. Robert II marched with Bohemond, Robert Curthose, Stephen of Blois, and Byzantine escorts; one day ahead of the remainder of the crusaders. This army was surrounded by the Seljuk sultan Kilij Arslan, at the Battle of Dorylaeum on 30th June 1097. The next day, the second army, led by Raymond IV of Toulouse, Godfrey of Bouillon, and Hugh of Vermandois; arrived and broke the Seljuk Muslim encirclement; resulting in the two armies joining together, with Robert II and Raymond IV, leading the combined army. The Seljuk Muslims were defeated, and the crusaders continued their march. At the end of 1097, the crusaders arrived at Antioch. The Siege of Antioch lasted many months.

In December, Robert II and Bohemond briefly left the army to raid the surrounding territory for food; then on the 30th they defeated an army sent to relieve Antioch, led by sultan Duqaq, the ruler of Damascus. The city of Antioch was eventually betrayed to Bohemond by an Armenian guard, and Robert II was among the first to enter the city, but only a few days later they were themselves besieged by sultan Kerbogha of Mosul. On 28th June 1098, the crusaders marched out to meet him in battle. Robert II and Hugh of Vermandois led the first of six divisions. Kerbogha was defeated, and the Muslim-held citadel finally surrendered to the crusaders. Robert II, along with Bohemond, Raymond, and Godfrey, occupied the citadel; but Bohemond soon claimed the city of Antioch for himself. Raymond also claimed it, but Robert II supported Bohemond in that dispute.

The dispute between these leading crusaders delayed the First Crusade even further. Raymond left Antioch to attack Maarrat al-Numan, which was captured. Robert II took part in this siege as well. Raymond then tried to bribe Robert II and the other leaders to follow him, instead of Bohemond. Robert II was offered 6,000 sous, but each attempted bribe was ignored. Raymond continued south to Jerusalem in January 1099, but Robert II and Godfrey remained behind in Antioch until February. They then re-joined Raymond's army at the Siege of Arqa. In June, Robert II and Gaston IV of Bearn led the vanguard which arrived at Ramla, and along with Tancred, Robert II led an expedition into Samaria to find wood in order to construct catapults for the Siege of Jerusalem.

When Jerusalem was captured on 15th July 1099, Robert II supported Godfrey's claim, over that of Raymond; and on 9th August marched out with him to meet the Fatamid army led by al-Afdal Shahanshah, which was coming to take back Jerusalem. Robert II formed part of the centre wing in the ensuing Battle of Ascalon, which resulted in a crusader victory. However, Godfrey and Raymond quarrelled over the possession of Ascalon, and even Robert II could not support Godfrey in this particular dispute. The city remained under the control of the crusaders, and their victory allowed for the creation of the Kingdom of Jerusalem. At the end of August, Robert II commenced his journey home with Robert Curthose and Raymond.

On the way back, they captured Latakia, which was returned to the Byzantine emperor, as promised years before. Raymond remained there, but both of the Roberts continued on their way home by way of Constantinople; after declining Alexius' request to stay there in his service. Robert II brought a precious relic back with him; the arm of Saint George, a gift from Alexius. The relic was placed in the church of Anchin Abbey in Flanders. After he returned, Robert II built the monastery of Saint Andrew in Zevenkerke, near Bruges. Because of his crusade, and the relics he brought home, he was nicknamed Robert of Jerusalem.

Hugh, count of Vermandois was born in 1057, and was the first count of Vermandois from the House of Capet. Hugh was a younger son of King Henry I of France, and Anne of Kiev; and the younger brother of Philip I. He became the first Capetian count of Vermandois after his mentally incapacitated brother-in-law, Odo, was disinherited. In 1085, Hugh helped William the Conqueror repel a Danish invasion of England. In early 1096 in Paris, Hugh and Philip decided to raise an army for the First Crusade. Although Philip could not participate, as he had been excommunicated, Hugh was said to have been finally convinced after an eclipse of the moon on 11th February 1096 acted as an omen for him.

In late August 1096, Hugh and his crusader army left France and travelled via the Alps and Rome to Bari, where he would cross the Adriatic Sea into the territory of the Byzantine Empire; unlike most of the other crusaders who travelled over land. He certainly considered himself to be of high importance, as evidenced by this message he sent to the Byzantine Emperor Alexius, demanding a proper welcome while on the crusade: "Know, Emperor, that I am King of Kings, the greatest of all beneath the heavens. It is fitting that I should be met on my arrival and received with the pomp and ceremony appropriate to my noble birth."

In her writings, Alexius' daughter Anna Comnena recorded a conversation between Hugh and Godfrey of Bouillon, whereby Hugh tried to persuade Godfrey to pledge his allegiance to Emperor Alexius. Godfrey however, refused, saying: "You left your own country as a ruler, with all the wealth and a strong army; now from the heights you've brought yourself to the level of a slave. And then, as if you had won some great success, have you come here to tell me to do the same?" Hugh replied: "We ought to have stayed in our own countries and keep our hands off other people's, but since we've come thus far and need the emperor's protection, no good will come of it unless we obey his orders."

Meanwhile, Hugh had reached the coast of Longobardi, and dispatched 24 envoys to the Doux (Duke) of Dyrrhachium with the following message: "Be it known to you, Doux, that our Lord Hugh is almost here. He brings with him from Rome the golden standard of Saint Peter. Understand, moreover, that he is supreme commander of the Frankish army. See to it then, that he is accorded a reception worthy of his rank and yourself prepare to meet him." Whilst sailing the Adriatic Sea from Bari towards Illyricum, Hugh's fleet was overwhelmed by a heavy storm, and most of the ships were lost. His own ship was thrown upon the shore near Epirus. When Hugh was found and brought to Dyrrhachium, he was treated to a banquet after being allowed to rest.

By order of the emperor, Hugh was given an armed escort to Constantinople. Alexius discretely but unmistakably restricted Hugh's freedom of movement until he was ready to swear by oath that all territories which had belonged to Byzantium before the Muslim

Turkish invasions would be returned. After the crusaders had successfully made their way across Seljuk territory and in 1098, captured the city of Antioch, Hugh was sent back to Constantinople to appeal for reinforcements from Alexius. The emperor was not interested.

So instead of returning to Antioch, Hugh made his way back to France. There, he was scorned for not having fulfilled his vow as a crusader to complete a pilgrimage to Jerusalem; and Pope Paschal II threatened to excommunicate him. He joined the Second Crusade of 1101, but was wounded in a fierce battle with the Turkish-led army of Kilij Arslan, and died from his wounds in Tarsus, in October 1101.

After all of the introductions, we sat around the vast table. William Guilhem then stood up.

'Honourable gentlemen of the cross, it is my pleasure to welcome you to Clermont and my heavenly paradise. What is mine is yours during your stay as my guests. I want you to feel totally at home and comfortable. I know you have all heard the rumour about our Holy Father's intention to ask you all to lead a pilgrimage to the Holy Land, to seek peace with the Muslim hoards. What an honour this will be for you all.'

If only he, and the others around the table knew Pope Urban's true intentions, I thought. As we were enjoying the sumptuous dinner, surrounded by servants at our beck and call, while the wine and ale flowed freely, Bohemond, stood to speak.

'I have a very reliable high level Church contact who sits in the inner circle of advisers to the imposter, Urban. He has told me that Urban will be launching a war against not only the Muslim hoards in the Holy Land, but also against our fellow Christians in the East. He is using the excuse of a crusade, as a means of conquering the Byzantine Orthodox Christians, and bringing them directly under his control, through the apparatus of the Catholic Church. This will be his true objective; a military invasion of the East. But that's not what he is going to tell us. He is going to tell us it will be a Christian crusade, with the blessing of our Lord. He is going to tell us the purpose of the crusade will be to free the Holy Land and Jerusalem from the clutches of the Muslim hoards. He is going to tell us that all Christians who participate in the crusade will be free of all their past sins, and will receive a direct passage into heaven in their afterlife. Urban wants the six of us to lead this military invasion. That's why he has called us here to Clermont. I have invited the most senior diplomatic envoy of the Byzantine Emperor Alexius, by the name of Cristos, to join us here, later this evening. Cristos is here in Clermont to deliver a message to Pope Urban II from Alexius, seeking Urban's help to arrange for a group of highly experienced knights, like us, to immediately travel to Constantinople, and to provide tactical military advice and leadership of the Byzantine army, in order to repel an imminent attack on Constantinople and surrounding regions by the Seljuk Turks.'

The hall erupted into a mixture of complimentary and critical noisy banter. I could see that Raymond of Toulouse was particularly offended by Bohemond's comments. But the others were supportive.

'This is an outrage', shouted Raymond. 'Are you insane, Bohemond? Do you realise that you have directly criticized our holy father, and the Church? You have engaged in blasphemy. You will be excommunicated! I will hear no further filthy and disgraceful talk from you!! This is not the end of the matter. I shall report this directly to Urban.'

Raymond stormed out of the hall. The other knights appeared to be happy to see him leave. There was an air of equal tension and excitement. The course of history was about to be changed. I definitely sensed a unity of spirit and purpose amongst the remaining knights. They appeared to totally embrace and support Bohemond.

'Urban isn't even our legitimate pope!' shouted Hugh.

'We must stand united and bring down this charlatan with imperial ambitions!' screamed Robert II.

'Here! Here!' they all responded, with great enthusiasm.

'Bohemond, can I speak with you privately?' asked William Guilhem, while the other remaining knights engaged in an animated discussion about the pope's intentions.

'You may. But my close friend and adviser Luca, will accompany us.'

So the three of us made our way into the lord's library.

'I don't know who passed on that information about Urban's real intentions, to you, but I need to share something very important with you. I have arranged for the legitimate holy father, Pope Clement III, to come to Clermont. He is due to arrive in the early morning, the day after tomorrow. He will be accompanied by a contingent of twenty knights, comprising his papal bodyguards. I am a member of a secret society of nobles scattered around Europe, with the express intention of overthrowing Urban and reinstating Clement back to his rightful place on the papal throne. We have been providing Clement and his followers with the necessary financial support to keep him safe, and to pursue his agenda as our legitimate pope. Urban is, as you say, an imposter. Our society has long believed Urban harbours imperial ambitions. His desire is nothing short of the Catholic Church exercising total political control not only over Europe, but also the Byzantine East, and Holy Lands, with Urban himself as the supreme leader'

'Lord Guilhem, you have orchestrated an honourable duty, to arrange for Clement to come here to Clermont' replied Bohemond. 'We must arrange for Clement to speak at the outdoor gathering in which Urban is planning to announce his crusade. For security reasons, it will be imperative we keep Clement's arrival an absolute secret. Luca, I know you have formulated a plan of action. Can you share it with us?

'Certainly Bohemond. On the morning of the day after tomorrow, we will deliver Clement incognito to the town square where Urban is due to speak. Bohemond, you and the other knights, in addition to his bodyguards, will then escort Clement to the stage, and surround him for protection as he speaks. Clement will then announce he is the legitimate pope and disclose to everybody present, the real intentions of Urban. With the Byzantine diplomatic envoy Cristos by his side, Clement will seek the approval of the high level church officials and nobility at Clermont to ignore the pleas of Urban for a military crusade, and instead, to give their full support for Bohemond and the other four knights staying here with us, to undertake a mission to the court of Emperor Alexius, to assist him in raising a Byzantine army to firstly remove the Muslims from his occupied lands; and then to negotiate with the Seljuk Muslim Turks to declare Jerusalem to be an independent and free city state; where Muslim and Christian pilgrims alike will be free to visit the city as pilgrims, side by side. Bohemond and the other four knights shall negotiate directly with Alexius, an appropriate reward for their efforts in assisting the Byzantine emperor. This reward will be in the form of five clearly defined Byzantine territories; one for each of the knights; with Antioch going to Bohemond. Urban will be detained by Bohemond, thus prevented from speaking, and he will be locked up in your castle prison, right here, lord Guilhem.'

'That's a good enough plan, Luca. Come, we have much work to do', said Bohemond.

'Yes we do', agreed William Guilhem.

Pope Clement III, known earlier as Guibert, was born in Parma, Italy. His family was related to the counts of Canossa. He was at the German imperial court by 1055, and was named imperial chancellor for Italy, a role he served from 1058 to 1063, with the backing and support of Empress Agnes. In 1072, King Henry IV named him bishop of Ravenna. Pope Alexander II was not enthusiastic since Guibert supported a rival to the papacy, Honorius, but he accepted Guibert after his archdeacon, Hilderbrand, compelled Guibert to take an oath of allegiance to the pope.

Not long after, Hilderbrand himself was elected Pope Gregory VII, and Guibert became one of the most prominent leaders of a radical movement opposing the Church reform program initiated by Pope Gregory. Guibert attended Gregory's first Lenten Synod in March 1074, and participated in passing decrees against simony (the making of profit from sacred objects or vows), and lax behaviour among the clergy. But since Guibert declined to attend the following year, in spite of an oath to do so, Gregory suspended him in 1075.

In February of that year, Pope Gregory VII excommunicated Guibert along with the other bishops who had adopted a resolution deposing the pope at the Worms Synod in January 1076. Guibert was again excommunicated at the Lenten Synod of 1078, because he had presided over a synod of Lombard bishops and abbots who had previously excommunicated Gregory at Pavia in April 1076. Finally, when King Henry IV summoned his German and Lombard bishops to a meeting at Brixen in June 1080, the bishops deposed Gregory yet again, and elected Guibert as pope. Henry immediately recognised the election as legitimate.

Four years later King Henry marched into Rome and took control of the city, forcing Pope Gregory to flee for safety to the Castel San Angelo. At this point, the people and clergy of Rome elected Guibert as pope; he took the name Pope Clement III, and was consecrated at the Lateran Basilica Cathedral on Palm Sunday, 24th March 1084.

A week later, on Easter Sunday, with Gregory still detained in the Castel San Angelo, Clement solemnly crowned Henry as the Holy Roman Emperor in Saint Peter's Basilica. Soon after this event, Gregory made his way to Salerno to visit his Norman ally, Robert Guiscard, Bohemond's father. Guiscard led an army back to Rome and forced Henry and Clement to leave the city; and helped reinstate Gregory back in Rome. I asked Bohemond about his view on this matter. He responded that his father was loyal to Gregory because he had assisted Guiscard in securing former papal lands in southern Italy in exchange for providing Gregory with protection. Bohemond was steadfast in his belief that the Church and its popes should not encroach upon the imperial power of emperors, kings, dukes, and statesmen; and therefore gave his full support to Clement.

After fleeing Rome, Clement went to Ravenna, where he became archbishop, in spite of the great support he still enjoyed among the people and clergy of Rome. For example, 13 of the cardinals recognised him as the legitimate pope. Indeed, Clement was back in Rome functioning as the pope during the reigns of the "alternative popes" Victor III (1086-87) and Urban II (1088-99). He was also able to broaden his support in German and Italian territories; as well as gaining influence in England, Hungary, Serbia, Croatia, Portugal, and Denmark.

Clement was active in pursuing negotiations towards a union of the Catholic and Orthodox faiths with the Orthodox leaders John II of Kiev, the Byzantine Emperors, and the Patriarch of Constantinople. In spite of these initiatives, in the 1090s the influence of his benefactor, Henry IV, declined in Rome; while support for Urban II increased. In 1098 Clement was forced out of Rome by the powerful noble Pierleoni family. Clement and his supporters sought sanctuary in the Castel San Angelo, but were forced to abandon that location on 24th August 1098. With Henry's troops withdrawn from Italy, Clement's only sphere of influence was around the diocese of Ravenna.

After Paschal II was elected pope, Clement prepared to press his claim to the papacy at Albano, but was forced to withdraw by Norman troops loyal to the pope. He reached Civita Castellana, and died there less than a year later. Clement's Roman supporters set up three successive "antipopes" – Theoderic (1100), Albert (1101), and Sylvester IV (1105-11); but these men never had the full backing of Holy Roman Emperor Henry IV, who would soon reach a compromise with the reformers, and keep his imperial right to invest and ordain bishops of the Church with their ring and staff.

Clement was an intelligent and principled man who sought his own direction in what were politically complex and tumultuous times. Though he relied heavily on Henry's support, he was much more than a pawn of imperial policy. Highly educated, Clement was responsible for some of the most articulate opposition to the Gregorian reformers, whose raw power-grabbing methods he opposed more than their goals. For example, Clement legislated against clerical marriage (Nicolaitism) and simony (profiteering) at a synod in Rome in 1089.

Unlike the majority of Gregorian reformers however, Clement maintained that the sacraments of schismatic priests, and his opponent's ordinations, were valid. Clement's position was more politically attractive to those caught between the two parties. In much the same way, he allowed his cardinals more influence, thus forcing Urban II to do the same in order to keep their loyalty. As a result, the College of Cardinals increased in importance during this period. It was this factor, which Bohemond and I were relying on, in order to convince the high-ranking cardinals and bishops here in Clermont, to switch their support from Urban to Clement.

Later that evening, Cristos arrived. There had been a number of death threats directed at him, since he arrived in Clermont one week ago, so he was heavily guarded. We were all seated around the dining table enjoying red wine from the nearby Guilhem family vineyard, when Bohemond began to speak.

'Envoy Cristos, we welcome you to the Guilhem Castle at such short notice. We are well aware your Emperor Alexius has sent you here to seek the pope's assistance in arranging a mercenary army to be led by the most esteemed knights of Western Europe to immediately travel to Constantinople to assist the emperor in repelling an imminent Muslim invasion of the lands surrounding Constantinople, and then ultimately an invasion of the great city itself.'

'Yes Bohemond, we are most concerned about this Muslim threat to our great capital city. They have already seized most of the Holy Land, including Jerusalem, and also large tracts of our Byzantine territory in the East.'

'We have asked you here tonight to inform you of some grave developments. Pope Urban will be announcing a crusade in a speech he is due to give on the morning after tomorrow. He will use the pretext of your emperor requesting his assistance as an excuse to start this crusade. But this will not just be a holy war against the Muslims to regain control of Jerusalem and the Holy Lands; it will also be a holy war against your Byzantine Empire and your emperor, in order to destroy Orthodox Christianity, remove Alexius, and bring your peoples directly under the imperial control of Pope Urban and the Catholic Church. We have arranged for the legitimate holy father, Pope Clement III to arrive here in Clermont, on that same morning. Under heavy guard, he will speak to the assembled clergy and nobles, and let them know of Urban's true intentions. He will require your support, in your capacity as an envoy of the Emperor Alexis. The imminent arrival of Clement must be kept highly confidential, Cristos.'

'You have my solemn word that I shall be tight-lipped. I can assure you that Clement will definitely have the support of my emperor. This is a mad grab for extreme power by Urban. Has he lost his mind? He will regret this action. My emperor Alexius has always acknowledged Clement as the true and legitimate pope.'

'Envoy Cristos, with the blessing of the legitimate holy father Clement III, it is my intention to travel to Constantinople with you, accompanied by these other esteemed knights gathered here tonight; Godfrey of Bouillon, Robert Curthose, Robert II of Flanders, and Hugh of Vermandois. We will be at the service of your great emperor, to assist him in any way we can, to formulate tactics and to lead his armies into battle against the Muslim hoards.'

I took note of the fact Bohemond did not mention what he and his fellow knights expected in return for their able assistance. But then again, I understood these were matters to be negotiated by Bohemond and his fellow knights, directly with Alexius. We continued drinking well into the night. There was a close bond forged between us all. We had the common objective of stopping Urban, and elevating the legitimacy of Clement to the papacy. When I finally got to my bed at around 1am, I collapsed into a deep sleep.

When I awoke, just as the sun was rising, I could hear a hive of activity and commotion within the castle, and its surrounds. Preparations were being made for a tournament of knights, to coincide with the visit of Urban and his Council. Bohemond told me this tournament was going to be on a grand scale because Urban had requested no expense be spared to put on a lively show for the visiting dignitaries. All of the knights staying in the castle were to be participants, along with numerous others. The medieval tournament was a forum for European knights to show off their military skills in mock battles, jousts, indulge in pageantry, display their chivalrous qualities, impress a noble lady, and win both riches and glory.

This tournament was to be between two groups of knights, numbering 50 on each side, wearing full armour, carrying lances, swords, and shields. On the one side, were the Norman and English knights; and they were to be facing off against a contingent of French, Italian, and Germanic knights. There were marshals to ensure no foul play, but as the field of conflict was a large one, inevitably there would be serious wounds and even deaths. There were not many rules to impose, being pretty much a free for all; and it was not considered unfair for a group of knights to attack a single opponent, or attack a knight who had lost his horse.

While honour and glory were strong motivators, there was too, the prospect of financial gain. Knights would often aim to steal weapons, armour, and anything else of value that their opponents were carrying; or even to capture them and demand a ransom which could be decided upon before the start of the tournament. There would be a lucrative cash prize for the winning team, at the end of the day's battle. The tournament was going to be held within the wider grounds of the Guilhem Castle, and was to run for the entire day. Numerous lavish tents were set up around the perimeter of the fighting area for the high ranking clergy and nobles. The most spectacular of all was for Urban and his entourage.

There were also large seated stands erected for the regular spectators; as well as stalls with refreshments, and areas set aside for sellers of horses, weapons, fine clothes, and a wide variety of hand-crafted products. Both groups of knights were to parade in front of the pope, and then past the spectators, shouting war cries and showing off their armour and coat of arms.

The tournament was to begin with each side lining up and preparing for the charge. At the sound of a bugle, each side would commence the mock battle. During the intermissions, the crowd was to be entertained with performances of drama accompanied by musicians, acrobats, pageants; and several banquets for the nobility in large marquee tents, during the course of the day.

The presence of eligible noble ladies added an element of romance to the event; increasing the desire of the knights to be as chivalrous as possible. Ladies might give certain token articles to specific knights they favoured, such as a veil which was then tied around the receiver's lance or sword. Costumes too, were an important element, with some knights dressing themselves up in bright assorted colours, or as legendary figures. The shields of the knights would display their family coat of arms.

The highlight of the day was to be the jousts, between the very best knights from both sides. A joust was when two knights would charge at each other on horseback, and try to knock the other off their horse with a lance. The winners of jousts were the true heroes of the day; and they would win large amounts of prize money.

All of the knights staying with me at the castle were scheduled to compete in jousts. I had learned that Bohemond and Raymond were two of the best jousters in Europe, and that they would be competing with each other in a jousting finale that was likely to be full of drama, in view of the animosity they had for each other, brought to a head when Raymond stormed out of the dining hall last night. So I was really looking forward to seeing them in action.

Of course, being a knight was not just about warfare and tournaments. Knights were expected to behave in a particular way. This was called the Code of Chivalry. The ideal knight was expected to be humble, loyal, fair, Christian, well-read, and possess good manners, especially towards women. Specifically, the knight's Code of Chivalry set out the following:

~ To follow the Church and defend it with his life.
~ To protect women and the weak.
~ To serve and defend the king.
~ To be generous and honest.
~ To never lie.
~ To live by honour and for glory.
~ To help widows and orphans.

Many knights took vows that they would abide by this Code.

For the entire day I accompanied Bohemond. He was very well known and popular amongst the high level clergy and nobility of Europe; of that, I had no doubt. Before the commencement of the tournament battle, in which Bohemond would play a leading role on the English-Norman side, he introduced me to many of the dignitaries who had come to Clermont either upon the instructions of Pope Urban, or to create friction and dissent.

Amongst the dignitaries I met were; Joannes, the cardinal of Porto; Dagobert, the archbishop of Pisa; Bruno, the bishop of Segni; Galterius, the cardinal of Albano; Rangerius, the archbishop of Reggio, Calabria; Richard, the cardinal of Marseilles; Teuzo, a cardinal of Rome; Albertus, the cardinal of Santa Sabina; Joannes Gattellus, the pope's chancellor; Hugues de Die, the archbishop of Lyon, and a papal legate; Amatus, the archbishop of Bordeaux, and a papal legate; Rainaldus, the archbishop of Reims; Richerius, the archbishop of Sens; Rollandus, the bishop of Dol; Dalmatius, the archbishop of Narbonne; Bernard de Sedirac, the archbishop of Toledo, and a papal legate; Hoellus, the bishop of Le Mans; Geoffrey of Vendome, a cardinal of Rome; Benedict, the bishop of Nantes; Petrus, the bishop of Poitiers; Ivo, the bishop of Chartres; Joannes, the bishop of Orleans; Roger, the bishop of Beauvais; Radulfus, the archbishop of Tours; and Hilgot, the former bishop of Soissons, and a close adviser to the pope.

The pope's chancellor Joannes Gattellus and I engaged in a stimulating and sometimes heated conversation about a wide range of subjects including the threat of Islam to Christianity; whether the schism between the Catholic and Orthodox Christianity could ever be healed; the achievements of Urban; the threat of Clement to the very fabric of Christianity (as he described it); the motives behind the assassination of Julius Caesar (he was a keen student of ancient Rome); and Urban's speech tomorrow (in which he gave nothing away).

Amongst the knights staying with me in the castle; Bohemond and Robert Curthose, both being of Norman origin, were positioned on the English-Norman side; whereas, Godfrey of Bouillon, Raymond of Toulouse, Robert of Flanders, and Hugh of Vermandois, were positioned on the French, Italian and Germanic side. The prestige of these knights was clear to see, for they were the leaders of each of their respective sides. It was a sight to behold to see 100 knights in their magnificent armour, colourful family coat of arms on their shields, and majestic highly trained horses, engaged in the mock battle. The battle was closely fought throughout the day.

Points were awarded by the judges for strategic battlefield tactics, bravery, poise, horse riding skills, chivalry, effective use of weapons, knocking an opponent off their horse, exemplary leadership and stamina, and the avoiding of unnecessary injury. In the early afternoon, the result of the mock battle was announced. The Bohemond-led English-Normans had marginally defeated the Raymond of Toulouse-led French, Italian, and Germanic knights. Both men were requested to come to the podium, positioned alongside the papal tent. Urban himself greeted them.

I was observing from a close position and could clearly see Raymond was seething with anger, clearly humiliated by the defeat; whilst Bohemond appeared very humble and gracious, at one point putting his arm around a clearly uncomfortable Raymond, appearing to console him. With both knights alongside him, Urban rose to the lectern at the centre of the staged podium.

'We have witnessed the greatest warriors in all of European Christendom today! The 100 most courageous and chivalrous knights of the Church. Our faith is in good hands, with these honourable men as our protectors. On behalf of your cohorts and supporters, Bohemond and Raymond, I congratulate you both for the outstanding tactics and leadership you displayed on the mock-battlefield today!'

I was surprised to see how gracious Urban was to Bohemond. Surely by now, Raymond had told him about the meeting last night. Well, if he knew about our plot to undermine him, and he surely did, he wasn't giving away an inch. It was an impressive performance in stoicism, I must say. What was he playing at? Why hadn't Urban arranged for us to be detained? The fact he had not detained us, made me think he knew nothing about Clement's arrival. It was imperative to our plan, that this remained confidential. So far, so good, I thought

The highlight of the day's tournament was undoubtedly the final joust, between Bohemond and Raymond. They were to joust three times. Whomever knocked his opponent off his horse the most number of times would be declared the winner. If both were knocked off once, or neither was knocked off at all, a panel of 5 judges were to decide the winner based on an elaborate point-scoring system that took into account many aspects of the jousting contest, including; how many times a knight was struck by a lance, where on the body they were struck, whether they lost their lance, and maintaining poised balance on the horse.

There must have been around 5,000 people gathered around to watch this fascinating clash of two extremely powerful personalities. I had a front row seat in the middle. Ironically, directly opposite me, on the other side of the track, was the papal box. Urban was clearly enjoying himself, laughing boisterously, and acknowledging the waves of individuals in the jam-packed crowd. Raymond arrived first. There was a deafening roar from the predominately French crowd as he demounted his black stallion, in full armoured regalia, to greet the pope. After receiving Urban's blessing, a strikingly beautiful blonde lady in her early twenties, made her way to the noble knight, and handed him a ribbon. I was to learn later this lady, Gisele, was the daughter of one of the most powerful noble families in the region. Raymond tied the yellow ribbon to the end of his lance, and then mounted his stallion, making his way to the northern end of the jousting field.

Then Bohemond made his appearance. There was restrained applause, although a number of his fellow Normans in the crowd, were screaming his name with great enthusiasm. I loved the way they rebelled against the protocol which had clearly been put in place by

Urban and his officials. I quickly glanced at Urban; his facial expressions spoke a thousand words. He clearly was angered by the disrespect shown by the small group of Normans in the crowd; but I sensed more than that from his demeanour. I sensed a deep hatred for Bohemond. Oh, he knew what was brewing all right! Bohemond looked magnificent riding his white stallion in a slow elegant trot, as he made his way to the papal podium. Again, Urban gave him his blessing.

I could see some words were exchanged, but couldn't hear what they were saying. Urban appeared displeased. Then suddenly the entire crowd erupted into spontaneous laughter and applause when not one, but five young gorgeous ladies made their way down from the noble stands. They all appeared very familiar to the great Norman knight. As they stood side by side, he knelt down in front of each of them, while kissing their right hands; each lady giving him a different coloured ribbon, which he duly attached to the saddle of his horse. He then gracefully made his way to the southern end.

The first joust was about to commence. The crowd was deadly silent. After the marshal waved his flag, both knights raced towards each other at full gallop, lances outstretched, separated by a white wooden barrier. Then suddenly, they clashed violently, both lances striking the target. Bohemond was struck in the upper chest near his right shoulder, and Raymond was struck in the middle of his chest. Of course, the thick armour cushioned the blows. Incredibly, neither knight fell off their horses, or so much as lost their balance, after being struck. The crowd was cheering hysterically. We were witnessing two of the greatest warriors in Europe in action, and it was compelling drama. Especially for me, because I knew the backstory behind the intense rivalry which was about to explode between these two heroic and proud men, tomorrow morning.

The second joust was even more thrilling! As both knights galloped towards each other at full speed, they brilliantly managed to completely avoid each other's lances, by contorting and angling their bodies with lightning reflexes. It was incredible to watch. Bohemond had narrowly missed being struck in the head by a handful of millimetres. I thought it was brutal of Raymond to be aiming for the head, when Bohemond continued to concentrate on his opponent's middle-upper body.

Then came the climax. The third and final joust. This time I could see both knights had their visors raised and were literally staring at each other for what seemed like an eternity. The crowd was abuzz. But as soon as they closed their visors, there was complete and utter silence. All I heard was a flock of birds flying overhead, and the horses. Both horses appeared agitated and needed to be expertly calmed by their respective riders. Then as the flag was waved they galloped at even greater speed towards each other. As they crossed paths Bohemond could see Raymond's Lance was again aimed towards his head. With consummate skill, Bohemond thrust his lance towards his opponent's right hand, and struck a forceful blow that resulted in Raymond letting go of the lance. Enough had been done to secure victory! Having dropped his lance, Raymond was the loser and Bohemond the victor.

Although only a small group, the Normans in the crowd screamed with joy, and I joined them! The majority of the crowd remained silent. Raymond directed his horse to the pope, spoke to him for a few minutes, and then galloped away from the tournament event. As the crowd dispersed rapidly, Bohemond approached the pope and knelt in front of him. Then without saying a word, rode off while his Norman supporters continued to cheer him with wild ecstatic enthusiasm. As I was about to make my way back to the castle, I caught a glimpse of a man in the crowd, dressed in black, but not as a member of the clergy. His eyes caught mine. It was Thero. I had no doubt. When I glanced in his direction again, he had vanished.

When I arrived at the castle, Bohemond was in an animated discussion with William Guilhem.

'Ah, Luca, did you enjoy the joust?'

'I certainly did, Bohemond. Raymond seemed humiliated.'

'Oh yes, he was in a big hurry to leave, wasn't he? Luca, lord Guilhem and I have been urgently summoned to see Urban. He wants us there in an hour. I want you to come along with us.'

'Certainly. Have you been told why he wants to meet?'

'No, Luca. But we know what this will be all about; don't we?'

It was a fifteen-minute walk to the Clermont cathedral. Urban was staying in the adjoining bishop's apartments. When we arrived, two papal guards escorted us directly to his living quarters. We sat and waited in a small library. Shortly after, Urban, his chancellor, Joannes Gattellus, and Raymond, entered the room.

'I must say, I was very surprised when you decided to purposely dislodged Raymond's lance by striking his hand. Very creative of you, Bohemond!' said Urban, sarcastically.

'Well, after constantly going for my head, I needed to remove his weapon, which he was using in an unchivalrous and reckless manner.'

'Now listen here, blasphemous swine! How dare you accuse me of being unchivalrous!', shouted Raymond.

Gattellius, ever the diplomat, brought order back in the room.

'Gentlemen, we are here to discuss an act of treachery. You have accused our holy father, Pope Urban II, of harbouring imperial ambitions, including the conquest of the Orthodox East. This is blasphemy! The people will wonder where you are if they don't see you tomorrow morning. Especially yourself Bohemond, the hero of today's tournament. But make no mistake, as soon as our holy father, Pope Urban II, has completed his monumental announcement, the three of you will be immediately detained and brought back to Rome for an urgent inquisition and trial. In the meantime, it will be futile if you try and escape. Our papal guards will be watching your every move'

As Gattellius spoke, Urban and Raymond were seething with rage, both of them gazing transfixed, at Bohemond. Then Urban lashed out.

'You Bohemond, your accomplice Guilhem, and the other rogue knights, will be permanently excommunicated from the Church, straight after my speech tomorrow. To think that I hand selected you and the other demonic knights, to represent me and my Church in the pilgrimage to the Holy Land and the Orthodox East! I shall damn the lot of you to hell, tomorrow! Raymond will lead the Church's true believers to the East.'

After venting his rage. Urban stood up, walked towards Bohemond, and slapped him hard in the face; first with his right hand, and then again with his left. I observed Raymond smiling as Urban lashed out.

Bohemond sat motionless and expressionless, as Urban, Gattellius, and Raymond, left the room. I breathed a heavy sigh of relief. Thank goodness Urban and his entourage knew nothing about the arrival of Clement in the morning. The secret had held tight. Later that evening, back at the castle, we received a visit from a messenger, letting us know Clement was safe, and resting in a small village less than ten kilometres outside of Clermont. Everything was going to plan so far, for what was going to be a history-changing and dramatic morning.

That night, as I lay on my bed, after drinking too much wine, I reflected upon my research on The Council of Clermont. Here was a perfect example of the surviving sources not reflecting the true intentions of the protagonist; in this case, Urban II. The Council of Clermont of 18-28 November 1095 was an impressive gathering of the elite of the Church and nobility of Europe, as we have seen. It was held in the cathedral of the city. Clearly, something big was about to happen. After nine days of ecclesiastical discussion and debate, 32 canonical decrees were issued; such as the reaffirmation of the prohibition of clerical marriage; and formally raising the clerical authority of the See of Lyons, above that of Sens and Reims.

There was too, the excommunication of both the Bishop of Cambrai, and King Philip I of France, the bishop for selling church privileges for personal gain, and the king for adultery. All really run-of-the-mill, stock-standard issues for the medieval Church; but it was Canon number 33, the last one to be issued, that would shake the medieval world. On the 27th November, the cream of the European clergy, and a crowd of laymen, gathered in a field just outside Clermont, for the finale of the Council. It was here that Urban II made his now famous speech, in an obviously pre-prepared set piece. The message, known as the Indulgence, was particularly addressed to Christian nobles and knights present, and those across Europe.

Urban II promised that all who defended Christendom and captured Jerusalem would be embarking on a pilgrimage; all their sins would be washed away, and their souls would reap infinite rewards in the afterlife. In case anyone was concerned, a group of church scholars later went to work and came up with the idea that a campaign of violence could be justified by references to particular passages in the Bible, and to the works of Saint Augustine of Hippo (354-430 CE). Further justification for war was the emphasis that this was a fight for liberation, not an unprovoked attack; and that the objectives were morally just and righteous ones.

Urban II had managed to hit a collective nerve in Europe with a powerful idea that weaved together the great themes of the age: religious fervour; deep concern for the afterlife; love of pilgrimage; and a hunger for military adventure for a just cause, amongst the nobility. The same winning formula would be used again and again by Urban's successors to gain widespread support for the many subsequent crusades in the next two centuries.

Although no contemporary sources exist in modern times, which outline the precise content of Urban II's Clermont speech; there is this short summary extract, which was a decree from the Council:

"Whoever for devotion alone, not to gain honour or money, goes to Jerusalem to liberate the Church of God can substitute this journey for all penance."

There are though, many medieval secondary sources which refer to the speech and its contents. But I realised now, even more than ever, that these sources needed to be treated with extreme caution, because they were written by supporters of Urban and the Crusades, as political propaganda. They do not fully express, what I now know to be Urban's true motives. These secondary sources highlighted the following:

- Jerusalem was the primary objective, with the defence of the Byzantine Empire a secondary aim.
- The suffering of Christians and desecration of the holy sites there, made the prompt and urgent timing of the Crusade an imperative.
- Those who fought would be rewarded in this life with material rewards and, in the next life, with eternal spiritual rewards.
- The Crusade would necessitate the end of the various damaging wars between the nobility of Europe.
- Only fit able fighting men should answer this call, and their property would be safeguarded in their absence.

The speech, whatever its precise wording, was met with immediate enthusiasm. Some of the audience followed the reaction of the bishop of Le Puy, Adhemar of Monteil, shouting out "God wills it!" The bishop then, as was almost certainly pre-arranged, came on the stage and received his cross, the symbol of a crusader's vow, from Urban II.

The choice of the cross as the banner of the campaign was a powerful visual reminder not only of the Crucifixion which after all, aligned with the liberation of Jerusalem, where Jesus was crucified; but also of what would then have been the well-known command from Jesus recorded in the Book of Matthew of the New Testament:

"If any man will come after me, let him deny himself, and take up his cross, and follow me."

Much more important than the effect on the immediate audience at Clermont, the Indulgence, once its message was spread, electrified medieval Europe, and witnessed an overwhelming response, with tens of thousands "taking up the cross" and vowing to crusade for Christendom. Indeed, it can be argued the speech was too successful, when not following the pope's advice, a rabble of untrained and unfit men, led by Peter the Hermit, a self-styled evangelist, was the first group to travel to the Holy Land via Constantinople; the so-called People's Crusade. This group, contained hardly any professional knights, and was unsurprisingly methodically crushed and wiped out in Asia Minor in October 1096, by the Seljuk Islamic army.

After the Council, Urban II wrote many letters of appeal, and as we have seen, embarked on a preaching tour of France during 1095-96 to recruit crusaders. Embassies and letters were dispatched to all of the corners of Christian Europe. Major churches such as those at Limoges, Angers, and Tours, acted as recruitment centres, where the Clermont speech was repeated. Many rural churches and monasteries also raised funds and drafted recruits. Across Europe, warriors inspired by notions of religious fervour, personal salvation, pilgrimage, adventure, and a desire for material wealth; gathered throughout 1096, ready to embark for Jerusalem. The departure date was set for 15th August of that year. Around 60,000 crusaders including around 6,000 well-trained and highly accomplished knights, would be involved in the first waves to enter the East and the Holy Land.

As we have seen, the First Crusade was a remarkable success. In 1097 Nicaea was captured, and a great victory was won at Dorylaion. In June 1098 Antioch was captured, and of course, Bohemond featured heavily in this campaign, and ultimately secured control for himself. Then, the big objective of the crusade was achieved when Jerusalem was captured on 15th July 1099. Another Muslim relief army was defeated at Ascalon in August of that same year.

Then Caesarea and Acre were taken in 1101. The Holy Land was finally back in Christian hands, and it seemed the Council of Clermont had achieved its purpose; even though Urban II died on 29th July 1099, never knowing the success of his First Crusade. History was to record that this First Crusade was the most successful. After six more crusades over around two hundred years, the Christians lost their control, and failed to retain Jerusalem and the Holy Land.

I was up just before sunrise, the next morning, 28th November 1095, the day the course of world history was going to change, if our mission was successful. The first thing we did is let the other four knights know that Clement was on his way to Clermont. Clearly surprised, but very excited, they embraced our mission with great enthusiasm. They understood we couldn't tell them earlier for security reasons.

Bohemond, lord Guilhem, the other knights, and I, set out on horseback to meet up with Pope Clement III and his entourage, who were secretly staying in a small village outside of Clermont. The plan was that we would escort them directly to the large field behind the Clermont cathedral, where Urban was due to give his speech. We were to arrive before the speech, once the crowd had gathered. When we arrived at the village, Clement was particularly pleased to see Guilhem and Bohemond, whom he both knew very well.

After courteous introductions and final preparations, including from his contingent of twenty armoured and fiercely loyal bodyguards; we made our way to Clermont. When we arrived outside the field, we could see the crowd, which I estimated to be over 3,000 people, had gathered. A stage had been erected in the centre. My heart was beating at a rapid rate, I was functioning purely on adrenalin, as we made our way into the field towards the stage.

The crowd quickly became eerily silent after they saw us enter the field. Clement was dressed in full papal regalia. He was completely surrounded by his twenty bodyguards, who created a protective guard of honour, as he demounted his horse and made his way to the stage podium. I remained in the background as Bohemond, Guilhem, and the other four knights literally stood on the stage behind Clement, along with the Byzantine envoy, Cristos. There was no sign of Urban and his officials. Clement then began to address the crowd.

'A sinister deed must be righted by us now! I am your legitimate holy father, duly elected by the cardinals of the Church some years ago. The role of pope is to represent Jesus and the holy Father on Earth. To show mercy, and humbly carry on the will and spread the message of Christ. To maintain the dignity and moral authority of the Church. There is no place for a pope to seek and exercise imperial power. There is no place for a pope to seek to conquer and subdue peoples of other lands. Urban is the current representative of a line of anti-popes who have not acknowledged the power of the imperial Holy Roman Emperor, and instead have sought the power for themselves. This must stop! This must stop here and now! I am your rightful merciful pope. Bohomond, I call upon you and your loyal knights to immediately find Urban, capture him, and place him under my custody until further notice.'

The crowd burst into an uproar. Clearly it was torn in two. I could see about half of those present were enthusiastically and passionately applauding the sentiments of Clement; and the other half were in a state of angry shock. Scuffles broke out throughout the crowd. Clement's security guards literally encircled the holy father, and aggressively pushed away a number of people who had angrily clamoured towards and then onto the stage to confront the legitimate pope. As Bohemond and his four knights immediately swung into action, and proceeded to find and detain Urban; the bodyguards quickly and decisively removed Clement from the stage, and delivered him safely away from the mob, and to the sanctuary of Guilhem Castle.

I couldn't believe how lightning fast these events unfolded. This was a brilliantly executed surprise attack on Urban, who didn't even get a chance to speak to the crowd. Bohemond and Guilhem had conceived of this plan, in my presence, in the library of the castle, the previous evening; and it had worked perfectly. I made my way back to the castle, which was a hive of activity, as preparations were made for the detention of Urban and his closest advisers, in the extensive network of underground dungeon cells. Sure enough, Bohemond and the other knights appeared with a clearly distressed Urban, and his right hand man Gattellius. Bohemond correctly reasoned it would be best to immediately lock up these two first, and then mop up the rest of the operation later, by rounding up the others in the inner circle.

Pope Clement III returned to Rome, and urgently implemented a complete restructuring and clean-sweeping of the Church hierarchy; removing all dissident cardinals, bishops, and other Church officials. He then issued a series of decrees reinstating the primary role of the Catholic Church to that of spreading the teachings of Jesus Christ and the holy scriptures, as outlined in the Bible. The Church ceased to be involved in political intrigue, and abandoned its imperial ambitions. The Holy Roman Emperor was fully supported by the Church as the legitimate political and imperial leader of European Christendom.

The emperor resumed his role of providing full protection to the Church. Clement also significantly improved relations not only with the Eastern Orthodox Christian Byzantines; but also with the Seljuk Turks and other Muslims. So much so, that an agreement was reached between the Catholic Church, the Orthodox Church, and the Seljuk and other Muslims, which allowed all pilgrims unrestricted access to Jerusalem and other areas within the Holy Lands, as long as none of those pilgrims caused any dissent leading to violence; if they did, a specially appointed Tribunal, comprising of Catholic, Orthodox, and Muslim, representatives, would adjudicate and hand down appropriate punishment to those offenders.

The Tribunal operated surprisingly well, and largely free of corruption and bias. Pope Clement III was instrumental in realigning the Catholic Church to its rightful place, as a spiritual institution spreading the message of Christianity, rather than a powerful imperial force. Bohemond was appointed to set up the Tribunal, and remained in the Holy Land.

My job had been done. I headed back to the 21st century, and a debriefing from Otto. When I arrived at the piano bar, exactly on time, I was surprised to see Otto was already there, sitting at our usual corner table, sipping his glass of water. He had ordered a gin and tonic for me. Wow! He was behaving like a human! The Billy Joel impersonator was playing a hauntingly beautiful rendition of "She's Always a Woman to Me" as I took my seat.

'Otto, since I've been taking these trips through the wormhole, I have been feeling fatigued and exhausted. Will there be any long lasting adverse effects on my health?'

'Your body will degenerate to the equivalent of one Earth year, for every trip you take back in time.'

'You didn't think that was worth telling me before I agreed to undertake this mission!?'

Otto could see I was clearly annoyed and upset. He studied my reaction curiously, as if I was a laboratory animal. Well, in one respect, I was!

'So I will effectively have aged twelve years, when I'm done with this?'

'Luca, biologically you are correct. But you are in such good health that the effects of the wormhole won't be noticeable to you nor anybody else.'

I didn't expect any kind of emotional reaction from Otto. After all, where he came from, emotions had been eliminated by their technology a long time ago. Ageing twelve years was a very small sacrifice for the opportunity of changing the future of the world for the better.

'Luca, I am getting reports from my contacts at home that Thero is determined to destroy our mission because he has ambitions to take control of your Earth, when your planet is on its knees after the calamities have struck. He is planning to appear as some kind of religious saviour, and create a global totalitarian regime, with himself as the supreme leader.'

'I saw him at the jousting event. I am puzzled, Otto. Other than his brazen attempt to kill Charlemagne, he has very much remained behind the scenes.'

'Underestimate Thero at your peril! He is watching your every move. Studying your modus-operandi closely. Trying to unnerve you. Biding his time, ready for the next strike. His attempted assassination of Charlemagne was just a warm-up to what he is capable of. Remember Luca, he only has to stop one of the twelve historical events, and he will have succeeded in his mission. The fact that he cannot kill anybody other than the major historical figure; does not preclude him from using his rat-cunning skills, and getting people on-side, to stop you in your tracks.

'Well, I have eight more missions to complete, so Thero will have many opportunities to strike. I will of course, be very vigilant.'

'Luca, you successfully prevented the Crusades. This was a major alternative turning point for that version of Earth. It meant that the two great religions of Christianity and Islam coexisted peacefully. Crucially, it also meant that antisemitism did not rear its ugly head anywhere near as much as it would have. So the Holocaust never happened in that world. It also meant that neither religion gained significant political and imperial influence; keeping religion in its rightful place as a means of spiritual belief and expression; and not as a political or ideological propaganda tool to be used to wage war and secure power through conquest. Make no mistake. The butterfly effect of these monumental changes we have achieved in the four missions so far, are having the desired effect on the future of your version of Earth. We just need to complete the job. That's all.'

I had four days before the next mission. Isabella and I booked into a chalet overlooking a lake, and surrounded by a forest, just outside of the town of Pemberton, in the far south-west corner of Western Australia, for three days. Nearby was a winery owned by a good friend of mine, Neil Scott. We spent our time making passionate love; going for long walks in the forest; rowing a boat in the lake; and having romantic dinners in the fine dining restaurant at Neil's winery. Both of us were connoisseurs of red wine. Neil provided us with some special wines to try, including a sublime ten-year vintage shiraz.

Isabella was broken. As a child growing up she adored her uncle Steve. He never married and was close to her dad, his twin brother. When her mum and dad divorced, Isabella was ten years old. Her mum was a heroin addict. After a harrowing journey to hell and back, she finally decided to get intensive treatment for her addiction. Isabella's parents tried to keep the marriage together, but the trauma of the heroin addiction broke them. Her uncle Steve moved in. This is when Isabella's life turned into a dark nightmare. Steve began to sexually abuse her. Always when her dad wasn't home. He said if she told anybody, they wouldn't believe her, and she would be taken away from her dad and placed with foster parents. She was terrified. Her dad had no idea. The abuse continued for five years.

At age fifteen, Isabella moved in with her mum, whom by now, had become totally rehabilitated and clean of the demonic drug. She was going to tell her mum. But suddenly, her whole life was thrown into turmoil when her dad committed suicide. He had gassed himself in the garage, from the exhaust of his car. Just before he died, he left a confidential note to Isabella. In the note he said he had found out what uncle Steve had done to her for five years. He confronted his brother and told him unless he left the country for good, he would call the police. Steve ended up moving to England, where he was not seen or heard from again. Isabella knew her dad was heartbroken and blamed himself for not protecting his daughter. So much so, that he took his own life. Isabella never told her mum. In fact, she never told anybody, except me.

.

She's Always a Woman to Me

She can kill with a smile, she can wound with her eyes
And she can ruin your faith with her casual lies
And she only reveals what she wants you to see
She hides like a child but she's always a woman to me
She can lead you to love, she can take you or leave you
She can ask for the truth but she'll never believe you
And she'll take what you give her as long as its free

Yeah she steals like a thief but she's always a woman to me
Oh, she takes care of herself, she can wait if she wants
She's ahead of her time
Oh, and she never gives out and she never gives in
She just changes her mind

And she'll promise you more than the garden of Eden
Then she'll carelessly cut you and laugh while you're bleeding
But she brings out the best and the worst you can be

Blame it all on yourself 'cause she's always a woman to me
Oh, she takes care of herself, she can wait if she wants
She's ahead of her time
Oh, and she never gives out and she never gives in
She just changes her mind

She is frequently kind and she's suddenly cruel
But she can do as she pleases, she's nobody's fool
And she can't be convicted, she's earned her degree
And the most she will do is throw shadows at you
But she's always a woman to me

Billy Joel (1977)

7

Christopher Columbus

Vallodolid, Spain, November 1485 CE

Over 500 years after the first Europeans arrived in the Americas, historians still debate the legacy of Christopher Columbus. Should he be remembered as a great explorer and discoverer, who brought European culture to a previously unknown world? Or should he be condemned as a man responsible for an "American Holocaust"; a man who brought devastating European diseases to unprotected native peoples; who disrupted the American ecosystem; and who initiated the Atlantic Slave Trade? What is Columbus's legacy – discovery and progress; or slavery, disease, and racial destruction? I pondered these questions deeply.

I knew there was a direct link between the discoveries of Columbus, and the utter breakdown in human rights arising from colonial conquest and slavery. The discovery of the New World by Columbus was to trigger centuries of European colonial imperialism, which was set to destroy rich and enduring indigenous cultures around the world. This is why Otto had included it on the list of missions. I had to stop Christopher Columbus from securing the necessary financing for his expeditions. This was to take me to Spain, and the court of King Ferdinand II, and Queen Isabella I.

The encounter that began in 1492 among the peoples of the Eastern and Western Hemispheres was one of the truly defining events in world history. This clash of civilizations not only produced an extraordinary transformation of the natural environment, and human cultures in the New World; it also initiated far reaching changes in Old World Europe. These transformations, not all of which of course were negative, were worth exploring in order to give me a sharper context of why I was undertaking this mission. New foods reshaped the diets of people in both hemispheres. Tomatoes, chocolate, potatoes, corn, green beans, peanuts, vanilla, pineapple, and turkey, transformed the

European diet; while Europeans introduced sugar, cattle, pigs, cloves, ginger, cardamom, and almonds to the Americas.

Global patterns of trade were overturned, as crops grown in the New World – including tobacco, rice, and vastly expanded production of sugar – fed growing consumer markets in Europe; not to mention cotton for clothing. There was an upheaval of the natural environment triggered by Columbus. Europeans cleared vast areas of forested land, and inadvertently introduced Old World weeds. The introduction of cattle, goats, horses, sheep, and pigs, also transformed ecosystems, as grazing animals ate up many native plants and disrupted longstanding indigenous systems of agriculture. The horse, which had been extinct in the New World for over 10,000 years, transformed the daily lives of many indigenous peoples. The introduction of horses by the Europeans encouraged many traditional farming peoples to become hunters and herders. Hunters mounted on horses were also much more skilled at killing game.

Columbus set off a chain of events that introduced massive disease and death into the New World. Diseases against which indigenous peoples had no natural immunities caused the greatest mass deaths in human history. Within one hundred years of contact with the Europeans, smallpox, measles, mumps, and whooping cough, had reduced the population of indigenous populations by up to 90 percent. From Peru to Canada, diseases reduced the resistance that Native Americans had from European conquerors. With the indigenous population decimated by disease, the Europeans gradually introduced a new labour force into the New World – enslaved Africans. Between 1502 and 1870, up to 15 million Africans were shipped to the Americas in the Atlantic Slave Trade; around 30 percent of them tragically did not survive the voyages, dying at sea and being literally dumped into the ocean.

Columbus's voyage of discovery also had another important result; it contributed to the development of the modern concepts of progress. To many Europeans, the New World seemed to be a place of innocence, freedom, eternal youth, and great opportunity. Columbus himself believed he had landed near the Biblical Garden of Eden. The perception of the New World as an environment free from the corruptions, injustices, and vices, of European life, would act as a powerful magnet to European colonisers and settlers with a sense of adventure. So while the collision of these worlds resulted in widespread death, enslavement, and destruction; it also inspired visions of a much better future.

In 1516, the English humanist Sir Thomas More (1478-1535) published "Utopia," his description of an ideal society where crime, injustice, and poverty, did not exist. More wrote this book only twenty-four years after Columbus's first voyage to the New World; and located his perfect utopian society in the Americas. More's book, which is written in the form of a dialogue, clearly contrasts the simplicity of life in Utopia with Europe's class divisions. In Utopia, property is held for the common good, gold is of no value, and all of the inhabitants eat the same food, and wear the same clothes. But there are aspects of the book that give us an insight into the entrenched European sense of superiority which existed at that time. His book justifies taking land from the indigenous peoples because, in the eyes of the Europeans, the natives did not cultivate it. Secondly, the prosperity and well-being of More's utopian society, ultimately is based on the widespread use of slave labour.

In 1484, Columbus asked King John II of Portugal to fund his venture of exploration and discovery. King John declined. Columbus then spent six years in Spain trying to convince King Ferdinand and Queen Isabella to invest in his venture. Finally, in 1492, the royal couple agreed to provide Columbus with three sailing ships, men, and supplies. The man I was going to meet with in Spain, to assist me in reversing this course of action, was Hernando de Talavera, the highly influential confessor and counsellor to Queen Isabella of Castile.

Talavera was born in 1430 in the town of Talavera de la Reina. He was the illegitimate son of a noble father and a commoner mother. He entered the University of Salamanca at the age of fifteen to study theology, eventually taking a position at the university, teaching moral philosophy. He then left his teaching role in 1460, and became an ordained priest. In 1466 Talavera entered the Monastery of San Leonardo de Alba, part of the Hieronymite Order. The Order of Saint Jerome, or Hieronymites, was a Catholic cloistered monastic religious order, and a common name for several congregations of hermit monks living according to the Rule of Saint Augustine.

In 1470 he was appointed prior of the Monastery of Nuestra Senora del Prado, in Valladolid, where he developed extensive reforms for the order. In the early 1470s, his religious writings and reform programs brought him to the attention of the newly-crowned Queen Isabella I of Castile. Cardinal Pedro Gonzalez de Mendoza, a key supporter of Isabella, introduced Talavera to the royal court. By 1475, Talavera had risen to become Isabella's confessor and counsellor; and in January 1476, he presented her with a treatise titled: "How All Loyal Christians Should Renew Their Spirits During Advent." More than just an Advent sermon, the paper was both an inspirational spiritual tract, and a politically astute guide that had a lifelong influence on the queen's approach to her reign.

Talavera also served on the royal council of advisers, and was relied upon to take on important assignments for the Crown. In 1479, he was sent to Portugal to ensure that Isabella's rival, Juana of Castile, entered a convent as had been previously agreed. He also headed a commission to look at royal prerogatives in the Canary Islands. At Isabella's request, Talavera mentored a young Juan Rodriguez de Fonseca, who later became the powerful de-facto minister of Spain's emerging colonial empire.

In 1485, when Christopher Columbus approached the Spanish Crown to propose his voyage of discovery, Talavera was his first contact at the royal court. He facilitated an introduction between Columbus and Isabella, and was instructed by the queen to establish a commission to establish the feasibility of the Columbus proposal. In 1490, the commission recommended against the plan. But in 1492, King Ferdinand and Queen Isabella overrode the commission board's decision, and instead decided to sponsor Columbus's expedition. Talavera was appointed Bishop of Avila in 1486. The population of Avila included prominent Jewish and Muslim communities.

His experience in dealing with these religious minorities would later significantly influence his approach to the Muslim population in Grenada, when he became archbishop there. After the Spanish conquest of Grenada in 1492, the rights of the Muslim majority to practice their religion was guaranteed in the terms of surrender put in place by Spain. In 1493, Talavera was appointed Archbishop of Grenada, a challenging assignment that demonstrated the Crown's trust in his abilities.

However, it also marked a turning point in his influence at the royal court, when Francisco Jimenez de Cisneros was named to replace him as Isabella's confessor and counsellor. Talavera's preferred approach was the peaceful conversion of the population to Christianity, explaining to them in their own language, the nature of the Christian religion, and its superiority over Islam. He promoted the study of the Arabic language, one that he learned himself, and encouraged his clergy to do likewise. The people of Granada respected Talavera, and were grateful for his adherence to the terms of the peace agreement; but his approach yielded few converts.

Meanwhile the influence of Cisneros at the royal court continued to grow, and when he was appointed Archbishop of Toledo, he became the most senior ranking member of the Catholic Church hierarchy in Spain. When he came to Grenada in 1499, Cisneros brought with him a much more aggressive approach to Muslim conversion to Christianity. Overriding Talavera's objections, his actions incited a revolt which threatened Cisneros' life, and was only put down by the timely intervention of the royal army.

To avoid further bloodshed, Talavera promised amnesty to any rebels who converted to Christianity; and over 50,000 people took advantage of his offer. After the rebellion in the city, Cisneros continued to push his aggressive efforts to convert Muslims in the countryside. A second rebellion erupted, and the royal army again was required to quash the rebels. Queen Isabella decided that a peaceful solution was not possible, and so in February 1502, she issued an edict requiring all adult Muslims in Castile to convert to Christianity, or face immediate expulsion.

Talavera had been opposed to the Spanish Inquisition for many years. After the death of his protector, Queen Isabella, in 1504, he was denounced by the notorious Inquisitor Diego Rodriguez de Lucero, and was accused of establishing a synagogue in his palace where allegedly he conducted Jewish ceremonies with family and other clerics. In the eyes of Lucero however, his real crime was his longstanding opposition to the Inquisition. His relatives and household servants were arrested, but Talavera himself was untouched until King Fernando authorized his arrest in June 1506. The papal nuncio Giovanni Ruffo appealed to Pope Julius II, who cleared Talavera of all charges, and ordered him released. Talavera died a short time later on 14th May 1507.

I arrived in the city of Valladolid on the 15th November 1485 to meet with Hernando de Talavera. The city is located in north-western Spain, where the Pisuerga and Esgueva rivers merge, 15 kilometres before they join the Duero river. Surrounding the city is a major winegrowing region. Valladolid was originally settled in pre-Roman times by the Celtic Vaccaei Gauls, and after the conquests of Julius Caesar, by the Romans themselves. It remained a small settlement until it was established as a lordship by King Alfonso VI of Castile, for count Pedro Ansurez, in 1072.

The city grew in prominence during the Middle Ages as the seat of the Court of Castile; and was also endowed with a cathedral, university (established in 1241), the Royal Palace, a Chancery, and the Royal Mint. During the time of Muslim rule in Spain, the Christian kings moved the population of this region further north, into more easily defended areas, and deliberately created a no man's land as a buffer zone, as protection against additional Moorish conquests. The city and its surrounding region was recaptured by the Spanish from the Moors in the 10th century. After King Alfonso IV of Castile gifted the lordship of Valladolid to count Pedro Ansurez in 1072; the count initiated a repopulation of the area which saw the settlement become a city. During the 12th and 13th centuries Valladolid grew rapidly into a major commercial, political, and religious centre.

In 1469, Queen Isabella I of Castile and King Ferdinand II of Aragon, were married in the city. Interestingly, in 1506 Christopher Columbus died in Valladolid, still convinced that he had reached the Indies, in a house that in modern times is a museum dedicated to him.

I arrived at the entrance gates to a monastery, just outside the city, surrounded by vineyards. As the gates opened, a monk approached me.

'We don't get many visitors here. I gather you are Luca Evangelista?'

'Yes padre.'

'I am padre Enrico. I am the prior of this monastery. Your uncle, Bishop Talavera is waiting for you. Come, let's go to him.'

Well, well, well. Talavera astutely had set me up as his nephew. This would mean I could stay close to him and accompany him to meetings at the Royal Court. The monastery was set up in the typical fashion of cloistered two-level buildings surrounding a central garden area. We entered the largest of the buildings and climbed the stairs into a library, where a distinguished looking gentleman was seated, reading a manuscript.

'Thank you, padre Enrico. You may leave us now. Luca Evangelista, welcome to Spain. Otto has timed your visit to perfection. Christopher Columbus is arriving in three hours to meet with us about his planned expedition. I hope you don't mind me introducing you as my nephew. Family ties are very important to us Spaniards. As my nephew, you will have unrestricted access to accompany me wherever I go.'

'I thought that was the case. It's a pleasure to meet you, Bishop Talavera.'

'You're my nephew, just call me Hernando. I have invited a number of other influential people who have the ear of Ferdinand and Isabella, along to the meeting later this afternoon. Now, let me show you to your room, so you can settle in here before Columbus arrives.'

It seemed to have become a pattern during these time travel missions, that shortly after I arrived, I would review my notes, reflections, and the lives, of the key characters of each mission. And so, once I settled into my modest room, I reviewed the life of Christopher Columbus.

During the 15th and 16th centuries, leaders of several European kingdoms sponsored expeditions overseas in the hope that explorers would discover great riches and new lands. The Portuguese were the earliest participants in what was known as The Age of Discovery. Starting in around 1420, small Portuguese ships, known as caravels, would sail along the coast of Africa, carrying spices, gold, slaves, and other goods; from Asia and Africa, into Europe.

Other European kingdoms, particularly Portugal's intense rival, Spain, were eager to share in the seemingly limitless riches and resources of the "Far East." By the end of the 15th century, Spain's "Reconquista" – the expulsion of Jews and Muslims out of the kingdom after centuries of war – was complete; and the Spanish King and Queen turned their attention to exploration and conquest in other regions of the world, including those yet to be discovered.

Christopher Columbus, the son of a wool merchant, was born in Genoa Italy, in 1451. When he was still a teenager he secured a job on a merchant ship, and remained at sea until 1476, when pirates attacked his ship as it sailed north along the Portuguese coast. Although the boat sank, the young Columbus managed to float to the shore on a piece of wood. He eventually made his way to Lisbon, where he studied mathematics, astronomy, cartography, and navigation. He also began to formulate into a plan, his dream of discovering new worlds.

At the end of the 15th century, it was virtually impossible to reach Asia from Europe by land. The trek was long, arduous, and extremely dangerous due to the presence of many hostile armies. Portuguese explorers solved this problem by travelling by sea instead. They sailed south in the Atlantic, along the West African coast, and then around the Cape of Good Hope at the far southern tip of Africa, and into the Indian Ocean. But Columbus had a different and innovative idea. Why not sail west across the Atlantic, rather than around the massive African continent? The young navigator's logic was sound, but his mathematics was flawed.

He incorrectly believed that the circumference of the Earth was much smaller than his contemporaries believed it was; as a result, he believed that the journey by ship from Europe to Asia should not only be possible, but comparatively easier, by navigating through an as-yet undiscovered Northwest Passage. He presented his plan to officials in Portugal and England; but he did not find a sympathetic audience until he presented his plan to the Spanish monarchs, Ferdinand of Aragon and Isabella of Castile. Columbus clearly wanted fame and fortune.

Ferdinand and Isabella wanted the same, along with the opportunity to outdo their fierce rival Portugal, and to export Catholicism to lands around the world. Columbus was a devout Catholic, and so was equally enthusiastic about converting natives to the message of God. Columbus ended up securing a contract with the Spanish royal rulers which promised him ten percent of whatever riches and resources he found; along with a royal title, and the governorship of any lands he encountered.

On 3rd August 1492, Christopher Columbus and his crew set sail from Spain in three ships; the Nina, the Pinta, and the Santa Maria. On 12th October, the ships reached land; not in the East Indies, as Columbus had assumed, but on one of the Bahamian islands – San

Salvador. For months, Columbus sailed from island to island, in what we now know as the Caribbean, looking for the "pearls, precious stones, gold, silver, spices, and other objects and merchandise whatsoever" that he had promised to his Spanish patrons; but he did not find much at all. In January 1493, after leaving several dozen men behind in a makeshift settlement on Hispaniola (modern-day Haiti and the Dominican Republic), he left for Spain.

He kept a detailed diary during his first voyage. Columbus's journal was written between 3rd August and 6th November 1492, and mentioned everything from the wildlife he encountered, such as dolphins and birds, to the weather, and the mood of his crew. More disturbingly, the journal also records his initial impressions of the local indigenous peoples, and his reasoning for why they should be enslaved. An excerpt from his diary says:

"They brought us parrots and balls of cotton and spears and many other things which they exchanged for the glass beads and hawks' bells. They willingly traded everything they owned. They were well-built, with good bodies and handsome features. They do not bear arms, and do not know them, for I showed them a sword, they took it by the edge and cut themselves out of ignorance. They have no iron. They would make fine servants. With fifty men we could subjugate them all and make them do whatever we want."

Around six months later, in September 1493, Columbus returned to the Americas. He found the Hispaniola settlement destroyed, and left his brothers, Bartolomeo and Diego Columbus behind to rebuild, along with some of his ships' crew and hundreds of enslaved indigenous people. Then he headed west to continue his mostly fruitless search for gold and other valuables.

His group now included a large number of indigenous people the Europeans had enslaved. In lieu of the material riches he had promised to the Spanish monarchs, he sent some 500 slaves to Queen Isabella, his main supporter. The queen was horrified. She believed that any people Columbus "discovered" were Spanish subjects who could not be enslaved. So she promptly and angrily returned the explorer's gift.

When I arrived back at the library, Bishop Hernando Talavera introduced me to the other men sitting around the table. There was

Father Antonio de Marchena, a Franciscan priest who was a friar in the convent of La Rabida, where after arriving in Spain from Portugal in 1484, Christopher Columbus requested asylum for himself and his son Diego. Marchena was the first confidant of Columbus in Spain, and after learning of Columbus's plans of exploration, had arranged the introduction to the royal court of Castile, via Talavera.

I was next introduced to Duke Medinaceli, who was a substantial property owner in Spain, and a close ally of Ferdinand and Isabella. He had provided significant funds for the ongoing war against the Muslim Moors.

Next I met Duke Medina-Sidonia, a fierce business rival of Medinaceli and one of the richest men in Spain. Although he was born out of wedlock, his birth was later legitimized by a royal decree issued by Ferdinand and Isabella, and as a result, he obtained the right to inherit the ducal title from his father, Juan Alonso de Guzman. He participated in the conquest of the Emirate of Granada, which resulted in the Moors losing power, and as a reward, Duke Medina-Sidonia was granted the title of Marquis of Gibraltar.

Finally, there was Cardinal Don Pedro Mendoza; the most senior Spanish representative of the Catholic Church in Rome. In addition to being an eminent cardinal, he was also a diplomat and a close advisor to Ferdinand and Isabella; often referred to as "the third king of Spain."

Mendoza was the fifth son of the poet Inigo Lopez de Mendoza, and studied at the University of Salamanca. After serving as a chaplain to King John II, he experienced a rapid rise in power, by successively becoming; Bishop of Calahorra in 1454; Bishop of Siguenza in 1467; Archbishop of Sevilla in 1474; Archbishop of Toledo and Primate of Spain in 1482. In 1473, as a result of the direct influence of Rodrigo Borgia, the future Pope Alexander VI, he was appointed as a Cardinal. Brought to the attention of the court of Castile by Alfonso de Fonseca, the Archbishop of Sevilla, by 1465 Mendoza had thrown his support and that of his powerful family, to Henry IV, in his struggle with the nobles.

Because the paternity of Henry IV's daughter and natural heir, Joan, was in doubt, his succession was unsettled. Mendoza then gave his full support to the claims of Henry's half-sister, Isabella, who in 1469 went on to marry Ferdinand of Aragon. Upon Henry's death in 1474,

Isabella declared herself to be the queen, and confirmed Mendoza as Chancellor of Castile, a post he had received from King Henry IV the year before. After a war over the succession, which ended successfully for Ferdinand and Isabella, Mendoza helped Isabella strengthen the monarchy, and deliver peace to the kingdom by pacifying the rebellious nobles, and by successfully negotiating with some of the most ambitious magnates in Spain. He was a humanist and translated Homer and Sallust for the benefit of his poet-father.

In 1483 he founded the College of Santa Cruz in Valladolid, as part of his new educational reforms for the clergy. Mendoza also helped Isabella reform the Spanish Church hierarchy and administration, advising her to appoint bishops from the middle class, rather than exclusively from the nobility. I knew the sources record Mendoza as a powerful supporter of Columbus. I also knew that without the financial support of the two extremely wealthy nobles present at this meeting, Mendoza would be hard-pressed to recommend the Columbus expedition to Isabella, whom Ferdinand had entrusted in making the final decision. So earlier in the afternoon, I had discussed with Talavera, the importance of us dissuading the dukes Medinaceli, and Medina-Sidonia, from investing in Columbus. This was going to be the key to stopping the expedition dead in its tracts.

Finally, the man himself, Christopher Columbus arrived. After Talavera introduced him to us, he made the Genovese navigator feel welcome.

'Welcome Columbus. We look forward to hearing your proposal.'

'Signor Talavera, I have been reading maps and accounts of sailors who have sailed west past the Canary Islands. I believe that the world is not flat, but round. I think that by sailing west, I can reach Cathay for spices and also the Indies, the land of gold.'

Talavera replied: 'Of course, you are no doubt aware of the great explorer, Henry the Navigator. He knew, as do all of us, that the world is indeed round. In fact, we too have sent ships exploring westward. We would like to know how you propose to reach Cathay, and what materials and supplies you will need.'

'Signor Talavera, I will need at least three ships, men to outfit them, and food and supplies for three months.'

Medinaceli interjected: 'Three months? Is that all the time you believe this voyage will take?'

'Yes. My calculations are based on a letter and a map made by the eminent scholar, Toscanelli, which has led me to believe the distance from Spain to Cipango (modern Japan) is seven hundred leagues.'

'Seven hundred leagues? Why, this is lunacy!' stated Medinaceli.

'Now, now, let's keep this meeting cordial gentlemen. Signor Columbus, mapmakers and scholars, of which I am one, believe that the distance is at least two thousand leagues' stated Talavera.

Medinaceli again interrupted: 'Signor Columbus, we don't know where you have got your information from, but it is wrong. Our scholars are very confident you have miscalculated, given their studies of location, and the distance between stars.'

Medina-Sidonia then spoke: 'What does he know? He used to be a weaver!'

'Please gentlemen, show our visitor some courtesy' Talavera pleaded. 'I apologize Signor Columbus. However, I agree. The distance you suggest is too short. The voyage is much longer and much riskier than you propose. Indeed, we are content to seek a route to the Indies by sailing around Africa. We have a number of captains who have been working their way down the coast of Africa, and once they round the tip, we believe it will be a short trip to Cathay and the Indies.'

Cardinal Mendoza spoke for the first time: 'Have you ever thought that there may be other lands between here and Cathay?'

'Of course, your eminence. Marco Polo wrote of Cipango and Seven Thousand Islands. I believe that God has granted me the gift of knowledge and revealed that it is feasible to sail to the Indies. I must carry out this journey!'

Mendoza continued: "So you want to carry our Christian faith to the unknown parts of the world? Is it true you have been rejected by Portugal?'

'Yes, your eminence. I met with King John of Portugal, and was rejected. This is a golden opportunity for Spain to venture where no other great power ever has, reaping the prestige and bounty of rewards.'

Mendoza replied: 'Why didn't you tell us about your approach to the Portuguese and their rejection of your proposal? The Portuguese have explored all along the coast of Africa and have established trading ports. It is true they are currently ahead of us when it comes to maritime exploration and discovery of new territories. Our Queen Isabella is full of faith, but Spain's treasury is empty! The war with the Moors rages on and on. Once the Spanish armies defeat the Moors, perhaps Spain can turn to a new world. If our king and queen are to invest in your proposal, they must be very sure of the return on their investment.'

'Give me three ships with men and supplies. I will show you I'm not mad. I can carry out this expedition. I alone have the knowledge required to successfully make this journey and make Spain even richer. But I have terms of my own which must be met.'

'And what are they?' replied Talavera.

'In return for undertaking the voyage I demand the title Viceroy and Governor-General of all territories I discover for Spain; and I also demand the title, Admiral of the Western Ocean. I demand one-tenth of all treasure, spices, gold, and precious stones found on the islands I discover. I will also own one-tenth of all land discovered and the profits, from these lands.'

Medina-Sidonia shouted: "These are outrageous demands! One-tenth, he is mad!

Talavera replied: That is quite enough Signor Medina-Sidonia! Is that all you are requesting Signor Columbus?'

'Yes.'

The meeting then ended. Columbus and Father Marchena left. I then decided to speak.

'Gentlemen, I have conducted a detailed investigation of Columbus's plans. As my uncle Hernando de Talavera knows, I have excellent contacts connected to the royal family in Portugal. They tell me Columbus is not sharing his true intentions with us. What he is really planning is to seize all property and treasures he discovers for himself, and to set himself up as the ruler of a newly created kingdom. He will enslave the natives and become their master and god. There will not be any benefit to the kingdom of Spain, nor to yourselves as his financiers, gentlemen. In short, Columbus is seeking fame, power, and riches for himself.'

'He is a charlatan, opportunist, fraudster, and imposter!' screamed Medina- Sidonia.

'He is not getting any of my money!' nodded Medinaceli, in total agreement.

'I think we are being too harsh on Columbus' stated Cardinal Mendoza. 'He seems very committed to this mission of discovery. Luca, have you considered that your sources in Portugal may have their own personal motives to seeing Columbus's mission fail? I don't think Portugal would want to be humiliated if Columbus succeeded in discovering the New World, and it was then to be found out that they rejected him before he came to us! I will be arranging for Columbus to personally meet with Queen Isabella, as she requested.'

'Your eminence, as Isabella's counsellor and confessor, I shall attend the meeting too. I also think it is important that her majesty hears first hand, my nephew Luca's concerns about Columbus's true intentions.'

'That's fine with me. Her majesty would want you to be there anyway, Bishop Talavera. I shall set up the meeting for tomorrow morning.

After the meeting I retired to my room. Columbus did seem like an amiable, sincere, and passionately driven man. I needed to remind myself of the ample primary sources which showed him to be a murderer, tyrant, and scoundrel. These specific cases clearly outline the unimaginable cruelty inflicted by Columbus and his crew during their time in the Caribbean. Columbus kidnapped a native woman and gave her to a crew member to rape. We have an extract from the diary of Michele de Cuneo, a crew member who participated in Columbus's second expedition, which says:

> While I was in the boat, I captured a very beautiful woman, whom the Lord Admiral (Columbus) gave to me. When I had taken her to my cabin she was naked, as was their custom. I was filled with a desire to take my pleasure with her and attempted to satisfy my desire. She was unwilling, and so treated me with her nails that I wished I had never begun. I then took a piece of rope and whipped her soundly, and she let forth such incredible screams that you would not have believed your ears. Eventually we came to such terms, I

> assure you, that you would have thought she had been brought up in a school of whores.

On Hispaniola, a member of Columbus's crew publicly cut off a native's ears to shock others into submission. After an attack by more than 2,000 natives, Columbus had an underling, Alonso de Ojeda, bring to him three native leaders, whom Columbus then ordered to be beheaded. Ojeda also ordered his men to grab another native, bring him to the middle of his village, and cut off his ears in retribution for the native's failure to be helpful to the Spaniards when fording a stream.

Columbus was also known to have kidnapped and enslaved more than 1,500 people on Hispaniola. According to his crew member Cuneo, Columbus ordered 1,500 men and women seized, letting 400 go and condemning 500 to be sent to Spain, and another 600 to be enslaved by Spanish men remaining on the island. About 200 of the 500 sent to Spain died during the voyage, and were thrown by the Spanish into the Atlantic. Columbus would force natives to collect gold for him or else they would die. He ordered every native over the age of 14 to give a large quantity of gold to the Spanish, or suffer a horrible death.

Those living in regions without much gold were allowed to give him cotton instead. Participants in this system were given a stamped copper or brass token to wear around their necks in what became a symbol of intolerable shame and humiliation. We have evidence of around 50,000 natives committing mass suicide rather than complying with the Spanish conquerors. A biography written by the historian, Laurence Bergreen, titled *Columbus: The Four Voyages* states:

> The Indians destroyed their stores of bread so that neither they nor the invaders would be able to eat it. They plunged off cliffs, they poisoned themselves with roots, and they starved themselves to death. Oppressed by the impossible requirement to deliver tributes of gold, Indians were no longer able to tend to their fields, or care for their sick, children, and elderly. They had given up and committed mass suicide to avoid being killed or captured by Christians, and to avoid sharing their land with them, their fields, groves, beaches, forests, and women: the future of their people.

Fifty-six years after Columbus's first voyage, only 500 out of 300,000 natives remained on the island of Hispaniola. Although population figures from 500 years ago are imprecise, Bergreen estimates there were about 300,000 inhabitants of Hispaniola in 1492. Between 1494 and 1496, 100,000 died, half due to mass suicide. In 1508, the population had reduced to 60,000; and by 1548, it was estimated to be only 500. Terrified, some natives fled to the mountains to avoid the Spanish troops, only to have dogs set upon them by Columbus's men.

Under his rule, Columbus also treated his Spanish colleagues in a degrading manner. While paling in comparison to his crimes against the native inhabitants, Columbus's rule over Spanish settlers was brutal. He ordered at least a dozen Spaniards to be whipped in public, tied by the neck, and bound together by their feet, for trading gold for food, to avoid starvation. He also ordered a woman's tongue to be cut out for speaking ill of himself and his brothers. Another woman was stripped naked and placed on the back of a donkey, and then whipped, as punishment for falsely claiming to be pregnant. He ordered Spaniards to be hanged for stealing bread. The historian Bergreen states:

> He even ordered the ears and nose cut off one miscreant, who was also whipped, shackled, and banished from the island. He ordered a cabin boy's hand nailed in public to the spot where he had pulled a trap from a river and caught a fish. Whippings for minor infractions occurred with alarming frequency. Columbus ordered one wrongdoer to receive a hundred lashes, which could be fatal, for stealing sheep, and another for lying about the incident. An unlucky fellow named Juan Moreno received a hundred lashes for failing to gather enough food for Columbus's pantry.

We have evidence that settlers under Columbus sold native girls as young as nine and ten into sexual slavery. In a letter to Dona Juana de la Torre, a friend of Queen Isabella, Columbus wrote:

> There are plenty of dealers who go about looking for girls; those from nine to ten are now in demand, and for all ages a good price must be paid.

There are cases where native slaves were beheaded when their Spanish captors couldn't be bothered to untie them. Benjamin Keen, a historian of the Spanish conquest of the Americas, notes that multiple primary sources confirm accounts of "exhausted Indian carriers, chained by the neck, whose heads the Spaniards severed from their bodies so they might not have to stop to untie them."

I was disgusted by all of this evidence. I was more determined than ever to stop Columbus from undertaking his expedition.The key to it all, was going to be whether I could somehow get the attention of Queen Isabella, and let her know first-hand, the degrading and murderous acts Columbus was going to inflict on hundreds of thousands of harmless innocent indigenous peoples; and even more disturbingly, the massive slave trade; and the savage Spanish conquistador-initiated rapes, pillages, genocide, and destruction, which was about to be unleashed in the New World.

That evening, Bishop Talavera invited me to sit in the audience of the Spanish Inquisition, of which he was, with great reluctance, at the insistence of Queen Isabella, one of five council members. The inquisition was headed by the brutal and fanatical grand inquisitor, Tomas de Torquemada, a man who had gained infamy in history for his widespread use of terror and torture to secure guilty pleas. The medieval inquisition had played a considerable role in Christian Spain during the 13th century, but the struggle against the Muslim Moors had kept the inhabitants of the Iberian Peninsula busy, and served to strengthen their faith.

When towards the end of the 15th century the Reconquista for the regaining control of Spain from the Moors was complete, the desire for religious unity became a matter of urgency. With the defeat and eviction of the Moors, Spain's Jewish population, which was amongst the largest in Europe, soon became a prominent target for religious persecution. Over a number of centuries, the Jewish community in Spain had flourished and grown in numbers and influence, though anti-Semitism had reared its ugly head from time to time.

During the reign of Henry III of Castile, from 1390 to 1406, Jews faced increased persecution and were pressured to convert to Christianity. The pogroms of 1391 were particularly brutal, and the threat of violence constantly hung over the Jewish community in Spain. Faced with the choice between baptism and death, the number of nominal converts to the Christian faith soon became very great. Many Jews were killed, and those who adopted Christian beliefs, the so called "conversos" faced continued suspicion and prejudice. In addition, there remained a significant population of Jews who had converted, but continued to practice their faith in secret. Known as "Marranos" those nominal converts from Judaism were perceived to be an even greater threat to the social order than those who had rejected forced conversion.

After Aragon and Castile were united by the marriage of Ferdinand and Isabella in 1469, the "Marranos" were denounced as a danger to the existence of Christian Spain. In 1478, Pope Sixtus IV issued a decree authorizing the Catholic Monarchs to name inquisitors who would address the issue. That did not mean the Spanish sovereigns were turning over to the Church the struggle for unity; on the contrary, they sought to use the Inquisition to support their absolute and centralizing regime, and most importantly, to increase their royal power in Aragon.

The first Spanish inquisitors, operating in Seville, proved to be so severe that Sixtus IV attempted to intervene. The Spanish crown now had in its possession a weapon too precious to give up, however, and the efforts of the Pope to limit the powers of the Inquisition, failed. In 1483 he was pressured to authorize the naming by the Spanish crown of a grand inquisitor for Castile; and during the same year also for Aragon, Valencia, and Catalonia, which were all placed under the power of the Inquisition in Castile.

The grand inquisitor acted as the head of the Inquisition in Spain. The ecclesiastical jurisdiction that he had received from the Vatican empowered him to name deputies and to hear appeals. In deciding appeals, the grand inquisitor was assisted by a council of five members and by consultors. All those offices were filled by agreement between the monarchy and the grand inquisitor. The first grand inquisitor in Spain was the Dominican, Tomas de Torquemada. His name became synonymous with the brutality and fanaticism associated with the Inquisition. Torquemada used torture and confiscation to terrorize his victims, and his methods were the product of a time when judicial procedure was deliberately cruel. After sentencing, the condemned were presented before a large crowd that often included members of the royalty; and the proceedings had a ritualized, almost festive, atmosphere.

The number of burnings at the stake during Torquemada's tenure was exaggerated by Protestant critics of the Inquisition; but nevertheless, it is estimated over 2,000 people were burnt at the stake. At Torquemada's urging, Ferdinand and Isabella issued an edict on 31st March 1492, giving Spanish Jews the choice of exile or baptism. As a result, over 160,000 Jews were expelled from Spain. The persecution and suppression of Muslims was prosecuted in the same fanatical manner.

That night I accompanied Bishop Talavera to the Inquisition Chambers, within the Royal Palace, and sat in the public gallery as Talavera chaired this particular hearing. Talavera commenced the proceedings with an opening statement.

'In the Royal Palace of the Inquisition of Castile, on the fifteenth day of November, one thousand four hundred and eighty-five, I, the Inquisitor, Bishop Hernando Talavera, being at my evening audience, have ordered Carlos Fernandez to be brought from the secret prison, to appear before me. He has sworn to declare the truth to me and to his audience and all others, until the conclusion of his trial; and to keep secret whatever he might see or hear, and everything which should befall him, concerning his trial. What is your name, birthplace, age, and occupation?'

'My name is Carlos Fernandez. I am a native of the city of Manresa, in the bishopric of Vique. I am thirty-one years of age. My trade is a blacksmith and farrier, your eminency.'

'What lineage and stock are your ancestors? Have you, or any of your relatives, been ever imprisoned, put under penance, absolved, or condemned by the Holy Office of the Inquisition, anywhere within the Spanish kingdom?'

'We are all Christians of pure blood. I have never heard or understood that any of my ancestors or relatives have suffered such a fate, and neither have I, until the present occasion.'

'Signor Fernandez, are you a baptized and confirmed Christian? Do you make it a regular practice to attend Mass, go to confession, and communicate at the times fixed by the Holy Mother Church?'

'I am a Christian. According to my parents, I was baptized in the cathedral church of Manresa. I do not know the name of the bishop who confirmed me. It has always been my regular practice to hear Mass, and take confession and communion, at the times prescribed by the Holy Mother Church. My last confession was in the town of Valles Campo de Tarragona, in the month of October last, on the day of Our Lady del Rosario. On this day, I received my confession from a Carmelite friar.'

'Can you read and write? Have you studied any science or natural philosophy?'

'I can read, but quite badly and slowly; having taught myself. I cannot write, and have never studied any of these disciplines.'

'Have you ever been out of the kingdom of Castile and Aragon; and if so, with which other persons?'

'I once visited the kingdom of Granada, but not in the company of any other person. While in Granada, I never had any communication with people of suspicious faith.'

'What have been the main events of your life, so far?'

'I was born in the city of Manresa, as I have said. I was brought up in the house of my father until the age of sixteen years, when I was sent to the town of Igualada, to Maestre Ando, a blacksmith and farrier, with whom I stayed for four months, learning his trade. After that, I resided in several places in Catalonia, and then visited Aragon and Granada, for short periods of time; until I came to live here two years ago.'

'Do you know the reason you have been arrested and detained in the prison of the Holy Office?'

'I do not know the reason, your Eminence. Nobody has told me the reason. All I can think of, is that the reason for my arrest relates to my ability to often cure people of fevers and other disorders, with rosemary water. A skill I have learnt from God and the Holy Mary our Lady, from whom I have received a particular gift for this purpose.'

'In what manner and at what time did you receive this gift?'

'I received this gift at a young age, having been born with a mole on my neck, and two others on my left hip. I had been sick for ten years, as a youth, with great lameness, and had entreated God and the Virgin to restore me to good health, and to grant me the power to cure others, so that I might in this way, help people.'

'What reason do you have for believing that God and our Lady have given you this healing power?'

'I was led to believe this from the good success which had accompanied my attempts to perform these cures on many people. None of these people paid me for curing them. Instead they provided me with charity in the form of food, water, shelter, and some donated coins. If you have received any testimony from anybody accusing me of performing these cures for monetary gain; then this is an offence against our Lord, and the reason I am imagining I have been arrested and imprisoned.'

'In this Holy Office, it is not customary to imprison any person without sufficient information that the person has committed, or seen committed, some act which is, or appears to be, contrary to our Holy Catholic Faith and Evangelical doctrine, which is taught and professed by the Holy Mother Roman Catholic Church, or against the proper and free jurisdiction of the Holy Office. You need to understand that you have been arrested and imprisoned as a direct consequence of credible information provided to us by a reliable person. You are now exhorted on the part of God our Lord, and his glorious and blessed mother, the Virgin Mary, to bethink yourself well, and to confess the whole truth to this Inquisition.'

'I have nothing to confess because I have done no wrong in the eyes of our Lord.'

'In that case, Carlos Fernandez, I hereby punish you to a burning at the stake, in order to remove the demons within you, and to release the purity of your soul into the hands of our Lord and the Virgin Mary. The burning shall take place the day after tomorrow, at noon. Guards, send him back to his prison cell.'

After formally closing the Inquisition Trial, Bishop Talavera and I walked the short distance from the Royal Palace to his bishop's residence.

'Luca Evangelista, I know you probably think burning people at the stake is barbaric. I can imagine in the 21st century from which you come, punishments are much less severe. I hope so, for I am a humanist and a man of deep Christian faith. I don't feel it is the will of our Lord for people to die such a horrible agonizing death. But

I'm sure you understand, my personal opinions are at great odds with the teachings and doctrines of the Church. If anybody was to know my true thoughts, I would undoubtedly be stripped of my position as bishop and brought before the Inquisition myself. This is why I haven't expressed what I have just told you to anybody else.'

This was all making sense to me. I knew that in the not too distant future, Bishop Talavera was going to be arrested for denouncing the Inquisition. Of course, I could not let him know this. He was clearly acting as an inquisitor out of loyalty to Queen Isabella and the Catholic Church. No wonder he felt so much guilt and dare I say, shame, in sending people accused of heresy to a cruel and brutal death by burning.

'I am a humanist too Bishop Talavera. Humanism is alive and well in the 21st century. It encourages open and critical thinking and the pursuit of knowledge and progress. This ideology of course, is the exact opposite of religious belief, which encourages rigid doctrines and an utter rejection of any enlightened thinking; regardless of the religion. There you go, now you know how I think. I would be a prime candidate for your Inquisition too, wouldn't I?'

'We both would, Luca. Now, let us get some good rest. Tomorrow morning, we will be meeting with Queen Isabella at the Royal Palace, to try and convince her not to support Columbus's expedition.'

I was excited about meeting Queen Isabella. Was it because my partner had the same name? It was much more than that. When researching her life for this trip, it occurred to me she was a complex monarch who wielded great power primarily for the benefit of her people. Yet she could be very stubborn and volatile. She had a love of learning and was a passionate student of history. Her life story is fascinating.

After her birth on 22nd April 1451, Isabella was second in the line of succession to her father, King John II of Castile, following her older half-brother, Henry. She became third in line when her brother Alfonso was born in 1453. Her mother was Isabella of Portugal, whose father was a son of King John I of Portugal, and whose mother was a granddaughter of the same king. Her father's father was Henry III of Castile, and his mother was Catherine of Lancaster, the daughter of John of Gaunt, the third son of England's Edward III. Isabella's half-brother became Henry IV, king of Castile, when their father, John II, died in 1454, when Isabella was three years of age. Isabella was raised by her mother until 1457, when the two children were brought to court by Henry to keep them from being used by opposing nobles. Isabella was well educated. Her tutors included Beatriz Galindo, a professor of philosophy, rhetoric, and medicine, at the University at Salamanca.

Henry's first marriage ended in divorce and without children. When his second wife, Joan of Portugal, gave birth to a daughter, Juana, in 1462, the opposing nobles claimed that Juana was the daughter of Beltran de la Cueva, the duke of Albuquerque; therefore, she is known in history as Juana la Beltraneja. The opposition's attempt to replace Henry with Alfonso failed, with the final defeat coming in July 1468, when Alfonso died of suspected poisoning. This is disputed though by many historians, who believe he more likely died from the plague. Nevertheless, Alfonso had named Isabella as his successor. Isabella was offered the crown by the nobles, but she refused, more than likely because she didn't believe she could maintain the crown in opposition to Henry. Henry was willing to compromise with the nobles and accept Isabella as his heiress.

Isabella married Ferdinand of Aragon, a second cousin, in October 1469, without Henry's approval. The cardinal of Valentia, Rodrigo Borgia, later to become Pope Alexander VI, helped Isabella and Ferdinand obtain the necessary papal dispensation; but the couple still had to resort to pretences and disguises to carry out the marriage ceremony in Valladolid. As a result, Henry withdrew his recognition of Isabella, and instead named Juana as his heir. After Henry's death in 1474, a war of succession erupted, with Alfonso V of Portugal, the prospective husband of Isabella's rival Juana, supporting Juana's claim to the throne. The dispute was settled in 1479 when Isabella was officially recognized as the Queen of Castile.

By this time, Ferdinand had become King of Aragon, and the two ruled both realms with equal authority, effectively unifying Spain in the process. Among their first acts were various reforms to reduce the power of the nobility, and increase the power of the crown. After her marriage, Isabella appointed Galindo as the tutor to her children. With the direct support of the queen, Galindo founded hospitals and schools in Spain, including the Hospital of the Holy Cross in Madrid. He also served as a close adviser to Isabella.

In 1480, Isabella and Ferdinand set up the Inquisition in Spain, as we have seen. This was one of many changes to the role of the Church that were initiated by the royal couple. The Inquisition was aimed mostly at Jews and Muslims who had overtly converted to Christianity, but were thought to be still practicing their faiths in secret. They were seen as heretics who rejected the Roman Catholic doctrines. Ferdinand and Isabella were given the title "the Catholic monarchs" by Pope Alexander VI in recognition of their role in "purifying" the faith.

Among Isabella's other religious pursuits was taking a special interest in the Poor Clares, an order of nuns. Isabella and Ferdinand planned to unify all of Spain by continuing a long-standing but stalled effort to expel the Muslim Moors, who held control of parts of Spain. In 1492, the Muslim Kingdom of Granada fell to Isabella and Ferdinand, thus completing the Reconquista. That same year, Isabella and Ferdinand issued an edict expelling all of the Jews in Spain who refused to convert to Christianity. Also of course, in 1492, Christopher Columbus managed to convince Isabella to sponsor his first voyage of exploration. Based on the traditions of that time, when Columbus became the first European to encounter lands in the New World, these lands were given to Castile.

Isabella took a special interest in the indigenous peoples of the New World. As we have seen, when Columbus brought some enslaved indigenous people back to Spain, Isabella was horrified and insisted they be returned and freed. She expressed her strong will that the "Indians" be treated with justice, humanity, and fairness.

By the time of her death on 26th November, 1504, Isabella's sons, grandsons, and her older daughter Isabella, queen of Portugal, had already died, leaving as Isabella's only heir "Mad Joan" Juana, who became queen of Castile in 1504, and of Aragon in 1516. Isabella was a patron of scholars and artists, establishing educational institutions, and building a large royal collection of artwork. She learned Latin as an adult and was widely read; also educating her sons and daughters. Her youngest daughter, Catherine of Aragon, became the first wife of Henry VIII of England, and mother of Mary I of England.

Isabella's Will, the only writing that she left, summarizes what she thought were her reign's achievements, as well as her wishes for the future. In 1958, the Roman Catholic Church began the process to canonize Isabella as a saint. After an exhaustive investigation, the commission appointed by the Church determined that she had "a reputation of sanctity" and was inspired by Christian values. In 1974, she was recognized with the title "Servant of God" by the Vatican, a step in the process of canonization.

Bishop Talavera and I made our way to the Royal Palace. Waiting outside the entrance to the Queen's Chambers were Christopher Columbus and Cardinal Mendoza. They were engaged in an animated conversation that appeared to be annoying Mendoza. Anyhow, when we arrived, Mendoza stood to greet us, and then arranged for an official to let Queen Isabella know we had all arrived to meet her. Shortly after, we were escorted to a lavishly appointed room. As soon as I walked in I saw Isabella walk towards us. She was a stunningly beautiful woman with long black glossy hair and piercing brown eyes. Although we had all entered the room, she looked straight at me, smiling.

'Thank you for coming to the palace, gentlemen. Bishop Talavera, this lovely man must be your nephew.'

'Yes, your majesty. May I introduce you to Luca Evangelista.'

'It is my deep honour and pleasure to meet with you, your majesty.'

Isabella reached out her right hand, and I kissed it. She couldn't take her eyes off me, and nor could I take my eyes off her. A familiar feeling of romantic chemistry was overcoming me. She was so gorgeous, charismatic, and vivacious.

'Your majesty, I introduce you to the explorer, Christopher Columbus', interjected Cardinal Mendoza, clearly bemused by the obvious attraction between Isabella and I.

'Welcome, signor Columbus. I have heard much about you and your proposed expedition to the New World. As you are no doubt aware, we are fighting a war against the Moors. The very survival of our greater Spanish kingdom is at stake. All of our resources are going towards this war. But it is my understanding from Cardinal Mendoza, that if I give my approval, two of the wealthiest nobles in the realm will provide you with the funds for your expedition. I am also aware of your 10% terms.'

'Your majesty, I have great confidence in my expedition and believe I can deliver to you, great wealth and prestige, particularly at the expense of the Portuguese.'

'Cardinal Mendoza and Bishop Talavera, what are your thoughts? Should I give this expedition my royal blessing?'

Mendoza spoke first. 'Your majesty, I believe such an expedition will excite and invigorate our Spanish subjects. Columbus's mission will explore places never seen before. Who knows what magnificent treasures he will find. His expedition will also deliver a powerful message not only to Portugal, but also to our other rival kingdoms that Spain is a great power, deserving of awe and respect. I support the involvement of the Crown in endorsing this expedition.'

'Thank you Cardinal Mendoza. And what do you think, Bishop Talavera?'

'Your majesty, I am not convinced signor Columbus has the necessary expertise, knowledge, and temperament, to undertake such an expedition. I have made discrete enquiries in Portugal and Genoa. I am told by a number of very reliable sources that Columbus is an ill-tempered and impatient man. He also has been involved in anti-Christian activities. I believe his motivation is self-interest and greed, not what is best for our kingdom. Rather than taking a huge risk with Columbus, I believe we should undertake our own expedition to the New World, led by a capable Spanish navigator. Your majesty, there are at least three highly suitable and eminent candidates, which I can discuss with you at a later date.'

'How dare you attack my good-character, Talavera!' screamed Columbus. 'Where did you get this ridiculous and totally untrue information from? I demand to know!'

Queen Isabella was clearly uncomfortable with Columbus's outburst. Cardinal Mendoza interjected on her behalf and was visibly angry as he spoke.

'Columbus! Stop this disrespectful insolence in the presence of her majesty right now! Sit down and do not utter another word unless you are instructed to speak. Do you understand?!'

'Yes, your eminence.'

There was an air of calmness in the room, as Isabella spoke.

'Gentlemen, I have heard enough. I will give this matter my careful consideration, and also speak with the proposed financiers, signor Medina-Sidonia, and signor Medinaceli. The meeting is now over. Luca Evangelista, can you please remain in my company? The rest of you can now leave.'

My heart pounded in anticipation. It was so intoxicating to be in the presence of this very powerful and extraordinarily beautiful woman. I remained calmly seated as the others left the room.

'Will you join me for lunch, signor Luca?'

'Yes your majesty, it will be my honour to.'

Isabella escorted me to the banquet hall of the palace. It was spectacularly decorated with large full scale paintings of herself and her husband, king Ferdinand, and past members of their respective royal families. The banquet table in the centre of the hall was huge. I estimated it could comfortably seat 50 people. There was a large ornately decorated fireplace on one side of the hall, that was giving off enough heat to keep the entire hall warm.

Isabella directed me to sit next to her on one side in the middle of the dining table. A delicious array of food had already been laid out in front of us by a team of servants, including a whole roast pig, loaves of freshly baked bread, an assortment of steamed vegetables, piles of fruit, a pot of soup, and a variety of cheeses and olives. While our plates were being prepared by two servants, another servant poured red wine into our gold-plated goblets.

'No doubt signor Luca, you are wondering why I have invited you to lunch with me, just you and I as you can see.'

'The thought did cross my mind, your majesty.'

'You fascinate me, Luca Evangelista. From the moment I laid my eyes on you, I felt an instant attraction. I can see in your eyes, you feel exactly the same.'

'Your majesty, may I be honest with you?'

'Of course! I crave honesty. When you are in a position like mine, one rarely gets it.'

'As soon as I saw you, I felt a deep connection with you, as if we had met before, in another life. And in that other life, we were romantic soulmates. I hope I haven't offended you in expressing this to you?'

'Offended me? Absolutely not. Excited me, is more like it, Luca! I don't often dream. On the night before last, I dreamt of an encounter with you. You were in my dream. You were urging me to take some course of action, but I didn't recall what the matter was that was of such great concern to you. I didn't think much of the dream when I awoke the next morning. But then, when you appeared in front of my eyes today, exactly the man I dreamt of, I was overcome with emotion. I too feel we have been together in a previous life. I also feel deeply, that you have been sent to me by our Lord and the Virgin Mary.'

I was touched by her sincerity. While we were enjoying the food and wine, animated in conversation, she kissed me on my lips. It was a gentle kiss, full of caring and devotion. I was overwhelmed and extended the kiss longer than what she may have planned. I could feel she was very happy I had added more passion to the kiss.

'I want you to know I am very concerned about the true motives of Columbus. When my uncle mentioned he had been making enquiries in England, Portugal, and Genoa, he in fact sent me to investigate. I have spent the last three months looking into the activities of Columbus, and talking confidentially with many people who have had dealings with him. He is not a man of good character, your majesty. He is looking to enrich himself as much as possible, and is seeking to conquer territories so he can secure himself as a tyrannical ruler over the lands he discovers, and the native peoples he may encounter, and even enslave them. I agree with my uncle. As an alternative, you should give your royal approval to a completely Spanish expedition to the New World, led by a capable and morally sound Spaniard, who will serve you and Spain entirely, with no ambition of personal enrichment.'

'Bishop Talavera is my closest counsellor and adviser. When he started expressing doubts about the Columbus expedition to me, I started having reservations. Now you have come into my dreams and my life! You have been sent to deliver a profound message to me, Luca! I like the idea of waiting longer, and when we are ready, once we have totally cleansed Spain of the Moors and Jews, we will then proceed to launch an "all-Spanish" expedition to the New World, manned by the very best people Spain can provide, with the very best intentions; treating the natives with due respect, not enslaving anybody, and totally for the benefit of our kingdom. I like this idea, and shall provide my full support to this option, instead of the Columbus option.'

'Well, for what it is worth, I am convinced you have made the right decision, your majesty.'

Then something totally unexpected happened. Queen Isabella started crying, firstly sobbing softly, and then shedding more tears. She grabbed my hand, and took me across the hall, down a number of passageways, and into her bedroom. Without saying a single word, she undressed me, then undressed herself; we then made passionate love on her bed. We were together for a couple of hours, devouring and caressing each other, again, with no words spoken at all. Our bodies communicated everything which needed to be said.

After we dressed, she kissed me once more on my lips, and asked me to leave; her only words were to wish me the very best on my mission, which I felt was an odd thing for her to say, because of course, I had not told her anything about my time travelling. As I left the royal palace, all I could ponder about was what Otto was going to think of this situation that I had just encountered. If she knew about my mission, how did she find out? Does making love to a person from the past, in any way activate a butterfly effect that may work against the very fabric of my mission? I needed to ask Otto these questions. Anyhow, I was going to find out soon enough, because my mission was over, and Otto was about to transport me back to the 21st century. I was also overwhelmed with guilt. Did I just cheat on my Isabella, when I made love with Queen Isabella?

This time, I arrived at the bar before Otto did. That's more like it, I thought. It seemed odd to me when Otto arrived first. What do Billy Joel and Otto have in common? Well, every time I met Otto at the bar, sure enough, the in-house entertainer was doing his usual round of the great showman's songs. This time it was "We Didn't Start the Fire."

'Otto, I need to tell you something a little embarrassing. You know how you told me I mustn't get emotionally involved with anybody from the past? Well, Queen Isabella and I had sex!'

'I know. I am aware of everything you do and say, when you are in the past. Having sex is fine, as long as it is initiated by the other person from the past, and not yourself; and of course, as long as a pregnancy doesn't come out of it, which in this case, it didn't. Queen Isabella was clearly enamoured of you, Luca.'

'Why didn't you tell me you entered the dreams of Queen Isabella, Otto?'

'I didn't, Luca Evangelista. I didn't.'

Otto proceeded to tell me that in that multiple universe version of the Earth, not only did Columbus not undertake his trip to the New World, but also the Spanish expedition happened nearly two years later. This two-year interval, and the command given to a number of humanitarian Spanish captains who led a series of expeditions, resulted in the discovery of not only much of the Caribbean and West Indies, but also both coasts of North America. The Spanish established settlements in all of these discovered territories, ahead of the Portuguese, British, French, and Dutch, but did not enslave and mistreat the indigenous peoples.

They led the way in working collaboratively and closely with the local natives, and rather than exploit the resources, and ship products back to Europe, the Spanish instead encouraged many of their people to settle in these newly discovered lands and extended their influence in that manner. Led by the example of the Spanish; the Portuguese, British, French, and Dutch, followed this same pattern of exploration and colonisation; and so as a result, the Atlantic Slave Trade never happened, and the cultures of these many diverse indigenous peoples were preserved and even flourished. Queen Isabella played a very crucial role in achieving this different result for the Spanish, by taking a personal interest in all of the expeditions.

After meeting Otto, I made my way to my Mum's place. My family was having dinner at her place to celebrate the 21st birthday of my nephew, Gino. I arrived early. My Mum was busy in the kitchen putting the finishing touches on the delicious traditional Italian food she had cooked and prepared. The entrée was platters of cold meats such as salami, ham, prosciutto, mortadella, and a variety of cheeses, as well as olives, and raw prawns marinated in lemon juice. This would be followed by her homemade lasagne. She had made the pasta sheets using her over 40-year old pasta-maker that she bought in Italy. The lasagne included eggs, small minced pork and veal meatballs, shredded salami and ham, provolone cheese, and our family's homemade tomato sauce. This sauce was simply delicious, and was based on a 500-year old recipe from the central Italian medieval village of my parents' birth, which had been passed down from one generation to the next.

I could see the main course was my Mum's veal and chicken cutlets, seasoned with herbs and spices, based on an old recipe. Accompanying the veal and chicken dish would be steamed broccoli, roast potatoes, peas, and my Mum's special salad. I knew my Mum would have prepared all of this delicious food herself, by getting up at 5am that morning and spending the whole day engaged in her labour of love. I say it is a labour of love, because I knew how much sheer joy and pleasure my Mum would get from just seeing our extended family all together enjoying her food, while engaged in laughter and animated conversation.

In fact, I knew that by the time we got around to having our family dinner that night, my Mum would be so exhausted that she wouldn't have eaten anything at all. Instead she would be overwhelmed with joy seeing us all together. This is why my Mum was literally the glue who held my family together. I came earlier to see how she was. It had not been long since my Dad died so tragically from being struck by a van. Although my Mum and Dad had more than their fair share of arguments, mostly over trivial things like my Dad doing the daily shopping for her and often coming back home with the wrong things; they were happily married, genuinely enjoyed each other's company, and were incredibly proud of the new life they had created in Australia; and the way in which they had brought up their kids, including me.

'Are you still dreaming of Dad?'

'Yes, Luca. Last night I felt his presence very strongly. He was in the room with me, believe it or not, my son. I had been watching television and dozed off on the couch. I know I had my rosary beads in my hand, because I was reciting my prayers before I fell asleep. I awoke when I felt a hand tugging at my shoulders. After I got off the couch, I saw that my rosary beads were wrapped around the photo of your father that I keep on the mantelpiece. How did those rosary beads get there Luca? I didn't put them there.'

My Mum was a devout Roman Catholic and very superstitious. Her religious beliefs were at the centre of her life. She often dreamt of dead people. When she described her dreams to me, I could feel that to her they were very real. She would often describe the conversations she had with the dead in great detail; whether it was her mother, her father, her grandparents; or her favourite uncle who died tragically in a work related accident in Italy at the young age of 35, leaving a distressed wife and three children all under the age of 6.

But the way in which she described my father, when he appeared in her dreams, was particularly vivid and intensely personal. I could see that she was still traumatized by the death of my Dad. On the afternoon of the day he died, we visited the site of the accident, and while my brothers and I were temporarily distracted, my Mum made her way to the side of the road where my Dad had lay hours earlier, dying, and used her handkerchief to collect some of my Dad's blood. Over the following days, she would show visitors the blood of my father, while crying with intense agonizing painful outbursts. This disturbed me greatly. I pleaded with my Mum to stop doing this; and eventually she did.

Any Road

Oh I've been traveling on a boat and a plane
In a car on a bike with a bus and a train
Traveling there and traveling here
Everywhere in every gear

But oh Lord we pay the price with the
Spin of a wheel – with the roll of the dice
Ah yeah you pay your fare
And if you don't know where you're going
Any road will take you there

And I've been traveling through the dirt and the grime
From the past to the future through the space and the time
Traveling deep beneath the waves – in
Watery grottoes and mountainous caves

But oh Lord we've got to fight
With the thoughts in the head with the dark and the light
No use to stop and stare
And if you don't know where you're going
Any road will take you there

You may not know where you came from
May not know who you are
May not even wondered how
You got this far

I've been traveling on a wing and a prayer
By the skin of my teeth by the breadth of a hair
Traveling where the four winds blow
With the sun on my face – in the ice
And the snow

But oooeeee it's a game
Sometimes you're cool, sometimes
You're lame
Ah yeah it's somewhere
And if you don't know where you're going
Any road will take you there

But oh Lord we pay the price
With the spin of the wheel with the roll of
The dice
Ah yeah, you pay your fare
And if you don't know where you're going
Any road will take you there

I keep traveling around the bend
There was no beginning, there is no end
It wasn't born and never dies
There are no edges, there is no size

Oh yeah, you just don't win
It's so far out – the way out is in
Bow to God and call him Sir
But if you don't know where you're going
Any road will take you there

But if you don't know where you're going
Any road will take you there

George Harrison (2002)

8

Otto von Bismarck

Berlin, Germany, November 1884 CE

After our family birthday dinner, I stayed up until 2am, reviewing my research notes for my next mission back in time. Otto told me I was due to travel to Berlin in 1884, at exactly midday tomorrow. This world of 19th century Europe was going to be much more familiar to me. The conference in Berlin I was going to be attending is little-known by most people living today in the 21st century. Yet, it played a significant role in unleashing the full forces of European Imperialism and literally led to the carve-up of the African continent, for the exclusive benefit of the European Powers.

When the conference was held, in 1884, the German nation was newly created. It previously consisted of a number of independent kingdoms and principalities, the largest and most powerful of which, were Prussia, Bavaria, and Saxony. Then in 1871, the Prussian ruler, King Wilhelm I, and his very politically astute chancellor, Otto von Bismarck, successfully unified these kingdoms and principalities into the nation state of Germany. Unlike the longer standing European Powers such as Britain and France, the newly-created Germany did not of course have any overseas colonies, literally being the "new kid on the block." Under the leadership of Wilhelm and Bismarck, Germany was determined to fast-track itself into a great European Power to rival Britain and France. Gaining colonies in Africa, was considered to be a big step for Germany to achieve its ambitions; so the accepted history says.

On the afternoon of Saturday, 15th November 1884, an international conference in Berlin was opened by Otto von Bismarck, the chancellor of the newly-created German Empire. There were representatives from the major European Powers, the United States, and the Ottoman Empire, seated around a horse-shoe shaped table, in a room with large windows, overlooking a spectacular garden. The only clue as to the purpose of the November gathering of white men, was hung on the wall, in the form of a very large map of the African continent, "drooping down like a question mark" according to the Nigerian historian, Professor Godfrey Uzoigwe.

Inclusive of a short break for Christmas and New Year, the Conference of Berlin would last 104 days, ending on 26th February 1885. In the over 135 years since, the conference has come to represent the late 19th century European Scramble and Partition of Africa. The delegates were hunched over a map of Africa on the table, armed with rulers and pencils, literally sketching out national borders on the continent, as they negotiated their respective imperial colonies, carving up Africa in the process, completely oblivious and disinterested in the rich variety of cultures, traditions, and histories, that they were obliterating in their lust for resources and power.

This conference set in motion something very destructive. It established the rules for the conquest and partition of Africa, in the process legitimizing for the Europeans, the idea of Africa being a playground for the exploitation of resources and peoples; and Africans themselves, having no say in the future of their continent. From the very beginning, the conference laid out the order of priorities. "The Powers are in the presence of three interests: That of the commercial and industrial nations, which a common necessity compels to the research of new outlets. That of the States and of the Powers summoned to exercise over the regions of the Congo an authority which will have burdens corresponding to their rights. And, lastly, that which some generous voices have already commended to your solicitude – the interests of the native populations." It also resolutely refused to consider the question of African sovereignty, and the legitimacy of laying claim to someone else's land and resources.

Professor Uzoigwe noted that: "Bismarck stated in his opening remarks at the conference that delegates had not been assembled to discuss matters of sovereignty either of African states or of the European powers in Africa." It was no accident that there were no Africans represented at the conference. Their opinions were clearly not valued and not considered necessary. The efforts of the Sultan of Zanzibar to get himself invited, for example, were ridiculed by the British in particular.

The American journalist Daniel De Leon described the conference as "an event unique in the history of political science; diplomatic in form, it was economic in fact."

While it was dressed up as a humanitarian summit to look into the welfare of the locals, its agenda was anything but that, purely political and economic in nature. Few on the European continent or in the African diaspora were fooled. A week before the conference closed, *The Lagos Observer* newspaper declared that "the world had, perhaps never witnessed a robbery on so large a scale." Six years later, another editor of a Lagos newspaper comparing the legacy conference to the slave trade, said: "A forcible possession of our land has taken the place of a forcible possession of our person." Theodore Holly, the first black Protestant Episcopal Bishop in the United States, condemned the delegates as having "come together to enact into law, national rapine, robbery and murder."

The outcome of the conference was the General Act, which was signed and ratified by all but one of the 14 nations at the table, the USA being the sole exception. Some of its main features were the establishment of a regime of free trade stretching across the middle of Africa, the development of which became the rationale for the recognition of the Congo Free State and its subsequent 13-year horror, the abolition of the overland slave trade, as well as establishing the principal of "effective occupation" for the European Powers.

The attempt to create a free trade area in Africa and therefore keep the continent from becoming both a spark for, and a theatre of conflict between the European Powers, was ultimately doomed. The principle of "effective occupation" was to become the catalyst for the military conquest of the African continent with far reaching consequences for its inhabitants. At the time of the conference, 80 percent of Africa remained under traditional and local indigenous control. The Europeans only had influence along the coastlines.

Following the conference, they started grabbing chunks of land inland, ultimately creating a hodgepodge of geometric boundaries that were superimposed over longstanding indigenous cultures and religions throughout Africa. Most of Africa ended up being conquered by the Europeans by the end of the 19th century. However, to get their claims over African land accepted, the European states had to demonstrate that they could actually administer the occupied area.

Often, military conquest proved to be the easy part. To govern, the European Powers found they had to contend with a confusing array of fluid tribal identities, cultures, and languages. Therefore, the Europeans went about reorganising Africans into units they could understand and control. As Professor Terence Ranger noted, the colonial period was marked "by systematic inventions of African traditions – ethnicity, customary law, and traditional religion. Before colonialism, Africa was characterised by pluralism, flexibility, and multiple identity. After colonialism, African identities of tribe, gender, and generation were all bounded by the rigidities of invented tradition." Imperial boundaries were imposed all over the continent, with scant regard to the damaging consequences to the indigenous peoples who had been living there for many centuries.

That first-ever international conference on Africa established a template for how the world deals with the continent. Today, in the 21st century, Africa is still seen primarily as a source of raw materials for the outside world, and an arena for more powerful countries to compete over. Conferences about the African continent are rarely held on the continent itself, and rarely care about the views of ordinary Africans. The sight of African heads of state assembling in foreign capitals to beg for favours is a re-enactment of the Sultan of Zanzibar's pleading to attend a conference where he would be the main course. Despite achieving independence for the most part in the 1950s and 1960s, many African countries have continued along the destructive path laid out in Berlin.

Former Tanzanian President Julius Nyerere declared: "We have artificial 'nations' carved out at the Berlin Conference in 1884, and today we are struggling to build these nations into stable units of human society. We are in danger of becoming the most Balkanised continent of the world." Ethnicity and tribalism continue to be the bane of African politics. "The Berlin Conference was Africa's undoing in more ways than one," wrote Jan Nijman, Peter Muller and Harm de Blij in their book, Geography: Realms, Religions, and Concepts. "The colonial powers superimposed their domains on the African continent.

By the time independence returned to Africa, the realm had acquired a legacy of political fragmentation that could neither be eliminated nor made to operate satisfactorily."

Now, over 135 later, I was determined to travel back to the Berlin Conference of 1884, and facilitate a change of history that would give the African continent a chance to develop and flourish independent of the European Powers, and for the primary benefit of the peoples of Africa. I had always wanted to travel to Berlin. In the late 19th century it was beginning to rival Paris as the most cosmopolitan city in Europe. But it had its fair share of problems.

Prior to 1870, visitors to Berlin found themselves confronted with little more than a swampy backwater. As the turn of the century approached however, the city underwent vast and rapid change, becoming one of Europe's most modern metropolises by the beginning of the 20th century. But along with industry and infrastructure, the changes also brought poverty and pestilence. When I first arrived in the centre of Berlin, at midday on Friday 14th November 1884, the day before the start of the conference, and on my birthday, I had a few hours to walk around the city.

I smelt the dust in the air, and saw many construction pits, as the city was coming of age. I saw a row of houses being torn down, and the skeletons of new ones standing nearly twice as high as the old building rows. Nearby, workers were levelling the sand for a new street. The city was so full of construction sites, and such a vast array of new buildings were coming into being, that anyone returning to the city after an absence of only a couple of months, was bound to feel out of place.

"I feel lost in Berlin. It has no resemblance to the city I had supposed it was. There was once a Berlin which I would have known, from descriptions in books; a dingy city in a marsh, with rough streets, muddy and lantern-lighted, dividing straight rows of ugly houses all alike, compacted into blocks as square and plain and uniform and monotonous and serious as so many dry-goods boxes. But that Berlin has disappeared. It is a new city; the newest I have ever seen. The main mass of the city looks as if it had been built last week," American author Mark Twain wrote, after living in Berlin for six months, starting in October 1891.

If a city can be seen as a living organism, then the years between 1870 and 1914 were Berlin's adolescence, a time when the sleepy capital of the Kingdom of Prussia became a booming metropolis, a place both contradictory and disorderly, always shifting between extremes, sometimes sparkling and sometimes abject, sometimes ruled by military discipline, and sometimes by bohemian excesses, but always willing to experiment, forging ahead impatiently toward the future.

Amazed by Berlin, Mark Twain called it "the Chicago of Europe," after the American city considered at the time to be the most modern in the world. "A new Berlin emerged, with modern facilities, asphalt paving, an enormous network of tram lines and with all the comforts modern technology could produce," reflected author Edmund Edel, who chronicled Berlin's bohemian scene in 1908. The city came to represent both promise and purgatory. The only thing everyone could agree on, it seemed, was a distinct lack of enthusiasm when Berlin became the capital city of the newly-created German nation, in 1871.

Even Chancellor Otto von Bismarck initially considered establishing the seat of the empire in the city of Kassel, instead. He found the Berliners to be too liberal, too subversive, and too prone to socialist ideals; and as if this wasn't enough, the liberal press in Berlin also bothered him. Yet the inhabitants themselves were largely unconcerned by their city's new role. "It's nothing at all, the king has become an emperor," noted Marie von Olfers, who ran a literary café in Berlin.

This elevation to imperial capital was only one push along with many other forces driving Berlin's transformation. In the years before and after the founding of the German nation, many different processes of change combined to create "the greatest shake-up that this city, which was successively the capital of the Principality of Brandenburg, the Kingdom of Prussia, and the German Empire, went through at any point in its history," says the historian, Michael Erbe.

Berlin caught up to other European cities at a breathtaking pace. The railroad provided the first catalyst, transforming Berlin in the 1840s into one of central Europe's most important railway hubs. Goods and commodities could now be transported long distances, an important development for mechanical engineering and for the trade in metals and textiles, as well for the electrical industry, which established itself in the city on the Spree River, drawing many jobseekers to Berlin. Industry was the true founder of the city, sociologist Werner Sombart argued in 1900. By 1864, over half of the city's inhabitants were not born in Berlin.

These new residents came primarily from Brandenburg, the region surrounding Berlin, and Silesia, in what today is the Czech Republic and Poland. The economic boom after 1871, sparked by the injection of 5 billion francs in reparations from the Franco-Prussian wartime enemy France, benefitted Berlin significantly, providing fertile ground for the establishment of banks, insurance companies, and largescale commercial enterprises. For example, 250 new businesses were registered in the year 1872 alone.

The German government kept pace, putting its stamp on the city with awe-inspiring halls of justice, schools, and palatial post offices; while the newly installed Kaiser's publicity displayed his power and tastes with grand museums, impressive café-lined boulevards, and military equestrian statues. The first place in which the new Berlin began to unfold was in the area around the city palace on the central boulevard, Unter den Linden.

Previously, people had lived in the upper floors of these buildings, while stores and workshops at the street level produced and sold daily goods and services; but now a modern city developed, where people worked, governed, and were entertained, but where hardly anybody now lived. During the day, nobles, townspeople, and some tourists would stroll along Friedrichstrasse, where they stopped to admire the city's first electrical interior lighting at Café Bauer, installed in 1884; or indulged in a cool pale ale at the Pschorr Brewery's beer palace; or took in theatre or opera at the Apollo Theatre, and the Berlin Opera House.

"The palaces receive their officers and civil servants; there is a constant coming and going; the crowd swarms out. The stock exchange employees drive to work with their own wagons or by cab; errand boys with 'express' written on their red caps, position themselves on the most advantageous corners. Students stroll through the university grounds, savouring the atmosphere of the academic quarter before going in. A hearse on its low wheels heads home, and now the knitting old lady takes up position in front of the opera, calling out the program and the lyrics of the opera that will play tonight. Finally, the guards draw up. The Kaiser approaches the window to greet them. Berliners gaping and foreigners stretching their necks from their cabs all raise their hats," wrote the young Frenchman Jules Laforgue, who served as a French reader for the empress, describing a morning in front of the Kaiser's palace in 1887.

In 1870, it was still possible to cross the city from one end to another in an hour by foot. Beyond the city's borders, woods and fields affirmed the agrarian nature of the region. In 1892, the German writer Theodor Fontane, described the area around a lake called Halensee, now in urban western Berlin, as a "desert panorama, crisscrossed with asparagus beds and railroad embankments."

Not long after, the newly constructed avenue Kurfurstendamm transformed the area into the downtown centre of the western part of the city. Stately elegant apartments with fifteen or more rooms lined the grand boulevard, where Wilhelm II had the Kaiser Wilhelm Memorial Church erected in 1895, in memory of his grandfather Wilhelm I. Writers, artists, and cabaret performers, met here at the Café des Westerns, which drew everyone, from composer Richard Strauss to poets Christian Morgenstern and Else Lasker-Schuler. "A circle of young men sits up front. Bleary-eyed, they have city dwellers' faces. Extremely elegant. Sometimes restless, tough, strained in their gaze. They talk of Nietzsche, of the most recent horse races, of the theatre premieres," is how the Berlin author and cultural researcher Hans Ostwald described one coffeehouse scene.

Major industrial corporations such as Siemens & Halske, AEG, and Borsig, moved from the city's centre towards its outskirts, seeking more space for their enormous factories. The city encroached onto the surrounding countryside, its boundaries with neighbouring cities such as Charlottenburg, Spandau, Schoneberg, and Lichtenberg, becoming indistinct.

Population growth was similarly dramatic in the city itself. Berlin's population in 1849 was only around 412,000, but by 1880 it had passed the one million mark. By 1914, 1.84 million people lived in the city, which had become Europe's most densely populated. Berlin's old baroque buildings were massively overcrowded even in the 1860s, and sanitary conditions were catastrophic.

With few available toilets, people relieved themselves in public if necessary, and disposed of wastewater and excrement in the street gutters, where thick, stinking filth made crossing any road, an adventure. British health expert, Edwin Chadwick, called Berlin the "most foul-smelling, dirtiest and most pestilent" capital city in the civilized world in 1872, declaring that its citizens could be "recognized by the smell of their clothes." Relief came in the form of an underground sewage system, a "radial system" that used pressure pipes and pumping stations to direct wastewater to sewage irrigation fields at the city's outskirts.

The before and after effect was astonishing. By 1900, Berlin was considered to be the cleanest city in Europe. This was one of the few successes achieved by Berlin's city planners. Administrative responsibilities were fragmented. Although Berlin had its own magistrates to administer justice, for example; in other areas such as public health, police, and the supervision of construction, the responsibilities fell to the Prussian authorities. As a result, for the most part, the metropolis was allowed to expand haphazardly, driven mainly by speculators' greed, rather than orderly city planning. Ruler-straight streets sprang up, always at 90-degree angles, and along them, kilometres of tenement houses with no front yards emerged.

The owners of these square-shaped lots squeezed in as many apartments as they could, behind grand, stucco-decorated facades, nesting as many as seven buildings behind one another, and leaving inner courtyards of just precisely the mandatory 28 square metres necessary to use a fire extinguisher. The wealthy lived in the front buildings that faced onto the streets, while the rest of the population squeezed together in the rear buildings, as well as the buildings' damp cellars and draft-filled attics.

To help pay the rent, many families took in boarders as well. The rooms were tiny, and stacked with as many beds as could be fitted in, often with up to six people living in a single room, and with laundry drying on lines, and clothes stacked in the corners. In 1871, one missionary in the city reported of a building in which 250 families lived, with 36 families along a single corridor.

Berliners differentiated clearly between the upscale parts of the city; those who could afford to do so, built villas in Grunewald or Lichterfelde, or took up residence in spacious apartments in Tiergarten or Charlottenburg; and working class neighbourhoods such as Luisenstadt and Wedding, which were home to unskilled labourers, whose wives worked from home, sewing clothing for the textile industry. These miserable and appalling living conditions were the downside of Berlin's evolution into a big city, and stood in dark contrast to the progress achieved by a constant stream of technological advancements towards the end of the 19th century.

The rapid pace of development meant that the well-off and newly rich quickly left the proletarian portion of the population far behind. By 1850, telegraph lines connected the city with Frankfurt, Cologne, Hamburg, Breslau, and Verviers in Belgium, which meant that news and information arrived quickly. Mail carriers sorted letters even as they were on their way to deliver them to the recipients. By 1881, the more technologically enlightened people began to install telephones. This increasing tempo in both communications and travel left people feeling even more stressed, hectic, and anxious in Berlin and elsewhere; but at the same time it made for an exciting time of unparalleled innovation.

Faster and faster modes of transportation interconnected the city, and those who could afford to, tried out each one, as soon as they could; first the horse-drawn omnibus, then the horse and steam-powered trolleys, and finally the world's first electric trolley, inaugurated by Werner von Siemens in Gross-Lichterfelde, at the time still a separate town from Berlin, in 1881. Soon these vehicles were creaking their way through the city streets, powered by overhead lines, as well as battery power in some of the more exclusive parts of town. Like blood pulsating through an artery, Europe's first viaduct railway line linked the city from end to end. "A tremendous edifice has arisen before us; such an assembly of bricks as perhaps has not been seen since the walls of Babylon and the aqueducts of Rome," enthused Bernhard Wolff, a Jewish Berliner, and son of a banker.

The very first Sunday after the opening, the new trains transported over 67,000 passengers. Tradesmen, bars, and restaurants took up quarters in the archways beneath the elevated tracks. "People in Berlin love transportation," declared the "City Documents," a series of 50 publications released by journalist and researcher Hans Ostwald in 1905. The height of modernity, meanwhile, came in the form of a combined elevated and underground train line; although this particular experience was at first enjoyed by only a small segment of the population. The elegant stations and train cars fitted out with red leather and mahogany, and especially the steep price, made this an exclusive form of transportation used mainly by salesmen, business people, and civil servants.

This bourgeois segment of society was a relatively new phenomenon in the city on the Spree. Its members worked in the powerful institutions of the banking quarter; the trading and insurance firms; as professors at the state universities and research institutes; or earned their living as doctors at new hospitals. The most numerous of this elite group though, were those employed by the government administration in the former Prussian, and now German, capital, which required more and more civil servants to run it.

Half of Berlin's residents came from the working class, while the other half consisted of the middle class and nobility; and the middle class were growing in power. The city's industrial boom had brought this segment of society, money and social standing, and now its members began to distance themselves – through education and a picture-perfect family life of velvet curtains and plush sofas – away from the proletarian lower classes, and the decadent nobility.

> All the gentlemen in whose company you find yourself are cultured, polite, well-bred people, albeit entirely unfamiliar with the smaller customs of great society, all occupied, each having his own well-ordered work, with presenting a healthy opinion on the literary and scientific efforts of the time. They have not the polish, the superficial gloss of the high society in the palace on Unter den Linden; they are no experts at tying ties and their garments date from the last years of the empire. Yet at the same time they are strangers to the petty idle chatter that blossoms in the environs of the Kaiser. They have a simple temperament and shy manners; yet their intellectual faculties

> are highly developed and in proper equilibrium; it is a pleasure to converse with them, and never without its benefits,

... wrote an anonymous French author in 1883, describing an evening at a middle-class home, at which the daughter of the family exhibited her talents on the piano for the assembled guests, after a dinner of roast venison, salad and fruit.

These Berliners got their information from a number of liberal Berlin newspapers, which gained in circulation and coverage. Publishers such as Leopold Ullstein, August Scherl, and Rudolf Mosse, built themselves grand headquarters near the city centre, and often addressed a variety of contemporary political issues in their papers, many of which came in a morning and evening edition. They were sometimes subject to blatant political influences, especially from Chancellor Bismarck himself, who is believed to have financed the newspaper "Deutsche Allgemeine Zeitung, from his own secret funds. Still, most of the new middle class remained largely apolitical. "When it comes to politics, these people are fully as incapable of rendering an opinion and just as indifferent as those in high society," a French observer stated.

Berlin's importance as a capital city could hardly be overlooked. Many elegant impressive buildings sprang up in the centre, while the city's government quarter, including the Reichstag parliament, was completed in 1894 after many delays. Yet many in the middle class had only a very limited interest in the decisions reached there, in part because the freely elected parliament hardly had the power to make real decisions. The real power was held by Kaiser Wilhelm, and his chancellor, Otto von Bismarck.

Far more important to Berliners than politics, and certainly more exciting, were entertainment and consumption. Berliners went to the theatre, opera, and vaudeville shows in great numbers. They marvelled at the first movies with their rattling film reels and accompanying live music, and went out to cafes with dancing, to card-playing clubs, and to amusement parks. These pleasure-seekers could find the programs for such events on advertising pillars erected around the city.

"At regular intervals all through the city are tidy round columns, around 18 feet high and as big around as a large barrel, with small black and white theatre programs and other notices posted on them. You can almost always find a group of people gathered around these columns, reading the notices," noted Mark Twain. New department stores likewise used advertisements to draw attention to the public. These stores presented a previously unheard of range of enticing products under one single roof, such as: dashing men's fashions, racy lingerie, thick carpets, sumptuous fabrics, and furniture. The palace of consumption built on Leipziger Strasse in 1897, by businessman George Wertheim, was even visited by Kaiser Wilhelm II and his wife.

Still, not everyone shared this optimistic view of progress. There were some who felt the city had lost its values, and who could no longer find their way amid the speed and restlessness of the new metropolis. "The older gentlemen and others who valued comfort above all else moaned and complained. They lost one lovely little old house after another. They watched as entire neighbourhoods, in which the Berlin of past centuries had mouldered, were taken away from them, torn down and replaced with newfangled buildings," complained Edmund Edel.

The old Prussian elite watched resentfully as these up-and-comers who were unconcerned with tradition, and many of whom were Jewish, gained high standing in Berlin society, while at the same time, the new middle class feared losing its own social status. Strains of anti-Semitism and anti-modernism crept into this society.

Then there were those who could do no more than cast longing looks at the city's new shop window displays, or dream of its opera premieres: the homeless, the destitute, the neglected working children, the prostitutes – people who had lost their footing within the rapid pace of development and modernism. Berlin was a city under high tension. The economic boom had ignited an explosion, and now all of the city's individual parts were pulling in many directions, straining separately towards the future, and held together only tenuously by the ideals of a German capital. The city didn't manage to find calm. Art critic, journalist, and admirer of Impressionism, Karl Scheffler, summed up the situation of late 19th century Berlin, in one sentence that has been quoted often ever since. Berlin, he wrote, was "damned always to become, and never to be."

After two hours of walking around the streets of central Berlin, I made my way to the government quarter, for my meeting with Heinrich von Kusserow, in the foyer of the Ministry of Foreign Affairs. It was an elegant building with a white marble floor, intricate ceiling, and a prominent chandelier in the centre of the lobby. When I arrived, I told the doorman I was there for a meeting with von Kusserow. I sat on a plush black leather couch as I waited.

'Ah, you must be Luca Evangelista.'

'It is my pleasure to meet you, Heinrich von Kusserow.'

'Now, now, just call me Heinrich, my good man. There is an excellent café nearby. Let's go there to talk.'

As we made our way to the café, I was struck by the number of finely dressed gentlemen earnestly going about their business of moving from one appointment to another. These were civil servants engaged in the precision management of the German government; a bureaucracy that operated like clockwork. When we entered the café, again, I was impressed by the beautiful interior decoration, white marble everywhere, large mirrors with gold frames, leather upholstered furniture, mahogany counter, stunning paintings, and the sweet aroma of the finest coffee.

Kusserow ordered two Turkish coffees, which were very popular in the European cafes of this time, before we made our way to a discrete area at the rear of the café. I had come across this café when conducting my research. It was Café Bauer, one of the first to open in Berlin, in 1877. In addition to the large hall on the ground floor, it also had a billiard room, and reading room, on the upper floor. Coffee houses in Berlin were a man's domain, and they had an air of sleaziness. Female waitresses were exposed to the gaze of men, to whom a woman of class would not expose herself.

This café was decorated with numerous murals; including the six-part cycle "The Roman Life" by Anton von Werner; it was also framed by stucco work by the Berlin sculptor, Otto Lessing. The over 800 European daily newspapers that were on display for the customers, was legendary. The owner, Mathias Bauer spent over 30,000 marks a year on these newspapers; making it a very popular venue for professionals and intellectuals.

'Many diplomats in my department come here to meet. This café has a number of discrete booths like this one, which are perfect for our line of business. Luca, I am very concerned about chancellor Bismarck's motives for the conference of European Powers he has organised, which as you know, starts tomorrow. Bismarck is going to give the impression he wants to acquire colonies in Africa, for Germany. He is going to create some sort of protocol whereby the other European Powers can formalise their pre-existing claims to the African continent, to pave the way for a European Powers grab for Africa. This will result in nothing short of the destruction of many longstanding civilizations, tribal groups, and cultures. Bismarck's real intention is to get the European Powers, particularly Britain and France, distracted, by them devoting a huge proportion of their resources into Africa, while he builds a huge German military machine to threaten them in the heart of Europe, when the time is right'

'When Otto told me you were my contact here in Berlin, I was surprised, Heinrich. The historical sources seem to imply you were very much in support of the colonisation of Africa by the European Powers.'

'No, that is not the case. I am a humanist. This is entirely something Bismarck's fierce ambition has set up, and we must stop it from happening, Luca. If we succeed in stopping this conference from achieving its imperial aims, over 80% of Africa will remain under the control of indigenous Africans, and I suspect that as a result, history will be changed for the better.'

'Heinrich, I have a strategy to sabotage this conference. I think the key to stopping this calamitous chain of events is to convince the two greatest powers in Europe, Britain and France, who have also secured the most prominent presence in Africa to date; that Germany is intent on using its industrial muscle to build a large military force, with the intention of expanding its empire within Europe, by engaging in war with the other European Powers. We need to convince Britain and France that this entire African conference is about Germany distracting the European Powers into putting much of their resources into Africa, thereby weakening their military resources in Europe, making it easier for Germany to achieve its hunger for a dominant position within

Europe. This is something I need to do. I don't want you to be compromised in any way. You are a high level German government official and a proud German citizen. This must not get back to you in any way.'

'Ever since Otto visited me, I have been feeling very anxious about how I can stop this conference from succeeding, without committing any treasonous act myself. Your strategy is very sound, Luca. There is one nation attending the conference, which is also against this grab for Africa succeeding. It is an emerging world power. I am talking about the United States of America. With my assistance behind the scenes, if you can convince the United States delegates that Germany is using this conference as a distraction to cover up its rapid military build-up in Europe, we may be able to convince them to discretely sidestep Germany, and handle the negotiations directly with the British and French.'

We left the Café Bauer and walked the short distance to the Hotel Kaiserhof, one of the finest in Berlin, where Heinrich von Kusserow had arranged for me to stay. It was a luxurious hotel in the centre of the city, located next to the Reich Chancellery, where Bismarck worked from, within the government quarter.

The hotel was founded in 1872, and consisted of 260 elegant rooms, all fitted out in a modern and luxurious manner. It was the first Berlin hotel in which every room had an electricity supply, its own bathroom, and telephone. The hotel also featured steam heating and pneumatic lifts. The upper floor of the hotel became the NAZI party headquarters in 1932, and at the same time was also the residence of Adolf Hitler; an interesting coincidence because I was going to be meeting him in a future time travel mission. During the election campaign of 1932, Adolf Hitler avoided the menu at the Hotel Kaiserhof for fear of being poisoned by rivals or political opponents, and instead was fed by his fanatical admirer, Magda Goebbels, the wife of the Minister of Propaganda, Josef Goebbels; and the woman who murdered her six young children by giving them cyanide capsules in the dying days of the Third Reich, for fear of her children living their lives without Hitler in charge.

Before leaving me at the hotel, Kusserow told me I was invited to the opera that evening. After checking in, I made my way to my room, showered, and lay on the bed, thinking about my research on the two most critical characters in this mission; Heinrich von Kusserow, and Otto von Bismarck.

Heinrich von Kusserow was the son of the Prussian Lieutenant General Ferdinand von Kusserow and his wife, Eveline, a daughter of Salomon Oppenheim. On 27th November 1844, King Friedrich Wilhelm IV raised his father Ferdinand to the hereditary nobility for himself and his family. In 1869 Kusserow married Antonie Springer, daughter of the banker and businessman Ernst Springer.

After becoming a widower, he married Fanny Meyer in 1890, the widow of a merchant. He had a son and five daughters from his first marriage, and a son from his second marriage. Kusserow attended schools in Cologne and Dusseldorf, and then studied law at the University of Bonn. After the usual general preparatory service at the courts, he joined the Prussian Foreign Service. Between 1860 and 1862 he was an attache in the-Hague, then legation secretary in Turin, before moving to the Prussian Foreign Ministry in Berlin.

In 1861, Kusserow anonymously submitted a pamphlet on the peaceful solution of the German question, which contained ideas that Otto von Bismarck later implemented as part of the unification of Germany. In 1863, he sent Bismarck a memorandum proposing the idea of a German central authority and parliament, to which Bismarck reacted with overwhelming approval. Between 1864 and 1865 he was legation secretary at the Prussian Embassy in Paris, and then in Washington DC until 1868. He then worked in the Federal Chancellery of the North German Confederation, before serving as a counsellor for the Embassy of the North German Confederation in London, during the Franco-Prussian War.

After the founding of the unified German nation, Kusserow was elected to the first German Reichstag in 1871, as a member of the Liberal Reich Party. During this period, he also published a paper on International Law as it related to the Sea in times of war. After the end of the legislative period, Kusserow returned to active foreign service in 1874. In the Foreign Office he initially worked in the areas of legation and trade policy. In 1879 he was appointed Privy Councillor of Legation. He was also Federal Commissioner in the Reichstag, and was responsible for international relations.

Kusserow was active in the Ministry of Foreign Affairs within business circles interested in colonial policy, and ultimately he became the head of the colonial department within the ministry. This is when he started working directly with Bismarck, who was very keen to use colonial policy to the advantage of Germany; culminating in the Africa Conference of 1884-1885. Bismarck's aversion to turning Germany into a colonial power is well documented. One of the reasons was the late unification of the country, at a time when the industrialized nations had divided much of the world territory already.

Another reason was that Germany already had enough problems to ensure peace within and outside its borders, and wanted to avoid the risk of entering into a conflict with Britain or France over potential colonies. However, many businessmen did not share the insular opinion of Chancellor Bismarck and persistently asked the government for facilities and protection for the opening of foreign markets. Kusserow was very familiar with this inner circle of the business elite as his two sisters were married to Adolph von Hansemann, the founder of what is today Deutsche Bank; and a steel magnate, respectively. In addition, Kusserow's mother was from the Oppenheim family, one of the most powerful banking dynasties in the world.

So by occupying the position of the Head of Colonial Affairs, Kusserow was in a strong position to influence Bismarck on matters regarding German expansion into Africa. Kusserow was given the role of organising the African Conference of 1884-1885. It was clear to Kusserow though, that this Grab for Africa was going to trigger an arms race; particularly between Britain, France, and Germany; and so he did not want the conference to be a vehicle for the European Powers to take control of Africa. Little was he to know that the Africa Conference would also set in train a chain of events which would ultimately lead to the outbreak of the First World War in 1914.

Bismarck's story is fascinating. He was responsible for transforming a collection of small German states into a unified German nation and empire, and was its first chancellor. Otto Eduard Leopold von Bismarck was born into an aristocratic family at Schonhausen, northwest of Berlin, on 1st April 1815. He attended a prestigious school in Berlin, followed by the University of Gottingen. He then entered the Prussian civil service but was bored by his job, resigning in 1838. For nearly a decade, he helped his father manage the family estates.

In 1847, Bismarck married Johanna von Puttkamer, who provided him with stability. It was a year of significant change in his life, when he also embraced the Christian tradition of Lutheranism, and began his political career in the Prussian legislature, where he gained a reputation as an ultra-conservative royalist. In 1851, King Frederick Wilhelm IV appointed Bismarck as the Prussian representative to the German Confederation. He then served as ambassador to Russia and France. In 1862, he returned to Prussia and was appointed prime minister by the new king, Wilhelm I.

Bismarck was now determined to unite the German states into a single national empire, with Prussia at its core. With Austrian support, he used the expanded Prussian army to capture the provinces of Schleswig and Holstein from Denmark. He then escalated a dispute with Austria and its German allies over the administration of these provinces, into a war, in which Prussia was victorious. Prussia then proceeded to annex further territory within Germany.

Unable to persuade the southern German states led by Bavaria to join with his North German Confederation, he provoked hostilities with France as a way of uniting the German states against a common enemy. The German victory in the Franco-Prussian War, won over the southern German states, and in 1871 they agreed to join a unified German nation and empire. Wilhelm I of Prussia became emperor.

As chancellor of the new Germany, Bismarck concentrated on building a powerful state with a unified national identity. One of his targets was the Catholic Church, which he believed had too much influence, particularly in southern Germany. He also worked hard to prevent the spread of socialism, partly by introducing health insurance and pensions. When it came to international matters, Bismarck aimed to make the German empire the most powerful in Europe. In 1879, he negotiated an alliance with Austria-Hungary to counteract the influence and power of France and Russia. Italy later joined the alliance. In 1884-1885 he of course presided over the Africa Conference, determined to distractingly coax the European Powers into expending military and economic resources in Africa, while he oversaw a German military build-up at home.

To avoid alienating Britain, Bismarck arranged the two Mediterranean Agreements of 1887, designed to preserve the status quo, against a Russian threat. In 1890, Bismarck resigned after ideological and policy differences with the new emperor, Wilhelm II. He retired to his estate near Hamburg and died there on 30th July 1898. He was 83 years old. As a rebellious youth he had been a heavy drinker, womanizer, a bully, and militarist; but he could also be charming and sympathetic. He had been a giant of European power politics until forced to resign when he had become too much of a reactionary for the imperial regime of Wilhelm II to stomach. When his wife Johanna died in her sleep in November 1894, the "iron chancellor" cried like a child. He spent his final years alone, resentful, pessimistic, and desperately bored. He had his huge black mastiff dogs for company, and visits from his family – sons and daughter, sister, niece, and daughter in law.

He felt far too young to do nothing, but he could find nothing to do except write his memoirs, in which he soon lost interest. "Bored" or "tired" he wrote over and over again in his diary, or "bored and tired." Kaiser Wilhelm II came to see him in December 1897 ("to see how long the old man will last") and there was forced politeness on both sides. Bismarck was confined to a wheelchair, and as the summer of 1898 rolled on, he developed an inflammation of the lungs. He had difficulty breathing and lay in his bed most of the time, talking or singing quietly to himself.

On 30th July he had a relapse and the family gathered around his bed that night as he mumbled distractedly. At last he took a glass of his favourite wine, drank it completely, cried "Vorwarts" ("Forward"), and sank down on his pillow. At around 11pm his daughter saw that he was no longer breathing. The Kaiser arrived on 2nd August to find the old statesman's coffin in a bedroom crammed with wreaths and flowers. He issued a statement honouring "the man in whom the Lord God created the instrument for realisation of the immortal idea of Germany's unity and greatness".

There was no state funeral. The instrument of Germany's greatness was buried in a tomb at his family estate at Friedrichsruh, with an inscription he had dictated, describing himself laconically as "a loyal German servant of Kaiser Wilhelm I." The first Wilhelm, not the second. It was a pointed rebuke from beyond the grave. As always, he would have the last word.

After resting in my room and freshening up, I made my way down to the lobby a little early to enjoy a glass of red wine at the bar before meeting with Heinrich. The bar was full of civil servants and businessmen. I was going to see "The Marriage of Figaro" at the Berlin State Opera House. While I was at the bar enjoying my wine, a man approached me.

'Are you Luca Evangelista?'

'Yes, I am. Who are you, sir?'

'My name is James Crompton. I am with the American delegation, here for the conference. My boss has been talking with your boss, Heinrich von Kusserow. Can we meet at the gardens behind this hotel, near the grand fountain, tomorrow morning at 10am? Please don't tell anybody we have met. Not even your boss. I have some important information I want to share with you tomorrow.'

With that, Crompton left the bar and vanished into the night.

Heinrich's timing was perfect. As he arrived, I was finishing up my glass of fine wine. I wasn't sure what was more impressive, the wine, or the crystal glass it came in. And what a nice touch to include fine dark chocolate with the wine! I decided to honour Crompton's request, and not tell Heinrich anything about the encounter and my meeting tomorrow morning. I assumed he would tell me what was going on, when he was ready to.

'It's good to see you are ready, Luca. The opera house is only a short walk away. With our overcoats, scarves, hats, and gloves on, we will be comfortable to walk in the cool breeze outside.'

'The Berlin State Opera House has an interesting history, doesn't it Heinrich?' I casually asked as we made our way from the hotel and into the chilly, dimly lit streets.

'Oh yes! It certainly does. The Berlin State Opera House was built in 1741 by the order of Frederick the Great himself, and staged its first performance, Carl Heinrich Graun's "Caesar and Cleopatra" in 1742, while the opera house was still being completed. It is a majestic theatre, built in the thrilling Prussian classicist style, and with a decadent Rococo interior. It is the most elegant opera house in Europe. In 1843 the building was destroyed by a fire of unknown cause; but reopened a few years later, after a total reconstruction.'

When we arrived at the opera house I wasn't surprised to see we were seated in the more secluded Royal VIP section, higher up, overlooking the rest of the audience and the stage; and who was seated alongside us? Well, there was Otto von Bismarck of course, and a number of other high level government officials who were part of the entourage. Heinrich introduced me to Bismarck and the others.

Before the performance, emotions ran high as the German national anthem was played. I couldn't get Hitler and the NAZI's out of my head! After the formalities we enjoyed a wonderful operatic performance of Figaro! The house was full. As I scanned the audience, it was obvious to me that the majority of people in attendance were from the nobility and upper-middle classes. I had read about how elegantly people in the 19th century dressed when they went to the opera. I wasn't let down. There were even well dressed and behaved children in the audience! The people were immaculately attired in dinner suits and silk gowns. The jewellery was dazzling as tiaras, rings, bracelets, and necklaces, glistened from the light of the grand chandeliers, dominating the opera house.

During the performance, Bismarck seemed quite uncomfortable with my presence, and kept looking at me with a stern expression. Heinrich had told him I was his nephew, but I could tell he was suspicious of me right from the outset. I needed to tread carefully. For all I knew, he may have arranged for someone to watch my movements already.

'Are you here for the conference, Herr Evangelista?'

Bismarck immediately engaged me with his eyes. I felt an uneasiness. As if he could peer directly into my soul. I couldn't help thinking: What is it with these world famous men, and their piercing eyes!?

'Yes sir. I am interested in pursuing a career in the diplomatic service, and thought this conference would be a golden opportunity for me to see European diplomacy at its best – overseen by a great statesman, in you Herr Bismarck.'

Well, that comment had its intended effect. Bismarck was taken aback by what I said – but soaked it all in, and loved the compliment – as all powerful men do. That was the extent of my conversation with him. But I definitely felt I was in the presence of a great man, as I continued to enjoy the rest of the opera.

I awoke early the next morning, went for a jog around the streets close to the hotel, and then had a continental breakfast in the dining room, before making my way to the grand fountain in the gardens at the rear of the hotel. There was nobody to be seen when I sat on a bench directly in front of the fountain. After a short wait, David Crompton approached, and sat alongside me.

'So Luca, tell me, how did you become involved in this conference?'

'My uncle Heinrich suggested I attend, to gain valuable political and diplomatic experience. I am looking to start a career in the diplomatic service.'

'I see. Well, your uncle speaks very highly of you. He has been secretly meeting with my boss, John Kasson, the American lead negotiator at this conference. You are no doubt aware, the United States does not want the African continent to be overrun by the European Powers. We are here in Berlin, to stop this from happening. We also do not want Germany to become a major military power to the extent of threatening the peace of Europe. At first, we were very surprised when von Kasserow approached us. We assumed, like the rest of the world, that Germany had arranged this conference to get a meaningful slice of African colonies, as well as setting some ground rules for the European conquest of Africa, so that the European Powers don't get into a conflict over Africa. But after checking out his story, we learnt that he indeed shares our concerns about European imperialism in Africa. We understand Bismarck is pursuing a strategy of coaxing the European Powers into African colonies, so while they invest heavy resources into colonial adventures, the German nation can strengthen its military capacity to exercise major control and power on the European continent. Bismarck doesn't want a major presence in Africa for Germany. It's an interesting strategy. I have arranged for my boss, and the British and French lead negotiators, to meet with you and I, this evening at 7pm, at the American Embassy. Will you be there, Luca?'

'I certainly will be there. What role do you want me to play?'

'I am confident the British and French will take us seriously. They will understand we both have access to highly sensitive and confidential information, and that we speak on behalf of our diplomatic superiors and political leaders. We will clearly state the real strategy Bismarck is pursuing here. A strategy which will lead to the total conquest and destruction of Africa; and a significant arming of Germany to a level in which it will represent a real threat to the peace in Europe.'

After the meeting with Crompton, I hurriedly made my way to the African Conference which was being held at Chancellor Bismarck's official residence in central Berlin. I wanted to hear Bismarck's opening address to the delegates. I was duly disappointed with the speech. It was very guarded, diplomatic in nature, and of course, gave nothing away of his true intentions.

What was at stake if this conference succeeded? The best summation of the results and legacy of the Berlin meeting of the European Powers, I felt, was that given in 1915 by W.E.B. DuBois, an African American scholar and activist, who revealed that the Congress of Berlin was already having an impact on Africa weeks before the first group of delegates arrived in Germany. What he stated, as quoted here, really went to the core of why I needed to succeed in this mission to stop the European grab for colonies in Africa.

DuBois wrote: "The Berlin Conference to apportion the rising riches of Africa among the white peoples first met on the fifteenth day of November, 1884. Eleven days earlier, three Germans left Zanzibar (whither they had gone secretly disguised as mechanics), and before the Berlin Conference had finished its deliberations they had annexed to Germany an area over half as large again as the whole German Empire in Europe. Only in its dramatic suddenness was this undisguised robbery of the land of seven million natives different from the methods by which Great Britain and France got four million square miles each, Portugal three quarters of a million, and Italy and Spain smaller but substantial areas. The methods by which this continent has been stolen have been contemptible and dishonest beyond expression. Lying treaties, rivers of rum, murder, assassination, mutilation, rape, and torture have marked the progress of Englishmen, German, Frenchman, and Belgian on the dark continent. The only way in which the world has been able to endure the horrible tale is by deliberately stopping its ears and changing the subject of conversation while the deviltry went on. It all began, singularly enough...with Belgium. Many of us remember Henry Stanley's great solution of the puzzle of Central Africa, when he traced the mighty Congo sixteen hundred miles from Nyangwe to the sea. Suddenly the world knew that here lay the key to the riches of Central Africa. It stirred uneasily, but King Leopold of Belgium was first on his feet, and the result was the Congo Free State. But the Congo Free State, with all its magniloquent heralding of Peace, Christianity, and Commerce, degenerating into murder, mutilation, and downright robbery, differed only in degree and concentration from the tale of all Africa in this rape of the continent already furiously mangled by the slave trade. That sinister traffic, on which the British Empire and the American Republic were largely built, cost black Africa no less than 100,000,000 souls, the wreckage of its political and social life, and left the continent in precisely that state of helplessness which invites aggression and exploitation. "Colour" became in the world's thought synonymous with inferiority, "Negro" lost its capitalization, and Africa was another name for bestiality and barbarism. Thus, the world began to invest in colour prejudice. The "Colour Line" began to pay dividends. For indeed, while the exploitation of the valley of the Congo was the occasion of the Scramble for Africa, the cause lay deeper. Already England was in Africa, cleaning away the debris of the slave trade and half consciously groping toward the new Imperialism. France, humiliated and impoverished, looked toward a new northern African empire, sweeping from the Atlantic to the Red Sea. More slowly, Germany began to see the dawning of a new day, and, shut out from America by the Monroe Doctrine, looked to Asia and Africa for colonies. Portugal sought anew to make good her claim to her ancient African realm; and thus a continent where Europe claimed but a tenth of the land in 1875, was in twenty-five more years practically absorbed."

After spending a depressing day witnessing the sheer greed of the European Colonial Powers as they horse-traded for possessions in Africa, I began to look forward to the meeting that evening with David Crompton, his superior, the head of the US delegation, John Kasson, and the British and French diplomats. I arrived at the American Embassy at 6.50pm. Five minutes later, David greeted me and led me into a secure room, where three men were seated.

'Luca Evangelista, may I introduce you to my boss John Kasson, Edward Malet from Britain, and Alphonse de Courcel from France.'

John Kasson was a lawyer, politician and diplomat from the US state of Iowa. He was elected to the House of Representatives six times, but repeatedly interrupted his congressional role to serve as a diplomat in many different capacities. Edward Malet came from a family of diplomats, and was a member of the Tory-sympathetic Lyons School of British diplomacy. Alphonse de Courcel was the French ambassador to Germany, and a highly skilled negotiator. After greetings and formalities, I proceeded to speak.

'Gentlemen, we are here to avert a major disaster, for Africa, and for Europe. Chancellor Otto von Bismarck has set a trap by organising this conference. He is hoping to put in place a protocol and framework so the major European Powers, particularly your countries, will deploy substantial resources acquiring colonies in Africa; stripping the diverse cultures, traditions, and self-determination of the African peoples for centuries to come, in the process. Meanwhile, Bismarck aims to engage in a major economic expansion and military build-up within Germany to rival and then exceed your two nations, to the point when Germany will provoke a conflict with Britain and France for control of Europe. This is his true objective, gentlemen. To avert this threat, your nations need to remain strong in Europe. To achieve this, you need to concentrate your resources on strengthening your respective economies and military power in Europe, to counterbalance Germany; rather than going down the rabbit hole of engaging in colonisation and imperialism in Africa. It is imperative you get this message through to your highest level of government, otherwise I fear war with Germany in Europe will happen within the next twenty-five years.'

It seemed that my plea to the Americans, British, and French, in conjunction with the highly confidential intelligence Heinrich von Kasserow provided them, had done the job. After frantic rounds of negotiations, within a month of our meeting, all three nations announced they would no longer continue to participate in the Berlin Conference, and issued a strong statement condemning any attempts by the European Powers to carve up Africa by exploiting the valuable resources and the peoples of the continent.

Britain and France announced they had no intention of acquiring further colonies in Africa. The message had come through loud and clear. Germany was intent on building up a significant military presence in Europe, and the only way to stop this threat, was for Britain and France in particular to deploy all of their significant economic and military resources within Europe, counteracting the German threat. The European Powers couldn't afford embarking on very costly colonial ventures in Africa. Imperialism had been dealt a major body blow.

Again, Otto arrived at the piano bar before me! I don't know why this fazed me. Maybe I felt more relaxed arriving first and having at least one gin and tonic to calm my nerves. I never got over my anxiety in the presence of Otto. He was not from this world. His whole manner of being was wired totally different to any human on this planet. I always felt like he knew more about the future of the planet than he was letting on to me. Something amazing happened when I arrived this time. Otto was drinking a gin and tonic!

'I thought you didn't drink alcohol?'

'Well no. I never said I couldn't drink alcohol. It's just we are unfamiliar with this substance, where I come from.'

'So your curiosity got the better of you?'

'We don't possess this emotion you call curiosity, Luca.'

'Otto, I am curious about something.?

'You humans are always curious. I believe you have a saying about curiosity killing the cat?'

'I'm curious about why I haven't encountered Thero in my recent travels.'

'Luca, Thero has been watching every single move you have been making. He knows you are expecting to encounter him. He has been expecting you to show your vulnerability and frailty as a human, and for you to stumble and eventually fail. Of course, because you haven't failed yet, he is definitely formulating a big plan to stop you in some future period. He wants you to fail monumentally. You can be certain of this. Always stay on guard for his unexpected arrival.'

'Luca! Is it you? Well fancy bumping into you here!?'

It was my high school girlfriend, Anita. I literally hadn't seen or heard from her since I left school nearly 20 years ago. I had been dating her before I hooked up with my ex-wife, Connie. Anita and Connie were best friends, and Anita was shattered when I stopped seeing her and started dating Connie. Anita seemed intoxicated.

'Anita! It's great to see you after all of this time. Have you been well?'

'Not too good actually. My husband was cheating on me, so I kicked him out of the house, last week. I'm a free spirit now! You know my husband. He went to high school with us.'

'Not Jimmy!?

'Yes Jimmy. When you dumped me, I finally relented and went out on a date with him. Remember? You know how much he pursued me. Anyhow, when you didn't want me anymore, I started going out with him, and the rest as they say, is history. I married him Luca! I married that no-good scum of a man! Can you believe that!?"

I could see Otto was enjoying this encounter, even though he seemed slightly bemused, while sipping on his gin and tonic with a straw.

'You know you were the love of my life, don't you Luca? Hey, I'm sorry it didn't work out with Connie, by the way. I bumped into her a couple of weeks ago. We agreed to keep in touch, and are catching up for dinner next Wednesday night.'

'That's great! You guys were always close.'

'I just want you to know that you broke my heart when you dumped me, and it hasn't mended since. Goodbye Luca.'

And with that, she went back to join her girlfriends at the other end of the bar.

'Sorry about that Otto.'

'Why are you sorry? I found the whole encounter very interesting. Now, let me debrief you about the European Powers and Africa. As a result of Britain, France, and the United States pulling out of the Berlin Conference; the three powers formed an alliance specifically aimed at containing the military power and ambitions of Germany. Britain and France did not expand their presence in Africa, and in fact, by the early 20th century, pulled out of Africa completely, even though they maintained their colonies in other parts of the world. Of course, the jewel in the crown for Britain was India, and for France it was Indochina. But it gets even better, Luca. In this multiverse version of the Earth; Britain, France, and the United States played a significant role in investing in, and developing, Africa; and also sowed the seeds for the spread of parliamentary democracy there. As a result, by the mid-20th century, 10 great stable democratic nations emerged along ethnic and cultural lines, in this continent. Africa became as economically prosperous as Asia, by the 21st century. Unfortunately, Germany believed it was being isolated by the three great powers, and did nevertheless become militarily strong enough to launch the First World War, in the 1930s! This was a prolonged war which Germany ultimately lost. There was no Second World War.'

'That's very interesting Otto. From now on, I'm going to be on much more familiar turf, because I will be travelling into the 20th century for the next few missions. With all the technology and sophistication that goes with this century though, and with a very determined Thero on the loose, I feel my missions are going to get much tougher and harder from now on.'

'I think you have assessed that correctly, Luca. I quite like these gin and tonics by the way. I am fascinated by this thing called love that you humans possess. I learnt tonight that love can linger for many years, even when a person has been rejected by the object of their love.'

'Love definitely works in mysterious ways Otto. And even though it's been part of the human condition since the earliest days of our species, we still don't understand it.'

'Well, we have not quite encountered love, in the manner it applies to humans, in any of the other hundreds of alien civilizations we have made contact with, Luca.'

'Otto, speaking of love, can I ask a special favour of you?'

'What is it, Luca?'

'As you know, my father died recently; suddenly, and in tragic circumstances. I am missing him deeply. I have had recurring dreams of my childhood, and the many fond memories I have with my Dad. A favourite one, is him teaching me how to kick a soccer ball in the park across the road where we lived, when I was three years old.'

'Do you know, Luca, in spite of our advanced technology, my people do not possess the ability to dream. In fact, we have not encountered any other civilizations that possess this ability.'

'That's fascinating. Otto, would it be possible for me to utilise the wormhole in between missions, to travel back in time, to when I was three years old, and observe my Dad kicking a soccer ball with me?'

'No, Luca. The wormhole cannot be used by travellers to observe themselves at a younger, or older age, for that matter. We have never actually tried to do this. But our computer modelling tells us it would cause a major unpredictable cataclysm in the fabric of time and space, that could have a potentially catastrophic adverse impact on the future of your Earth, as well as multiple other versions of your planet in multi-verses.'

'Oh, I see.'

Otto was looking at me with obvious puzzlement, as tears began to well in my eyes.

'Can I use the wormhole to stop Isabella's uncle from molesting her?'

'No, Luca. The wormhole cannot be used to change the life of anybody related to you; or anybody who has an emotional connection with you.'

Tears were now freely flowing down my cheeks. I didn't try to wipe them off.

'What you can do, Luca, is travel back in time to observe your father at any time before you were born. You will be able to speak with him, but you cannot tell him you are his son, of course.'

My eyes lit up! I screamed with joy; jumped out of my seat, and gave Otto a big kiss on the cheek!

Ship of Fools

We're setting sail to the place on the map
From which no one has ever returned
Drawn by the promise of the joker and the fool
By the light of the crosses that burned
Drawn by the promise of the women and the lace
And the gold and the cotton and the pearls
It's the place where they keep all the darkness you need
You sail away from the light of the world on this trip, baby

You will pay tomorrow
You're gonna pay tomorrow
You will pay tomorrow

Oh, oh, oh
Save me, save me from tomorrow
I don't want to sail with this ship of fools, no, no
Oh, save me, save me from tomorrow
I don't want to sail with this ship of fools, no, no
I want to run and hide right now

Avarice and greed are gonna drive you over the endless sea
They will leave you drifting in the shallows
Or drowning in the oceans of history
Travelling the world, you're in search of no good
But I'm sure you'll build your Sodom like you knew you would
Using all the good people for your galley slaves
As your little boat struggles through the warning waves,
but you don't pay

You will pay tomorrow
You're gonna pay tomorrow, yeah
You're gonna pay tomorrow

Save me, save me from tomorrow
I don't want to sail with this ship of fools, no, no, no
Save me, save me from tomorrow
I don't want to sail with this ship of fools
Where's it comin' from?
Oh, where's it goin' to?
It's just a, it's just a ship of fools

All aboard now

Karl Edmond De Vere Wallinger – World Party (1987)

9

Franz Ferdinand

Sarajevo, Bosnia, June 1914 CE

After leaving Otto at the bar, I called in to see Isabella. When I arrived, I found her to be very upset. I felt uneasy about leaving Isabella on her own while undertaking the time travel missions. She was emotionally fragile and vulnerable. After attending many auditions, nothing was happening with her acting and theatrical performing career. She was alienated from her mother and other close family members. Her friends had noticed she was behaving oddly, and always in dark moods.

'What's the matter sweet baby girl? Please don't shut me out of your life. I know you are hurting. Talk to me.'

'I don't know why I'm existing, Luca. There's no purpose to my life. I'm waking up most mornings and feeling down even before my days begin. I don't feel I belong in this world. Do you understand me?'

'You've got me, honey! You've got me! We have each other. What we share is so special. It won't be long before these time travel missions will be over, and then we can resume building a wonderful life for each other.'

'I think what you're doing to make the future better, is wonderful, baby. You are my hero. I am in constant fear of your safety, of course. But I am so incredibly proud of you. I am deeply in love with you Luca. I know you feel the same about me too. This is not about you, our relationship, or our future together. It's about this guttural empty feeling which has taken hold of me in a vice-like grip and won't let me go.'

'Sweetheart, we have discussed getting help. I think you need to see a clinical psychologist, so hopefully we can get to the bottom of what this is, which is making you feel so depressed.'

'No!!! I've already told you a thousand times!! I'm not going to place myself in a system which puts labels on vulnerable people, and then turns them into a psychological condition, fed by pharmaceuticals, designed to make people comfortably numb! My emotions! My passions! My creative energy! They all come from deep within me! I'm not going to have that energy force taken out of me Luca! I will deal with my state of mind in my own way. I will be fine. You don't need to worry about me.'

I felt so saddened seeing her react in this way. She clearly needed help. I was becoming very concerned for her well-being and state of mental health. I feared she may become suicidal. My worst nightmare was Isabella crying out to me for help, and taking her own life, while I was on a time travel mission. I wouldn't be able to help her. I was so concerned that I had arranged for her best friend, Jane, to keep an eye on her; but Isabella, being so fiercely independent, asked Jane to back-off.

As emotionally fragile as she was, Isabella could also be incredibly strong, and protective of me. I remember one memorable New Year's evening a couple of years ago, we had been invited to a formal dinner party by a wealthy friend of hers. I even had to hire a tuxedo – something a working class boy like me can never get accustomed to. Anyhow, during the evening, a couple of thirty-something year old pompous arrogant stockbrokers seated opposite us, struck up a conversation with Isabella.

'Honey, has anybody told you that you have the most gorgeous blue eyes?' said one of them, clearly full of red wine.

'I get that all the time from sleazy guys like you,' was Isabella's instinctive response.

I felt an overwhelming urge to intervene, but I didn't. I knew Isabella usually handled these situations with her customary gusto.

'What are you doing with a nerdy schoolteacher? We can show you how to live the life of your dreams.' said the other one, also intoxicated.

'You mean you can show off all of your toys to me? Do you take me for a fool? Do you honestly think I would give up an intelligent, caring, sensitive, strong protective man, who is my rock; for a couple of superficial shallow dickheads like you?'

I couldn't help it. I just burst out laughing, while the two "dickheads" left the table and weren't to be seen by us for the remainder of the evening.

When I finally arrived home later that evening, I reviewed my notes about the assassination of Franz Ferdinand, making sure I understood the sequence of events, leading up to this dire act. I was due to travel back to Sarajevo tomorrow, arriving there at 9am on the 28th June 1914, the day of the assassination. My contact person was Franz von Harrach, Franz Ferdinand's bodyguard and close friend. My mission was to prevent the assassination from happening, and therefore averting a chain of events which culminated in the First World War.

On 28th June 1914, Gavrilo Princip, a Serbian nationalist, assassinated the Austrian heir to the throne, Archduke Franz Ferdinand and his pregnant wife Sophie, in the Bosnian capital, Sarajevo. This outrageous act of brutality was aimed at undermining the Austro-Hungarian Empire which had annexed Bosnia into its multi ethnic realm in 1908. The murder of the royal couple ushered in the so-called July Crisis which ended with the outbreak of the First World War in August 1914. The assassination has been described as the spark that would set light to a continent already riddled with international tensions. However, a European war was not inevitable. Right up to the last moment, some European statesmen were desperately trying to avoid an escalation of the crisis by advocating meditation, while others did everything in their power to ensure that a war would break out.

The murder of the Archduke caused widespread international outrage, even though assassinations of prominent individuals were rather more common at that time than they are today. For example, the Austrian Emperor himself, Kaiser Franz Joseph, nearly succumbed to an assassin in Sarajevo in May 1910; while an Italian anarchist had murdered his wife, Empress Elizabeth, in 1898. Other royal assassination victims included the Serbian King Alexander and his wife, in 1903; the Italian King Umberto, in 1900; and the Greek King George I, in 1913. However, we do not remember these acts of violence because their consequences were less serious; on the other hand, we remember the date and place of this infamous assassination in Sarajevo because the events that followed it led directly to the First World War.

The six assassins can be traced back to the Serbian capital Belgrade, where each of the young men who waited for the hapless Archduke in Sarajevo along the pre-published official route, were radicalised by

Serbian nationalist organizations. Serbia had been a threat and irritant to Austria-Hungary, particularly since it won the Balkan Wars of 1912 and 1913, and as a consequence had nearly doubled its territory, and increased its population from 3 to 4.5 million. The government's aim was to unite even more Serbian territory and people with Serbia; and those people happened to live in multi-ethnic Austria-Hungary, including Bosnia, which had been annexed by Austria-

Hungary in 1908.

Three of the young conspirators had left impoverished lives in Sarajevo for Belgrade. Trifko Grabez, Nedeljko Cabrinovic, and Gavrilo Princip, were all members of the revolutionary organisation Mlada Bosna (Young Bosnia). In the Serbian capital they succumbed to the anti-Habsburg propaganda of several underground organisations such as the Black Hand, a conspiratorial officers' group which stood for the idea of a greater Serbia. In the Austrian capital Vienna, the assassination was immediately perceived as a Serbian provocation, even though actual evidence of Serbian involvement in the plot was hard to come by.

It was not known at the time that one of the instigators of this act was indeed a member of the Serbian establishment; the head of the Serbian military intelligence service, Dragutin Dimitrijevic (also known as Apis), and members of the Black Hand were behind the assassination, just as they had been behind the unsuccessful attempt to kill Kaiser Franz Joseph in 1910. The would-be assassins were trained in the use of weapons in Belgrade, and equipped with four revolvers and six small bombs from the Serbian state arsenal in Kragujevac. In Bosnia, they were joined by three more conspirators; Danilo Ilic, Veljko Cubrilovic, and Civijetko Popovic. The youngest in their group was only 17.

They lined up along the previously announced route that Franz Ferdinand and his wife would take on that Sunday morning, travelling from the train station to the Sarajevo Town Hall. However, the first attempt to kill the Archduke failed. Nedeljko Cabrinovic threw his bomb on the Appel Quay, but it bounced off the open convertible car. It exploded underneath the car behind, injuring a few of the passengers and some spectators. The Archduke was unharmed, while his wife suffered a small wound to her cheek. The couple were hurriedly taken to the Town Hall, and this could have been the end of it all – another failed assassination attempt, just like all the earlier ones. But Franz Ferdinand ignored advice to cancel the rest of the tour, and insisted the couple visited some of the injured in the hospital before continuing with the official program.

As a compromise, it was agreed that the convoy should follow a different route and not, as planned, travel down Franz-Joseph-Strasse. However, tragically, this change of plan appears not to have been communicated to the driver in the first car, who turned into the street as previously arranged. In the hastily conducted reverse manoeuvre, the Archduke's car came to a halt right in front of Gavrilo Princip who had positioned himself, by chance, at the exact same spot.

A few metres away from his target, Princip managed to shoot the Archduke in the neck, and his wife in the abdomen. Sophie died in the car, and Franz Ferdinand died shortly after reaching the residence of the Governor. The conspirators could not know, and certainly had not planned, that a world war would result from this act of violence; but in the weeks that followed, a series of decisions were made in Europe's capitals that ensured the death of this one man would be the trigger for the deaths of millions.

I arrived at the Sarajevo Railway Station at 9am on the 28th June 1914. It was a tight schedule. The royal train carrying Archduke Franz Ferdinand, his wife Sophie, who was the Duchess of Hohenburg, and his entourage including my contact, Franz von Harrach, was due to arrive at the station from Ilidze Bosnia, at 9.50am. The motorcade was to leave the station at 10.10, pass by the army barracks, and arrive at the Sarajevo Town Hall at 10.30am. It was during this time interval when the six assassins were supposed to strike. From 10.40 to 11.40am the royal couple were scheduled to open and tour the State Museum.

This was then going to be followed by a lavish lunch at the governor's residence from noon to 2pm, after which the couple were to return to the railway station. I knew that while I was waiting for the train to arrive, the assassins were in their respective positions along the route to be taken by the motorcade. It was going to be impossible to change the route. History needed to take its course on this journey, including the attempt to blow the royal couple up.

What I was here to stop, was the route of the second journey from the Town Hall to the hospital, which Franz Ferdinand insisted on doing, to visit the people injured by the bomb blast. I was hoping this was going to be the shortest of my time travel missions to date. Arrive in the morning, stop the assassination, and then get back to the 21st century by the end of the day. On this mission, I was taking on the role of an additional bodyguard appointed by Franz von Harrach, and would be riding in the car with the royal couple and von Harrach. I had studied the map of the route relentlessly and knew exactly where each of the six assassins were positioned. There weren't going to be any surprises for me on this first journey because I knew exactly what was about to unfold.

While I waited at the station, I collected my thoughts about Franz von Harrach. He was the son of Alfred Karl Graf von Harrach, and his wife Princess Anna von Lobkowicz, who were large landowners in Janowitz, including the owners of a glassworks business. Harrach became a member of the Austro-Hungarian royal household and was stationed at the main palace. During his time there he developed a close friendship with the Archduke Franz Ferdinand, becoming one of his most trusted advisers, and a bodyguard; accompanying him on many trips, including the fateful journey to Sarajevo.

On Sunday, 28th June, 1914, Harrach, as a member of the Voluntary Automobile Corps, provided Franz Ferdinand with his six-seater double Phaeton automobile, for the ride through the streets of central Sarajevo. The planned route started from the railway station, to the "defensive camp" of the Austro-Hungarian army on the outskirts of the city, and then onto the Town Hall; and from there to the State Museum, and then for a lavish lunch at the Konak of Sarajevo, the official residence of the governor of Bosnia and Herzegovina. In the back of the royal vehicle would be seated Archduke Franz Ferdinand and his wife Sophie; in front of them, on folding seats, were the governor Oskar Potiorek, and the adjutant Franz von Harrach. In the front seats sat the chauffeur-driver, Leopold Lojka, and the court chamber rifleman, Gustav Schneiberg, who wore a gala uniform.

During the trial of the assassins, Harrach indicated that he clearly heard a shot during the first attack before the bomb fell. He also said that before the second assassination attempt he stood on the running board of the automobile on the side of the quay, when driving from the Town Hall, to cover the royal couple with his body in the event a bullet was fired from the bank.

In his testimony, Harrach stated: "When we came to the bend in the road leading to Franz-Josef-Strasse, shots were fired, but from the opposite side where I was not standing. As the car quickly reversed, a thin stream of blood spurted from His Highness's mouth onto my right cheek. As I was pulling out my handkerchief to wipe the blood away from his mouth, the Duchess cried out to him, 'For God's sake! What has happened to you?' At that, she slid off the seat and lay on the floor of the car, with her face between his knees. I had no idea that she too was hit and thought she had simply fainted with fright. Then I heard His Imperial Highness say, 'Sophie, Sophie, don't die. Stay alive for the children!' At that, I seized the Archduke by the collar of his uniform, to stop his head dropping forward, and asked him if he was in great pain. He answered me quite distinctly, 'It is nothing!' His face began to twist somewhat, but he went on repeating, six or seven times, ever more faintly as he gradually lost consciousness, 'It's nothing!' then came a brief pause followed by a convulsive rattle in his throat, caused by a loss of blood. This ceased on arrival at the governor's residence. The two unconscious bodies were carried into the building where their death was soon established."

I had gained a valuable insight into the motivations of the assassins, from this eyewitness account given by Bonjove Jevtic, one of the leaders of the Black Hand, the terrorist arm of the Serbian Nationalist Organisation, Narodna Odbrana: "A tiny clipping from a newspaper, mailed without comment from a secret band of terrorists in Zagreb, capital of Croatia, to their comrades in Belgrade, was the torch which set the world afire with war in 1914. That bit of paper wrecked old, proud empires. It gave birth to new, free nations. I was one of the members of the terrorist band in Belgrade which received it. The little clipping declared that the Austrian Archduke Francis Ferdinand would visit Sarajevo, the capital of Bosnia, June 28, to direct army manoeuvers in the neighbouring mountains. It reached our meeting place, the café called Zlatna Moruna, one night the latter part of April, 1914. To understand how great a sensation that little piece of paper caused among us when it was passed from hand to hand almost in silence, and how greatly it inflamed our hearts, it is necessary to explain just why the Narodna Odbrana existed, the kind of men that were in it, and the significance of that date, June 28, on which the Archduke dared to enter Sarajevo. As everyone knows, the old Austrio-Hungarian Empire was built by conquest and intrigues, by sales and treacheries, which held men of the upper classes were ardent patriots. They were dissimilar in everything except hatred of the oppressor. Such were the men into whose hands the tiny bit of newsprint was sent by friends in Bosnia that April night in Belgrade. At a small table in a very humble café, beneath a flickering gas jet we sat and read it. There was no advice nor admonition sent with it. Only four letters and two numerals were sufficient to make us unanimous, without discussion, as to what we should do about it. They were connived in Sarajevo all the twenty-two conspirators were in their allotted positions, armed and ready. They were distributed five hundred yards apart over the whole route along which the Archduke must travel from the railroad station to the Town Hall. When Francis Ferdinand and his retinue drove from the station they were allowed to pass the first two conspirators. The motor cars were driving too fast to make an attempt feasible and in the crowd were many Serbians; throwing a grenade would have killed many innocent people. When the car passed Gabrinovic, the compositor, he threw his grenade. It hit the side of the car, but Francis Ferdinand with presence of mind threw himself back and was uninjured. Several officers riding in his attendance were injured. The cars sped to the Town Hall and the rest of the conspirators did not interfere with them. After the reception in the Town Hall, General Potiorek, the Austrian Commander, pleaded with Francis Ferdinand to leave the city, as it was seething with rebellion. The Archduke was persuaded to drive the shortest way out of the city and to go quickly. The road to the manoeuvers was shaped like the letter V, making a sharp turn at the bridge over the River Milgacka. Francis Ferdinand's car could go fast enough until it reached this spot, but here it was forced to slow down for the turn. Here Princip had taken his stand. As the car came abreast, he stepped forward from the curb, drew his automatic pistol from his coat and fired two shots. The first struck the wife of the Archduke, the Archduchess Sofia, in the abdomen. She was an expectant mother. She died instantly. The second bullet struck the Archduke close to the heart. He uttered only one word, "Sofia", a call to his stricken wife. Then his head fell back and he collapsed. He died almost instantly. The officers seized Princip. They beat him over the head with the flat of their swords. They knocked him down, they kicked him, scraped the skin from his neck with the edges of their swords, tortured him, all but killed him. The next day they put chains on Princip's feet, which he wore till his death. I was placed in the cell next to Princip's, and when Princip was taken out to walk in the prison yard, I was taken along as his companion. Awakened in the middle of the night and told that he was to be carried off to another prison, Princip made an appeal to the prison governor. 'There is no need to carry me to another prison. My life is already ebbing away. I suggest that you nail me to a cross and burn me alive. My flaming body will be a torch to light my people on their path to freedom."

Suddenly, I could hear the sound of the steam train making its way towards the station; then I saw it, a glistening black coal-fired showpiece of the Industrial Revolution. After a piercing screeching of its brakes, the train was motionless at the station platform, as a puff of steam was let off. I was a fair distance away, further along the platform. Dignitaries came out of the station building; the governor, mayor, military officers, government officials, all waiting for the doors to open and the royal entourage to exit the train. Then suddenly, the royal couple exited onto the platform first, followed by the others. They all conversed on the platform, shaking hands, bowing, and engaging in pleasantries and laughter, while Lieutenant Colonel Count Franz von Harrach, in full imperial military uniform, left the party and walked towards me.

'Franz von Harrach, it is my pleasure to meet you.'

'The pleasure is all mine, Luca Evangelista. We have a golden opportunity to put history right. I have been overwhelmed with emotion ever since Otto's visit a few days ago. Come, the Archduke wants to meet you. He knows you are an additional bodyguard hand-picked by me.'

'Franz, if we can't change the route to the hospital, we must work swiftly and decisively to stop Princip from firing the two shots, by apprehending him minutes before the royal car makes that fateful "V" turn.'

'Agreed, Luca, agreed'

I took a deep breath as we made our way along the platform to the royal party and officials. It was going to be a day of high drama, to say the least.

'Your highness, may I introduce you to Luca Evangelista, the elite bodyguard I was telling you about.'

'I am honoured to meet you, sir' I said confidently as I looked straight into the Archduke's piercing blue eyes.

'Welcome to my security detail, young man. If the rumours of impending rebellion in this city are true, you are going to have a very busy and eventful day.'

'I stand ready and committed to serve and protect you and the Archduchess, your highness.'

'Thank you, Luca.'

The Archduchess Sophie was more beautiful than her photographs showed; she reached out her right hand for me to kiss, as she smiled shyly. Heavily pregnant, I was determined to ensure not only the Archduke's life was saved, but hers as well. General Oskar Potiorek, the Governor of the Austrian provinces of Bosnia-Herzegovina had assigned the seating arrangements for the motorcade of four cars. In the front car was Fehim Curcic, the Mayor of Sarajevo, and Doctor Gerde, the city's Commissioner of Police. Franz Ferdinand and Sophie made their way into the second car to be driven by Leopold Lojka, and were joined by Gustav Schneiberg, Oskar Potiorek, Count von Harrach, and myself.

The car's top was rolled back so that the crowds could get a good view of the royal couple. Other dignitaries were in the third and fourth cars. The local police force was in charge of the security arrangements for the royal visit. Before the arrival of Franz Ferdinand in Sarajevo, thirty-five potential troublemakers were arrested and taken into custody. A hundred and twenty policemen were placed along the route the royal party was going to take to the City Hall; but it was decided that the 70,000 Austro-Hungarian soldiers stationed in Sarajevo were going to remain in their barracks.

Unknown to the Sarajevo police force, six members of the Black Hand group also lined the route. They were spaced out along the Appel Quay; each one had been instructed to try and kill Franz Ferdinand when the royal car reached his position. The first conspirator on the route to see the royal car was Muhamed Mehmedbasic, who, standing outside the Austro-Hungarian Bank building, lost his nerve and allowed the car to pass him by without taking any action. Mehmedbasic later said that a policemen was standing behind him, and feared he would be arrested before he had a chance to throw his bomb. I actually spotted him and our eyes met as we drove past the bank building.

While the royal motorcade was proceeding, it wasn't the first conspirator I was worried about; it was the second one, Nedjelko Cabrinovic, because I knew what was about to happen. I had to maintain maximum discipline, and not respond in any way; instead allowing the historical events to unfold. And sure enough, it happened. At 10.15am, I saw Cabrinovic step forward from the crowd, and hurl his bomb at the Archduke's car. The car I was in. The driver immediately accelerated when he saw the mortal object flying towards him. The bomb let off a loud explosion under the front wheel of the next car behind us.

Two of the occupants, Eric von Merizzi, and Count Boos-Waldeck, were seriously injured, along with a dozen spectators hit by bomb splinters. After throwing his bomb, Nedjelko Cabrinovic swallowed the cyanide he was carrying, and then I saw him jump into the Miljacka River. Four men, including two detectives, raced after him and managed to arrest him in the shallow water of the river. The poison had failed to kill him, and he was taken to a local police station. Meanwhile, the driver of our car, Leopold Lojka, accelerated at such a great speed to the City Hall, that the other assassins from the Black Hand, including Gavrilo Princip, had clearly aborted their missions to kill Franz Ferdinand. As the car was speeding, I could see clearly shocked, confused, and angry spectators, lining the streets.

When we arrived at the City Hall, there was pandemonium, with officials racing confusingly in all directions. There were collective sighs of relief and spontaneous raptured applause though when they saw the Archduke Ferdinand and his wife Sophie enter the building unharmed. The hall became silent as Fehim Curcic, the Mayor of Sarajevo, stood on the podium and began to speak. I could nevertheless still sense much tension in the air.

'Our hearts are full of happiness over the most gracious visit with which Your Highnesses are pleased to honour our capital city of Sarajevo, and I consider myself happy that Your Highness can read in our faces the feelings of our love and devotion, of our unshakable loyalty, and of our obedience to His Majesty our Emperor and King, and to the Most Serene Dynasty of Hapsburg-Lorraine. All the citizens of the capital city of Sarajevo find that their souls are filled with happiness, and they most enthusiastically greet Your Highnesses' most illustrious visit with the most cordial of welcomes, deeply convinced that this stay in our beloved city of Sarajevo will ever increase Your Highnesses' most gracious interest in our progress and well-being, and ever fortify our own most profound gratitude and loyalty, a loyalty that shall dwell immutably in our hearts, and that shall grow forever.'

There was a deafening and prolonged round of applause as the Archduke then made his way to the podium. I was currently functioning on sheer adrenalin after witnessing the day's events so far. I also had an overwhelming urge to swing into action, knowing more drama was yet to come.

'It gives me special pleasure to accept the assurances of your unshakeable loyalty and affection for His Majesty, our Most Gracious Emperor and King. I thank you cordially for the resounding ovations with which the population received me and my wife, the more so since in them an expression of pleasure over the failure of the assassination attempt.'

Again, there was a thunderous round of applause from everybody present, along with shouts of 'Long Live the Emperor! Long Live the Archduke! Long Live the Duchess!' I must say, considering there had been a serious attempt on his life, the Archduke seemed cool, calm, and collected, as he mingled and socialised with the assembled dignitaries. During the official reception at the City Hall, Franz Ferdinand asked about the members of his party that had been wounded by the bomb. When the Archduke was told they were badly injured in hospital, he insisted on being taken to see them.

A member of the Archduke's staff, Baron Morsey, suggested this might be dangerous; but Oskar Potiorek, who was responsible for the safety of the royal party, replied, "Do you think Sarajevo is full of assassins?" However, Potiorek did accept it would be better if Duchess Sophie remained behind at the City Hall. When Baron Morsey told Sophie about the revised plans, she refused to stay, arguing: "As long as the Archduke shows himself in public today, I will not leave him." So it was agreed the royal couple would be taken to the hospital. In a change to the course of history, Harrach and I ensured the drivers were aware of the revised route we would be taking. Surely, by doing this, we had snuffed out the opportunity for Princep to fire the two fatal bullets, I thought, with great relief.

As we left the front entrance of the building to get into the waiting cars, there was a large appreciative crowd lining the streets. Potiorek, Harrach, and myself, escorted the royal couple down the steps towards the pavement and the awaiting cars. Suddenly a man in a black overcoat burst his way through the crowd! He was holding a gun in his right hand! Pumped with adrenalin, I raced towards him as he was about to lift his arm and take aim at the Archduke.

As people were screaming in terror I dove straight onto him and managed to unbalance him as he fired a shot into the air. We were engaged in a fierce struggle on the steps, then rolling down the steps, kicking and punching each other frantically on the pavement! I managed to wrestle the gun out of his hand. He had me by the scruff of the neck with both hands, trying to choke me. I broke free and gave him a thunderous punch to the front of his face, mustering all the power and force I possessed. He lay unconscious on the pavement, bleeding from the nose, surrounded by an angry mob who were being restrained by a number of police officers as they tried to seek retribution. I was shocked to see it was Thero! Thero had tried to assassinate the Archduke.

The police managed to bring him back to consciousness and then took him away to the nearby police headquarters for questioning. I instinctively knew of course, that they weren't going to get any information from him at all; they weren't going to be able to identify him; and certainly, he was going to escape by literally vanishing into thin air, as he left this time period, and travelled back into the future through the wormhole. I needed to talk to him.

After arriving at police headquarters, Harrach arranged for me to meet privately with Thero for ten minutes, in a secure room within the holding cells. As I entered the bare concrete room with a bright overhanging light, a small wooden table, and two chairs, I could see Thero was sitting upright with his eyes serenely closed, as if he was meditating. His eyes shot open immediately as I sat opposite him.

'When they told me you were visiting me Luca Evangelista, I decided to delay my entry into the time portal. So within minutes of us concluding this discussion, I shall vanish into thin air.'

'Why did you decide to wait for me to see you?'

'Why? Why? Why? Indeed. You fascinate me. You seem to possess a level of perseverance and determination that I didn't realise existed in humans. I wanted to look you in the eyes and show you my determination to destroy your mission. You will not succeed. You haven't seen anything yet. Do you understand?'

'Why are you so hell-bent on sabotaging the mission and sealing the terrible fate of this planet and its people, Thero?'

'There was a time when I had great optimism about humans and their potential. When I first visited your planet, around 5,000 years ago in Egypt, I encountered a group of humans with profound vision, courage, integrity, and deep wisdom; somewhat like your attributes, Luca. I sowed the seeds of the great civilization of Egypt! I secured a dynasty for them, and gave them access to highly advanced technology in architecture, construction, engineering, and the sciences, particularly in medicine and astronomy. My expectation was, that the seeds of technology I had sown back then, would germinate and evolve into a highly sophisticated, ultra-advanced civilization, where the pursuit of knowledge would be the ultimate goal, and resources would be shared equally among the continents and diverse peoples, certainly by the 21st century; but instead, humans have regressed, rather than progressed. You still fight brutal wars. You still have massive inequality. You still have widespread poverty. You have economic systems that are rapidly depleting the resources of your planet, and encourage outright greed and exploitation of people. You are destroying the climate and ecosystems of this planet. You have used human knowledge to develop destructive technology. What is there for me to appreciate about you humans and the sorry state of affairs that exist on your planet in the 21st century? You had your chances. Humans do not deserve to be saved'

'There are many good people on this planet who are devoting their lives for a better world, Thero.'

'Not enough of you, I'm afraid. The powerful Elite of 300 men who really control this planet and its destiny, are conspiring to kill the majority of the world's population, and enslave the few million who they will choose to keep alive.'

'Are you talking about the Illuminati, or the Bilderberg Group?'

'You are as naïve as the vast majority of your world's population, Luca. They don't have any name attached to them. These incredibly powerful, immensely wealthy families have been pulling the big strings on this planet for centuries; led by the Rothschild's in Europe, and the Rockefeller's in the United States. Their front man, who holds enormous influence within the institutionalised global power structure, is still Henry Kissinger, even though he is 98 years old.'

'Does this powerful elite know about the time travel missions?'

'I do not know. It is quite possible because they have an extensive network of spies in very high places across all facets of your society, spread around the world. If they do know, they will stop at nothing to prevent you from succeeding. Just as I will. The Elite 300, have financed and engineered many major wars, revolutions, and global events, in recent centuries; including the Industrial Revolution, Napoleonic Wars, American Civil War, French Revolution, European Imperialism, First World War, Spanish Flu, Russian Revolution, Great Depression, Second World War, Chinese Communist Revolution, Cold War, Computer Age, European Union, Globalisation, New World Order, War on Terrorism, Internet, Artificial Intelligence, Global Financial Crisis, Covid-19; and the emerging trend under the umbrella of the United Nations, of a World Government, which they will well and truly direct and control. I have told you enough. I must go now. See you soon though, Luca Evangelista.'

My head was spinning and I was reeling as I left the building, entered the wormhole, and made my way back to the 21st century.

'Well Luca, you avoided the First World War. The positive spin-offs from this war never happening on that version of the Earth are too numerous for me to even begin to articulate to you here and now. Suffice to say, the overall mission is progressing well. The Russian Revolution is coming next. This one is full of intrigue, passion, competing agendas, and skulduggery in the extreme. Vladimir Lenin, Leon Trotsky, and Joseph Stalin, await you'

'I'm as ready as I will ever be for all of it, Otto' I replied, probably not as confidently as I should have, as we sat in the piano bar, both sipping our gin and tonics. 'What do you know about the Elite 300 men who control the world?'

'We see this pattern on many of the planets with more advanced civilizations we visit. Over a period of time, power gets concentrated in the hands of an elite group of families, they conspire together to expand their power and influence even further, on a global scale, usually at the expense of the rest of the population, and the well-being of the very planet they inhabit. Ultimately they formalise their power into a whole-planet totalitarian government. So these Elite 300 men as you describe them Luca, is nothing new or surprising to me. They are not relevant to our mission.'

Now I had to contend with not only Thero trying to stop me when travelling back in time; but also the possibility of thugs, hired by the Elite 300, trying to stop me here in the 21st century, as well.

With Otto's blessing, before embarking on my next mission, I was going to travel down the wormhole to the small central Italian village of my parents' birth. Located in the Apennine Mountains, it is over 950 years old, and surrounded by a pine forest. My family has a villa in the village, which my parents, myself, and my three older brothers all pitched in to buy. It is our family sanctuary. It is located next door to where my Mum was born, and a very short distance from where Dad was born. The upstairs master bedroom has polished floorboards, and its own wrought iron balcony with a spectacular view of lush green farming land in the foreground, and the mountains in the background. At night, the mountains are dotted with "jewels" of light, each one representing a medieval village, perched high up.

Isabella and I had shared a very memorable five days in our family village. We would awaken in the morning to the sounds of cows mooing, birds singing, and the church bells ringing; as rays of sunshine engulfed our master bedroom. Our taste buds were overwhelmed with the aroma of freshly baked bread, and roasted coffee, coming from the nearby bakery and café. My relatives were exceedingly generous, constantly inviting us to lunches, dinners, and treks into the surrounding fields; where many of them still had traditional farms, from which they gained not only the majority of their food, like meat, cheeses, olives, tomato sauce, and an assortment of fruit and vegetables; but also their own 100% organic wines.

I arrived in Montagano at 10am, on the 15th July, 1958. I was standing right in the centre of the piazza (town square). I knew exactly where I needed to go. As I walked to the outskirts of the village, alongside the pine forest, and into the fields, I saw many men and women working on the land. They all greeted me with friendly smiles. Many asked where I was from, or if I was looking for anybody in particular. I simply said I was an Australian tourist with relatives in the region, visiting that area for a few days.

Then, I arrived at the small Evangelista family farm. A variety of vegetables were being grown. From a distance, I could recognise my grandfather Giuseppe, and grandmother Teresa, working the land. Not far away were two men in their late teens and early twenties. I had seen sufficient family photos to recognise them as my uncles Domenico and Roberto. Further in the distance, at the foot of the mountains, I could make out a younger man, tending to a flock of around twenty sheep. As I walked closer, I was flooded with emotion. Standing a few hundred metres in front of me, with shorts, and a distinctive cap, was my Dad. Being the youngest, his job was to shepherd the family sheep.

My Dad loved working in the fields. When he came to Australia, his first job was working on a very large sheep and wheat farm in central Western Australia. Each year, he would go with his youngest brother Antonio, to a family vineyard owned by Croatians, to handpick grapes for our homemade wine. Even when my Mum and Dad returned to Italy on holidays, my Dad would spend a lot of time on farms owned by relatives and friends; helping them out for sheer enjoyment.

'Can I help you, signor?' said my Dad.

'I'm fine thank you. I am from Australia, and am here on a holiday visiting my relatives in the nearby village of Petrella.'

He was walking towards me. It was surreal seeing him so young. He was fifteen years old. By now, I was overwhelmed with emotion. I couldn't do anything about the tears flowing down my cheeks. I knew what I wanted to say. But I wasn't allowed to say it. My Dad could not know I was his son.

'Are you okay?' he said, while pulling out his handkerchief and giving it to me.

'My father died a short time ago. I was thinking of him, and now I'm upset. I'm sorry. What's your name?

'I'm so sorry to hear that. My name is Filippo.'

'What's your name?'

'Luca.'

'I like that name. I like it so much that it's one of the names I will be giving to my future son. I am going to have four sons, you know! I also have dreams of starting a new life and family in Australia. You look very familiar. Have we met before?'

Well, that was it, for me. I cried so hard that Filippo came and comforted me.

'I understand how horrible it must be to lose your father. I often have terrible nightmares about losing mine.'

I had experienced something very special. Something that I knew no other human being could ever hope for. To meet one of their parents, before they were born.

I wished Filippo all the very best, and made my way back towards the village, and then to the 21st century. I would be forever grateful to Otto for giving me this life-changing opportunity.

We Didn't Start the Fire

Harry Truman, Doris Day, Red China, Johnnie Ray
South Pacific, Walter Winchell, Joe DiMaggio
Joe McCarthy, Richard Nixon, Studebaker, Television
North Korea, South Korea, Marilyn Monroe

Rosenbergs, H-Bomb, Sugar Ray, Panmunjom
Brando, The King And I, and The Catcher In The Rye
Eisenhower, Vaccine, England's got a new queen
Marciano, Liberace, Santayana goodbye

We didn't start the fire
It was always burning
Since the world's been turning
We didn't start the fire
No, we didn't light it
But we tried to fight it

Joseph Stalin, Malenkov, Nasser and Prokofiev
Rockefeller, Campanella, Communist Bloc
Roy Cohn, Juan Peron, Toscanini, Dacron
Dien Bien Phu Falls, Rock Around the Clock
Einstein, James Dean, Brooklyn's got a winning team
Davy Crockett, Peter Pan, Elvis Presley, Disneyland
Bardot, Budapest, Alabama, Krushchev
Princess Grace, Peyton Place, Trouble in the Suez

We didn't start the fire
It was always burning
Since the world's been turning
We didn't start the fire
No, we didn't light it
But we tried to fight it

Little Rock, Pasternak, Mickey Mantle, Kerouac
Sputnik, Chou En-Lai, Bridge On The River Kwai
Lebanon, Charles de Gaulle, California baseball
Starkweather Homicide, Children of Thalidomide

Buddy Holly, Ben-Hur, Space Monkey, Mafia
Hula Hoops, Castro, Edsel is a no-go
U-2, Syngman Rhee, payola and Kennedy
Chubby Checker, Psycho, Belgians in the Congo

We didn't start the fire
It was always burning
Since the world's been turning
We didn't start the fire
No, we didn't light it
But we tried to fight it

Hemingway, Eichmann, Stranger in a Strange Land
Dylan, Berlin, Bay of Pigs invasion
Lawrence of Arabia, British Beatlemania
Ole Miss, John Glenn, Liston beats Patterson
Pope Paul, Malcolm X, British Politician Sex
J.F.K. blown away, what else do I have to say?

We didn't start the fire
It was always burning
Since the world's been turning
We didn't start the fire
No, we didn't light it
But we tried to fight it

Birth control, Ho Chi Minh, Richard Nixon back again
Moonshot, Woodstock, Watergate, punk rock
Begin, Reagan, Palestine, Terror on the airline
Ayatollah's in Iran, Russians in Afghanistan
Wheel of Fortune, Sally Ride, heavy metal, suicide

Foreign debts, homeless Vets, AIDS, Crack, Bernie Goetz
Hypodermics on the shores, China's under martial law
Rock and Roller Cola wars, I can't take it anymore

We didn't start the fire
It was always burning
Since the world's been turning
We didn't start the fire
But when we are gone
It will still burn on and on and on and on
And on and on and on and on...

We didn't start the fire
It was always burning
Since the world's been turning
We didn't start the fire
No, we didn't light it
But we tried to fight it

We didn't start the fire
It was always burning
Since the world's been turning
We didn't start the fire
No, we didn't light it
But we tried to fight it

We didn't start the fire
It was always burning
Since the word's been turning
We didn't start the fire
No, we didn't light it
But we tried to fight it

Billy Joel (1989)

10

Vladimir Lenin

Moscow, Russia, April 1922 CE

I WAS DUE TO TRAVEL DOWN THE WORMHOLE THE NEXT MORNING, and appear outside Vladimir Lenin's residence in Moscow, on 23rd April, 1922, one month before he suffered his first stroke. My helper was going to be his longstanding and very loyal wife, Nadezhda Krupskaya. That night, I reflected upon my intense research of the monumental rivalry and clash of wills between Vladimir Lenin's two obvious successors; Leon Trotsky and Joseph Stalin.

Among the Bolshevik leaders, it was Leon Trotsky who seemed most likely to take over the Soviet Union after Lenin's demise. However, in the ensuing political struggle, Trotsky completely succumbed to his nemesis, Joseph Stalin, which first led to his exile, and then ultimately to his brutal assassination with an ice pick, in Mexico. How did this titanic clash of personalities begin?

The first open conflict between the two leaders of the Revolution happened in the summer of 1918 during the defence of Tsaritsyn (later called Stalingrad, now Volgograd), which was besieged by the anti-Bolshevik White Army during the Russian Civil War. As a hub of supplying bread to Central Russia, the city was of significant strategic importance. Stalin, then the People's Commissar (Minister) for Nationalities, arrived in Tsaritsyn in June to sort out the problem of organising food supplies.

Having secured the support of Lenin, he broadened his powers to include the defence of the city. "The line south of Tsaritsyn has yet to be re-established," Stalin wrote to Lenin on 18th July. "I give everyone who needs it a tongue-lashing. I hope we will soon restore it. If our military 'specialists' (shoemakers!) had not been asleep on the job, the line would not have been breached. And if it is re-established, it won't be thanks to, but in spite of, the military." It was the question of these "military specialists" – former tsarist officers – that defined the early relationship between Stalin and Trotsky.

The future "father of nations" (as Stalin would be known) resolutely opposed their appointment to high level posts in the Bolshevik Red Army, considering them unreliable, and many still loyal to the Tsar, so therefore he believed they were prone to betray the Revolution at the blink of an eyelid. A contrary point of view was held by the People's Commissar for Military Affairs, Leon Trotsky. Through his efforts, well-trained professional military personnel from the ex-Tsar's Imperial Army were transferred to the service of the Bolsheviks, to such an extent that the Red Army boasted over 250 tsarist generals.

Stalin used his position to make sure that the former tsarist general Andrei Snesarev was removed from his post as the leader of the North Caucasian Military District. Junior commanders were less fortunate. Suspecting them of counterrevolutionary activities, Stalin ordered the arrest of the entire artillery command, up to and including minor administration officials. They were placed on the so-called "death barge" (a floating jail common during the Russian Civil War) in the middle of the Volga river, where many soon perished from the inhuman conditions.

Trotsky's subsequent appointment of Pavel Sytin, also a former tsarist general, as commander of the Southern Front, provoked another outburst from Stalin: "The Central Committee of the Party must discuss the question of the behaviour of Trotsky, who slights the most prominent members of the Party in favour of traitors." Stalin blatantly ignored Trotsky's order to give Sytin full authority over military operations, and he even set up an alternative command centre. On many written instructions from the People's Commissar for Military Affairs, Stalin simply scrawled "Disregard." Stalin and Trotsky never saw eye to eye on any issue concerning the defence of Tsaritsyn.

Gradually, their conflict evolved into open, aggressive hostility toward one another. Stalin telegraphed this message to Lenin on 3rd October, 1918: "The fact is that Trotsky is incapable of singing without falsetto or acting without flashy gestures. I would have nothing against this if the interests of the common cause did not suffer. This not being the case, I request, before it is too late, to restrain Trotsky and clip his wings, for I fear that his madcap orders will sow discord between the army and the command staff, and completely ruin the Front." The very next day, an enraged Trotsky dispatched his own telegram from Tambov, to head of state, Lenin, with an urgent request to recall Stalin from the city. Seething with anger, he even muddled the words in the telegram: "Tsaritsyn (instead of Stalin) must either obey or get out." In the end, Lenin sided with Trotsky and recalled Stalin to Moscow on 19th October.

Despite this factional rift at the heart of the military command, the city of Tsaritsyn was held by the Red Army for another year. It fell only in the summer of 1919, as a result of an unsuccessful counteroffensive by the Red Army. It was then in November 1918, that Stalin, having been recalled from Tsaritsyn, and harbouring a deep malicious resentment and thirst for vengeance in his soul, wrote a short article on the anniversary of the Revolution. The purpose was to strike a blow at Trotsky's reputation and prestige, and to deploy the authority of the Central Committee, headed by Vladimir Lenin, against him. "An undercurrent of anger flowed through this jubilee article," Trotsky himself later wrote in his memoirs. The Tsaritsyn conflict was only the first stage in the long and ultimately violent confrontation between the two post-Lenin powerful heavyweights of the Bolshevik revolutionary movement.

It was midday on the 23rd April, 1922, when I arrived outside of the main entrance to the Kremlin Senate Palace in central Moscow, the official residence of the Soviet President Vladimir Lenin. His wife, Nadezhda Krupskaya, was my contact, and she was waiting for me at the entrance. It was going to be very difficult to keep secret the fact Lenin was due to suffer the first of three strokes, in four weeks. Of course, like all events not yet occurring, I needed to keep this secret as well, or the wormhole would collapse, I would be stuck in Moscow 1922, and my mission would fail.

'Comrade Luca Evangelista, I have been expecting you. Otto told me you would arrive at exactly midday, and here you are. My husband has been so fatigued in recent weeks, and has been spending much of his time confined to his bed. Ever since the attempt on his life in 1918, his state of health has gradually deteriorated.'

'Madam Krupskaya, it is my honour to meet you. I understand your husband is in ill-health. Stalin has been actively taking advantage of your husband's incapacitation, by building a power structure of loyal followers, holding many of the key positions within the Party apparatus, with himself securely entrenched as the General Secretary of the Central Committee of the Communist Party, effective from 3rd April, 1922, just over three weeks ago. It is imperative that over the next three days, we persuade your husband to exercise his full power and authority in a forceful and unequivocal manner within the Communist Party, to position Leon Trotsky as his heir apparent, not Joseph Stalin.'

'Yes Luca, we have a formidable challenge ahead of us because Stalin is an extremely aggressive operator who will stop at nothing to enhance his political ambitions, whereas, as you no doubt already know as a historian, Leon Trotsky is a highly intelligent, charismatic, and often arrogant person, who often rubs people the wrong way, and does not possess the sheer ruthlessness and killer-instinct that Stalin has.'

'Your husband is the heart and soul of the Revolution. The majority of Bolsheviks love and support him. We just need to ensure his messages find their way to the influential Party members, and to the proletariat masses. At the moment, Stalin is actively preventing this.'

'I know Luca. I know. All I can say, is you are going to be a welcome breath of fresh air to my dear husband. He is getting weaker by the day. He still has the fire in his eyes, and his mind is still razor sharp. Your determination and energy is going to make all the difference, I believe.'

'I will do my best. There is much at stake here.'

Madam Krupskaya proceeded to take me on a tour of the Kremlin Palace, which was within the wider grounds of the Kremlin complex of buildings. Initially constructed from 1776 to 1787, the palace originally housed the Moscow branch of the Governing Senate, the highest judiciary and legislative office of Tsarist Imperial Russia. The Kremlin Palace was located in the northern section of the Kremlin grounds. It was shaped like a triangle, with one side directly adjacent to the Kremlin Wall, and parallel to Red Square.

The building had three floors, and was painted in the same yellow colour as many other administrative buildings within the Moscow Kremlin. The triangular structure had an inner courtyard, and was divided by hallways. In the middle of the main façade was an arched passage fashioned like a triumphal arch leading to the courtyard. Inside was Rotunda Hall, once called the Pantheon of Russia. Its green dome, carrying the national flag as seen from Red Square, was an iconic symbol of Soviet propaganda. Inside the palace building, was the large "Catherine Hall" which was designed as a parade room, where especially important state ceremonies and banquets were held. It was a circular hall with extensive ornamentation depicting Catherine the Great as the Greek goddess Minerva.

The Presidential Residence consisted of two sections, one for the presidential administrative staff offices, and the other as a residence for the President. All of the administrative rooms were located along the outer facades, and were connected through corridors running along the perimeter of the inner courtyard. The President's executive office, decorated in white and green colours, was located in the Oval Room. Meetings and negotiations were held there. It was also where state awards were presented. The Oval Room was decorated with a malachite fireplace, a mirror with a bronze clock, and candelabrums on the mantelpiece. The tall sculptures of Peter the Great, Catherine the Great, Nicholas I, and Alexander III, were removed by the Bolsheviks when they took control. Since the 1917 Russian Revolution and relocation of the capital to Moscow, the Kremlin Palace served as the seat of the Soviet government, including the Politburo.

Vladimir Lenin had his study and private apartment on the third floor. What struck me about the private apartment was its opulence; including chandeliers, leather furniture, precious works of art and sculptures, tapestries, and oriental rugs. As Madam Krupskaya explained to me; all of these extravagant items were seized from the imperial court of the tsar, and were the property of the state, not her husband. She showed me to my room, situated on the third floor. Although small in size, and sparsely furnished, it had a view of the courtyard and surrounding immaculate gardens.

As I lay on the bed and closed my eyes for a brief rest, I collected my thoughts on the eventful life of Nadezhda Krupskaya. She was the daughter of a military officer, and was born in St. Petersburg on 26th February, 1869. A radical from a young age, Krupskaya was a committed Marxist, and was a member of several banned extremist organisations during czarist rule. She taught literacy in an evening school for adults, and in 1894 met fellow revolutionary, Vladimir Lenin. Two years later, Lenin was arrested and sentenced to three years of internal exile in Siberia. Krupskaya joined Lenin in the Siberian city of Shushenskoye, and they eventually married in July, 1898.

While living in exile, the couple translated from English to Russian, "The Theory and Practice of Trade Unionism" by Sidney and Beatrice Webb. Released from exile in February, 1900, Krupskaya, Lenin, and fellow revolutionary activist, Julius Martov, decided to leave Russia. They moved to Geneva where they joined up with George Plekhanov, Pavel Axelrod, and other members of the Liberation of Labour organisation, to publish "Iskra" ("Spark"). The Marxist paper was named after a passage from a poem: "The spark will kindle a flame." Leon Trotsky and a number of other revolutionaries joined the venture soon after.

At the Second Congress of the Social Democratic Labour Party held in London in 1903, there was a dispute between Lenin and Julius Martov. Lenin argued for a small Party of professional revolutionaries with a large following of non-party sympathisers and supporters. Martov disagreed, believing it was better to have a large Party of professional activists. Martov won the vote, 28-23, but Lenin was unwilling to accept the result, and formed a faction known as the Bolsheviks. Those who remained loyal to Martov became known as the Mensheviks. Those members who joined the Bolsheviks included Krupskaya, Joseph Stalin, and later, Leon Trotsky. During the First World War, Krupskaya and Lenin lived in Switzerland. After the overthrow of Tsar Nicholas II in April, 1917, they returned to Russia. Lenin then joined with Leon Trotsky in plotting against the provisional government which was led by the democratic reformer, Alexander Kerensky.

When that government collapsed in October 1917, Lenin and the Bolsheviks triggered a mass workers uprising, which led to the Russian Revolution; and took control of Russia. Krupskaya had opposed Lenin's call for an early revolution, but after its stunning success, she hid her political differences with her husband. In November 1917, Krupskaya was appointed as the Deputy People's Commissar (Minister) of Education and Enlightenment.

Lenin's health deteriorated after he was shot in an assassination attempt on 30th August, 1918. Two bullets entered his body, and it was considered too dangerous to remove them. Lenin suffered a stroke in May 1922, followed by a second one in December of that same year.

Four days later, he dictated his famous "Testament" where he personally assessed the capabilities of all the main party leaders, including Trotsky and Stalin. Three days after writing this Testament Lenin had a third stroke. As a result, he was no longer able to speak or write, and although he lived for another ten months, he ceased to exist as a powerful figure within the Soviet Union. Krupskaya published her memoirs, "Reminisces on Lenin" in 1926. She died on 27th February 1939, a broken and lonely woman, scorned and ostracized by the Stalinist regime.

The events leading up to the incapacitation ofVladimir Lenin, and the power struggle between Stalin and Trotsky, can be traced back to the final stages of the First World War, in February and March, 1917, when the first revolution in Russia had overthrown Tsar Nicholas II, and an unelected provisional government had declared Russia to be a democratic republic. However, the provisional government failed to carry out land reform, kept Russia in the war, and delayed holding promised elections. Consequently, this government became increasingly unpopular.

In October and November, 1917, a second revolution had taken place, at the insistence ofVladimir Lenin. This Bolshevik Revolution succeeded, transforming Russia into the world's first workers' State. This new State, renamed the Russian Socialist Federal Soviet Republic, was then plunged into three years of civil war. Though the Bolsheviks finally won power in 1921, the massive economic and political upheaval all this turmoil and warfare had created led to many sharp policy differences between the leading Bolsheviks.

The most important disagreement was over economic policy. At the start of the Civil War, an economic program known as "War Communism" had been adopted as an emergency measure. Grain had been requisitioned from peasant farmers in villages and towns all over the country, to ensure adequate supplies for the Soviet Red Army, and the industrial city centres; all private trade had been banned; and all factories, mines, and banks, were nationalised, or effectively taken over by the government.

However, this policy, along with the damage suffered as a consequence of the Civil War, and the restrictions on democracy during the war, had led to the Kronstadt Rising in March 1921, in which workers, sailors, and soldiers, staged a serious revolt in protest. Though this revolt had been ruthlessly crushed, Lenin persuaded the 10th Party Congress of 1921 to adopt a New Economic Policy (NEP) to replace War Communism. The NEP introduced a partial step-back towards small scale capitalism. This limited revival of capitalism, and the aftershock of the Kronstadt Rising, also led Lenin to introduce a ban on political and ideological factions within the Communist Party; and also a ban on opposition parties in the Soviets. Several communists opposed this ban, and later, Lenin stated that it was a purely temporary measure, intended to cope with the acute political and economic crisis the Soviet Union was facing.

In May 1922, Lenin had the first of a series of strokes, which increasingly restricted his ability to take an active part in politics. Yet there were significant political differences over the internal political governance of the Communist Party, and what attitude to take about furthering a world workers' revolution. Leading communists began to consider what would happen if Lenin died. The most important communists after Lenin were the other members of the Politburo at that time.

The Politburo (short for "Political Bureau") was the Russian Communist Party's body responsible for making political decisions between Congresses. Though, in theory, the Politburo was responsible to the Central Committee (CC) which elected it, and to the Party Congress (which elected the CC); in practice, the Politburo soon came to dominate the other two bodies. In 1921, it comprised: Lenin, Trotsky, Zinoviev, Kamenev, Bukharin, Rykov, Stalin, and Tomsky. Of these, Leon Trotsky seemed the most likely to replace Lenin. After him, Zinoviev and Kamenev were strong political leaders (of the Petrograd and Moscow Communist Party branches, respectively) and had long been associated with Lenin; their weak spot was that they had been opposed to the October-November Revolution, at first. Bukharin too, was a well-known and popular revolutionary leader.

Stalin was not well-known, and seemed unlikely to emerge as a major leader. However, he had been appointed Commissar (Minister) for the Nationalities after the revolution and, in April 1922, had been appointed General-Secretary of the Communist Party. This position included appointing and dismissing communist officials within the Party.

Many of the leading communists resented Trotsky's rapid rise to the top of the Party after August 1917. Zinoviev and Kamenev in particular believed they should take over from Lenin, and turned to Stalin for help to stop Trotsky succeeding. These three became known as the "triumvirs." As early as December 1922, they began moves to prevent Trotsky from obtaining majority support. Though Lenin's strokes kept him from active involvement in politics, his awareness of these political and personal tensions caused him growing concern, and led him to propose to Trotsky that they should form a Joint Bloc for Democracy against growing signs of bureaucracy in the Party and the State. Towards the end of December 1922, Lenin suffered a second stroke.

Concerned about what might happen after his death, he dictated his initial thoughts for what he believed would be his last Testament, outlining the strengths and weaknesses of all the leading communists. He was particularly worried by Stalin's attitudes towards the non-Russian nationalities. After 1921, Lenin had come to favour a looser federation of autonomous states, rather than a more centralised unitary State, which Stalin was trying to push through. Lenin was also very concerned about Stalin's use of force against those in the Soviet Republic of Georgia who were against his plans.

These concerns led Lenin to add a Postscript to his Testament in January 1923, recommending Stalin's removal from all official Party and government positions. Here is an extract from Lenin's Testament: "Since he became General Secretary, Comrade Stalin has concentrated in his hands immeasurable power, and I am not sure that he will always know how to use that power with sufficient caution. On the other hand, Comrade Trotsky is distinguished not only by his outstanding qualities (personally he is the most capable man in the present Central Committee) but also by his excess of self-confidence and a readiness to be carried away by the purely administrative side of affairs. Stalin is too rude, and this fault, entirely supportable in relations amongst us Communists, becomes insupportable in the office of General Secretary.

Therefore, I propose to the comrades to find a way of removing Stalin from that position and to appoint another man who in all respects differs from Stalin only in superiority; namely, more patient, more loyal, more-polite, less capricious, and more attentive to comrades."

From the time he wrote his Testament, until his death the following year, Lenin urged Trotsky on several occasions to launch a campaign against bureaucracy, and for the restoration of Communist Party "democracy" (majority-rule). By January 1923, the triumvirs' alliance had been finalised. Soon a "whispering campaign" was underway, concerning Trotsky's non-Bolshevik past, and his earlier disagreements with Lenin.

However, Stalin appeared to be in serious trouble in March 1923, when his arrogance and rudeness to Lenin's wife had led Lenin to send him a harsh letter, on 5th March, threatening to "break relations" with him entirely if he did not retract and apologise. Kamenev was aware of this rift, and of Lenin's intention to politically "crush" Stalin. At this stage it really seemed like Stalin's ambitions were doomed to failure. But then, Lenin suffered a third stroke, which left him paralysed and speechless for most of the remaining time, until his death in January 1924.

This is why Otto had decided to send me to Moscow in April 1922, a month before Lenin suffered his first stroke, and by which time it became apparent that Stalin was using his position as the recently appointed General Secretary of the Party to launch himself into the front runner to take over the leadership from Lenin, and completely sideline Trotsky. Stalin already had the Politburo stacked with his supporters.

With the help of his wife Nadezhda, who was already deeply distrustful of Stalin and his fierce personal ambitions; and with the full involvement of Leon Trotsky, working closely with Lenin; I needed to trigger a chain of events to ensure Trotsky rather than Stalin, would gain the majority support of the wider membership of the Communist Party; in order to thwart the ambitions of Stalin, and to position Trotsky as the heir apparent of Lenin for the leadership of the Party, and the Soviet Union.

After a short rest, there was a knock on the door.

'Comrade Evangelista, President Lenin is ready to see you now.'

He introduced himself as Leonid, a Party official working on Lenin's staff. Leonid escorted me to Lenin's presidential office, at the other end of the building. When I entered, the great man himself was seated at his desk, with his wife standing alongside him. The desk was made of crafted mahogany, the carpet was red, and there was an elegant chandelier hanging from the centre of the large room. Bookshelves full of books lined two walls.

'Comrade Luca Evangelista, it is my pleasure to meet you. My wife has told me you are a visiting professor of politics from London, specialising in the securing and maintaining of power, acquainted with some of our Marxist friends in the United Kingdom, and that you will be here for three days only.'

'Yes that is correct Mr Lenin. It is my great honour to meet you and spend the next three days in your esteemed company.'

'I know Nadezhda has fully debriefed you of the imminent threat Stalin poses to the future of the revolution and of this great nation. I was very unhappy in the sudden manner he secured the position of General Secretary of the Party some weeks ago. He has wasted no time in removing many of my supporters from key positions and replacing them with his cronies. He has also orchestrated a ruthless campaign amongst Party comrades to discredit the reputation of Trotsky. I know we must act quickly.'

'Yes sir, time is of the essence.'

Of course, Lenin was not aware he was going to be further incapacitated with his first stroke, in four weeks.

'Comrade Luca, I have arranged for you and Leonid to meet comrade Trotsky, at the Metropol Hotel, tomorrow morning at 10 am. Can you do that?'

'Absolutely! I am looking forward to meeting him.'

'Excellent. I have taken all the necessary steps to ensure your meeting with Trotsky will be secure and private. I trust my dear friend Leonid with my life; so can you. I want you to fully debrief Trotsky on the situation regarding the clear and imminent threat posed by Stalin. Leonid will have all the background information you desire. Trotsky knows that he is my favoured candidate to replace me as the Party head and leader of the government. He also knows that I am willing and able to implement whatever plan you and he come up with. The purpose of your meeting with him will be to devise a plan that removes Joseph Stalin from all positions of power within the Communist Party and the government; and replaces him with Leon Trotsky. I know I can get majority Party support for this. I still have great influence within the Party. Just give me a workable plan. My health is deteriorating by the day. Time is of the utmost essence.'

I could see Lenin was an ailing man. He was virtually devoid of energy and spoke in a very weak voice. But when I looked into his eyes, I saw all of the fire and relentless passion which made him into the great revolutionary figure he was. Before I left his office, he invited me to join himself, his wife, and Leonid, for a private dinner at 6pm that evening, in the presidential dining room of the Metropol Hotel.

I had about three hours to kill, so I decided to put on an overcoat and go for a walk through the streets of central Moscow. Nadezhda didn't think it was a good idea me walking through the streets of Moscow on my own. She was concerned for my safety. She said Stalin had an extensive network of spies, including some unidentified staff working in the presidential offices. She suggested that their highly trusted aide, Leonid, accompany me on my walk, which was fine with me.

As we ventured outside, my first impression was how "European" the centre of this city was, with its well-paved boulevards, and attractively lit-up shop windows (even though many of the shelves inside were empty and dusty). Electric trams and buses were plentiful. There were an abundance of placards and advertisements, some of them very beautifully illustrated. Theatre, picture-palace, and music-hall announcements were suspended across the streets like huge banners. There were loudspeakers in every square. The streets were crowded.

Many people, especially the women, were surprisingly well-dressed and manicured. Numerous foreign newspapers could be bought at the kiosks. Alcohol was plentiful. Although wine could only be bought in special shops, vodka was in abundant supply everywhere. Leonid turned out to have a very interesting background. He was a confidante of Lenin, and had been working closely with him since 1917. He was previously a factory manager.

'The communists drink more than anyone else, Luca. Not because they are worse than the others, but because they have more money to spend. As a rule, it is not easy to distinguish a communist from an ordinary workman. Yet they do differ. The communists are more adaptable, supple, and better able to look after their own interests. The ordinary workers are often resentful of the communists because they think they get everything they want. They think the communists are given priority in this system, and they're right! For example, the communists get first priority for available housing, and for job promotions', explained Leonid to me as we were walking the streets.

'So Leonid, are you saying there already is a feeling amongst the common workers that the communists have a sense of privileged entitlement, and that the ideals of the Revolution are not being achieved?'

'Yes comrade Luca. So much so that the word "bourgeois" is now widely used to describe a typical communist. All who join the Communist Party do so for the sake of some material advantage, or to be one of a privileged group. There is no doubt in my mind that the Communist Party is forming the nucleus of a future bourgeoisie middle-class. Many of the communists are almost American in their business instincts, self-indulgence, and competitiveness.'

'Tell me about the Soviet colonies on the outskirts of town, Leonid? What do the common workers think of them?'

'The quarters where the working classes live lie towards the outskirts of the city. Amongst the older houses, the newly built, gigantic, barrack-like tenements are conspicuous. On the outskirts and beyond are allotments and bungalows meant for holiday residence, but they are now serving largely to house the surplus population of Moscow. These little huts are grouped all along the railway lines. Some 10,000 workmen live up to thirty miles away from Moscow, and travel into the city every day. The number of landlords are enormous. Nearly all the former landlords have retained their houses and joined the Communist Party, for obvious reasons. In addition to these, there are the new landlords. These are the communists who have acquired the villas and houses over which they were placed in charge. But most of the houses are in the hands of the Communist government, in the form of housing trusts. Theoretically, they are rented out to workmen, especially to the railway workers. But in reality, these government-administered housing trusts are blatantly corrupt, renting the houses out to their own people at very attractive rates, that is, to the communists and their relatives. So Luca, in spite of all the laws to the contrary, there are many communists who have a house in the city, as well as a villa or bungalow in the country. This privilege is shared by those who have enough money to pay bribes. All of these corrupt dealings are done openly. There is no attempt to conceal the sums of money that are paid. Do you see what's going on?'

'Yes, but I didn't really think corruption was so widespread, so soon after the Revolution!'

'Now Luca, regarding the Soviet colonies, things are even worse. In these so called colonies, that is to say, the conglomeration of huts and houses on the outskirts of the city, and along the railway lines; a new kind of life is developing. Each colony has its Soviet; in which hygiene, welfare-work, the fire brigade, sewerage, and so on are discussed in regular bureaucratic meetings attended by the local communist administrators. In the cluster of colonies in which my relatives live for example, there is a chemist's shop, an ambulance, and a hospital, so that they are not badly off for medical aid. But the welfare work is, generally speaking, very primitive. There are hardly any sewers, and the streets are littered with dirt and rubbish. In Spring, when the snow melts, and in Autumn, you literally wade through the slush. There is a Communist Cell in every colony which attends to the cultural needs of the residents. Its headquarters is usually the local police station. Some of the colonies have clubs where films are shown. If they're not propaganda films, French films are usually preferred. There are also regular lectures on Marxism, government policy, and what they call: the significance of physical culture. But these lectures are poorly attended. The young people prefer to spend their spare time drinking or playing cards, or both. Never has so much vodka been consumed in Russia, as now.'

'I see Leonid. I see. How did you and comrade Lenin become such close friends?'

'Ah, that is an interesting story, comrade Luca. I met him here in Moscow in early 1917 in the most extraordinary circumstances. He was giving a speech at one of the workers' halls. Curious about this revolutionary firebrand, I decided to attend. The hall was jam-packed with proletariat workers from all manner of industries. There was excitement in the air as Lenin came onto the stage to speak, after a number of minor speakers rallied the audience into a frenzy of excitement. His speech didn't let anybody down. He was mesmerising as he proceeded to savage the tsarist regime for its neglect of the common Russian people, and for continuing to involve the mother country in the Imperial War. As was customary for him, after he completed his speech, he came into the crowd to mingle. I was amazed that such a popular man had no security surrounding him. As he approached the people near me, I decided to come up to him and let him know how much I enjoyed his speech. Just as I got near to him, a man with a knife lunged at the great man. As soon as I saw the attacker, I pushed Lenin aside, so the man's knife just grazed Lenin's arm. It was intended for his heart. Anyhow, Lenin was so grateful for my deed, he asked me that evening to join his entourage and become one of his bodyguards. I believed in his revolutionary ideology, and really believed he would influence Russia for the better; so I did. The assassination attempt was kept secret, because it wouldn't look good if people found out a worker tried to kill our revolutionary leader.'

After returning to my room briefly to freshen up, I was accompanied by Leonid to the Metropol, literally only a five-minute walk across the road from the Kremlin. Opened in 1905, the Metropol Hotel was situated on Theatre Square in the historic heart of Moscow. Like the other grand hotels of the era; such as the Waldorf Astoria in New York, Claridge's in London, and the Ritz in Paris; the Metropol set the standard in the city for luxury and service. It was the first hotel in Moscow to have hot water and telephones in the rooms, international cuisine in the restaurants, and an American bar off the lobby.

Within days of its opening, the Metropol became the preferred stamping ground not only for cosmopolitan travellers, but also for the glamourous and wealthy of the city. Twelve years after its opening, the Metropol found itself serving as a fortress in a pitched battle with forces loyal to the Tsar defending the eastern flank of the Kremlin within the hotel's suites, while the communist Bolsheviks returned fire from the streets below. In the ensuing battle, nearly every window in the hotel was shattered.

In fact, when the American journalist John Reed arrived in the city, shortly after witnessing the fall of the Hermitage in St. Petersburg, he was assured by the Metropol's unflappable front desk captain: "We have some very comfortable rooms, if the gentleman does not mind a little fresh air." When the victorious Bolsheviks decided to return the capital to Moscow, after 400 years in St. Petersburg, the city did not have the necessary infrastructure to house the new government.

So, the Bolsheviks seized the Metropol, threw out the guests, renamed it the Second House of the Soviets, and used it to accommodate communist officials, and various departments of the fledgling State. In fact, it was in Suite 217 of the Metropol that Yakov Sverdlov, the first chairman of the All-Russia Executive Committee, locked the constitutional drafting committee in the room, vowing he wouldn't unlock the door until they had finished their work. Within a matter of hours, the committee re-emerged with a new constitution which officially heralded the victory of the Proletariat over the tsarist forces of privilege.

Right then and there, the Metropol's existence as a grand hotel should have come to an end. But when the major European nations began restoring trade and diplomatic relations in the 1920s, the Bolsheviks realised that the hotels of Moscow were going to provide Western visitors with their first impression of the new Russia. Should weary ambassadors or businessmen spend their visit in some austere hostel with shared bathrooms, humble furnishings, and limited services, they might draw the conclusion that Communism was failing! So, in order to signal their success, the Bolsheviks found themselves removing the bureaucrats and apparatchiks, and restoring the Metropol to its original glory, complete with uniformed bellhops in the lobby, silver service in the restaurants, and American jazz in the bar.

Leonid and I arrived fifteen minutes early, and enjoyed a cocktail at the American jazz bar, just alongside the lobby. Two saxophonists and a drummer were accompanying a pianist in an upbeat jazz number, as we both ordered a "Bloody Mary," a fashionable bourgeoisie drink only invented the year before, in Paris. After about ten minutes, the hotel manager discreetly advised us that Lenin and his wife were comfortably seated in the upstairs presidential dining room, waiting for us.

When we arrived, I was immediately overwhelmed by the sheer opulence of the dining room. Covered in plush red carpet, a grand crystal chandelier, classic marble columns, wall and ceiling paintings; it also had a floor to ceiling window with a spectacular view of the Kremlin, lit up brilliantly at night. Also visible was the Bolshoi Theatre, and the main Moscow avenue of Tverskaya.

There was a set menu, comprising an expert blending of traditional Russian cooking, with some local Moscow culinary traditions. We began our Russian gastronomic experience with shots of horseradish vodka, paired very well with our appetizers, comprising raw fish, and two kinds of caviar on blini, which are Russian pancakes made from wheat. Then we went on to pelmini, a traditional Russian dumpling with soup. Usually, pelmini was made with meat, but on this occasion the chef created this delicacy with fish, which was just sublime. Next came a very traditional borscht soup dish. This one came with freshly chopped herbs and sour cream. For the main course, we had a roast beef, and a grilled fish dish, accompanied by an assortment of steamed vegetables and mashed potatoes. Finally, we ended the magnificent meal with a dessert of honey cake with raspberries. We ate this with a shot of honey vodka.

This was one of the most exquisite dining experiences of my life. Here I was, in the heart of Moscow in 1922, dining with the leader of the Bolshevik Revolution, Vladimir Lenin, and his wife Nadezhda, and closest adviser Leonid; all die-hard communists, in absolute luxury and opulence befitting the greatest kings and queens of Europe. The ironic juxtaposition did not escape me.

What was also fascinating about this dining experience, was that Lenin and his wife did not utter a single word about the dire situation we were about to confront – the power struggle between Stalin and Trotsky. The entire conversation was superficial pleasantries. I figured the reason there wasn't serious discussion that evening, was because the presidential dining room was probably bugged by Stalin loyalists, and Lenin knew it. Anyhow, after a very pleasant dinner, where I gained a valuable insight into the magnetic charismatic personality of Lenin, and the utter loyalty Nadezhda had towards her husband; we made our way the short distance back to the Kremlin Palace, where I retired to my room, and reflected upon the life ofVladimir Lenin.

Lenin was born Vladimir Ilyich Ulyanov in Simbirsk, a large town of around 45,000 people located along the Volga River. His family was of mixed ethnic heritage, with Russian, German, Swedish, and Jewish, ancestries. Only a generation before, the Ulyanovs had been peasant serfs. Lenin's father, Ilya, completed a university education, became a teacher, and rose within the system to become a school inspector.

Their humble origins furnished the Ulyanovs with empathy towards Russia's peasant and working classes. They were also politically informed and liberal-minded. In her memoirs, Lenin's sister recalled the family home being filled with passionate discussion and debates about the situation in Russia. Tragedy struck the Ulyanovs twice in the 1880s. His father Ilya, died in 1886; and in the following year, Vladimir's older brother, Alexander, a university student, was arrested and hanged for his alleged involvement in a plot to assassinate Tsar Alexander III.

This event led to the Ulyanovs being condemned and ostracised as revolutionaries. Both his father's death, and his brother's execution, had a significant impact on Vladimir Ulyanov. He lost faith in God and religion, and his political position began to shift from liberalism to radical socialism. Vladimir became interested in the same radical ideas as his late brother, particularly the work of the revolutionary socialist philosopher, Nikolai Chernyshevsky. In the autumn of 1887, Vladimir entered Kazan University to study law. His enrolment was secured with the help of a written reference from his former headmaster, the father of Alexander Kerensky, the future leader of the provisional government just before the Bolshevik Revolution.

It was at university when Vladimir Ulyanov became first involved in radical Marxist groups. Both the university, and the local authorities, quickly identified him as a "person of interest". Within weeks of commencing his studies, Vladimir was expelled. He managed to complete his studies independently in 1891; though his subsequent political activities meant he didn't get to practise law.

Entering adulthood, Vladimir Ulyanov became obsessive about socialism and revolution. He read voraciously, consuming books about philosophy and socialist theory, political propaganda, and reports from or about revolutionary groups around the world. When not reading, he was writing or speaking in workers' circles, or at underground meetings. In the early 1890s, Ulyanov formed an alliance with Julius Martov, the future leader of the Menshevik communist faction. It was also at this time that he married one of his fellow socialists, Nadezhda Krupskaya. His political activities brought him to the attention of the tsarist regime. For much of the 1890s, he lived and worked under assumed names, and sometimes in disguise.

He was eventually captured in 1895, and sentenced to three years' isolation in Siberia. In 1900, Ulyanov began another period of exile, this time in several cities of Western Europe. It was during this period that he adopted the codename "Lenin," possibly a derivation of the Lena River in Siberia. In 1902, Lenin published: "What is to Be Done? – Burning Questions of our Movement." In this treatise, he outlined his vision of an organised movement to bring about a socialist revolution. It called for a small party that was tightly run, carefully planned, hard-working, disciplined, and secretive.

In Lenin's view, membership of this party should be restricted, in order to keep out infiltrators, interlopers, and the half-hearted. Ideological and tactical decisions would be made by an intellectual elite, and not subject to the whims and self-interest of the masses. Each party member would be a "professional revolutionary" devoting all of his or her time, energy, and zeal, to the socialist cause. Lenin himself was the living embodiment of this idea. He lived an austere existence with few creature comforts or social pleasures. His only interests were socialism and revolution; broken occasionally by ice-skating, playing chess, or listening to Beethoven.

Lenin was not just dedicated to the theory of revolution; he also took an interest in the physical and logistic aspects. According to the historian, Orlando Figes, the Bolshevik leader prepared instruction guides for everything from bomb use to bank robbery. He wore leather, and undertook physical exercise and weightlifting to convey the impression of strength and masculinity. Lenin's radical political views and prolific revolutionary activities made him a wanted man in Russia.

He spent many years out of the country, living in exile in cities like Munich, Prague, Paris, and Manchester. Lenin was in London and caught off guard by the events of the 1905 Russian Revolution. He returned briefly, but was back in exile by 1907. In April 1917, Lenin returned to Russia with the assistance of the German government, which gave him the opportunity to undermine and destabilise the new Provisional Government. On arrival, Lenin delivered a speech at Finland Station that became the basis for his famous April Theses; which was a document of ten points focusing Bolshevik efforts on opposing the Provisional Government, promoting a socialist revolution, and laying the groundwork for a proletariat-led government.

Lenin was forced back into exile in mid-1917 following the spontaneous "July Days" uprising, which he neither endorsed or exploited. As government troops combed Petrograd looking for the Bolsheviks leader, he shaved off his trademark beard, donned the clothes of a fisherman, and slipped across the water into Finland.

Lenin returned to Russia in September 1917 to oversee the Bolshevik resurgence. His determination to overthrow the Provisional Government made him the driving force behind the October Revolution. Afterwards, Lenin immediately took charge of the Soviet government, issuing its first decrees, and shaping its economic policies. During his leadership of the Bolsheviks and the Soviet state, Vladimir Lenin was subjected to several threats and assassination attempts. The most notable of these occurred on 30th August 1918, when Fanya Kaplan, a lone assassin with populist sympathies, fired two shots into his upper body in Moscow.

Lenin survived this attack, but the complications and effects of his injuries contributed towards the shortening of his lifespan. According to the historian, Robert Service, who gained access to the Bolshevik leader's medical records, Lenin's awareness that his time was limited, contributed to his obsession, impatience, and authoritarianism. Whatever the causes, the final three years of Lenin's life were marked by poor health. He suffered from tinnitus, insomnia, and severe headaches; and then endured three significant strokes in May 1922, December 1922, and March 1923.

From this point on, Lenin spent much of his time at his Gorki mansion. He remained sharp-minded, kept abreast of political developments, and continued writing briefs and letters to party officials. Joseph Stalin was put in charge of his convalescence; and proceeded to manipulate Lenin to his own advantage.

Vladimir Lenin died on 21st January 1924. His funeral, held in freezing conditions in Red Square, was attended by around 60,000 people. The Politburo voted to preserve Lenin's body, and place it on display to the public; a decision opposed by his widow, Nadezhda Krupskaya. About the legacy of Lenin, the historian, Nina Tumarkin, said:

> The real Lenin was neither hero, nor gentleman – but he was a genius in revolutionary politics. Lenin the cult figure was later lauded for his enormous modesty. This is partly true and partly false. Lenin was neither greedy nor vain. He coveted neither material possessions, nor the luxury or enjoying the knowledge that tens of millions of people might admire an inflated version of his biography. He was supremely self-confident and had no need of such vanities. What he sought throughout his life was the means to impose his will on a populace that bore little resemblance to him in temperament or talent.

My understanding of Lenin's ideology was reinforced by the following quotations attributed to him:

- Freedom in capitalist society always remains about the same as it was in ancient Greek republics. Freedom from slave owners.
- There are decades where nothing happens; and there are weeks where decades happen.
- Despair is typical of those who do not understand the causes of evil, see no way out, and are incapable of struggle.
- A lie told often enough becomes the truth.
- Without Revolutionary theory, there can be no Revolutionary Movement.
- Give me just one generation of youth, and I'll transform the whole world.
- Can a nation be free if it oppresses other nations? It cannot.
- Sometimes – history needs a push.

- The best way to control the opposition is to lead it ourselves.
- The Capitalists will sell us the rope with which we will hang them.
- The way to crush the bourgeoisie is to grind them between the millstones of taxation and inflation.
- Every society is three meals away from chaos.
- While the State exists, there can be no freedom. When there is freedom, there will be no State.
- Three keys to success: read, read, read.
- Imperialism: The final stage of Capitalism.
- I can't listen to music too often. It affects your nerves, makes you want to say stupid nice things, and stroke the heads of people who could create such beauty while living in this vile hell.
- The goal of Socialism is Communism.
- It is more pleasant and useful to go through "the experience of the revolution" than to write about it.
- We are not utopians, we do not "dream" of dispensing at once with all administration, with all subordination. These anarchist dreams, based upon incomprehension of the tasks of the proletarian dictatorship, are totally alien to Marxism, and, as a matter of fact, serve only to postpone the socialist revolution until people are different. No, we want the socialist revolution with people as they are now, with people who cannot dispense with subordination, control, and "foremen and accountants".
- Whenever the cause of the people is entrusted to professors, it is lost.
- There are no morals in politics; there is only experience. A scoundrel may be of use because he is a scoundrel.
- All official and liberal science defends wage-slavery, whereas Marxism has declared relentless war on that slavery.
- The intellectual forces of the workers and peasants are growing and getting stronger in their fight to overthrow the bourgeoisie and their accomplices, the educated classes, the lackeys of capital, who consider themselves the brains of the nation. In fact, they are not its brains but its shit.

- Attention, must be devoted principally to raising the workers to the level of revolutionaries; it is not our task to descend to the level of the "working masses".
- Revolution can never be forecast; it cannot be foretold; it comes of itself. Revolution is brewing and is bound to flare up.

The years between 1922 and 1928 witnessed a desperate struggle for power between Trotsky and Stalin. Lenin knew this was going to happen. There was nothing to prevent it. Lenin found Trotsky able but overconfident. Lenin knew that Stalin had concentrated a great deal of power in his own hands. He was afraid Stalin didn't know how to use it. Fortunately, Lenin left history a Testament of his anguished thoughts in 1922.

In the struggle of the mid-1920s, Trotsky argued for a more highly trained managerial force in industry, and for economic planning as an instrument that the State could use to control social change. He wanted agriculture to be completely mechanized, and peasant individualism to be weakened. Trotsky also maintained that only a world revolution would permit Russia to carry socialism to its proper conclusion. Socialism, in other words, could not succeed in one country. He believed there needed to be a world socialist revolution, otherwise Russian socialism was doomed to failure. The opponents of Trotsky's left deviation found their voice in Nikolai Bukharin, the editor of *Pravda*, the Party's newspaper.

A defender of the New Economic Plan (NEP), Bukharin managed to soften the rigorous Marxist doctrine of the class struggle. He believed socialism was sure of success. Bukharin did not believe in rapid industrialization. His vision of socialism would be attained gradually over time. He favoured cooperatives among peasants, but opposed collectivization in which the peasants owned everything "collectively." In foreign affairs, Bukharin was eager to work with non-communist groups who might be useful to Russia. In his rise to power, Stalin used Bukharin's ideas to discredit Trotsky, then, partly because Bukharin's policies were failing, he adopted many of Trotsky's policies, and eliminated Bukharin.

Stalin was not a theoretician. His Marxism took the form of opportunism and catechism. He was not an intellectual, as Trotsky was. He could mimic Marxist ideology, but could not elaborate upon the theoretical underpinnings of his statements. Stalin was a Party worker, and it was in the Party apparatus where he felt the most comfortable. He came to favour rapid industrialization. At the end of 1927, he ordered the collectivization of agriculture, because its output was small when compared to the industrial sector. Agriculture, like industry, he said, must be transformed into a large-scale unified State enterprise.

In opposition to Trotsky, Stalin maintained that socialism was possible within Russia alone. An independent socialist state could indeed exist. This did not mean that Stalin abandoned the idea of a world revolution. What it did mean is that until the world revolution did take place, Russia would have to serve as the world's shining example of socialism. In international affairs, this doctrine allowed the Soviet Union to pursue a policy of "peaceful coexistence" with capitalist states when necessary. Of course, this also meant that the Soviet Union would support socialist revolutions whenever possible. Stalin's idea of "socialism in one country" gave inner strength to those communists who had doubts about the prospects of a world revolution.

And while Trotsky continued to argue a western Marxist version of the future revolution, Stalin convinced everyone that the revolution in socialism that he himself had helped to create was a Russian idea, thereby bolstering his overtly nationalist posture. By the end of the Civil War, Stalin was Commissar of Nationalities. In this position he dealt with the affairs of 65 million, out of a total of 140 million, inhabitants of the new Russian Soviet Republic. In 1922, Stalin proposed the new Union of Socialist Soviet Republics (USSR) as a substitute for the existing federation of republics. In the USSR, Moscow would control war, foreign policy, and trade; and would coordinate finance, the economy, food, and labour.

Stalin was also Commissar of the Workers' and Peasants' Inspectorate. His duties here included the elimination of inefficiency and corruption from every branch of the civil service, and to train a loyal cadre of civil servants. Although the Inspectorate never did what it was supposed to do, it did give Stalin direct control over thousands of bureaucrats, and as a result, over the entire machinery of government. Lenin attacked Stalin's work in the Inspectorate, in late 1923, but by then it was too late. Stalin had managed to secure an ever-widening circle of loyal officials into key positions within the Party, while he himself controlled the affairs of the State. As we have seen, Stalin was also a member of the politburo, the five-man group of party bosses elected by the Central Committee. Here, his job was the day-to-day management of the Party.

He was the permanent liaison officer between the Politburo and the Orgburo, which assigned Party personnel to their duties in factory, office, and army units. Besides these important posts, we have seen that Stalin also became General Secretary of the Party's Central Committee, in April 1922. In this role, he prepared agendas for Politburo meetings, and passed on decisions down to the lower levels of the Party and government. In essence, he controlled all Party appointments, promotions, and demotions. He made sure that local trade unions, cooperatives, and army units, were led by loyal communists, responsible in all cases to Stalin himself. He also kept detailed files on all managers of industry, and all Party members. This is how a simple Georgian peasant captured so much power for himself in the two years before Lenin's death. Stalin knew exactly what he was doing.

In a centralized one-party state like the Soviet Union, a man of Stalin's immense ambitions, who held so many key positions, had an enormous advantage in the struggle for power. The Soviet State was new. It suffered a great deal because its revolutionary leader and great prophet, Vladimir Lenin, had been incapacitated for the last few years of his life. Although Stalin held numerous key positions, none of his positions were as important as the Ministry of War; and the head of this ministry was none other than Leon Trotsky.

So the point here, is that at this time in the early 1920s, the likelihood of Stalin assuming power, was not generally recognised; until it was too late. Inside the Politburo, Stalin formed a three-man triumvirate with Zinoviev and Kamenev. Zinoviev was chairman of the Petrograd Soviet, and head man of the Communist International. Kamenev was Lenin's deputy, and president of the Moscow Soviet. The three taken together – Stalin, Zinoviev, and Kamenev – were "old Bolsheviks." In other words, these three men had been behind Lenin, and the Bolshevik cause right from the very start. This could not be said about Trotsky. Before 1917, Trotsky had been a Menshevik, and served as an independent member of the intelligentsia.

The triumvirate of Stalin, Zinoviev, and Kamenev, proved to be completely unworkable. Each man used the secret police in order to suppress all plots against them. All three resisted Trotsky's demands to reform the Party. The three, at Stalin's prompting, initiated the cult of Lenin, immediately before his death in 1924, so that any act by Trotsky would have appeared as a violent act against the now dead iconic leader of the revolution. Any Trotsky supporter within the Party was assigned a post as far away from Moscow as possible. Stalin and the others also prevented the publication of Lenin's Testament, so that the rank and file, the ordinary Party members, would have no knowledge regarding Lenin's grave doubts about Stalin's leadership abilities. Instead, they published everything Trotsky had ever said which might have been at odds with Lenin.

Early in 1925, Stalin and his allies forced Trotsky to resign as the Minister of War. The triumvirate was then dissolved. Stalin allied himself with Bukharin, and other right-wing members of the Politburo, to which he now appointed his loyal followers. Using all of his accumulated powers, Stalin struck against his former allies on all questions of policy.

As a result, Zinoviev and Kamenev, moved into an alliance with Trotsky in 1926. Stalin then proceeded to charge Zinoviev with plotting with the army, and so Zinoviev was expelled from the Politburo. Next, Trotsky was expelled from the Politburo, and Zinoviev was ousted as president of the Communist International. In December 1927, a Communist Party Congress expelled Trotsky from the Party, and exiled him to Central Asia. With Trotsky exiled from the country, Lenin dead, and Zinoviev and Kamenev stripped of political power, Stalin assumed total control and was ready to implement his "revolution from above."

The next morning, I awoke early and went for a walk around the walled perimeter of the Kremlin, followed by a light breakfast with Lenin and Leonid.

'Comrade Luca, Trotsky is a very impressive, highly intelligent, and charismatic man. What he lacks is modesty, and the ruthless cunning streak which Stalin possesses in spades. When you and Leonid meet with him shortly, you will need to take this into account, and come up with a plan of action which involves the sidelining of Stalin and his loyal cronies. The long term future of our socialist Revolution lays in the hands of Trotsky, who is a true believer. With the right people holding key positions around him, and providing him with necessary support, Trotsky will excel. Stalin is an opportunistic dictator, and if he takes over, our Revolution will die under the suffocating grip of his iron fist.'

'I understand comrade Lenin.'

When Leonid and I arrived at the Metropol, we were taken to a suite which was often used as a secure meeting room by Lenin. Waiting for us was Trotsky.

'Comrade Trotsky, may I introduce you to Luca Evangelista, a professor of political science, visiting us from London.'

'Good to see you Leonid, and a pleasure to meet you Luca. Comrade Lenin has told me about you. Sit down gentlemen.'

After a short but pleasant conversation about the grandeur and history of the Metropol Hotel, I proceeded to express my concern and outline my strategy.

'Comrade Trotsky, you are a gifted man. The Revolution and the subsequent success of the Bolsheviks in the Civil War would not have been possible without your formidable intellect and exceptional leadership. I know that comrade Lenin considers you to be his natural successor. I also know you enjoy widespread support amongst Lenin's followers within the wider Bolshevik Party, but virtually no support in the current Politburo.'

'I don't currently have support within the Politburo, Luca, because Stalin has put his people in there. The real power lies within the rank and file members of the Party in any event, not the Politburo?'

'If I may be direct with you, sir, while you have been doing the rounds delivering speeches throughout the country, engaged in your deep thinking and writing, and working towards the spread of Communism internationally; Stalin has been astutely and aggressively active behind the scenes, undermining you, and using his powerful position as General Secretary, to appoint his followers into key positions throughout the Party apparatus. He's achieved much, already, in the few weeks he has been holding that position.'

'Stalin is an ignorant fool. He's an embarrassment to our cause. He is crude, arrogant, and stupid. I know of his extreme ambition to accumulate power, and gain the support of Lenin to position himself as the next leader of the Party and the State. We will never let that happen.'

'With the greatest respect, you are severely underestimating his capabilities, and his sheer brutish force of will to get what he wants. Comrade Trotsky, you are not a political manipulator like he is. I understand this. But he is taking full advantage of your aloofness and your disinterest in forging political connections within the Party. You haven't made a move to secure your power base; whereas he has.'

'Lenin has been giving me similar warnings about the threat posed by Stalin, comrade Luca, but I have kept reassuring him that when the time comes for our great leader to step down, the majority of the Party will vote for his heir-apparent as the new leader; and as you say, I am Lenin's anointed heir-apparent.'

'Comrade Trotsky, in his role as General Secretary, Stalin has full control over the flow of information within the Party. In the short time he has held this position he has remade it into the most powerful position in the Party. He is suppressing messages from Lenin that are critical of him, or favourable to you, and manipulating Party communications, discrediting you at every opportunity.'

'Well then, what do you propose we do, comrade Luca?'

'I have come up with a detailed plan. Indulge me please, while I explain it. We know the supreme decision-making body is supposed to be the Congress of the Communist Party. All of the 1,225 delegates are loyal members of the Party, representing all regions of the State. This is where Lenin intended the real power to be held, but of course, Stalin has eroded its power. We will rectify this. But more of that later. Currently the Congress only meets once a year; and in between these annual meetings, the Party is ruled by the seventy-odd members of the Central Committee of the Party, which is meant to provide executive leadership. All of these members, who are the most influential Party members, are elected by the Congress. Then, we have the Politburo, which is meant to be the highest ranking policy-making authority within the Party. It is supposed to come up with policies in accordance with the ideology of the Central Committee; again Stalin has abused this process for his own personal ambitions. All of the Politburo ten members, including Stalin and Lenin, have been elected by the Central Committee. Incredibly, all of the other eight members; Nikolai Bukharin, Lev Kamenev, Mikhail Kalinin, Vyacheslav Molotov, Gregory Zinoviev, Alexei Rykov, Mikhail Tomsky, and Valerian Kuybyshev; are close allies of Stalin! Finally, we come to the Secretariat, which is responsible for managing the day to day affairs of the Party and the State. Its five members are also elected by the Central Committee; which appointed Stalin as the General Secretary. In that role, Stalin has yielded immense power in placing his cronies in many key positions throughout the Party. Gentlemen, as a matter of urgency, comrade Vladimir Lenin must call an extraordinary meeting of the Central Committee, the seventy-odd members of which are the real Party powerbrokers, and the majority of whom, still revere Lenin. At this meeting, Lenin needs to renounce Joseph Stalin, and formally anoint you, comrade Trotsky as his heir-apparent and successor, and clearly explain his reasons for this decision in a forceful way, mustering up all of his revolutionary zeal and passion, so that there can be no doubt whatsoever amongst the members of the Central Committee. Immediately following Lenin's speech, a formal vote should be held, resolving to vacate ALL of the positions currently held within the Politburo, and the Secretariat. Then, a vote should be conducted to appoint the NEW members of both bodies. These new members should be Trotsky-Lenin loyalists, all to be nominated by Lenin; with yourself, comrade Trotsky, to be appointed as General Secretary of the Secretariat. Before this meeting of the Central Committee is announced, Lenin must also arrange for Stalin's arrest and strict detention, and a purge of all Stalin diehard loyalists within the Party, so he and his followers cannot participate in this process in any way. Comrade Trotsky as the Minister of War, you have full control of the army. You must use the resources of the army to round up and detain all Stalin loyalists. But violence must not be used, otherwise Stalin's supporters will use that against you, including the possibility of inciting another civil war. Force but not violence.'

'That's a ruthless plan, comrade Luca.'

'Comrade Trotsky, this plan is a walk in the park, compared to the widespread brutal violence Stalin is willing to unleash, in order to preserve his lust for power. Removing Stalin and his cronies from positions of power is absolutely necessary for the long term survival of the Revolution, and the creation of a truly Marxist State.'

'Very well then, let's present your plan to Lenin, Luca Evangelista.'

I didn't waste any time in presenting my plan to Lenin and his wife, that afternoon. He was totally supportive of the plan. We agreed time was of the essence. I worked closely with him in putting together a written message to all Party members, from Lenin. It was a modified version of his Testament, that this time was not going to be suppressed by Stalin, because Lenin himself would be delivering it to a full meeting of the Central Committee. After much discussion and amendments, we came up with this message:

"The stability of the Central Committee is vital for the continual progression of our Socialist Revolution. Our Party is currently fractured into two classes, and this is creating much instability. If we do not remedy this fracture, here and now, we are doomed to failure. The primary cause of our Party fracture is the ongoing power struggle between comrades Stalin and Trotsky. Comrade Stalin, having become General Secretary, has unlimited authority concentrated in his hands, and I am not sure whether he will always be capable of using that authority with sufficient caution. Stalin is too rude, and this defect, although quite tolerable in our midst, and in dealing among us Communists, becomes intolerable in a General Secretary. Comrade Trotsky, on the other hand, is distinguished not only by his outstanding ability and intellect; but he is also the most capable man in the current Central Committee to advance the cause of the Socialist Revolution, particularly if he is surrounded by loyal and capable Party administrators. So it is for these reasons that I now hereby call upon all members of the Central Committee to vote for the removal of comrade Stalin from all positions within the Party, and to expel him from the Party. I also call on members to vote for comrade Trotsky, my declared successor, to the position of General Secretary. In addition, I am seeking your vote to declare all current Politburo and Secretariat positions vacant, with the exception of mine, and comrade Trotsky's."

Satisfied with my role in changing the course of Russian history, later that afternoon, I went for a jog around the walled perimeter of the Kremlin. As I was jogging, a sudden blow to the back of my head rendered me unconscious. When I awoke a few hours later, feeling very dizzy and groggy, I was blindfolded, handcuffed, and very cold. I was sitting on a damp concrete surface in what appeared to be a holding cell of some sort. I could hear two voices echoing in the background. Suddenly I heard footsteps coming in my direction, and then the screeching sound of a key unlocking a metallic door. The next thing I knew my blindfold was removed. I was shocked to see that the two men standing in front of me were Stalin and Leonid.

'Comrade Leonid! You betrayed Lenin?'

'Shut up Luca Evangelista! I know who you are and where you really come from, but your efforts have amounted to nothing. You are an American spy! The natural successor to Lenin will always be comrade Stalin. Do you understand?'

'How dare you undermine me!!' shouted Stalin.

He proceeded to savagely kick me with such force, that I thought I was going to die. When I regained consciousness, I was laying on my back, feeling excruciating pain in my head, stomach, and back. I was certain I had some cracked ribs. I could see a pool of blood on the floor next to my head. The two of them were still standing over me.

'Are you ready to tell us the truth now, miserable scum!? We know who you are! You have been sent here by your capitalist masters to sow the seeds to overthrow our revolutionary government, by installing the American puppet and traitor of socialism, Trotsky, haven't you!?' growled Leonid.

'He's not answering, beat him up some more' Stalin said, in a soft voice.

This time, Leonid grabbed me by the chest with clenched fists, and dragged me onto my feet, pushed me up against the concrete wall, and proceeded to inundate me with savage punches to my head and chest. I clenched my handcuffed fists and meekly tried to protect my face from his brutal assault.

Just as I was on the verge of losing consciousness for a third time, I heard loud screams as five soldiers stormed into the holding cell. They immediately subdued Stalin and Leonid.

'Comrades Joseph Stalin and Leonid Lebedeva, you are hereby under arrest, by the authority of our great leader Vladimir Lenin, and our Minister of War, Leon Trotsky.'

'How dare you! You will pay for this!' screamed Stalin, as he and Leonid were led out of the cell by four of the soldiers.

The remaining soldier had a first aid kit, and attended to my wounds.

'Luca Evangelista, when you did not return from your Kremlin jog, comrade Lenin became alarmed. He contacted comrade Trotsky, who, being suspicious of Leonid Lebedeva, had arranged for him to be placed under surveillance by army intelligence officers, a couple of weeks ago. It was these officers who observed Lebedeva assaulting and kidnapping you, and who followed him to this abandoned prison facility, which Stalin likes to use to torture political opponents.'

'I never imagined Leonid Lebedeva would be spying for Stalin. He and Lenin were so close.'

'Stalin is an incredibly shrewd political operator who knows how to corrupt, bribe, and blackmail people into doing his dirty work,' said the soldier as he escorted me back to the Kremlin Palace.

At the palace, I was attended to by Lenin's personal doctor. Thankfully, my injuries were not severe. No bones were broken, and no organs were damaged. It was mainly lacerations and bruising. I rested in the palace for a few hours. Later, feeling somewhat better, I met with Lenin and his wife, who thanked me, and reassured me that the Central Committee meeting would go ahead. Lenin showed me surveillance photos of a mysterious man who had been secretly meeting with Leonid on a number of occasions in the last couple of days. It was Thero!

They weren't able to identify him of course, and I decided to play dumb and tell Lenin I had no idea who this man was. So, Thero had told Leonid I was an American spy. Of course, he couldn't tell Leonid I was from the future. If he had, he would have breached a sacred oath from his home planet. I left for the 21st century, certain that Lenin was absolutely determined to purge the Party of all Stalin loyalists, and position his successor, Leon Trotsky, to take control of the Party and the Soviet Socialist State.

The piano bar was a hive of activity when I arrived. The Billy Joel impersonator was in full flight, performing "Uptown Girl" while a number of people in the audience were happily singing along, egged on by cocktails. I was feeling lethargic, so ordered an espresso martini to pick me up. Otto arrived not long after me.

'How are you feeling Luca? You took some heavy blows.'

'I'm sore, but otherwise fine. I'll be back to normal in a few days, ready for the Hitler mission, Otto.'

'Lenin delivered a fiery and passionate address to the members of the Central Committee. Days before the crucial meeting of Party leaders, Trotsky personally oversaw a massive army effort to round up and arrest thousands of Stalin loyalists throughout the country. It was Trotsky at his finest. His leadership skills were on full display. Following Lenin's speech, a clear majority of the Central Committee members voted to remove Joseph Stalin from all his positions; to expel him from the Party; to vacate all Politburo and Secretariat positions, other than Lenin and Trotsky; and to appoint capable Lenin-Trotsky loyalists to both bodies. The Central Committee meeting was a resounding success. But more than this Luca, Trotsky went on to become an outstanding Soviet leader, and successfully created a Marxist Socialist State, with none of the purges, famine, repression, and savage violence experienced under Stalin. The Soviet Union became such a shining beacon of Socialism, that the Revolution spread to other countries, including Germany, France, and Italy. Trotsky also skilfully managed the rivalry with the United States to such an extent, that although there was still a Cold War, conflicts such as Berlin, Korea, Vietnam, and Cuba; did not happen in that version of Earth.'

'Wow! That's impressive, Otto.'

Isabella was waiting outside her apartment when I arrived later that evening. She looked anxious, distressed, and sleep deprived.

'Baby, please sit down' she said, as she gave me a glass of neat gin.

'What's happening, sweetheart.'

I could see she was very uncomfortable. She was shaking, as she poured herself some gin as well. It seemed like an eternity before she finally spoke.

'I've been seeing Gary. It started with us just having drinks, and him listening to me and keeping me company, baby. I had no intention of cheating on you!'

Gary was a close friend of Isabella. She met him when they were both studying at the academy of performing arts. I was shocked. My mind was racing with flashes of the many instances when we were out socialising and Gary would be very tactile, often touching her hands, while they were engaged in some animated conversation. I cleaned up the gin in two gulps to numb my pain, before I spoke.

'How long have the two of you been intimate?'

'It's been a couple of months, baby.'

'Why, Isabella? Why!?'

'He was just a friend!' she screamed. 'I never had any intimate feelings for him whatsoever! But it turns out he was secretly in love with me, baby! I never realised that. I never saw the signals. I needed somebody to talk to. Somebody to share my innermost feelings with. Somebody to distract me from my demons. He was always here for me. You weren't around. I'm so sorry Luca.'

Suddenly, she burst out crying, sobbing and sobbing, louder and louder. I could see she was tormented. She couldn't cope with telling me all this. I made it easy for her. Although I was in a complete state of surreal trance-like shock, I got up, kissed her on the cheek, wished her all the very best, and left her apartment, with her anguished cries echoing in my aching head. I never wanted to see her again.

It's the End of the World as we Know it (and I Feel Fine)

That's great, it starts with an earthquake, birds and snakes,
an aeroplane – Lenny Bruce is not afraid.
Eye of a hurricane, listen to yourself chum,
world serves its own needs, don't misserve your own needs.

Feed it up a knock, speed, grunt, no, strength, no.
Ladder, structure clatter with fear of height, down height.
Wire in a fire, represent the seven games, in a government for hire
and a combat site.

Left her, wasn't coming in a hurry with the furies breathing down
your neck.
Team by team reporters baffled, trumped, tethered crop.
Look at that low plane, fine then.

Uh oh, overflow, population, common group, but it'll do.
Save yourself, serve yourself. World serves its own needs, listen to your
heart bleed.
Tell me with the rapture and the reverent in the right-right.
You vitriolic, patriotic, slam, fight, bright light, feeling pretty psyched.

It's the end of the world as we know it.
It's the end of the world as we know it.
It's the end of the world as we know it and I feel fine.

Six o'clock – TV hour. Don't get caught in foreign tower.
Slash and burn, return, listen to yourself churn.
Lock him in uniform and book burning, blood letting.
Every motive escalate. Automotive incinerate.

Light a candle, light a motive. Step down, step down.
Watch a heel crush, crush. Uh-oh, this means no fear.
Cavalier, renegade and steer clear! A tournament, a tournament, a tournament of lies.
Offer me solutions, offer me alternatives and I decline.

It's the end of the world as we know it.
It's the end of the world as we know it.
(It's time I had some time alone)
It's the end of the world as we know it
(It's time I had some time alone) and I feel fine.
(I feel fine)

It's the end of the world as we know it. (it's time I had some time alone)
It's the end of the world as we know it. (It's time I had some time alone)
It's the end of the world as we know it
(it's time I had some time alone) and I feel fine.

The other night I tripped a nice continental drift divide.
Mount Saint Edelite.
Leonard Bernstein. Leonid Brezhnev. Lenny Bruce and Lester Bangs.
Birthday party, cheesecake, jelly bean, boom!
You symbiotic, patriotic, slam but neck, right? Right.

It's the end of the world as we know it. (It's time I had some time alone)
It's the end of the world as we know it. (It's time I had some time alone)
It's the end of the world as we know it (It's time I had some time alone)
and I feel fine.

It's the end of the world as we know it.
It's the end of the world as we know it.
It's the end of the world as we know it (It's time I had some time alone)
and I feel fine.

It's the end of the world as we know it. (It's time I had some time alone)
It's the end of the world as we know it. (It's time I had some time alone)
It's the end of the world as we know it (It's time I had some time alone) and I feel fine.

It's the end of the world as we know it. (It's time I had some time alone)
It's the end of the world as we know it. (it's time I had some time alone)
It's the end of the world as we know it (It's time I had some time alone) and I feel fine…

Bill Berry, Peter Buck, Mike Mills, Michael Stipe. R.E.M. (1987)

11

Adolf Hitler

Vienna, Austria, June 1908 CE

I MUST SAY, THIS NEXT TIME TRAVEL TRIP WAS THE ONE I WAS LOOKING forward to the most, along with the JFK trip. As a history teacher I have found that nothing else in history fascinates students more than the rise and fall of Hitler. Having researched him in so much detail, I was really looking forward to seeing for myself how close the actual man was to the image of the man, built up over many decades by a myriad of historians, and people that supposedly knew him.

The year was 1907 when Adolf Hitler left his hometown of Linz in Austria and arrived in the capital city, Vienna. He was supported by a small orphan's benefit that he qualified for after his father's death in 1903. He also received money from his beloved mother, Klara. It was not a large amount, but it was enough for him to get by on. Hitler was later joined by his childhood friend, August Kubizek; the man who was to be my contact when I arrived in Vienna. Hitler and Kubizek rented a room at Stumpergasse31, from Czech immigrant Maria Zakreys, between 22nd February to early in July, 1908. This room was in a central location close to Mariahilfer Strasse, one of the city's main shopping boulevards, and provided a good base for the young men to explore and enjoy the capital city.

The pair would often go for long walks in and around the centre of the city, and attend concerts, plays, and the opera. Both of them moved to Vienna with the hope of being accepted to study and become artists; Hitler wanted to become a painter, and Kubizek a musician. As a result, Hitler applied to the Vienna Academy of Fine Arts, and Kubizek applied to the Vienna Conservatory. What Kubizek did not know, however, was that Hitler had already applied to study at the Academy in 1907, prior to moving to Vienna. At this first attempt, he passed the initial exam, but was subsequently rejected, because his drawing skills were judged to be "unsatisfactory".

It appears that Kubizek was Hitler's closest friend, going back to his childhood in Linz, and probably his only true friend while in Vienna. Therefore, we can only look to him to provide details into Hitler's life during this period; and Kubizek's memoir: "Adolf Hitler, My Childhood Friend" which was published in 1953, does exactly that. Kubizek describes their living conditions as squalid and depressing. Hitler himself is described as a temperamental man who could fly into fits of rage, and long, often incoherent rants, about an unfair society in which Hitler thought he was a victim of an oppressive system that stopped him from progressing in life.

Kubizek describes a work-shy man who preferred to obsess relentlessly on personal projects, rather than "proper" paid work. For example, he obsessed over solving Vienna's housing crisis, by designing multiple occupancy accommodation for Austrian workers. He would also stay up all night writing operas and plays, which, according to Kubizek, he never finished. Hitler thought ordinary jobs were beneath him, he clearly did not want to become a cog in the wheel of society, and instead focused what misplaced attention he had, on lofty schemes he was neither qualified for, or able, to complete. He called these projects, his "studies." He worked on these studies all night, and slept during the day.

From their flat, Hitler would walk to watch political debates in the nearby Parliament building. In his autobiography, "Mein Kampf" he said that it was after watching these debates that he would grow to despise the country's paralytic political system, and democracy, in particular. Away from the flat and their studies, the two young men would also attend the Court Opera, standing in the cheap seats. This is where Hitler developed a passion for the opera of Richard Wagner, in particular.

They also went to the theatre and watched many plays. Kubizek noted how after each performance, Hitler would give detailed reviews in the form of lengthy and critical monologues. This even led to Kubizek suggesting that he should seek work as a drama critic, and write for a newspaper, providing some much-needed money for them to live on. Like all of the many other attempts by Kubizek to get his friend into employment, Hitler debated him on why each job was not suitable for him. These usually escalated into fully-blown arguments.

In November 1908, Kubizek returned to their flat after a two-months absence for compulsory Austrian military service, to discover his childhood friend had abruptly moved out, with no explanation. Hitler didn't even leave a forwarding address. The pair would not meet again until 1938. Hitler's sudden departure from the flat was a shock to Kubizek, but with the benefit of hindsight, the tell-tale signs were there. In the year Hitler moved from Linz to Vienna, he suffered two tragedies; his mother's death, and a second rejection from the Vienna Academy of Fine Arts.

Hitler was very close to his mother, Klara. In *Mein Kampf* he wrote that he had "honoured my father but loved my mother." Klara died on 21st December 1907, just a few months after he moved to Vienna. He described her death as a "dreadful blow." He temporarily moved back to Linz in her final weeks, to be with her. Not only was it painful on an emotional level, the death of Klara was also the beginning of a downward spiral into further poverty for Hitler, because Klara provided her son with financial support. This was an essential lifeline as the orphans' benefit he received due to his father's death, was not substantial enough to live on alone – and as we know, Hitler was fundamentally lazy, averse to work, and refused to support himself; instead he was keeping busy with his "studies" and pet projects.

In his book, *Adolf Hitler: My Childhood Friend* Kubizek made this observation about Hitler's mother, shortly after Hitler left her for Vienna.

> Frau Klara seemed more careworn than ever. Her face was deeply lined. Her eyes were lifeless, her voice sounded tired and resigned. I had the impression that, now that Adolf was no longer there, she had let herself go, and looked older and more ailing than ever. She certainly had concealed her condition from her son to make the parting easier for him. Or perhaps it was Adolf's impulsive nature that had kept up her vitality. Now, on her own, she seemed to be an old, sick woman.

Things took another turn for the worse a few months later when, in October 1908, Hitler reapplied for a place in the Academy of Fine

Arts. He was rejected for the second time. On this occasion his work was judged to be so poor that he wasn't even invited to take the formal entrance exam. So confident was Hitler in his skills as an artist, he described his rejection from art school as a "bolt from the blue." This was in direct contrast to his friend Kubizek, who had been accepted to study music at the Conservatory, and progressed well in his course. His lecturer even gave him students of his own to teach.

Kubizek completed his studies in 1912, and was hired as a conductor of the orchestra in the Austrian city of Marburg. In 1914, he married Anna Funke, and over the next few years she gave birth to three sons; Augustin, Karl, and Rudolf. When the First World War broke out, he joined the Austro-Hungarian Infantry, and although wounded in 1915, made a full recovery and returned to action.

After the war he became an official in the municipal council of Eferding, Upper Austria. In 1933, Kubizek sent Adolf Hitler a letter congratulating him on becoming Chancellor of Germany. Hitler replied, but did not meet Kubizek until 9th April 1938, during a visit to Linz. They met in a hotel lounge and reminisced for an hour. Hitler offered to revive his old friend's musical career by appointing him as the conductor of a prominent orchestra, but Kubizek, by now 50 years old, declined the offer. But he did accept Hitler's offer of funding his three sons through music school, and for years to come, Hitler would send birthday presents to Kubizek's elderly mother.

Hitler also hired Kubizek to write two short propaganda booklets about Hitler's early life. August Kubizek reminded Hitler of an occasion when, together in Linz, they went to see a performance of Wagner's "Rienzi." Hitler had come out mesmerized, as if in a trance. Hitler gripped Kubizek's hands and spoke of a mission that he was one day to receive from the people, in order to guide them out of slavery, to the heights of freedom.

Hitler remembered the occasion well, looked wistfully at his old friend, and said, "It began at that hour...." In 1939 and 1940, Hitler invited Kubizek to sit with him at the Bayreuth Festival in Bavaria, an annual celebration of the music of Richard Wagner. The occasions were, according to Kubizek in words reminiscent of Hitler's style, "the happiest of my earthly existence." Kubizek was arrested in December

1945, and was imprisoned and interrogated by United States Army officers. He was not released until 8th April 1947. His book, *Adolf Hitler: My Childhood Friend* was published in 1953, in which he declared,

> No power on earth could compel me to deny my friendship with Adolf Hitler.

August Kubizek died, aged 68, on 23rd October 1956, the very day the Hungarian Revolution broke out.

Details are scarce about Hitler's life between November 1908, and February 1910, when he moved into a men's dormitory on Meldemannstrabe27. However, records do disclose two locations where he stayed during this time. On 18th November 1908, Hitler signed for accommodation in Apartment 16, at Felberstrasse22. Occupants here could either rent a room, or a single bed in a dormitory. Given Hitler's fragile financial situation at this time, it is likely he opted for the bed in a dorm. This meagre accommodation was Hitler's home until August 1909.

Then, in the summer of 1909, an already struggling Hitler suffered yet another financial blow. His aunt had loaned him money, and now this source of income had dried up. Hitler moved out of the dorm accommodation, and moved into Sechshauserstrasse58, which was a rundown building in the remote 15th district ofVienna. His stay there did not last long though. An eviction notice dated 16th September 1909, shows that a student called Hitler was told to leave. The note does not provide a reason, but it is accepted that it was for not paying his rent. Just like one year earlier, when he departed from Kubizek, he did not leave a forwarding address.

It is believed that over the next three months, he lived on the streets, slept on park benches, and begged for money. Vienna had a large population of homeless people during this time. Park benches, alleys, and doorways were all common places for Vienna's homeless. Train stations, coffee houses, bars, and low-cost lodgings known as flophouses, were also popular destinations amongst Vienna's homeless. Another popular place at the time was the Prater amusement park, which was largely closed during the winter months. A bench in Prater was highly sought after, and fiercely competitive amongst Vienna's displaced.

During this time, Hitler would have relied heavily on charitable organisations for food and shelter. A relative of Maria Zakreys, his first Viennese landlord at Stumpergasse31, recalls seeing Hitler queuing up at the Merciful Sisters Hospital, for free food. The woman recalled seeing what she thought was once a neat young man now looking dishevelled, standing in line for soup and a piece of bread, in ragged clothes. The encounter took place just around the corner from Stumpergasse31, so being familiar with the area, Hitler would have known of the organisation's charitable activities. The situation for Hitler was so dire during this time that in a desperate attempt to raise some money, he sold his possessions; including his art supplies, general clothing, and overcoat.

His predicament must have been very extreme, because the harsh Austrian winter was closing in, with the temperature plummeting, and not having an overcoat would have made him more vulnerable to the cold conditions. Also, his art supplies were his only means of making money, other than begging on the streets.

After what would have been a gruelling three months relying on charity and living on Vienna's cold streets, Hitler succumbed to the winter and entered a homeless shelter in Meiding, an outer suburb of Vienna, in December 1909. Meiding was a workers' suburb, and the "Asylum for the Homeless" was located behind Meidinger cemetery, far from the residents, to hide its wretched occupants from view. The Meiding shelter was a large facility housing 1,000 of Vienna's most hopeless and destitute. Residents at the asylum could only be granted one weeks' accommodation at a time, making it difficult to plan for the future.

People often queued the length of the street to try and get a bed in the Meiding shelter. There are even numerous newspaper reports from the time that detail people dying on the pavement outside, whilst waiting for a bed, during extremely cold winter nights. Residents were forced to adhere to the shelter's strict rules and regimen. This included a mandatory bedtime, with entry to dorms controlled by locks. Lights-out was at a specific time. The bed would have been a simple cot in a group dormitory.

Residents also had to leave the premises by 9am, and were not permitted to enter during the day. The shelter literally stripped people of their dignity and sense of individuality, and must have sunk Hitler to a new low in his life to that point. The chaperoned public showers, and group delousing procedures would have aggravated and distressed him. And there was no privacy at mealtime as well, with everybody dining in a huge hall. While at the Meiding shelter, Hitler became acquainted with Reinhold Hanisch.

According to Hanisch, a typical day for them would start at 9am, when they would take a long walk through the central Vienna city streets to St. Katherine's Convent to queue up for soup, which would be distributed by the nuns at noon. They would then head to the train station, or a charity-run "warm-room" where poor people could seek some relief from the cold weather. In the afternoon, the pair would try their luck with the Salvation Army for some more food, before heading back to the homeless shelter. Hanisch was more experienced and accustomed to life on the streets than Hitler, and was good at spotting an opportunity.

It was during this time that the pair became business partners and started making some money together. Hanisch noted that Hitler was not good at begging, but he could paint. However, for the same reasons that made him bad at begging, Hitler was also a poor salesman. It struck Hanisch that Hitler should paint, and he could be his agent, selling his paintings and postcards across the city; building relationships with art dealers and frame-makers, many of whom were Jewish, eventually creating a list of regular customers. This business venture provided Hitler and Hanisch with much needed stability, and as a result, the pair saw an improvement in their situations when, in February 1910, they moved into the Mannerheim hostel for men, located at Meldemannstrabe27.

It had been a difficult fifteen months, and Hitler would have felt that he had benefited from a change in fortune when he moved into the Mannerheim hostel. He now had a business that provided relatively stable income. The price of a bed was reasonable, at 10 kronen per month, and another 15 kronen gave him a good supply of decent food. Other amenities and facilities available at the Mannerheim hostel which would have pleased Hitler, was a library with two reading rooms, a resident doctor, and bathroom facilities. There was also a clothes workshop, and laundry facilities. However, it seems that Hitler only had one set of clothes during the three years he spent at the hostel. Hitler would also have benefited from his own room. He was classified as a permanent tenant, which afforded him certain privileges, such as new linen every week, a bed, a table, an electric lamp, and a mirror.

There was a lock in his bedroom door too, which meant he could securely keep his belongings, and gain a sense of independence, after long periods of staying in group dormitories. His time at the Mannerheim definitely brought some stability back into Hitler's life. His painting was a key factor in achieving this stability. Business between Hitler and Hanisch was steady. Hitler would sit by the window in one of the reading rooms and paint local scenes, and landmark buildings in Vienna. These were often postcards and watercolours that were sold to taverns, or would be placed in empty picture frames for frame-makers and art dealers. He also sold his paintings to tourists.

For a while, the business venture blossomed, as Hanisch effectively hawked across Vienna selling Hitler's paintings wherever he could. After a while, Hitler knew what sold best – paintings of local scenes and landmarks. The profits were split 50-50, and the paintings typically fetched between 5 and 10 kronen. The business relationship however, would not last. Hitler left the hostel for a week with a man called Josef Neumann, to explore another business opportunity. Neumann was linked to Vienna's Jewish art trade, and Hitler thought he would be a better agent. Something happened during that week that left Hitler visibly shaken, and his relationship with Hanisch and Neumann never recovered. Hitler decided to cut out the middlemen, and started selling directly to art dealers. It is not known what actually happened during that week with Neumann, but it certainly had a lasting impact on Hitler.

The relationship with Hanisch really turned sour when Hitler accused him of stealing paintings, and owing him money. Hitler even testified against his former business partner in court in 1910, in an unrelated fraud case, to spite him. In later years, Hanisch reflected on his time with Hitler in Vienna: "He (Hitler) was never an ardent worker, was unable to get up in the morning, had difficulty in getting started, and seemed to be suffering from a paralysis of the will." In 1937, when Hitler was Fuhrer of Germany, Hanisch was arrested for speaking to the press about Hitler's early days in Vienna. It is alleged that whilst he was imprisoned, Hitler sent a direct order to the guards to kill him.

Hitler also became somewhat of an institution within the hostel. Fellow residents would gather around him to watch him paint. A keen interest in politics never left Hitler, and residents recall how he was an avid reader of the daily newspapers. He also borrowed books from the library on German history, German mythology, political pamphlets, and philosophy. Furthermore, in the Mannerheim hostel, he had an audience to perform his monologues for; he was known to give speeches on politics to the other residents.

After a positive three years in the Mannerheim, Hitler's time in Vienna came to an abrupt end when he managed to avoid conscription to the Austria-Hungary army. He failed the army's medical test, but is quoted as saying he did not want to serve, because of the mixtures of races in the army. He also foresaw the collapse of the Habsburg Empire, which contributed to his reasoning. He received the last of his father's estate in May 1913, and with that he moved to Munich. He survived for a time by continuing to sell his paintings in the same manner as he did in Vienna. But then in August 1914, he enlisted in the German Army to fight in the First World War.

I arrived in Vienna, outside the main entrance to the building at Stumpergasse31, on a bright sunny day, on 15th June 1908. I had read so much about Hitler's early years in Vienna, that the surroundings seemed quite familiar to me. I had also visited Vienna on a number of occasions when in Europe, and this was definitely a city which hadn't changed much over the years. Many of the beautiful buildings and landmarks in this great city had been preserved into the 21st century. I immediately recognised the smiling young man walking towards me.

'You must be August Kubizek!'

'Yes. It's my sincere pleasure to meet you here, Luca Evangelista. Come, there is a lovely café nearby.'

As we made our way to the café, I recognised the Burg Theatre, the Town Hall, and the Parliament building. There it was! We were making our way to the Café Landtmann. Opened in 1873, it was an instant hit, and adored by the residents of Vienna. I knew it was also the favourite café of Sigmund Freud, and Leon Trotsky, who were living in Vienna at the same time as Hitler. I wondered if Hitler and either Freud or Trotsky, were ever in the café at the same time.

A weird thought also occurred to me if I would see Trotsky for a second time during my time travels; the first time being in the Moscow of 1922, and the second time in the Vienna of 1908. From my research, I knew that it was a tradition for newly-minted graduates of the nearby University of Vienna, to come to the Café Landtmann, to celebrate. Coffee-house culture defined Vienna throughout the 18th, 19th, and early 20th centuries when hundreds of cafes opened around the city.

Viennese coffee houses played a role similar to that of clubs in the Anglo-Saxon tradition; they served as meeting places for thinkers, politicians, poets, and artists, alike; fuelled by caffeine and cakes. When we arrived at the café, we sat at one of the red leather booths, surrounded by velvet upholstery, and plush drapes. Kubizek ordered Viennese coffee, the café's classic pre-pealed soft-boiled eggs, and its famous apple strudel with rich custard sauce. The rich aroma of Vienna's local and dark roasted coffee beans filled the air. The unique taste of the coffee could be attributed to the fresh mountain water from the snow-covered mountains, around seventy kilometres south of the city.

'Luca, Otto has told me how important it is for us to make sure Adolf gains acceptance into the Vienna Academy of Fine Arts. Of course, he said he couldn't explain to me the reasons why. He also told me you are from the future, and that you cannot disclose anything to me about Adolf, nor the future you come from.'

'Yes, August. I will greatly appreciate it if you respect Otto's rules. Now, what I can tell you though, is that Adolf already applied to the Vienna Academy last year, and was rejected. The reason he was rejected is because the examiners considered him not to be proficient in the drawing of human figures, and facial expressions, even though they considered him to be a satisfactory artist of buildings and natural landscapes. In fact, the examiners considered Adolf was more suitable for architecture rather than artistic painting, and encouraged him to apply for the Architecture course within the Academy. He declined, primarily because he needed to complete his secondary education to gain admission; and he didn't want to do that. We must convince Adolf he needs lessons from a human figure and portrait painter.'

'Yes Luca, I agree. With that end in mind, I have already made enquiries, and have been given the name of just such a painter, who I understand, is prepared to spend time with Adolf, to fine tune his human and portrait skills to a level acceptable to the Academy; his name is Egon Schiele. He is being mentored by the well-known painter, Gustav Klimt, who has a connection with the Academy. Klimt is noted for his paintings, murals, and sketches, primarily of the female body, which are often defined by a distinct eroticism. The paintings he completed around 1900 for the ceiling of the Great Hall of the University of Vienna, have been marked with controversy because they are considered by many to be pornographic. Schiele, on the other hand, has mastered the art of self-portraits, twisted body shapes, and expressive faces, from Klimt. When Schiele was 14 years old, his father died from syphilis, and he became a ward of his maternal uncle, who recognised Schiele's talent for drawing, so he arranged for him to be tutored by the artist, Ludwig Karl Strauch. In 1906, Schiele successfully applied at the Vienna Academy of Fine Arts. His main teacher was Christian Griepenkerl.'

'Hang on, August. This is very interesting! Guess who was the head examiner when Adolf unsuccessfully applied to the Academy last year?'

'Oh Luca, don't tell me it was Griepenkerl?'

'Absolutely, it was!'

'Well, we've hit the jackpot then! We must arrange for Adolf and Egon Schiele to meet, but first, I want to introduce you to Adolf. Meet me at the park at the end of this road in an hour.'

'That will be fine, August.'

Walking the streets of Vienna on my own, after the café meeting with August Kubizek, I remembered an interesting and ironic fact about Egon Schiele, when I had researched him, amongst other young Viennese artists from this time. Schiele's art was admired by many Jewish art collectors whose collections were looted by the Nazis; in Germany from 1933, in Austria as a result of the Anschluss, from 1938, and in France from the German occupation of 1940.

As a result, numerous restitution cases in the 21st century involved artworks by Schiele. For example, Egon Schiele's "Woman in Black Pinafore" (1911) and "Woman Hiding Her Face" (1912) were owned by the Jewish cabaret artist and film star Fritz Grunbaum, before the Nazis deported him to the Dachau extermination camp. Schiele's "Krumau" (1916) was owned by the Jewish art collector Daisy Hellmann, until it was seized by the Nazis in 1942. Hellmann first made a restitution claim in 1948, but her heirs were not able to recover the Schiele painting until 2002. Austria's Nazi looting organisation, the Vugesta, had auctioned "Krumau" in Vienna, in February 1942, where the Sanct Lucas gallery bought it on behalf of an investor, Wolfgang Gurlitt. In 1953, the City of Linz, ironically Hitler's birthplace, acquired it for the Neue Galerie in Linz. The 1917 painting by Egon Schiele, "Portrait of the Artist's Wife" was confiscated by the Nazis, when the owner, Karl Maylander, a Jewish businessman in Vienna, was killed in Auschwitz. "Four Trees" (1917) was owned by Josef Morgenstern, who was arrested and deported to Auschwitz, where he was murdered.

The art gallery of the Jewish art dealer, Lea Bondi Jaray, owner of the famous "Portrait of Wally" (1912), was seized by the Nazis prior to his escape to London. In 1954, "Portrait of Wally" was purchased by Rudolf Leopold, and became part of the collection of the Leopold Museum, when it was established by the Austrian government, which purchased more than 5,000 artworks that Leopold had owned. After a 1997-98 exhibit of Schiele's work at the Museum of Modern Art in New York, the painting was seized by order of the New York County District Attorney, and was tied up in litigation by the heirs of its former owner, who claim that the painting was plundered by the Nazis, and should be returned to them. The dispute was settled on 20th July 2010, and the painting was subsequently purchased by the Leopold Museum for US$19 million.

When I arrived at the park, I could see Hitler and Kubizek in the distance, standing alongside a small group of about twenty young men, watching and listening to somebody delivering a speech. As I got closer, I could hear what the person was saying, even though I couldn't see him, because he was obstructed by the people gathered in front of him. He was speaking in a fiery voice, building up to a rant and rave.

'We are led by a corrupt, indecent, decadent family, that has had a stranglehold on our beloved Austria, for centuries. They have forced us to mix with so many inferior Jewish, Slavic, and Gypsy races, that we have become contaminated with their venom. We must stand up and fight for mother Austria! The Austrians are Germanic – we belong in the German Empire!'

As I was getting closer and closer, I caught a glimpse of this animated speaker, in between the people gathered around him. It was Thero! He was clearly trying to make an impression on young Hitler. Unbelievable! Suddenly, Kuzibek and Hitler parted from the small crowd of onlookers and walked towards me.

'Adolf, I would like to introduce you to Luca Evangelista. We met earlier today at the Café Landtmann. He is a professor of Art History, visiting Vienna from London.'

Hitler didn't say a word. I was fascinated to see he had nothing to say about Thero's speech, although as I was approaching them minutes earlier, I did observe that Hitler was listening intently and seemed to be enjoying it. Instead he gazed straight into me, with those hypnotic pale blue, clear eyes, as if he was looking directly into my soul. Then he gave me a faint smile, and limply stretched out his right hand for me to shake, which was surely a sign of approval.

I was getting a taste of what was to come with this man, and his ability to mesmerise a whole population of people, while taking them on a path that ultimately led to the utter destruction of Germany, and the shattering of his 1,000 Years Reich dream. But that was all in the future. Here and now, this man was totally insignificant; and I had to keep it this way, for the future of humanity and the world.

'August tells me you are a painter, Adolf. What type of paintings do you mainly do?'

'Mainly landscapes and buildings.'

'I am here to help you gain admission into the Vienna Academy of Fine Arts, Adolf.'

Hitler was visibly upset, and began to shake, as he stared at August.

'Adolf, you can trust Luca. When he told me he was intimately familiar with the admission requirements of the Academy, I had to introduce him to you.'

'To gain admission into the Academy, you must demonstrate to the examiners that you are proficient at drawing the human form, in all of its varieties, Adolf.'

August had pointed out to me that Hitler had this peculiar trait of never accepting his friend's advice. So we came up with a plan. It would be me who would recommend Egon Schiele as his art tutor, not August. Although Hitler gave the impression he wasn't paying much attention to me, I knew instinctively that he was. He was displaying similar behaviour to me, when I didn't want to acknowledge somebody was making perfect sense. So I continued.

'The world of art is changing rapidly, Adolf. A modern impressionist form of art is now in vogue. The art pioneered by painters like Claude Monet in Paris. It is no longer acceptable for a painter just to reproduce landscapes and buildings. The Academy is at the forefront of this impressionist movement. One which, when it comes to humans, involves expressing the full range of emotions in the form of art. Facial expressions of all sorts. Humans engaged in the act of living their lives. Spontaneous joy and anger; and all of the other emotions in between. It's now all about capturing facial expressions and the diversity of the human condition, as far as the Academy is concerned. To be accepted into the Academy, you need to be proficient in this form of painting, Adolf.'

Again, there was a prolonged silence, and that penetrating gaze; but finally he spoke.

'Ever since I was a child, I have wanted to become a professional painter. The Academy came close to shattering my dream, when they rejected me last year. I passed the preliminary portion; which required me to draw two of the assigned iconic Biblical scenes, in two sessions of three hours each. The second portion required that I provide a previously prepared portfolio to the examiners. They told me my work contained, in their words, too few heads. They came to the conclusion that I had more talent in architecture than in painting. But I think these were just excuses. Excuses to reject my application. I think they took a personal dislike of me. I think they wanted to thwart my ambition to become a successful and world-renowned painter.'

'Adolf, I can assure you there was no dislike of you in any form. I am familiar with the admission requirements of the Academy. I have spoken to the chief examiner, Christian Griepenkerl. To be admitted, a painter must demonstrate proficiency in drawing people and their emotions, in a variety of forms. The Academy assesses the quality of art by both the talent of the painter, and the subject of the paintings. Historical paintings are considered to be the most prestigious, followed by portraits and other paintings depicting the human form. Landscapes, buildings, and still-life, are at the bottom of their rankings. Paintings which depict stories of people, and classical depictions of the human form, are held in the highest regard. To gain admission to the Academy this time, you must set aside your pride, bitterness, and hatred; and instead develop a focus on the human body in your art. This is where the young painter, Egon Schiele, will be of valuable assistance to you. Will you let him tutor you?'

When I looked to see where Thero was, he was nowhere to be seen. He had simply vanished. Anyhow, my job was done. I just hoped I had done enough to get Hitler admitted into the Academy.

'Otto! You never cease to surprise me. Are you enjoying that espresso martini?'

'You're fifteen minutes late, Luca. Seeing you weren't here, I went to the bar and asked for a popular cocktail I could try. So he gave me this! I'm acquiring a taste for alcoholic cocktails.'

'Sorry I'm late. My mother hasn't been well. She's not coping with Dad's death. I've come from her place straight to the bar.'

'Well, you finally got to meet Adolf Hitler.'

'It's ironic that one of my most anticipated time travel missions, lasted for less than twenty-four hours, Otto.'

'There was no need for you to stay in Vienna any longer. The job was done, and it was a resounding success. Hitler went on to take art lessons with Egon Schiele, for three months. He turned out to be an excellent painter of the human form. When Hitler applied with the Academy for the second time in October 1908, he comfortably passed his examinations, and was admitted into the Academy. He then went on to become an accomplished painter and architect, living for the remainder of his life in Vienna.'

'Architect?'

'Yes Luca. His passion for buildings never subsided, so after completing his painting studies, he enrolled in the Academy's architecture course.'

'So he pursued a career as an architect and painter.'

'Not only that. Hitler never enlisted in the First World War. In this version of Earth, the outcome of the First World War didn't change. But the big changes happened from the 1920s. Although devastated by the impact of the Great Depression, Germany's fledgling democracy survived. Some outstanding political leaders emerged who were able to navigate Germany on a socialist democratic path, between the extremes of communism on the Left, and nationalism on the Right. Here's the big thing Luca. Although there were numerous regional conflicts in Europe and Asia, the Second World War never happened. But the Cold War between Communist Russia and Capitalist America, still did happen. A very strong European Union ultimately emerged, led by Germany. So there you have it. A resounding success.'

I chuckled. That clearly wasn't Otto's first espresso martini. He appeared to be drunk!

Enola Gay

Enola Gay
You should have stayed at home yesterday
Ah-ha, words can't describe
The feeling and the way you lied

These games you play
They're going to end in more than tears some day
Ah-ha Enola Gay
It shouldn't ever have to end this way

It's 8:15
And that's the time that it's always been
We got your message on the radio
Conditions normal, and you're coming home

Enola Gay
Is mother proud of little boy today?
Ah-ha this kiss you give
It's never ever going to fade away

Enola Gay
You shouldn't ever have to live this way
Ah-ha Enola Gay
You should've faded our dreams away

It's 8:15
And that's the time that it's always been
We got your message on the radio
Conditions normal, and you're coming home

Enola Gay
Is mother proud of little boy today?
Ha-ha this kiss you give
It's never ever going to fade away

Andy McCluskey, Orchestral Manoeuvres in the Dark (1980)

12

Robert Oppenheimer

Los Alamos, United States of America,
October 1944 CE

MY NEXT TIME TRAVEL MISSION WAS GOING TO TAKE ME TO the remote settlement of Los Alamos, in New Mexico, United States, in late 1944; in an attempt to delay the development of the atomic bomb. The story of the Manhattan Project began in 1938, when German scientists Otto Hahn, and Fritz Strassmann inadvertently discovered the process of nuclear fission. A few months later, Albert Einstein and Leo Szilard sent a letter to President Franklin D. Roosevelt warning him that Germany might try to build an atomic bomb. In response, Roosevelt formed the Uranium Committee, a group of top military and scientific experts to determine the feasibility of a nuclear chain reaction.

Nevertheless, the initial research moved slowly, until the spring of 1941, when a British atomic energy committee issued a report affirming that an atomic bomb was theoretically possible, and urged full cooperation with the United States, in the development of such a bomb. The US government responded by reorganising its atomic research under the S-1 Committee, which was in turn under the jurisdiction of the newly created Office of Scientific Research and Development, led by engineer and Under Secretary of Defence for Research and Engineering, Vannevar Bush. As the project progressed from research to development, however, Bush realised that the S-1 Committee did not have the resources for full scale construction, eventually opting to turn to the Army for support.

Prior to the formal creation of the Manhattan Project, atomic research was ongoing at a number of universities around the United States. At the "Rad Lab" (Radiation Laboratory) at the University of California at Berkeley, research was underway under the direction of Ernest Lawrence. Lawrence's most significant discovery came with his invention of the cyclotron, known as an "atomic smasher" which could accelerate atoms through a vacuum, and use electromagnets to induce collisions at speeds of up to 25,000 miles per second. Lawrence believed his machine could separate Uranium-235 by electromagnetic separation, one of the four possible uranium isotope separation methods that would ultimately be considered during the Manhattan Project.

Also during this time, Berkeley professors Emilio Segre, and Glenn Seaborg, proved that the element 94, which they named plutonium, could also be used in nuclear reactions, offering another possible path to the bomb. Meanwhile, at Columbia University in New York, a team of scientists, including Enrico Fermi, Leo Szilard, Walter Zinn, and Herbert Anderson, conducted experiments using chain-reacting nuclear "piles" to measure the neutron emission from fission. Production was moved to the Metallurgical Laboratory at the University of Chicago, in February 1942. In December of the same year, Chicago Pile-1 went critical, creating the world's first self-sustaining chain reaction. This experiment not only proved that nuclear energy could generate power, but also demonstrated a viable method to produce plutonium.

The Manhattan Project was officially created on 13th August, 1942. Its first major funding came in December, when President Roosevelt ordered an initial allotment of $500 million. The headquarters of the project was in Washington D.C., while numerous project sites were scattered across the country. The Manhattan Project's weapons research laboratory was located in Los Alamos, in New Mexico. Under the direction of Robert Oppenheimer, the Los Alamos laboratory would conduct the bulk of the remaining research, and construction of the bomb.

Physicists, chemists, metallurgists, explosives experts, and military personnel, converged in the secret town, which grew to be the home of thousands of project workers and their families. Meanwhile, the Army was charged with supplying, supporting, and guarding the top-secret work being done at Los Alamos. Another important Manhattan Project site was located at Oak Ridge, Tennessee. By this time, the Manhattan Project was pursuing both a uranium and plutonium based atomic bomb. Oak Ridge became the home of the uranium enrichment plants, K-25, Y-12, and S-50; and the pilot plutonium production reactor, the X-10 Graphite Reactor.

Equally important was the site at Hanford, Washington, where the full-scale plutonium production plant, the B Reactor, was constructed, and was eventually joined by other reactors. Dozens of other sites were also involved with the Manhattan Project. In Cambridge, Massachusetts, scientists conducted further research at Harvard University, and the Massachusetts Institute of Technology. In Dayton, Ohio, the Manhattan Project tasked the Monsanto Chemical Company with separating and purifying the radioactive element, polonium, which was to be used as the initiator for the atomic bombs.

In Canada, the Manhattan Project coordinated its efforts with the Montreal Laboratory, and the Chalk River Nuclear Laboratories in Ontario, the site for one of the world's first heavy water nuclear reactors. Meanwhile, the 509th Composite Group of the Army Air Force, which would drop the atomic bombs on Japan, trained at Wendover Airfield in Utah, and in Cuba, before shipping out to the launching point for the atomic bomb attacks, at Tinian Islands in the Pacific. It is estimated that over 600,000 people worked on the Manhattan Project.

Undoubtedly though, the major facility of the Manhattan Project was the bomb research and development laboratory at Los Alamos, located in the mountains of northern New Mexico. Codenamed "Project Y" the laboratory that designed and fabricated the first atomic bombs began to take shape in the spring of 1942, when James Conant suggested to Vannevar Bush, that the Office of Scientific and Research Development and the Army form a committee to study bomb development. Bush agreed, and forwarded the recommendation to Vice President Henry Wallace, Secretary of War Henry Stimson, and General George Marshall.

By the time of his appointment in late September, General Leslie Groves had orders to set up a committee to study military applications of the bomb. Meanwhile, sentiment was growing among the Manhattan Project scientists that research on the bomb project needed to be better coordinated. Robert Oppenheimer, among others, advocated a central facility where theoretical and experimental work could be conducted according to standard scientific protocols. This would ensure accuracy, and speed-up any progress. Oppenheimer suggested that the bomb design laboratory operate secretly in an isolated area, but allow for the free exchange of ideas among the scientists on the staff.

Groves accepted Oppenheimer's recommendation, and began seeking a suitable location. By the end of the year, they had settled on an unlikely site for the laboratory; an isolated boys' school on a mesa, high-up in the Jemez Mountains. Groves selected Oppenheimer to head the new laboratory at Los Alamos. He proved to be an excellent director, despite initial concerns about his administrative inexperience, leftist political sympathies, and lack of a Nobel Prize, when several scientists he would be directing were prize winners. Oppenheimer insisted, with much success, that the scientists at Los Alamos remain as much of an academic community as possible; and he proved to be adept at satisfying the emotional and intellectual needs of his highly qualified and distinguished staff.

Although Oppenheimer and Groves were of completely different temperaments, they worked effectively together. The Groves-Oppenheimer alliance, though not one of friendship and intimacy, was marked by mutual respect, and was a major factor in the ultimate success of the Manhattan Project. Oppenheimer had a chance to display his powers of persuasion early on in the project, when he had to convince scientists, many of whom were already deeply involved in war-related research in university laboratories around the country, to join his new organisation. Complicating his task were initial plans to operate Los Alamos as a military laboratory.

Oppenheimer accepted Groves' rationale for this arrangement, but feared that the military chain of command was not suitable for scientific decision making, and soon found that many of the scientists objected to working as commissioned military officers. The issue came to a head when Oppenheimer tried to convince the renowned physicists, Robert Bacher, and Isidor Rabi, from the Massachusetts Institute of Technology's Radiation Laboratory, to join the Los Alamos team. Neither thought a military environment was conducive to scientific research. At Oppenheimer's request, Conant and Groves wrote a letter explaining that the secret weapon-related research had presidential authority, and was of the utmost national importance. The letter promised that the laboratory would remain civilian, at least throughout 1943, after which, as a result of heightened secrecy and national security requirements, it would require to be militarised in the final stages of the project.

In the meantime, it was clear that Oppenheimer would oversee all scientific work, and Groves would oversee the military and security aspects. Oppenheimer spent the first three months of 1943 tirelessly crisscrossing the country in an attempt to recruit a first-rate staff; an effort that proved to be highly successful. Even Bacher signed on, though at the time, he promised to resign as soon as the project became militarised. Instead, Bacher stayed on until late 1945, because Oppenheimer agreed to keep his experimental research laboratory as a civilian facility. As soon as Oppenheimer arrived in Los Alamos in mid-March of 1943, recruits began arriving from universities across the United States; including California, Minnesota, Chicago, Princeton, Stanford, Purdue, Columbia, Iowa, and the Massachusetts Institute of Technology.

Virtually overnight, Los Alamos became the ultimate ivory tower boomtown, as scientists and their families, along with particle accelerators and other experimental equipment; including two Van de Graaff generators, a Cockroft-Walton machine, and a cyclotron; arrived in caravan-fashion at the city of Santa Fe, and then made their way up to the mesa along the single primitive road. The staff included many contemporary and future stars of the scientific community, including; Luis Alvarez, Hans Bethe, Norris Bradbury, Enrico Fermi, Richard Feynman, Eric Jette, George Kistiakowsky, Seth Neddermeyer, John von Neumann, Emilio Segre, Cyril Smith, Edward Teller, Victor Weisskopf, Robert Wilson, and many more. In the spring of 1943, a sizeable contingent of British scientists also arrived at Los Alamos. It was a remarkable gathering of the world's most brilliant scientists, who were to settle within this remote outpost of the Manhattan Project.

Early work on the design of the atomic bomb began even as scientists continued to arrive at Los Alamos throughout 1943. The properties of uranium were reasonably well understood; but those of plutonium less so; and of course at that stage, knowledge of fission explosions was entirely theoretical. The theoretical consensus was that fission chain reactions did take place with sufficient speed to produce powerful releases of energy (and not simply result in the explosion of the critical mass itself), but only experiments could test this theory.

In addition to calculations on uranium and plutonium fission, chain reactions, and critical masses; work also needed to be done on the ordnance aspects of the bomb, or the "Gadget" as it came to be known. Two subcritical masses of fissionable material would have to come together to form a supercritical mass, for an explosion to occur. Furthermore, they had to come together in a precise manner, and at high speed. Measures also had to be taken to ensure that the highly unstable subcritical masses did not pre-detonate because of spontaneously emitted neutrons. Always in the background loomed the hydrogen bomb; a thermonuclear device considerably more powerful than either a uranium or plutonium device.

Any hydrogen bomb would likely require an atomic fission bomb as a detonator, however. For this reason, research on the hydrogen bomb, or "Super-bomb" was always a distant second in priority at Los Alamos; but Robert Oppenheimer concluded that this research was too important to ignore. After considerable thought, he gave Edward Teller permission to devote himself to the hydrogen nuclear weapon that ultimately would dominate the Cold War.

The first few months at Los Alamos were occupied with briefings on nuclear physics for the technical staff, and with planning research priorities and organising the laboratories. Enrico Fermi took control of critical mass experiments, and standardisation of measurement techniques. Plutonium purification work became a high priority at Los Alamos, and increased attention was paid to metallurgy. An engineering division was set up to collaborate with the physicists on bomb design and fabrication.

The laboratory was organised into four divisions – theoretical, under Hans Bethe; experimental physics, under Robert "Bob" Bacher; chemistry and metallurgy, under Joseph Kennedy; and ordnance, under Navy Captain William "Deke" Parsons. As the overall director in charge, Robert Oppenheimer shouldered all of the burdens of the project, managing the numerous mundane matters such as living quarters, mail censorship, salaries, promotions, and other "quality of life" issues that would become inevitable in an intellectual pressure-cooker environment with few social amenities. Oppenheimer relied on a group of advisers to help him keep the "big picture" in focus, while a committee made up of the Los Alamos group leaders provided the day-to-day communications between divisions.

By December 1943, theory and experimental data concluded that a bomb using either uranium or plutonium would detonate, if it could be designed and fabricated into the correct size and shape. But many details still remained to be worked out, including calculations to determine how much uranium-235 or plutonium would be needed for an explosive device.

Bob Bacher's experimental physics division patiently generated the measurements needed to calculate critical and efficient mass. The same group utilised particle accelerators to produce the large numbers of neutrons needed for its cross section experiments. Bacher's group also compiled data that helped identify tamper materials that would most effectively push neutrons back to the core, and enhance the efficiency of the explosion. The chemists' job was to purify the uranium-235 and plutonium, reduce them to metals, and process the tamper material. The metallurgy division had to turn the purified uranium-235 and plutonium into metal.

Significant progress was made as the metallurgists adapted a stationary-bomb technique. Captain Deke Parsons, in charge of ordnance engineering, directed his staff to design two artillery pieces of relatively standard specifications, except for their extremely light barrels – one for a uranium bomb, and one for a plutonium bomb. The guns needed to achieve high velocities, but they would not have to be durable since they would only be fired once. Here again, early efforts centred on the more problematic plutonium weapon, which required a higher velocity due to its higher risk of pre-detonation. Two plutonium guns arrived in March 1944 and were field tested successfully. In the same month, two uranium guns were ordered.

Because the gun-type bomb design seemed so simple and practical, Deke Parsons had assigned implosion studies as a low priority, and placed the emphasis on the more familiar artillery method. Consequently, Seth Neddermeyer performed his early implosion tests in relative obscurity. Neddermeyer found it difficult to create symmetrical implosions at the low velocities he had achieved. When the Princeton mathematician, John von Neumann, a Hungarian refugee, visited Los Alamos late in 1943, he suggested that high-speed assembly and high velocities would prevent pre-detonation, and achieve more symmetrical implosions. A relatively small, subcritical mass could be placed under so much pressure by a symmetrical implosion that an efficient detonation could occur. Less fissionable material would be required, bombs could be ready earlier, and the extreme purification of plutonium would be unnecessary.

Von Neumann's theories excited Robert Oppenheimer, who assigned Parsons' deputy, George Kistiakowsky, the task of perfecting implosion techniques using this methodology. Because Parsons and Neddermeyer did not get along, it was Kistiakowsky who worked with the scientists on the implosion project. While experiments on the gun and implosion methods continued, Parsons directed much of his effort towards developing bomb hardware, including arming and wiring mechanisms, and fusing devices. Working with the Army Air Force, Parsons' group developed two bomb models by March 1944, and began testing them with B-29 bombers. "Thin Man" named for President Roosevelt, utilised the plutonium gun design; while "Fat Man" named after Winston Churchill, was an implosion prototype.

In the summer of 1944, however, it became clear that, because of the plutonium problem, a gun-type design would not work for the plutonium bomb. The implosion method was now transformed from an intriguing possibility into a difficult necessity. Glenn Seaborg had warned that when plutonium-239 was irradiated for a length of time, it was likely to pick up an additional neutron, transforming it into plutonium-240, and increasing the danger of pre-detonation (meaning that the bullet and target in the plutonium weapon would melt before coming together). On 17th July 1944, the difficult decision was made by Oppenheimer to cease work on the plutonium gun method – there would be no "Thin Man" atomic bomb. Plutonium could only be used in an implosion device, but in the summer of 1944 an implosion device looked like a long shot.

Abandonment of the plutonium gun project eliminated a shortcut to the development of the atomic bomb. This necessitated a revision of the estimates of weapon delivery Vannevar Bush had given the President in 1943. The new timetable, presented to General George Marshall by Leslie Groves on 7th August 1944 – two months after "D-Day" and the allied invasion of France – promised small implosion weapons of uranium or plutonium in the second quarter of 1945, if experiments proved to be satisfactory. More certain was the delivery of a uranium gun-type bomb by 1st August 1945; and the delivery of one or two more by the end of that year. Marshall and Groves agreed that Germany might well surrender by the summer of 1945, therefore making it probable that Japan would be the target of any atomic bombs ready by that time.

Oppenheimer acted quickly to maximise the laboratory's efforts to master the technology of implosion. Only if the implosion method could be perfected, could a plutonium bomb be developed. Without either a plutonium gun bomb or implosion weapon, the burden would fall entirely on uranium, and the less-efficient gun method. Oppenheimer directed a major reorganisation of Los Alamos in July 1944 that prepared the way for the final development of an implosion bomb. Robert Bacher took over G Division (for "Gadget") to experiment with implosion, and design a bomb. Kistiakowsky led X Division (for "explosives") in work on the explosive components. Hans Bethe continued to head up theoretical studies; and Parsons now focused on overall bomb construction and delivery.

Field tests performed with uranium-235 prototypes in late 1944 eased doubts about the gun-type method to be employed in the uranium bomb. It was becoming clear that uranium-235 could be used in a gun-type nuclear device to meet the 1st August deadline Groves had given to General Marshall and the Joint Chiefs of Staff. The plutonium, produced at such expense and effort, however, would not fit into wartime planning unless a breakthrough in implosion technology could be found quickly.

None of the Los Alamos bomb design work would be of any use if Oak Ridge or Hanford did not come through with enough uranium-235 or plutonium for at least one bomb. Spending on the Manhattan Project had reached $100 million per month by mid-1944, yet it was still far from clear that enough of either fissionable substance could be produced before the end of the war. In the summer of 1944, Oak Ridge's Y-12 Electromagnetic Plant was plagued by operational problems. At Hanford, the first production reactor had not yet been completed. In addition, officials feared that not enough of the uranium-containing slugs to feed the pile, would be available. Even assuming that enough uranium or plutonium could be delivered by Oak Ridge or Hanford, there was no guarantee that the Los Alamos laboratory would be able to design and fabricate an effective atomic bomb in time.

Only the most optimistic in the Manhattan Project would have predicted, as Groves did when he met Marshall in August 1944, that a bomb or bombs powerful enough to make a difference in the current war, would be ready by 1st August 1945. With the surrender of Germany in April 1945, only Japan remained as a possible wartime atomic threat. Japanese physicists had noted the discovery of fission before the war, and they did inform the Japanese Army of the danger. Some research was conducted at a Tokyo laboratory into various methods of uranium enrichment, but comparatively little progress was made.

In early 1943, a group of Japanese experts concluded that, while it was true that the United States was probably trying to build an atomic bomb, it might take Japan ten years or more to build one. Accordingly, little further research into nuclear energy was conducted in Japan beyond the construction of one cyclotron in Kyoto.

Of course, the main rival to the United States for the development of an atomic bomb, was the Soviet Union. Few aspects of the Manhattan Project remained secret from the Soviet Union for long. Given the size of the Soviet espionage network within the United States, and the number of Americans who were sympathetic to communism, it seems highly unlikely that the penetration of the "secretive" Manhattan Project by spies, could have been prevented.

In most cases, the individuals who chose to provide information to the Soviet Union did so for ideological reasons, not for the money. They were usually volunteers who approached Soviet intelligence themselves. Also, in most cases, they were not aware that anyone else had chosen to do the same thing. Soviet espionage directed at the Manhattan Project probably hastened by at least 12-18 months, the Soviet acquisition of an atomic bomb. When the Soviet Union conducted its first nuclear test on 29th August 1949, the device they used was virtually identical in design to the atomic bomb the Americans used on Hiroshima, four years earlier.

Fortunately for the Manhattan Project, during the winter of 1944-45, substantial progress was made on uranium enrichment at Oak Ridge, thanks to improved performance at each of the major production facilities. By the spring of 1945, even though uranium enrichment was still an enormously complicated and laborious process, the project was clearly on the right track. "Little Boy," the atomic bomb dropped on the Japanese city of Hiroshima on 6th August 1945, contained uranium that had been enriched at Oak Ridge.

The uranium path to the atomic bomb had indeed been proven to be viable, and timely enough to produce a weapon before the end of the war. At Hanford, the reactor was completed and began functioning in September 1944. The amount of plutonium shipped to Los Alamos grew rapidly over the spring and summer. By the beginning of August 1945, three plutonium atomic bombs had been constructed at Los Alamos; one of which was detonated over the Japanese city of Nagasaki on 9th August 1945. The plutonium path to the bomb had proven to be as effective as the uranium path.

I arrived in the small town of Lamy on the 15th October, 1944. Otto had provided me with all of the necessary identification and security clearance papers. I had taken the identity of a PhD student in nuclear physicis from the University of Manchester in the United Kingdom. This meant that none of the American and Eastern European scientists would know anything about me and my background. Los Alamos was so secret that it was not on any map. No one who went to live and work at Los Alamos was allowed to tell friends or family members where they were going. A single post office box, P.O. Box 1663, served all of the Los Alamos residents.

Babies born during the Manhattan Project had "P.O. Box 1663" listed as their birthplace on their birth certificates. I heard of a case where Sears & Roebuck department store delivery men became suspicious when orders for a dozen baby bassinets came from the same address. By the end of the war, over five thousand people had been assigned the P.O. Box 1663 address. The reason I arrived in Lamy was that it was the first stop for many of the scientists, engineers, and all of the others assigned to work on the top-secret project at Los Alamos. Ten miles from Santa Fe, Lamy was the nearest stop on the Atchinson,

Topeka, and Santa Fe railway line. Young men and women assigned to work at Los Alamos arrived in the small town of Lamy, not knowing where they were, or where they were going.

After I arrived in Lamy, I was met at the railway station by a military driver who took me to 109 East Palace Avenue in the larger town of Santa Fe. This building, constructed as a Spanish hacienda in the 1600s, was located just off the plaza in downtown Santa Fe, and served as the administrative hub of the Manhattan Project. Once inside the building, Dorothy McKibbin was the first reassuring smiling face I saw. After examining all of my papers, and issuing me with an ID and security passes, Dorothy informed me that my journey was scheduled to continue for another 35 miles along the winding road up to the Pajarito Plateau, or "the Hill" as Los Alamos was called; but I told her I would be meeting my contact in Santa Fe.

In the early months of the project, Dorothy was dispatching an average of 65 people each day. The steady stream of arrivals meant the office was often a chaotic hive of activity. Not only did she issue passes and IDs, she also directed newcomers to their homes, received shipments of household items to be distributed to the Los Alamos residents, and tended to personal matters as required. Dorothy McKibbin was the perfect person for her job, and quickly became indispensable as the gatekeeper at 109 East Palace Avenue; and a close friend and confidante of Robert Oppenheimer himself. When I met her, she greeted me with a warm smile, an engaging personality, and was reassuringly calm and efficient.

I was going to be meeting my contact at La Fonda, a Spanish-style favourite watering hole for the scientists and their wives, who would regularly venture down from Los Alamos, for a taste of civilization. La Fonda was located at 100 East San Francisco Street, in downtown Santa Fe, only a short walk from the administration building. Fearing that they might loosen-up too much and reveal the project's secrets, covert government agents monitored Los Alamos residents as they unwound there; so I needed to be very discreet when I met with my contact there. Santa Fe residents were trying to figure out what the secret project was at Los Alamos. Worried that they might guess correctly, Oppenheimer asked physicists Bob Serber and John Manley to go to

Santa Fe with their wives to spread the rumour that Los Alamos was making electromagnetic rockets.

I was due to meet my contact outside the entrance to the La Fonda, at exactly 1pm. I arrived five minutes early. Then suddenly, a black Buick pulled up into the carpark. I recognised the man who got out, immediately. It was Robert Bacher, a brilliant physicist who joined the Manhattan Project from the Massachusetts Institute of Technology's Radiation Laboratory. I understood why Otto had chosen him. He wasn't comfortable working in a military environment, and had serious reservations about the morality and ethics of the atomic bomb.

'Luca Evangelista, I take it?'

'It's my pleasure to meet you Robert.'

'Just call me Bob. All of my friends do. Do you feel like an icy cold beer?'

I could see why so many people had nostalgic memories of the La Fonda. It was jam-packed. Many men were congregated around the long bar, drinking, laughing, and animated in conversation. Then there were lamp-lit tables of couples, mainly husbands and wives, eating lunch. The place was decorated with patriotic American memorabilia; a large framed photograph of FDR, flags, soldiers, aircraft carriers, fighter planes, marines, and numerous iconic posters of the war effort, musicians, and movie stars. This place oozed 1940s America! Glenn Miller's "American Patrol" was blaring in the background as we made our way to a discrete table in the back corner.

'For the record, I want you to know I had no choice. I didn't want to be part of the Manhattan Project. Oppenheimer put a huge amount of pressure on me. He said it was my patriotic duty. He got the big generals to twist my arm; Groves, and FDR's right hand man, Marshall. Refusing to be a part of this just wasn't an option for me. But you probably know that I only signed on for the scientific phase, and that as soon as the project becomes militarized, which is expected to occur from the start of 1945, I will resign and be out of here'

I knew Bob wasn't going to resign, but I couldn't tell him that.

'I totally understand, Bob. I would bet there are many other scientists working on this project who are just as troubled as you are, but also feel like they've been pressured into it, and haven't got the courage to put their feet down and resist being part of the militarisation phase, as you have.'

'True. I know of many scientists who are very uncomfortable with all of this. I won't mention names now. This place is not secure enough. Thankfully, with the music on in the background, and the noise from all the chatter going on in here, nobody is listening in to us now. But I don't want to take any unnecessary risks'

'As the head of the experimental physics division, Bob, your role is critical in the development of the bomb. Without your division coming up with accurate measurements to calculate the precise critical mass required for an efficient explosion, causing maximum destruction; your utilisation of particle accelerators to produce the large numbers of neutrons that will be needed for the bomb; and also your effort in compiling the data to help identify the most effective way to push the neutrons back to the core, to enhance the efficiency of the explosion; the atomic bomb will be a non-starter, it won't get past first base.'

'Let's get out of here. You're staying with me and my wife in Los Alamos. You know that, right? We can talk some more, in the car.'

As we drove up to the Hill, in Bob's Buick Special Series 40 sedan, as solid as a tank, soft leather interior, polished wood dashboard, more Glenn Miller music on the radio, and the powerful engine guzzling fuel as if there was an infinite supply. I methodically outlined my plan to Bob.

'Okay Bob. You need to do everything you possibly can, to ensure there is no atomic bomb developed by mid-1945. I am not naïve enough to believe we will stop the development of nuclear weapons forever. Of course they will ultimately be developed! But if we can ensure there is no atomic bomb by July-August of 1945, the United States will have no choice other than to defeat the Japanese with conventional military power, including a full-scale invasion of the Japanese mainland.'

'What about the Germans, Luca?'

'Bob, you know the rules. I cannot tell you about future events. Of course, the United States and its allies are fighting this war on two fronts; against Germany in Europe; and against the Japanese in the Pacific.'

'We know that the Germans are frantically trying to develop an atomic bomb too, Luca. It wouldn't surprise me if the Soviets are as well. We keep hearing rumours of German and Soviet spies who have infiltrated the Manhattan Project.'

'All too true, Bob. So your mission is crystal clear – to delay the development of the bomb by at least three, but preferably, five years. This is a critical mission. Do you believe you can pull it off?'

'I'll move heaven and earth to give it my best shot, Luca. The bomb is evil and goes against everything humanity should stand for.'

Bob and his wife Jean were staying in a neat bungalow; one of many lining up both sides of one of the main roads of Los Alamos.

'Honey, I'd like to introduce you to Luca Evangelista.'

'It's lovely to meet you Luca. You must be feeling tired. Let me show you to your room. You will have to excuse us; this place is quite modest. Nothing like the beautiful home we had in Boston. I'll make you a coffee and some sandwiches'

'Oh, this is perfectly fine, Jean. I appreciate your hospitality.'

'Come Luca, let me show you to your room.'

After freshening up, Bob and I sat in his lounge, gin and tonics in hand.

'So Luca, as far as everybody here is concerned, you will be my right hand man, working closely with me in the experimental physics division, which as you know, I am in charge of. I have unrestricted access to Oppenheimer. In fact, we meet daily, and he updates me on the overall progress of the project. So we are in a great position to delay this thing. We're in the bowels of the project, Luca. If I don't get the results they're after, in experimental physics, the development of the bomb will proceed at a snail's pace. It's as simple as that.'

'Groves and Oppenheimer are very astute and highly driven men, as you know, Bob. We're going to have to tread carefully and avoid too much of a spotlight on us, and your team. This is going to be a very sensitive and dangerous mission.'

'I have no doubt the future of our planet is at stake Luca, even though I know you cannot share any of that future with me. That's why we must succeed.'

Bob had been invited to a dinner party at Edith Warner's place that evening. A number of other physicists and mathematicians would be attending. New arrivals coming from Lamy, if they came in by train, or coming by car through Santa Fe and 109 East Parade, were told to cross the Rio Grande River at the Otowi Bridge. Right across the Otowi Bridge was a little house, and a wonderful woman by the name of Edith Warner lived there. In the 1920s, Edith had come from the Midwest for health reasons. The house itself was on the San Ildefonso Indian reservation. She thought she was in heaven. She wanted to get away from the hustle and bustle of modern America. Edith raised her son there, and developed close bonds with the native Pueblo Indians on the reservation.

At the time, the railway went through there, so she became like a mail agent, delivering packages to the Pueblo Indians. Then one day in 1942, a man that she had known because he had come by on his trips up into the mountains, visited her, and said: "Your life's going to change." This man was Robert Oppenheimer. He had stopped there because he loved going to the mountains of New Mexico; and the Jamez Mountains in particular, were attractive to him, when he would ride horses out into the wilderness. He stopped and warned her there was going to be an imminent change in this sleepy little part of New Mexico. Here was this woman who was looking for isolation, and to get away from modern America; and all of a sudden the future America came knocking on her door. Edith Warner began to host dinner parties in her home, and scientists such as Oppenheimer, Teller, and Niels Bohr, sought out her food and company. Along with her partner, Atilano Montoya, an American Indian elder of the San Ildefonso Pueblo, Edith Warner represented an intersection between the local New Mexico culture, and the lives of the Manhattan Project scientists. Both communities accepted her as part of their own. To be invited to one of her dinners, was a privilege. I would be going to the dinner that night.

That evening, Bob and I made our way down the Hill, to Edith's place.

'You're going to enjoy the dinner tonight, Luca. Edith's dinners are legendary around here. Edith invites six people to these dinners. Her Indian partner Atlilano, helps with the cooking. They come up with all sorts of delicious meals that blend modern American, Pueblo Indian, and Mexican food. Tonight we will be with some interesting characters. There's the brilliant Hungarian mathematician, John von Neumann, who I'm sure you know much about. He's an intellectual freak, you'll see for yourself. Not from this world, many say, half-jokingly. Also there will be two other mathematicians; the fellow Hungarian, Peter Lax, and the Polish, Stanislaus Ulam. And there's also a young physicist, Geoffrey Chew.'

We were the first to arrive. Over the next thirty minutes, the others made their presence felt. Edith was everything I had imagined. A wonderfully warm, generous, genuine, humble host, who made us all feel very welcome. Her partner was very quiet, greeting us all with a friendly smile. While enjoying a garden-to-table feast of stewed meats flavoured with wild herbs and vegetables from her garden, including ten varieties of squash; followed by her deliciously famous chocolate cake with raspberries; the conversation flowed freely and widely around the table.

Bob was interested to know about Geoffrey Chew's background. He had not been at Los Alamos for long. Apparently, it was customary at these dinners, for a newly arrived scientist to give an outline of his history and background, when invited to Edith's for the first time; so Geoffrey did.

'I was born in Washington D.C. on 5th June, 1924. I am the fourth and youngest sibling in a family where my father is fully English. My mother is one-quarter Burmese, which means that I am one-eighth Burmese. But the Burmese connection was concealed from my three siblings and I, until my oldest sister made a trip to Europe before the war, and uncovered this fact. I don't know why, but my mother is ashamed of her Burmese background. As children growing up, my father treated my brother and sisters rather roughly and disrespectfully, but he treated me very well. I got a scholarship at George Washington University. My father wanted me to take an engineering degree. He never heard of anybody who called himself a physicist. I didn't really know what physics was at that point. But he wanted me to do something economically useful in order that I could have a decent job and support myself financially. Jobs were so much on the minds of everybody still at that point, because of the aftereffects of the Great Depression. The closest

I would come was chemistry. It was agreed that chemistry was sufficiently important to business that if you had a degree in chemistry, you would probably be able to get a job.'

'So, how did you get into physics, Geoffrey?' quizzed Bob.

'At George Washington University, I had the extreme good fortune, in my junior year, of taking a course from George Gamow, who as you all no doubt know, is a Russian theoretical physicist who had escaped to the United States a few years earlier, and who has a gift for teaching physics. I enjoyed his courses more than any of the chemistry courses that I had. I continued to suppose that I was going to get a degree in chemistry, but I kept on taking physics courses because they were more interesting. Then eventually, I enjoyed physics so much, that I majored in it.'

'How did you become involved in the Manhattan Project?' asked Bob.

'During the first half of my senior year last year, a curious event occurred. One of my sisters who was aspiring to a career in commercial art, had a friend, Jean Craighead, who was a reporter for the Washington Post. Jean had been investigating as a feature story in the Post, various cases coming before the special board set up by the government, to consider possible increases in salaries in special cases. As you all know, all salaries have been frozen by the government, for the period of the war. This reporter, Jean, was getting interesting material for a possible story. She had come upon a young experimental physicist graduating from the University of Washington in St. Louis. He had applied to this government board for an increase in salary. As a graduate student, he had been getting a relatively modest salary. Now, he had his degree, and he was applying for an increase, probably a substantial increase. What caught the attention of this reporter, was that he was a nuclear physicist. She wondered why anybody doing nuclear physics would be considered important to the war effort; because like my father thought, physics was not considered economically relevant. People who studied physics were not contributing to the general economy. They were considered to be doing something very abstract, interesting, but not useful, let's say. So Jean Craighead was puzzling over this question: Why would a nuclear physicist be considered important to the United States' war effort? She mentioned this to her friend, my sister, Ruth Chew. Ruth said to Jean, "Well, of course, I have no idea. But I have a brother who is taking a course in nuclear physics at George Washington University. Why don't you call him up and ask him?" Now, it happened that shortly before I received this telephone call, George Gamow was giving a class in nuclear physics, which I attended; and explained that this process called nuclear fission had been discovered in Germany, just a few years before, and that it opened the theoretical possibility of an atomic weapon that would be much more powerful than any that had heretofore been possible. He said that it was probably good for the world that such a weapon was not practical, because it required an isotope of uranium that was extremely rare; that the common form of uranium did not undergo fission; and that it didn't seem as if there was going to be enough of this fissionable uranium to ever build anything practical. When Jean Craighead called me on the phone and asked me if I had any idea about why the United States would consider nuclear physics relevant to the war effort, I told her what Gamow had told us. Then I forgot about it.'

'What happened next?' Bob asked with increased interest.

'Well, shortly thereafter, on a Sunday morning, I got a telephone call from someone who wished not to be identified, who said that he would like to have a confidential meeting with me. He didn't want anybody else in my family to know about it. Of course, this was completely astounding to me, but I said, "Okay. If you come to the front door of the house, on such and such a time, I will let you in, and then I will take you upstairs to my bedroom. We can talk up there. The rest of my family need not know that you are in the house." This was what happened. We started talking in my bedroom upstairs. At first, he was trying not to reveal anything to me, but just to find stuff out – I later figured it out; that morning the Washington Post had carried a feature story by Jean Craighead, with a drawing at the beginning of the story which showed an atomic bomb exploding over Berlin. He was from the Army Intelligence, and had immediately called Jean Craighead, and asked her how she got this information. They were presumably assuming that somebody within the Manhattan Project had given her the information. She said, oh, no, she had just based it all on this conversation she had with a brother of her friend. At the beginning of the conversation with the Army Intelligence man, I could tell he was sceptical of what she was telling, because I was nineteen years old, and obviously had no contact with anybody in the Manhattan Project. But I told him, "Well, whatever she had to say about nuclear fission in the article was accurate, and it was consistent with what George Gamow, my teacher, had told his class. That was the information I had passed on to her." Well, that was the end of that story, as far as I was concerned. I never heard anything more directly about it. But shortly thereafter, George Gamow took me into his office. He said, "I have a friend who is a faculty member here at George Washington until recently, whose name is Edward Teller, who has written to me asking if there were any graduating seniors who might be suitable for coming to work for the project he was working for. At that point, I had already, without understanding what I was doing, accepted an offer from another branch of the Manhattan Project, which was in New York, and was connected with Columbia University. I told Gamow this. He said, "What Teller is doing is much more interesting than whatever is going on in New York. You should by all means go and work with Teller." I accepted Gamow's recommendation. Anyway, as soon as I finished the work for my degree, last year, I was put into communication with somebody at the University of Chicago. The instruction was that I would take a train from Washington to Chicago. I was not told where I would end up, but I would wait in the railway station where the train deposited me. Somebody from the University of Chicago would come and give me a ticket that would take me to my destination, which was not Chicago, but I was not told where it was. I can remember sitting in that railway station for several hours, nothing happened. Then eventually, somebody came over to me and said, "Is your name Geoffrey Chew?" I said, "Yes." He said, "Oh, I was looking for a Chinese person." It turned out he had been waiting there for two hours, because he assumed that anybody with the name "Chew" was Chinese.'

'Tell us about your first trip to Los Alamos' I asked.

'He handed me a ticket. The ticket was to take me on the Santa Fe Railroad to a station called Lamy, which was not Santa Fe itself, but a short distance away from Santa Fe. So I got on this train. I spent a night on the train. There were two other young men on the train with me, coming from Harvard, who also descended from the train, in Lamy. When I got off the train in Lamy, I was met by somebody that I had never seen before, who introduced me to himself as Edward Teller. So that was my first encounter with Edward Teller, getting off the train. It was pretty late in the day. It was dark. He then drove me to Los Alamos. I can remember being very nervous, because the road crossed some precipitous terrain along the sides of cliffs and so on. This individual, whom I had never met before, was speaking with an accent that was not anything I had ever heard before, and was intense. He was trying to bring me completely up to date during that drive, on what happened up until then in the Manhattan Project. I can remember that he scared me, because he would keep looking at me while driving. I was afraid he was going to run over the side of a ravine, but he didn't. During this drive from Lamy to Los Alamos, one of the points that he emphasised was an idea related to another Hungarian mathematician. It was your theory, John von Neumann.'

'Oh, that's interesting. What did Edward tell you about my work, Geoffrey?'

'What Teller told me on that drive, is that largely because of your influence, John, a way of exploding a nuclear-fission based weapon was being emphasised at Los Alamos. This of course, was the concept of a circular-spherical implosion.'

'You're now working closely with Teller, aren't you, Geoffrey?', Bob asked.

'Yes. I work as an assistant to Teller. I'm helping him pursue his research on fusion, rather than fission.'

Bob then interjected.

'You know that Oppenheimer has decided the idea of fusion is far too distant; and that fission research must therefore take priority over fusion research, don't you?'

'Well, yes. But Oppenheimer has allowed Teller to continue with the research on the fusion possibility.'

'Thank you Geoffrey. Another fellow scientist who is a recent arrival is Peter Lax. Peter, tell us a little about yourself.'

'Sure Bob. I was born in Budapest, Hungary. I came to America with my family at the age of 15, to flee Nazi persecution.'

'Tell us a little about your childhood and your parents.'

'My parents are doctors. My father was a prominent doctor in Hungary, and has established himself as a successful physician in New York. He is a wonderful father, and will do anything for me.'

'And how about your mother?'

'My mother is a very intelligent woman, and interested in many things. She is good at mathematics.'

'What was Budapest like during your childhood?'

'Well, it was a city of a million. It's a very beautiful city. It lies on the Danube – Buda. It used to be two cities, Buda and Pest. It became Budapest the same year that greater New York was put together, Brooklyn and Manhattan. Buda is an ancient city, over a thousand years old. Buda was the brother of Attila. Hungarians and Huns are supposed to be brothers. So in Hungary, Attila was a good guy. I was utterly surprised when I came to America, what he stood for here.'

'I know you had an early interest in mathematics. How did your parents encourage that interest, Peter?', enquired Bob.

'Well, I was tutored by a wonderful mathematician, Rozsa Peter. She was a logician. She wrote a popular book that was, and still is, popular in America, called Playing with Infinity.'

'We are the product of the Hungarian miracle, aren't we Peter?', beamed John von Neumann, in a gloating manner.

'Oh yes, we certainly are, John!'

'Let these guys know what the Hungarian miracle is all about, Peter'

'I once asked Marcel Riesz, who was a very distinguished Hungarian mathematician, how come mathematics was so popular and prominent in Hungary? He told me that the tradition goes back to a mathematician of the early nineteenth century, Johann Bolyai. I don't know if you guys have heard of his name. I know you certainly have, John. He was one of the discoverers of non-Euclidean geometry; Bolyai and Nikolai Lobachevsky, about the same time. His father was also a mathematician who had studied in Gottingen, and was a friend of Carl Friedrich Gauss. His father wrote to Gauss, describing his son's great discovery, that there is such a thing as non-Euclidean geometry. And Gauss wrote back, "Oh yes, I have thought of that too." And this crushed young Bolyai, and he didn't do anything afterwards. The 1920s and 30s in Hungary was particularly a time when there were a lot of brilliant mathematicians in Hungary. And you, John von Neumann, are considered to be the greatest. When I came to America, I carried letters from Hungarian mathematicians to you, John, saying that you should look after me. And you very soon came to visit me at my parents' apartment, and interviewed me.'

'You gained national prominence after winning a high school math competition, didn't you Peter?', asked von Neumann.

'That's right. It was a competition started by Roland Eotvos, who was a physicist and a Minister of Education in Hungary. It was a high school competition in his honour, in mathematics and physics. I think we were assigned three problems, and we had four or five hours to solve them. It was a very well-designed competition, because all of the leading mathematicians were winners. They participated in it. It's very impressive.'

'Your performance, in particular, was outstanding because you weren't even in senior high school when you took it the first time, Peter', explained von Neumann.

'I was fourteen, when I took the first test. And then took it again when I was fifteen.'

'What was Hungary like when you left, and what was the trip to America like?', I asked, out of sheer historical curiosity.

'I was spared the worst of it. There were anti-Jewish laws. The Jews weren't being deported or killed. There were labour camps, but they were not death camps. My father had influential friends; he was able to get people out of the camps. Anyway, we left just in time. We sailed on the 5th December, 1941. Three days out, Pearl Harbor came. It was a neutral ship, so it became a belligerent ship. I remember the ship was lit up at night, the first three nights. The third night, they turned the lights off. But we didn't run into any German submarines or navy. It was a ten-day trip. When we started our trip, America was a neutral country. When we arrived, America was at war with Hungary. So we were taken to Ellis Island. But in a few days, they figured out that the Lax family was not at war with America. So they let us go.'

'How did your connection with Richard Courant happen?', asked Bob.

'My parents know the mathematician, Gabor Szego. He's Hungarian, and head of the mathematics department at Stanford University. Szego recommended that I study with Richard Courant. Courant is a very interesting man. He has built two great institutes; one in Gottingen in Germany, and then he was kicked out by Hitler, because he is Jewish; and then another great institute at New York University. He is a very remarkable man, although if you look at him superficially, he doesn't look like a great administrator. He is prone to mumbling. But people who can judge people recognise that he is a man who can build something. It is relationships with people that is his great strength, along with his very broad view of mathematics.'

'So he became your mentor, Peter?', continued Bob.

'Yes, yes. I remember the first time we went to see him, in the spring of 1942, shortly after we came to America. The first thing that happened, as soon as my father got his license to practise, he became Courant's doctor. So our two families were involved closely.'

'How did you get from New York University to Los Alamos?', asked Bob.

'I'm sure that Courant must have recommended me, but then I was drafted. When I turned eighteen in May this year, I was drafted into the Army. Courant contacted the Army, to make sure I was placed where my mathematical talent would be of use. So the Army sent me to Texas A&M University, where I studied mathematics for one semester. But then I was picked out of there and sent to Oak Ridge first for some basic training and security clearances. They then moved me on. I wasn't told very much. I was told to get into a train. The Atchison, Topeka, and Santa Fe Railroad doesn't go through Santa Fe, of course. I got out at Lamy. There was a car waiting for me, and a few other guys, and we went off into the hills. I recognised Santa Fe, because when we came to America, my father got his car, and we drove around America, and we visited Santa Fe.'

It turned out to be a fascinating evening. Because it was getting late, I was off the hook, and didn't have to give my backstory, after Peter Lax. I had the opportunity to chat with John von Neumann. There was definitely something "out of this world" about him. I couldn't help thinking that he was the key to stopping the development of the atomic bomb by mid-1945. I couldn't take this thought out of my mind. When we arrived back at the Bacher residence at around 10pm, I reviewed my research notes on the life of John von Neumann.

John von Neumann was born Neumann Janos Lajos, on 28th December, 1903, in Budapest, Hungary. The son of wealthy and respected parents, von Neumann's father was a banker, and his mother was the daughter of Austro-Hungarian aristocrats. In 1913, the Austro-Hungarian Emperor, Franz Josef, made von Neumann's father a member of the nobility, granting the family an honorary hereditary title of "Margitta", now Marghita, Romania. The young von Neumann was immediately singled out among his peers as a true child prodigy, especially in mathematics. He is believed to have had a photographic memory, which helped him absorb considerable knowledge from a very early age. By the age of six, he was dividing two, eight-digit numbers in his head, and by age eight, had mastered calculus.

His father believed that all his children needed to speak the major languages of Europe, beyond their native Hungarian, so von Neumann was taught English, French, Italian, and German. As a boy, he also had a deep interest in history, and read the entire 46-volume "General History in Monographs" by the German historian, Wilhelm Oncken. Encouraged by his teachers, von Neumann excelled in his studies, but his father did not believe a career as a mathematician would be financially lucrative. Instead, von Neumann and his father agreed that he would take up chemical engineering, and he went to study in Berlin at age 17, and later in Zurich. Chemistry was one of the few fields that seemed to hold no interest for John von Neumann; though he did receive a Zurich diploma in chemical engineering, while also earning a Ph.D. in Mathematics at the same time.

John von Neumann published early, starting at the age of 20, when he wrote a paper defining the ordinal numbers, which is still the definition we use today. He wrote his Ph.D. dissertation on set theory, and made several contributions to this field, in the course of his life. By 1927, von Neumann had already published twelve noteworthy papers in mathematics. By 1929, he was up to 32 published works, grinding out major contributions at a rate of roughly one academic paper every month. During this time, he held senior research positions at the universities of Berlin and Hamburg. Von Neumann also converted to Catholicism that same year, following the death of his father in 1929.

On New Year's Day in 1930, John von Neumann married Marietta Kovesi, an economics student at Budapest University, with whom he would have his only child, Marina, in 1935. While von Neumann might have seemed destined for a promising career in Germany, in October 1929, he was offered a position at Princeton University in New Jersey, which he fatefully accepted, traveling to the United States with his wife in 1930. By 1933, John von Neumann became one of the original six mathematics professors at the newly founded Institute for Advanced Study in Princeton, a post he would remain in for the rest of his life.

When he moved to New Jersey, like many American immigrants before him, von Neumann anglicised his Hungarian name. In 1937, he and his wife divorced, and in the following year von Neumann remarried, this time to Klara Dan, whom he first met in Budapest during his final visits to Hungary in the lead up to the Second World War. In 1937, von Neumann became a naturalised citizen, and in 1939, his mother, siblings, and in-laws, all emigrated to the United States.

Of course, one of John von Neumann's most significant contributions to history was his work on the Manhattan Project during the Second World War. True to form, von Neumann couldn't let a mathematical challenge go unresolved; and one of the more difficult problems was how to model the effects of explosions. Von Neumann threw himself at these problems in the 1930s, and became an expert in this field. If he had a specialty, it would have been on the mathematics of shaped charges, which are used to control and direct the force of their explosive energy. This put him in fairly regular consultation with the US military, particularly the US Navy.

When the Manhattan Project began its work in the early 1940s, von Neumann was recruited for his expertise. In 1943, von Neumann made his most significant and lasting impact on the Manhattan Project. The Los Alamos laboratory discovered that plutonium-239, one of the fissile materials used by the project, was incompatible with the laboratory's working atomic bomb design. A physicist at the lab, Seth

Neddermeyer, had been working on a separate, implosion-type bomb design that showed promise; but many considered it to be unworkable. To detonate a nuclear explosion, you need to trigger a runaway fission chain reaction in the bomb's reactant. The rate of the chain reaction is exponential, so controlling the explosion long enough for sufficient fissile material to undergo the required reaction is a significant challenge.

The implosion-type bomb required even more sophisticated controls to generate the reaction, but it also would not require nearly as much material as the prevailing gun-type bomb design being developed at Los Alamos. An implosion-type device uses a series of controlled conventional explosions to compress the fissile reactant in its core. Under this pressure, the fissile material quickly starts a nuclear fission chain reaction that is held in place by the force of the implosion, allowing more fissile material to release its energy. Controlling these explosions to create the exact right implosive force to produce the desired reaction, was a challenge that John von Neumann took on with considerable passion.

He believed that using less material shaped into a sphere, and properly compressed by an implosive force, could generate a more efficient and effective explosion that used as much of the available fissile material as possible. He was often one of the few voices arguing for the implosive method, and eventually worked out the mathematics that showed how it could be done if the implosion managed to maintain a spherical geometry with at least 95% accuracy. Von Neumann also worked out that the effectiveness of the blast would be increased if it was detonated above the target by some significant distance, rather than having it detonate upon hitting the ground. This greatly increased the lethality of the atomic bomb, and also reduced the amount of radioactive fallout produced by the nuclear explosion.

Von Neumann was selected as part of the team of scientists who would consult the military on possible Japanese targets for the bombs. He suggested the cultural capital city of Kyoto, arguing that its destruction might be enough of a "body blow" to force the Japanese to surrender and achieve a quick end to the war. He wasn't alone in this suggestion, but the Secretary of War, Henry Stinson, vetoed the targeting of Kyoto, because of its many historic buildings and important religious shrines; and the cities of Hiroshima, and Nagasaki, were chosen instead. Von Neumann was present during the Trinity Test on 16th July, 1945, where the first atomic weapon was detonated. Unlike some of his contemporaries in the Manhattan Project, von Neumann did not seem to have any of the reflective anguish, regret, or even a passing doubt about his work on the atomic bomb.

In fact, he became one of the most vocal proponents of nuclear weapons development, and supported the doctrine of Mutually Assured Destruction ("MAD") as the only way to prevent another catastrophic world war. Like a lot of Americans in the early Post-War era, John von Neumann was concerned about America falling behind the Soviet Union in nuclear weapons development. By the late 1940s to early 1950s, it was becoming evident that the idea of strategic bombers dropping more Fat Men atomic bombs on the enemy, was being superseded by rocket delivery technology. Missiles, von Neumann believed, were the future of nuclear weapons; and due to his contacts with German scientists working on the Soviet Weapons Program, he knew the Soviet Union saw it the same way he did.

The race was on to build small enough Hydrogen bombs that could fit into a warhead on top of an intercontinental ballistic missile. Von Neumann aggressively pushed to close the "missile gap" with the Soviets. After the war, Von Neumann served on the U.S. Atomic Energy Commission, advising government and military leaders on technological development and strategy; and is widely credited as the architect of the MAD strategy, which would go on to be adopted as the de facto U.S. policy during the Cold War.

John von Neumann met Alan Turing in the early 1930s while Turing was working on his Ph.D. at Princeton; but he had known of him even before then. In 1937, Turing had published his landmark paper "On Computable Numbers" which casually laid the theoretical foundation for modern computing. Von Neumann recognised the significance of Turing's discovery and furthered the development of computer science in the 1930s, including long discussions with Turing at Princeton around the idea of artificial intelligence. As a mathematician, von Neumann approached computer science from a more abstract perspective, especially since there weren't really any working computers in the 1930s; but that would change after the Second World War.

Von Neumann was deeply involved in the development of the ENIAC, the first programmable electronic computer that was "Turing-complete", meaning that it was able to recognise and decide on other data-manipulation rule sets rather than only the one it started with. It was von Neumann who modified ENIAC to run as a stored-program machine. This latter discovery made modern programs as we understand them today, possible. Von Neumann himself wrote several of the first programs to run on ENIAC, and used it extensively to run simulations on his nuclear weapons research, as part of the Atomic Energy Commission. Without question, von Neumann's most lasting contributions to the field of computer science are the two fundamental concepts used in every computer running today – von Neumann architecture, and the stored-program concept.

In 1955, John von Neumann was diagnosed with cancer, after a growth was found on his collarbone during a doctor's visit; and he didn't take the revelation well. By all accounts, von Neumann was terrified of the coming end. Eugene Wigner, a lifelong friend, wrote: "When von Neumann realised he was incurably ill, his logic forced him to realise that he would cease to exist, and hence cease to have thoughts. It was heartbreaking to watch the frustration of his mind, when all hope was gone, in its struggle with the fate which appeared to him unavoidable but unacceptable."

His disease progressed throughout 1956, and he was eventually admitted into the Walter Reed Army Medical Center, in Washington DC. He had a constant security detail to guard against his divulging classified top-secret information, due to his deteriorating condition. Von Neumann invited a Catholic priest to consult with him on his deathbed, and was given his last rites, though the priest later said that von Neumann didn't appear to be comforted by them. On 8th February, 1957, von Neumann succumbed to cancer at the age of 53, and was buried at Princeton Cemetery, New Jersey. Whether John von Neumann's cancer was a result of radiation exposure he suffered during his time with the Manhattan Project, has long been debated; but there's no question that humanity lost one of its greatest scientific minds, well before his time.

Von Neumann's assistant, P.R. Halmos, wrote the following about him, in 1973: "The heroes of humanity are of two kinds; the ones who are just like all of us, but very much more so; and the ones who apparently, have an extra-human spark. We can all run, and some of us can run the mile in less than 4 minutes; but there is nothing that most of us can do that compares with the creation of the Great G-minor Fugue. Von Neumann's greatness was the human kind. We can all think clearly, more or less, some of the time, but von Neumann's clarity of thought was orders of magnitude greater than that of most of us, all the time."

John Neumann's brilliance is unquestionable, though his legacy, especially his work on nuclear weapons, is more complicated than his friends and admirers would probably want to admit. It takes a different kind of mind indeed to look at an atomic bomb, and innovate ways to make them even more deadly, to take even more lives. There was much more to John von Neumann than anybody realised when he was alive. I was about to uncover the truth about him. But I am jumping ahead of myself, now.

The next morning, I accompanied Bob to the experimental research laboratories. It was a hive of activity as hundreds of scientists in white lab coats went about their research, working within stifling, tight-fitting spaces, surrounded by an assortment of scientific instruments, many of which I couldn't recognise. They were all on a mission, unified in their determination to develop the bomb, so it seems. But that wasn't the reality. For amongst these dedicated scientists, I spotted an instantly recognisable "boyish" face.

There he was – Klaus Fuchs. He was a German theoretical physicist who became one of the most infamous spies to work on the Manhattan Project; secretly passing on information about the atomic bomb to the Soviet Union. Fuchs, who had fled Germany in 1933, went to England, where he received a Ph.D. in physics, and another in science. He became a British citizen in 1942, and the following year he travelled with a team of British scientists to Columbia University in New York, to work on the Manhattan Project. In New York, an agent for the Soviet KGB nicknamed "Raymond" approached Fuchs and recruited him to spy on behalf of the Soviet Union.

In 1944, Fuchs transferred to Los Alamos where he worked on imploding a fissionable plutonium core. He was also present at the Trinity Test of the first detonated atomic bomb in April, 1945. The entire time he was at Los Alamos, Fuchs passed on intelligence to Soviet agents. Awareness of Fuchs's espionage did not come to light until 1949. He initially denied the charges, but ultimately confessed in 1950. After trial proceedings that lasted a total of 90 minutes, Fuchs received a sentence of 14 years in prison, and lost his British citizenship.

Of course, I couldn't mention any of this to anybody, not to Bob Bacher, nor to Robert Oppenheimer. As I was chatting with Bob, the man himself made an entrance to the laboratory, the larger-than-life Robert Oppenheimer.

'Robert, let me introduce you to my latest recruit, Luca Evangelista.'

'I have been looking forward to meeting you, Mr Oppenheimer, you are a great inspiration to me.'

'Why thank you, son. I believe you have come from a British university?'

'Yes sir, I completed my physics degree at the University of Manchester. As you are no doubt aware, the university's Department of Physics and Astronomy has an outstanding historical record of achievements, including Ernest Rutherford's detection of the atomic nucleus.'

'One of the greatest physicists ever. I studied at Cambridge with Ernest Rutherford in the late 1920s', Oppenheimer replied.

How brutally ironic it was to see Klaus Fuchs literally standing a few metres away from Robert Oppenheimer!

I reflected on the legacy of Robert Oppenheimer, and his revered place in 20th century world history. Robert Oppenheimer's name is not only synonymous with the Manhattan Project and the development of the atomic bomb; but also with the dilemma facing scientists when the interests of a nation, and their own moral conscience, collide.

Oppenheimer's early education was at the Ethical Cultural School in New York. He took mathematics and science classes, but also enthusiastically studied Greek, Latin, French, and German. He had a feel for languages, and often learned one quickly, just to read something in its original language. He learned Dutch in six weeks in order to give a scientific lecture in the Netherlands. He also maintained an interest in the classics, and eastern philosophy, throughout his life. He was always an intense person; tall, thin, contemplative, and probing. After the oral exam for his Ph.D., the professor administering it, is reported to have said, "Phew! I'm glad that's over. He was on the point of questioning me."

Oppenheimer obtained his Ph.D. in Germany after graduating from Harvard in 1925, and studying at Cambridge University under Ernest Rutherford. In 1929, he returned to the United States, holding positions at Berkeley, and Cal Tech. He was an extraordinary teacher, and an excellent theoretician. His analyses predicted many later finds, such as the neutron, positron, meson, and the existence of neutron stars.

Absorbed in his studies, and the theoretical world of physics, he was often somewhat distracted from the "real world." But the rise of fascism in the 1930s caught his attention, and he took a strong stand against it. By 1939, Niels Bohr brought news to the United States that German scientists had split the atom. The implication that the Nazis could develop extremely powerful weapons, prompted President Roosevelt to formally establish the Manhattan Project in 1942. In June 1942, Robert Oppenheimer was appointed its director. As we have seen, preliminary research was being done at Columbia University, the University of Chicago, and in Oak Ridge, Tennessee; but Oppenheimer set up a new research facility at Los Alamos, in New Mexico.

There, he brought the best minds in physics, chemistry, mathematics, and engineering, to work on the challenge of creating an atomic bomb. In the end, he was managing more than three thousand people, as well as tackling theoretical and mechanical problems, as they arose. On the 16th July, 1945, Oppenheimer witnessed the first explosion of an atomic bomb, in the New Mexico desert. "We knew the world would not be the same," he said. Within a month, two atomic bombs were dropped on Japanese cities; first Hiroshima, and then Nagasaki. Japan then surrendered unconditionally on 10th August, 1945.

After the war, Oppenheimer chaired the U.S. Atomic Energy Commission. He opposed the development of an even more powerful hydrogen bomb, which was being overseen by Edward Teller. When

President Truman finally approved it, Oppenheimer did not argue, but his initial reluctance, and the Cold War political climate, turned against him. In 1953, at the height of U.S. anti-communist feeling, Oppenheimer was accused of having communist sympathies, and as a result, his national security clearance was taken away. He had, in fact, had friends who were communists, mostly people involved in the anti-fascist movement of the 1930s.

This loss of security clearance effectively ended Oppenheimer's influence on science policy. He held the academic post of director of the Institute of Advanced Study, at Princeton University; and in the last years of his life, he thought and wrote much about the problems of intellectual ethics and morality. He died of throat cancer in 1967.

We can understand a lot about the philosophical, moral, and ethical dilemmas Oppenheimer confronted, from some of his quotations:

- Now, I am become Death, the destroyer of worlds.
- In battle, in forests, at the precipice in the mountains, On the dark great sea, in the midst of javelins and arrows, In sleep, in confusion, in the depths of shame, The good deeds a man has done before, defend him.
- We knew the world would not be the same. A few people laughed, a few people cried. Most people were silent. I remembered the line from the Hindu scripture, the Bhagavad-Gita; Vishnu is trying to persuade the Prince that he should do his duty, and to impress him, takes on his multi-armed form and says, 'Now I am become Death, the destroyer of worlds.' I suppose we all thought that, one way or another.
- It is a profound and necessary truth that the deep things in science are not found because they are useful; they are found because it was possible to find them.
- When we deny the EVIL within ourselves, we dehumanize ourselves, and we deprive ourselves not only of our own destiny but of any possibility of dealing with the EVIL of others.
- It is perfectly obvious that the whole world is going to hell. The only possible chance that it might not is that we do not attempt to prevent it from doing so.

- Knowledge cannot be pursued without morality.
- It was a heroic time. It was not the doing of any one man; it involved the collaboration of scores of scientists from many different lands. But from the first to last, the deeply creative, subtle, and critical spirit of Niels Bohr guided, restrained, deepened, and finally transmuted the enterprise.
- Mr. President, I have blood on my hands.
- There is no place for dogma in science. The scientist is free, and must be free to ask any question, to doubt any assertion, to seek for any evidence, to correct any errors.

Robert Oppenheimer was clearly tormented by his role in the development of the atomic bomb. This torment remained with him for the rest of his life.

That evening, after dinner, Bob and I were in his lounge room, refreshing with gin and tonics.

'Luca, I know you have grave suspicions about John von Neumann. So do I. He has a mysterious visitor staying with him. The man claims to be a Hungarian nuclear physicist. He arrived yesterday morning. He says his name is Jan Szoke. Nobody has heard of him. Not even the other Hungarian scientists here at Los Alamos. I have been told that John was able to personally obtain all the necessary papers and security clearances for him, to the satisfaction of Oppenheimer. Apparently he's only staying for a few days.'

'Bob, who is the one man that is intellectually capable of solving the remaining problematic challenges which stand in the way of developing the atomic bomb to its ultimate destructive capabilities? It's not Robert Oppenheimer, is it?'

'No Luca, it's John von Neumann, without a shadow of a doubt.'

'Yes. He is the key. So, what we need to do Bob, is to immediately get von Neumann out of the equation. Now, I don't mean that we harm him in any way.'

'What do you mean then, Luca?'

'We need to kidnap him, and shuttle him to a destination far away from here; preferably to another remote town. I have formulated a plan, Bob. All we need is somebody who you can totally trust, who can accommodate John von Neumann, for up to 12 months. Of course, we will reward this person handsomely.'

'My goodness, Luca Evangelista! That is a bold and dramatic plan!'

'Trust me, the future of our planet is at stake.'

Bob, got up from the sofa, walked across the room to check there was nobody within earshot. He didn't have to do this, because his wife had gone out for a card night with a number of the other wives.

'Okay, Luca. Listen carefully. I think I have the perfect person. In high school, there was a guy who was brilliant at mathematics. But he was the archetypical nerd. A loner with no friends. Constantly bullied. His father died tragically in a car accident when he was young. His mother was an alcoholic, but singlehandedly raised him. I took him under my wing, and we became the best of friends. Rick Logan, is his name. After high school and college, we went on to study at university together – he majored in mathematics, and I in physics. After we graduated, we stayed close. He became a high school math teacher. But after his mother died, he too became an alcoholic, and quit his job. He was literally homeless, ravaged by the drink, and had no money. So, without my wife, or anybody else knowing, I arranged for him to leave Boston, and seek detox help at a clinic located just outside of the small Massachusetts town of Stockbridge. Anyhow, after a year in there, he came good. Got his act together. He took up writing fiction, and oil painting. When I was transferred here, to make sure he wasn't too far away from me, I set him up in a rented secluded chalet, outside the small town of Trinidad, 230 miles north of here in Colorado; about a 4-hour drive. He lives there with his gay partner, Gary, who looks after him really well. Rick owes me, Luca. He owes me big time. Also, he is dead-set against the development of the atomic bomb. The ultimate evil, he says. I trust him one hundred percent. Rick's like a close brother to me. I think he's our man.'

'He sounds like the ideal person. Does he have a secure room, at the chalet, where John can be kept, literally under lock and key? Also, we need to protect Rick. What's the escape plan for him, after he releases von Neumann in twelve months? Can Rick be connected back to you?'

'Well, it gets even better. There are actually two separate chalets. He and Gary live in one, and he uses the adjoining one for his writing and painting. The chalets are surrounded by a forest. Rick wanted total privacy and seclusion with Gary, to assist him with his recovery. He didn't want to see, or have anything to do, with anybody else. So, John can be accommodated in his own chalet, alongside Rick and Gary. They are brick and tile chalets – very secure. Because I have been financially supporting Rick, I have been very careful to be discreet, and have left no paper-trails that trace him to me, whatsoever. Now, if we blindfold and drug, von Neumann, he will have no idea where his destination is. So, after 12 months, Rick and Gary will drive him to another remote location, and literally drop him off. Meanwhile, as an extra precaution, in 12 months I will arrange for Rick and Gary to "disappear" to another remote town, so they will never be tracked down by the authorities.'

'Okay. There's a lot at stake here, so the risks are well worth taking. Let's swing into action'

'There's more, Luca.'

'What is it, Bob?'

'Nobody knows this. You will be the only person I have shared this with. I have installed a listening device in the home of John von Neumann. I did this a couple of days ago, when I knew John was in a meeting with Oppenheimer and some government officials who had come in from Washington. I did this to help you, Luca.'

'Well, that's brilliant!'

'I've checked the recordings for anything of interest, and found

something intriguing. I don't know what to make of it. Let me play it back, for you.'

We made our way to the study, where Bob had a Magnetophon tape recorder set up.

'Okay, this is the interesting bit.'

'Remember, you are now Jan Szoke. I owe everything to you. I still don't know why you chose me?'

I recognised that was the voice of John von Neumann.

'Five thousand years ago, in the desert of Egypt, alongside the great Nile, I chose Khufu. I transferred to him, the necessary scientific, mathematical, engineering, construction, agricultural, medical, and philosophical knowledge to help him not only to engineer and construct the Great Pyramids of Giza; but to also lay the foundations for a great civilization; which I expected would go on to flourish, and start a chain reaction of other civilizations, built on innovation and progress, that would achieve wonderful things for the humans of this planet. Instead, over the centuries and millennia, there was war, famine, inequality, greed, hatred, totalitarianism, exploitation of the planet's precious resources, overpopulation, pandemics, climate change, mass extinctions of plant and animal species, and an over-reliance on technology. This planet is now experiencing a slow death, von Neumann. So I came to visit you when you were a young man. I transferred to you, the intellectual knowledge and power to develop weapons of mass destruction – ones that can swiftly and decisively put humans out of their misery once and for all – nuclear weapons!'

Bob stopped the recorder.

'That's Thero, Bob. He's not a Hungarian scientist. I can't tell you anything else, but I'm sure you can figure it out.'

'Why is he here, Luca?'

'To stop me. He knows I'm here. I will deal with him. How soon can you contact Rick, and let him know our plan?'

'I can't call him from here. The phones are tapped. Same in Santa Fe.

Since I arrived here, I have always driven out to the small town of Vadito, a 45-minute drive, north-east from here, to make my personal phone calls, including all calls to Rick. I will let him know tomorrow morning.'

'Time will be of the essence, Bob. We will need to literally overpower,

drug, and kidnap von Neumann when he gets home tomorrow night. I will then drive your car, with von Neumann, to a halfway point between here and Rick's place. You cannot be connected with this kidnapping in any way Bob. You need to continue to delay the atomic bomb project from here. This all needs to be done tomorrow night. As I said, I will deal with Thero, tomorrow morning. He won't get in our way.'

It was clear from the recordings, that Thero was staying with von Neumann, and would be in his home for all of tomorrow morning. Bob told me von Neumann had a set routine, and was extremely punctual. He would leave his home at 6.30am, and arrive back home at 6.30pm; working a 12-hour day. So, my plan was to break-in to von Neumann's place through a back window that had been left unlocked by Bob, then use my martial arts skill to overpower Thero, and render him unconscious, using ether that Bob had provided to me. Bob was then going to make the short drive to von Neumann's place.

He and I would place Thero, unconscious, blind-folded, gagged, and tied-up, into the trunk of Bob's Buick; and then transport him a short distance to a secure storage shed, within the perimeter of the research laboratories Bob was in charge of, sufficiently remote from the main building that nobody would find him. Bob, possessed the one and only master key to the storage shed. Thero only needed to be kept in that shed for up to 24 hours. This would give me enough time to deliver John von Neumann to Rick and Gary. Of course, Thero could only remain in the past for as long as I was. So, when I took the wormhole to the 21st century, Thero would vanish from Los Alamos, as well.

I was up early the next morning, ready for what was going to be a very eventful day. I arrived at von Neumann's place at 7.00am. There was nobody to be seen. The street was eerily quiet. I made my way to the rear of the house and entered through the unlocked window. I quietly made my way into the laundry, then kitchen, and then as I approached the lounge room, I could see Thero sitting there, upright, in his customary black, his back turned away from me. I had the damp ether cloth ready as I slowly approached him, dead silent.

Then, in an instant, Thero shot out of his chair, turned around, and literally jumped on me, knocking me to the ground. As we brawled on the floor, Thero on top of me, knocking furniture, and shattering vases, smashing against the liquor cabinet, sending bottles of gin and scotch hurtling in every direction, I frantically thrust the damp ether cloth into his face with my right hand, while gripping the hair on the back of his head brutally hard, with my left hand, to keep his head still. He was desperately trying to break away from me. But I held firm. Suddenly, he was dazed and in a sleep-like trance, and ultimately he collapsed onto my chest, completely limp and unconscious. I managed to subdue him without him saying a single word. I didn't have much time to blindfold him, gag him, and tie his hands and feet.

I had arranged with Bob to park his car in the enclosed side carport of the house, at exactly 7.30am. Ten minutes to go. Finally, I heard the Buick pull up into the carport. Bob and I placed Thero into the trunk, and then made our way to the secure storage facility on the perimeter of the lab. Everything worked like clockwork. Nobody saw us. Thero was locked in the shed, tied and gagged, still unconscious. Even when he regained consciousness, he could scream and make endless noise, and nobody would hear him because the laboratory buildings were quite a distance away. The shed was securely locked. All we had to do now was to repeat the process again, when John von Neumann arrived home at 6.30pm.

I had no trouble subduing von Neumann. I was hiding in the house when he arrived, so managed to spring him by complete surprise. After rendering him unconscious with the ether, I tied, blindfolded, and gagged him; and placed him in the trunk of Bob's Buick. I was heading for the small town of Wagon Mound, New Mexico, about 125 miles from the Colorado border; a 2- hour drive. I easily cleared the security guard posts on the outskirts of Los Alamos, and Santa Fe. Once outside the city limits of Santa Fe, I took him out of the trunk, laid him down on the backseat, and ungagged him, so we could talk, while I continued the journey.

'Why did you team-up with Thero, for God's sake?'

'Why? He found me when I was a freshman at university. He made me into a brilliant scientist. He expanded my mind to the point that I became super-human.'

'Yes, but you knew what his motive was! He wanted you to come up with an atomic bomb, which ultimately would lead to the destruction of humanity!'

'He never told me his motives at first. He just said, he wanted to give me an intellectual gift that would significantly advance human knowledge.'

'Well, super-human, von Neumann, you knew what your mission was at Los Alamos, didn't you?'

There was a significant silence, before von Neumann replied, with a softer voice.

'Thero promised me I would be saved from any human calamity. He promised to take me to his planet, where I would live for eternity, and continue to make a scientific contribution to his civilization. But, I promise you, Luca, over the last few days, since the arrival of Thero, I was having second thoughts about continuing with his mission. Only this morning, I was seriously considering escaping from Los Alamos, having nothing further to do with the Manhattan Project, and heading back to Hungary, to pursue my own research, for the benefit of humanity. Don't you see? I was having cold-feet even before you arrived. You rescued me, Luca Evangelista. You rescued me from a terrible fate.'

'Well, I don't believe you.'

Suddenly, the dark desert highway was infiltrated by a bright light, which was getting brighter and brighter, as I looked in the rear vision mirror. Lights began to flash. It was a police car, getting closer and closer.

'Right, John. Here's your chance to prove to me that you are telling the truth. There's a police car coming up. I want you to use your hands to knock out the partition between the back seat and the trunk, and then wriggle yourself into the trunk. If they see you, it's all over for humanity. Please redeem yourself, and do as I say.'

It was a highway patrol car. I pulled the Buick up to the side of the desert road. The police car stopped directly behind me. Two officers came towards me. I wound down the window, and waited anxiously.

'Good evening sir, do you realise that your tail lights aren't working?'

'Thank you for letting me know, officer. I will have them fixed first thing tomorrow morning.'

'Can I see your licence, please?'

One of the officers shone a torch into the car, while the other directed his torch onto my drivers' license. As far as they were concerned, I was on my own. Von Neumann was well-hidden, in the trunk.

'Okay, that's fine. Sorry to bother you, sir. Have a good evening.'

And that was it. I felt a huge sigh of relief. I continued my journey through the pitch black desert to Wagon Mound; with von Neumann still in the trunk. When I arrived on the outskirts of the town, Rick and Gary were waiting in their car, along the side of the highway. We placed von Neumann, still blindfolded and tied, into the trunk of their car. I told Rick and Gary that von Neumann was unlikely to present himself as a problem to them, because he was remorseful for what he had almost succeeded in inflicting upon humanity. I told them he would probably welcome 12 months of exile, as long as they supplied him with plenty of books. I then made my way back to Los Alamos, arriving late into the night, parked the Buick in Bob's driveway, and then took the wormhole to the 21st century.

'This was a crucial mission for changing the future for the better, Luca.'

I stirred my gin and tonic, and studied the animated expressions on Otto's face. He was definitely becoming more human-like.

'As a direct result of taking von Neumann out of the Manhattan Project in October 1944, and due to the courageous efforts of Bob Bacher, stalling the experimental physics laboratory work, the Manhattan Project actually failed.An atomic bomb was never detonated. The war in the Pacific continued for another three years, after the United States launched a massive invasion of Japan, supported by the Soviet Union. Ultimately, the Americans and Soviets prevailed, and the Japanese surrendered in 1948. In 1950, the United States, Soviet Union, Britain, France, and China, signed a landmark agreement, banning the use of atomic energy, and the development of nuclear weapons. This agreement was diligently and successfully policed by a newly established, well-resourced International Atomic Energy Commission. As a result, that alternate version of the Earth never developed nuclear weapons.'

As Otto was debriefing me, the magnitude of this last mission overwhelmed me like a ton of bricks.A world with no nuclear weapons! David Bowie's *Heroes* was echoing throughout the piano bar during an intermission. In that surreal fleeting moment, my phone lit up with a message: "Hi baby. I'm pregnant. I know you're the father." I looked into Otto's eyes, and cried, and cried, and cried.

Heroes

I, I will be king
And you, you will be queen
Though nothing will drive them away
We can beat them just for one day
We can be heroes just for one day

And you, you can be mean
And I, I'll drink all the time
'Cause we're lovers, and that is a fact
Yes we're lovers, and that is that

Though nothing will keep us together
We could steal time just for one day
We can be heroes for ever and ever
What d'you say?

I, I wish you could swim
Like the dolphins, like dolphins can swim

Though nothing, nothing will keep us together
We can beat them forever and ever
Oh, we can be heroes just for one day

I, I will be king
And you, you will be queen
Though nothing will drive them away
We can be heroes, just for one day
We can be us, just for one day

I, I can remember (I remember)
Standing, by the wall (By the wall)
And the guns, shot above our heads (Over our heads)
And we kissed, as though nothing could fall (Nothing could fall)

And the shame was on the other side
Oh, we can beat them forever and ever
Then we could be heroes, just for one day

We can be heroes
We can be heroes
We can be heroes just for one day
We can be heroes

We're nothing, and nothing will help us
Maybe we're lying, then you better not stay
But we could be safer just for one day
Oh-oh-oh-oh, oh-oh-oh-oh, just for one day

Brian Eno, David Bowie, Andrea Schroeder (1977)

13

John F. Kennedy

Dallas, United States of America, November 1963 CE

SHOULD I REACH-OUT TO ISABELLA? MY HEART SAID YES, BUT MY rational mind was resisting. Was the baby really mine? I knew she didn't want to hurt me anymore. So, for her to contact me, I instinctively knew she must have been certain I was the father. Not having a child, had created a big void in my life. All three of my brothers had kids. I had three nieces and three nephews. I came from a traditional Italian background where kids were a big part of family life. I knew my mother was disappointed I didn't have kids. She tried not to show it, but particularly since the death of my father, I sensed that she saw me as incomplete, without my own family. To be a man, and not to be married with kids, was not Italian. I loved Isabella. But she was broken. She didn't want to be mended. Did I seriously expect she and I could live together as a family unit, and raise a child?

I don't know why, but as I sat in my study, at 7.30am, the blinds open, and bright rays of sunshine lighting up the room, I made myself a gin and tonic. I needed to calm my nerves. Mixed feelings abounded. What to do about Isabella and her pregnancy. Pent-up excitement, tinged with anxiety, about my next mission. To Dallas, 22nd November 1963, I was going. To stop the assassination of President John Fitzgerald Kennedy. This mission was different to all of the others. It was shrouded in mystery. There were endless conspiracy theories. Who killed JFK? Lee Harvey Oswald, acting alone? Lee Harvey Oswald, as part of a conspiracy? The CIA? The FBI? The Mafia? The Russians? The Cubans? Lyndon Johnson? Extreme Right Wing Generals? Combinations thereof?

I knew a lot about the events surrounding the assassination, and the life of JFK. It was a topic that fascinated me. I loved teaching it. A showcase of teaching JFK was my mock-trial; where students would take on the roles of actual characters: Oswald, Jackie, Governor

Connolly, Lyndon Johnson, secret service agents – include the heroic Clint Hill who literally jumped on Jackie, to prevent her from falling off the car, as it sped to Parkland Hospital immediately after the fatal shot was fired, FBI agents, Dallas police officers, witnesses. Two of my brightest students would take on the roles of defence lawyers; two others as prosecution lawyers; twelve students would form the jury; I was the judge. I conducted the trial just like a real one. Following correct judiciary procedure and protocol. The kids loved it. At the end, I would direct the "jury" to make a final decision, based on the well-established legal principles of evidence. Was Lee Harvey Oswald guilty of firing the shot which actually killed the President, beyond a reasonable doubt?

I had visited the museum on the sixth floor of the Texas School Book Depository building in Dallas Texas, three times. I saw the "snipers den," the grassy knoll, and picketed fence. I paced up and down Dealey Plaza, vividly imagining what the scene must have been like, when the shots were fired. Pandemonium. Panic. Horror. Shock. Fear. Nightmarish. Grisly. Surreal. Brutal. Screaming. Terror. The shattering of a dream. How many shots were fired? Three? Six? How many assassins were there? One? Two? Three? I was going to go back in time, and try to prevent the assassination, without really knowing who actually did it, and where the fatal shot was fired from.

How was I going to do this? Was I going to race straight-up to the sixth floor of the Texas School Book Depository building, and assume that Lee Harvey Oswald was the lone gunman; as the government-backed investigation, The Warren Commission, concluded? What if Oswald didn't fire the fatal shot? Then, my mission would fail miserably, and I wouldn't get a second chance to change history for the better. Otto was at pains to point out to me, that even he didn't know who fired the fatal shot, and where that shot came from. I needed to figure it all out myself.

From my own extensive research over two decades, I was convinced the mastermind behind the planning and execution of the assassination was the very powerful and mysterious CIA Counterintelligence Agent, James Jesus Angleton. His father was an NCR executive who had once participated in General Pershing's pursuit of the revolutionary Mexican leader, Pancho Villa, and his girlfriend, Carmen Moreno. James grew up in Boise, and later Dayton, in Ohio, where NCR was headquartered. At the age of fourteen, his family moved to Milan, Italy, where NCR manufactured cash registers.

Angleton spent his summers at British preparatory schools, and Malvern College. He participated in International Boy Scout Jamboree events in Scotland, Hungary, and Holland. When the NAZIs took over the Boy Scouts in Germany, Angleton made friends with some anti-NAZI leaders, and carried their letters back to the founder of the International Boy Scout movement in England. Both father and son would serve in the Office of Strategic Services (OSS), the U.S. intelligence agency, before the CIA was formed. Angleton's father was described by Max Corvo, a top OSS officer in Italy, as "ultra-conservative, a sympathiser with Fascist officials, who certainly was not unfriendly with the Fascists."

When he reached college age, Angleton attended Yale University in the U.S., where he first showed a tendency to stay up all night. Insomnia was to plague him for most of his life. Although many who knew him described him as brilliant, Angleton's academic record at Yale, was nothing special. But Angleton did manage to impress teachers with his aura of secretive mysteriousness, his maturity beyond his years, and his self-confidence. After graduating in the lowest 25% of his class, Angleton enrolled at Harvard University Law School.

His move to Harvard was not the consequence of any strong ambition to study law. Rather, like many young men at the time, he was putting his future on hold, but giving himself many options, by immersing himself within the "Harvard network." While studying at Harvard, Angleton met and married his wife, Cicely D'Autremont. The marriage took place a few weeks after Angleton had been drafted into the Army. Shortly after that, as a result of the combined efforts of his OSS father, and his former Yale English professor, Norman Pearson, then heading up the OSS operation in London; Angleton was transferred to London to study the political and security situation in Italy, working for X-2, a counterintelligence unit of the OSS.

It was during this period that Angleton met Kim Philby, the man who would become an infamous Soviet spy. Philby rose to a position of significant influence within the British intelligence establishment, until he was finally exposed as a Soviet agent, and fled to Moscow. Angleton was devastated by this serious betrayal, despite having been warned by fellow-agent and good friend, Bill Harvey, that Philby seemed to be acting like a mole. In October 1944, Angleton was transferred to Rome as the commanding officer of the Special Counterintelligence Unit Z, a joint American-British spying setup.

Around six months later, Angleton was promoted to the Chief of the X-2 unit in Italy. He was the youngest X-2 chief in the OSS. His staff included Raymond Rocca, who would loyally serve by his side until Angleton's expulsion from the CIA in 1974. Angleton's activities in Italy were very successful. X-2 was focused on destabilising the very powerful and influential Communist Party of Italy, to ensure it never got to form a government.

During this time, his activities were not only limited to acts of loyalty to his fellow intelligence agents; but could also be directed to more personal, vindictive measures. Blackmailing vulnerable people was his modus operandi. He mixed with a variety of unsavoury characters, including high-ranking members of the Mafia in Italy and the United States, many of whom, he kept as contacts, to assist him with his future counterintelligence endeavours.

After the war, Angleton did not wish to immediately return to his new wife, nor his son, born in his absence; and chose instead to remain in action in Europe. X-2 was folded into the Strategic Services Unit (SSU), effectively a War Department unit, and a temporary holding place for the by then defunct, OSS. Two years after the war, Angleton returned to the United States to his wife and son, and worked for the temporary intelligence agency that would eventually become the Central Intelligence Agency – the CIA.

Within a short time, he would achieve notoriety for his late hours, and for being, according to his secretary Gloria Loomis, "a terrible taskmaster." Before the CIA was created, many in the U.S. Congress feared that the creation of a new intelligence agency would lead to a police state similar to the one they had defeated in Germany. But the loudest protest for the formation of the CIA came from the very powerful and influential FBI Director, J. Edgar Hoover, who feared the

CIA would directly encroach upon the FBI's spheres of influence. Was J. Edgar Hoover blackmailed into supporting the creation of the CIA? In his book about J. Edgar Hoover, "Official and Confidential" the author, Tony Summers, outlined that Meyer Lansky, a top Mafia figure, had blackmail power over Hoover through his possession of photos that showed Hoover and his lifelong friend and close FBI associate, Clyde Tolson, engaged in homosexual activity.

Summers claims that Angleton also had possession of these photos. In his book, Summers names two sources for this allegation: former OSS officer, John Weitz, and private investigator, Gordon Novel. Weitz claimed he had been shown the pictures by James Angleton, at a dinner party hosted by Angleton in the fifties. Novel said that Angleton had shown him the explosive photos in 1967, when Novel was involved in New Orleans District Attorney, Jim Garrison's case against alleged JFK conspirator, the businessman and CIA operative, Clay Shaw. "I asked him if they were fakes," Novel recounted, "but he said they were real, that they'd been taken with a special lens. They looked authentic to me."

Novel's explanation of why Angleton showed him the pictures is even more interesting. He explains: "I was pursuing a lawsuit against Garrison, which Hoover wanted me to drop, but which my contacts in the Johnson administration and at CIA wanted me to pursue. I'd been told I would incur Hoover's wrath if I went ahead, but Angleton was demonstrating that Hoover was not invulnerable, that the Agency (CIA) had enough power to make him come to heel. I had the impression that this was not the first time the sex pictures had been used. Angleton told me to go see Hoover and tell him I'd seen the sex photographs. Later, I went to the Mayflower Hotel and spoke to Hoover. He was with Tolson, sitting in the Rib Room. When I mentioned that I had seen the sex photographs, and that Angleton had sent me, Tolson nearly choked on his food."

Novel stated that Angleton told him the photos had been taken in 1946; during the 1945-1947 timeframe, Hoover was battling hard to prevent the creation of the CIA. Also during this period, Angleton was involved with the Mafia, who were assisting him in the Italian anti-communism campaign. Whether the Mafia gave Angleton the compromising photos, or vice versa, we will never definitively know.

Right from the inception of the CIA, Angleton's reputation as a mysterious and very powerful spymaster, took hold. Even the heads of the CIA feared him. The first CIA Director Allen Dulles, worked closely with Angleton, and understood his formidable power. Thomas Braden, a CIA media operative was confronted by Dulles over a remark Braden had made about one of Dulles' professional relationships. Braden recounted what followed: "You'd better watch out," Dulles warned him. "Jimmy's (Angleton) got his eye on you." Braden said he drew the obvious conclusion - that James Angleton had bugged his bedroom and was picking up pillow talk between himself and his wife, Joan. But Braden said he wasn't surprised by the incident, because Angleton was known to have bugs all over Washington, and beyond.

Braden described how Angleton would enter Dulles's office "first thing in the morning" to report the results of the overnight bugs and phone-taps: "He used to delight Allen with stories of what happened at people's dinner parties. Jim used to come into Allen's office, and Allen would say – 'How's the fishing?' And Jim would say – 'Well, I got a few nibbles last night.' It was all done in the guise of fishing talk." Braden was upset because "some senator or representative might say something that might be of use to the Agency. I didn't think that was right. I think Jim was amoral."

Angleton routinely used information gathered through clearly illegal phone taps, to blackmail people into supporting his efforts. No wonder his CIA associates, politicians, and other government people, feared him. Just about everyone in the CIA who knew Angleton, came to fear him, and avoided crossing his path. This extended from subordinates to the highest officials, including Allen Dulles, and his then deputy, Richard Helms. Angleton was called "no-knock" because he had unprecedented access to senior agency officials. According to Braden: "He always came alone and had this aura of secrecy about him, something that made him stand out – even among other secretive CIA officers. In those days, there was a general CIA camaraderie, but Jim made himself exempt from this. He was a loner who worked alone."

Angleton knew that knowledge was power, so not only would he go to extraordinary lengths to obtain information; he would also lord his knowledge over others; especially newly-appointed CIA directors.

One of his CIA contemporaries said: "He would put each new director through the embarrassment of having to beg him to indoctrinate them in important CIA matters. Jim was enormously clever, he relished his bureaucratic power, and was expert at using it. He was utterly contemptuous of the chain of command. He had a keen sense of what the traffic would bear in relation to his own interests. It worked like this – when a new director came in, Jim would stay in his own office out of sight. If a top staff meeting was requested, he simply wouldn't attend, and would offer endless delays. He was a master at waiting to see the new director alone, on his own terms, and with his own agenda."

Angleton's most powerful patrons were Allen Dulles and Richard Helms. As his biographer, Tom Mangold, described it: "He was extended such trust by his supervisors that there was often a significant failure of executive control over his activities. The result was that his subsequent actions were performed without bureaucratic interference. The simple fact is that if Angleton wanted something done, it was done. He had the experience, the patronage, and the clout." Angleton ran the Counterintelligence unit, within the CIA. The primary role of Counterintelligence is to protect agents from a foreign intelligence organisation uncovering CIA assets and operations. Another important role is the ability to disseminate disinformation to foreign intelligence services in an effort to create for them, a false picture of reality, causing them to act in ways that may be ultimately against their own interests.

In addition to overseeing counterintelligence, Angleton also had control over the CIA's relationship with the FBI. Angleton's complete counterintelligence empire employed over 200 people. Inside this large group was a small handful of Angleton's most trusted, loyal, and closed-mouthed associates, called the Special Investigations Group (SIG). When the alleged assassin of President Kennedy, Lee Harvey Oswald, defected to the Soviet Union in 1959, there were only five members of the SIG, which was headed by Birch D. O'Neal. Included in the SIG at that time were also Ann Egerter, and Newton "Scotty" Miler. The SIG unit is very important in the case of the Kennedy assassination because, for whatever reason, SIG held a file on Lee Harvey Oswald, four years prior to the assassination.

What was the real role of the SIG? Angleton described the primary task of the SIG to the Church Congressional Committee investigating the JFK assassination, very vaguely, as follows: "The primary task was the penetration of the Agency and the government, and historical penetration cases are recruitment of U.S. officials in positions, code clerks. It had a very tight filing system of its own, and it was the only component in counterintelligence that had access to the security files, and the personnel maintained by the Office of Security." The Office of Security's primary role was to protect the CIA from harm. This involved monitoring the CIA's own employees and assets to ensure that no one leaked data about the CIA, or betrayed the CIA in any way.

Because of the nature of what was done there, Office of Security files were the most closely guarded in the Agency. It is significant therefore, that Angleton's SIG group had access to these files. It is also significant that the Office of Security also had a file on Lee Harvey Oswald. According to Angleton's close associate, Raymond G. Rocca: "The SIG was set up to handle especially sensitive cases in the area of security or personnel, and in particular, cases involving security of personnel who were also of operational interest, as operators."

In other words, the SIG was an interface with the Office of Security. The two operated, hand in hand. When asked what would cause the SIG to open a file on someone, Rocca gave this response: "I would imagine that they would have had the occasion whenever a question arose that concerned people that came within the purview of the mission that I have described, namely, the penetration of our operations, or the advancement of our particular interests with respect to the security of those operations. I mean, there were many sensitive areas that involved aspects, that involved sources and access to materials that were of higher classification that what you have shown me."

When the Church Committee asked why the SIG had opened a file on Lee Harvey Oswald in particular, Rocca offered this cryptic response: "Let me go back and open a little parenthesis about this. What I regard now, in the light of what you said, is probably a too narrow view of what SIG was interested in. They were also concerned with Americans as a security threat in a community-wide sense, and they dealt with FBI cases, with the Office of Security cases, and with other cases on the same level, as they dealt with our own, basically. It would be with respect to where and what had happened to DP (Directorate of Plans) materials with respect to a defection in any of these places." When further questioned about whether Oswald had anything to do with the DP at this time, Rocca did not offer a direct response.

Was Lee Harvey Oswald in Mexico City, weeks before the assassination of President Kennedy? If so, what was he doing there? On the face of it, it appears that Oswald travelled to Mexico City to visit the Cuban and Soviet embassies in order to get visas to visit both of these countries. His visa applications were denied. But was there more to the trip than just applying for visas? Shortly before the assassination, Oswald's CIA file was transferred to the Mexico City CIA headquarters desk, which was run by John Whitten, and supported by desk officer Charlotte Bustos. Bustos, Ann Egerter – working for Angleton, and Stephen Roll – Angleton's liaison officer on Soviet matters, drafted the two now infamous communications that cause much suspicion of the CIA's involvement in the Kennedy assassination.

Although the two communications were drafted at the same time, the cable to the CIA in Mexico City describes Oswald as 5'10", 165 pounds, and with light brown hair; whereas the teletype from the CIA to the State Department, Navy, and the FBI, describes Oswald as being approximately 35 years old, 6' tall, with an athletic build, and a receding hairline. Neither of these descriptions were accurate. Why would Angleton's people be collaborating with the Mexico City desk officer to mislead other government agencies, unless they were trying to hide or protect Lee Harvey Oswald's true identity?

Immediately after the assassination, Bustos found a photo of Oswald that was taken by the CIA's Mexico City surveillance operations. Phil Agee, Joseph Burkholder Smith, Daniel Watson, and Joseph Piccolo, all CIA employees, recalled hearing about, and in the latter two cases, actually viewing such a photo. According to Agee, Bustos found the photo within an hour or two after the President's assassination. Based on numerous accounts, Bustos had a "fantastic memory," yet, she could not recall what she was doing on the day of the assassination. It was one of Angleton's staff members, Anne Goodpasture, who supplied the photo the CIA showed to the FBI, as a possible picture of Oswald.

Curiously, in a later interview to congressional investigators, Goodpasture said that CIA headquarters refused to send a photo of Oswald to Mexico City, and she was never sure why.

We know from Oswald's CIA file that indeed news clippings from his Soviet defection, with his photo, were present; so the CIA did have an authentic photo of Oswald to share with the FBI, and the other government/military agencies. Was Bustos' picture, a true picture of Oswald? Or was it a picture of just another person who was not in fact, Oswald? If Bustos' photo of Oswald was genuine; for the CIA to have supplied agent Goodpasture's "Mystery Man" photo, in place of the real photo, suggests a deliberate effort to cover-up and deceive. In that case, Bustos' forged picture would have to be "disappeared" by the CIA, so that the evidence of their deception would never see the light of day.

Also, if Bustos' picture was not Oswald, but another man who looked like him instead, that also suggests a deliberate effort to deceive; as the picture was shown to at least two others within the CIA, as evidence that Oswald had been in Mexico City; a point which has never been fully proven. To date, the CIA has consistently taken the only safe road available, by claiming (despite multiple credible accounts to the contrary) that no such picture of Lee Harvey Oswald in Mexico City was ever found.

Anne Goodpasture testified that at one point during her CIA career she had worked for James Angleton as a counterintelligence officer; and that it was the CI group that sent her to Mexico City in 1957. Asked to explain the difference between CE (counterespionage) and CI (counterintelligence), Goodpasture replied: "Counterespionage was the activity, and Counterintelligence was the product." Angleton said of Goodpasture: "I personally have had very little dealings with her, but my men had had a lot of dealings with her. She was always in on very sensitive cases." Goodpasture was also involved with Staff D, which was seriously involved in several coup attempts, and assassination plots – including Cuba and Castro.

To the congressional investigators, Goodpasture downplayed her involvement in Staff D, claiming that she was simply involved in duplicating and distributing materials. Goodpasture maintained that in 1963 her sole duty was to the Mexico City CIA station. She was later to receive an Agency career achievement award, for having discovered Oswald at the Cuban embassy in Mexico City. As we have seen, Goodpasture was responsible for delivering the fake Oswald "Mystery Man" photo, supposedly taken in Mexico City. She was also the main liaison and in most cases, sole point of contact, between the CIA Mexico City station, and all other U.S. government departments and agencies.

Asked about her first recollection of the JFK assassination, she answered: "I think I heard about it from a phone call from our outside person on the phone tap operation, and I believe it was around lunchtime when there weren't too many people there, and as they all filtered back in, there was office gossip; but I have tried to remember. I've heard so many people say, I can remember, I was standing at the telephone, or I was in the drugstore, or I was in church; and I really don't remember who all were there at the time. Dave Phillips said that someone from the military attache's office came up and told him about it, and I don't remember that. I don't even remember him being in the station at the time."

Amongst her duties in Mexico City, it has become clear that Goodpasture ran all of David Phillips' operations. Phillips, was the CIA's chief of Western Hemisphere operations, and was the CIA man who most closely tied James Angleton into the JFK assassination story. Phillips appears to have been seen in the presence of Oswald, by Antonio Veciana, a Cuban exile who was recruited by the CIA to kill Fidel Castro. When the congressional investigators tracked down the many false "Castro killed Kennedy" leads, they kept tracing back to CIA assets run by Phillips.

Dan Hardway, an attorney engaged by the House Select Committee on Assassinations, had this to say about David Phillips: "I'm firmly convinced now that he ran the red herring, disinformation aspects of the plot. The thing that got him so nervous was when I started mentioning all the anti-Castro Cubans who were in reports filed with the FBI for the Warren Commission; and every one of them had a tie I could trace back to him. That's what got him very upset. He knew the whole thing could unravel."

Angleton was close friends with CIA Mexico City station chief, Win Scott, and ran numerous operations with him. Scott, in turn, was so close to Phillips that he recommended Phillips become his deputy in the Mexico City station, while waiting for the next deputy, Alan White, to arrive. Phillips also had a close connection to JM/WAVE – the code name for the highly secretive, covert CIA intelligence-gathering and training station, based just outside Miami, Florida. It was the operational headquarters of "Operation Mongoose," the name given to a covert action program to sabotage and subvert the Castro regime in Cuba; including assassination attempts against Fidel Castro himself.

The line between Des Fitzgerald's Special Affairs Staff – a division of the CIA responsible for covert and paramilitary operations, and the actions of JM/WAVE, is very blurred. During the weekend of the JFK assassination, CIA Director, John McCone's executive assistant, Walt Elder, saw Fitzgerald; and Fitzgerald told Elder he had met with Rolando Cubela, a former pro-Castro revolutionary leader, who was now working for the CIA under Operation Mongoose. Fitzgerald did not tell Elder he had given Cubela a poison pen to be used against Castro; nor that Fitzgerald had pretended to be in Mexico City as an emissary of Bobby Kennedy.

Fitzgerald literally did not directly mention the JFK assassination to Elder over that weekend, which Elder thought was strange. But Elder had the distinct impression that Fitzgerald was particularly upset that weekend. Elder was struck by Fitzgerald's clear discomfort, and claimed that "Des was normally imperturbable, but he was very disturbed about his involvement." The normally smooth operator was "shaking his head and wringing his hands. It was very uncharacteristic. That's why I remember it so clearly," Elder said in 1993. He thought Fitzgerald was "distraught and overreacting."

Des Fitzgerald's wife has stated that the first and last time she ever saw her husband break down in tears was when Lee Harvey Oswald was shot dead by Jack Ruby, on the Sunday morning of the weekend of the JFK assassination; an event ghoulishly captured on live television. She claims her husband had been distressed from the moment of the assassination, and sat silently, watching the news unfold, along with millions of others around the world. When Jack Ruby performed his ghastly deed, Fitzgerald began to cry, and said, cryptically, "Now we'll never know."

James Angleton went to extraordinary lengths to protect the interests of the CIA, and to cover-up the CIA's involvement in the assassination of President Kennedy. On 12th October, 1964, nearly 11 months after the assassination of JFK, a woman named Mary Pinchot Meyer was brutally shot and killed while going on her daily walk along the C&O Canal Trail, near the exclusive Georgetown area of Washington D.C. where she lived. The police charged a black man named Ray Crump Jr, with the crime. Since the murder took place in the nation's capital, the trial was in a federal district court.

Meyer had been married for 13 years to a high level CIA official named Cord Meyer. The Angleton's and Meyer's were very close, and they were especially bound together by their mutual interest in art and culture. Also, James Angleton and Cord Meyer were close associates, within the CIA. The Meyer's divorced in 1958. Crump vehemently professed his innocence of the crime. Convinced of his innocence, a renowned Washington D.C. criminal-defence attorney named Dovey Roundtree, agreed to represent him free of charge.

At Crump's trial, the federal prosecutor summoned a man named Ben Bradlee to the witness stand, as the prosecution's first witness. At the time, Bradlee was the Washington bureau chief for Newsweek magazine. He would later go on to become the executive director of the Washington Post newspaper. Bradlee's wife was Mary Meyer's sister. After Bradlee took the witness stand, the prosecutor, Alfred Hartman, asked him the following question: "Now, besides the usual articles of Mrs Meyer's avocation, did you find there, any other articles of her personal property?" Bradlee replied: "There was a pocketbook there," adding that it contained "keys, a wallet, cosmetics, and pencils."

What Bradlee said, was a half-truth. What he failed to reveal in response to the prosecutor's question was a secret that he was determined to protect – that he had also found the personal diary of Mary Meyer. Unbeknown to the prosecutor, or to Crump's defence attorney, was that on the night of the murder, Bradlee had gone to Meyer's home to retrieve her diary. When he arrived there, he encountered James Angleton burglarizing her home, in his own attempt to retrieve Meyer's diary. Angleton's wife, and Mary Meyer, had been good friends. Bradlee found the diary, and turned it over to Angleton, who then proceeded to read it, and destroy it. A blatant act of obstruction of justice, and destruction of evidence.

As it turned out, Mary Meyer had been having a secret affair with President John F. Kennedy in the months prior to his assassination. By all accounts, it was an extremely intimate affair; one in which Kennedy appears to have actually fallen in love with Meyer, who had been a long-time peace activist. Given that Kennedy had thrown down the gauntlet before the U.S. national-security establishment, with his famous Peace Speech at American University, in June 1963, in which he declared the end to the Cold War; it is likely that at the time, he was engaged in pillow talk with Meyer about the vicious and monumental struggle he was engaged in, with the U.S. national-security establishment, who wanted the Cold War with the Soviet Union, not only to continue, but to escalate. It his highly likely that Meyer's diary included Kennedy's sentiments, and identified particular people within the national-security establishment, who were a threat to him.

In fact, Meyer alluded to this possibility, in a telephone call after the Kennedy assassination, to her close friend, Timothy Leary, in which she sobbingly and fearfully stated: "They couldn't control him anymore. He was changing too fast. They've covered everything up." Mary's murder had all of the characteristics of a highly professional hit-job, along with a very sophisticated cover-up, involving the framing of an innocent man. By the time the secrets surrounding the discovery, and the destruction, of Meyer's diary were disclosed, the statute of limitations had expired on such crimes as obstruction of justice, destruction of evidence, perjury, and conspiracies to commit these crimes.

Prosecutor Hartman later stated that he had been "totally unaware of who Mary Meyer was, or what her connections were," and that having that knowledge "could have changed everything." Washington D.C. Police Detective Bernie Crooke later stated: "I'd have been very upset at the time if I'd known that the deceased's diary had been destroyed." Defence lawyer Dovey Roundtree expressed shock at learning of the diary's significance. "How differently my line of cross-examination would have run, had I been aware, on July 20, 1965, of the story Mr. Bradlee told thirty years later in his autobiography. James Angleton's awareness of the diary's existence, and his interest in finding it, reading it, and destroying it – all of that unsettled me deeply when I read Mr. Bradlee's 1995 account, as did his insistence that the diary was a private document. Had I been aware of it, I would have felt compelled to pursue it."

On 29th July, 1965, the jury found Ray Crump Jr., not guilty of murdering Mary Meyer. In a deathbed interview in February 2001, Cord Meyer was asked who he believed had murdered his ex-wife. Recanting an earlier statement that he had made in a 1980 book he had written, that pointed to a "sexually motivated assault by a single individual," this time, on his deathbed, Meyer responded: "The same sons of bitches that killed John F. Kennedy."

We have seen earlier that Winston ("Win") Scott was the CIA's station chief in Mexico City, and a close associate of James Angleton. Scott retired in 1969 and wrote a memoir about his time in the FBI, OSS, and the CIA. He completed the manuscript, "It Came To Little," and made plans to discuss the contents of the book with CIA director, Richard Helms, in Washington D.C., on 30th April, 1971.

Four days before the agreed meeting, Scott died of a heart attack. According to Win Scott's son, Michael, James Angleton took possession of his father's manuscript. Angleton also confiscated three large cartons of files including a tape-recording of the voice of Lee Harvey Oswald. Michael Scott was also told by a reliable CIA source that his father had not died from natural causes. Scott eventually got his father's manuscript back from the CIA. However, 150 pages were missing. Chapters 13 to 16 were deleted in their entirety. In fact, everything about his life in the CIA, after 1947, had been removed, on the grounds of national security.

When the Select Committee on Intelligence Activities, and Select Committee on Assassinations was announced by the U.S. Congress in the early seventies, and began its investigation of the assassination of JFK in 1976, there were numerous potential witnesses and persons of interest, who died in mysterious-suspicious circumstances around that time, including; Malcolm Wallace, a hitman and LBJ bodyguard, (1971); Lucien Sarti, a French drug trafficker and hitman, (1972); Charles Willoughby, an extreme right-wing retired U.S. general, (1972); Thomas Davis, an anti-Castro gunrunner and associate of Jack Ruby, (1973); Richard Cain, a notoriously corrupt Chicago police officer and close associate of Sam Giancana, (1973); Dave Yarras, associate of Jack Ruby and one of Giancana's Mafia hitmen, (1974); Sam Giancana, head of the Chicago Mafia who shared a mistress with JFK, (1975); Jimmy Hoffa, head of the Teamsters Union and Kennedy-hater, (1975); Roland Masferrer, an anti-Castro operative who worked with the CIA, (1975); Johnny Roselli, a Chicago mobster recruited by the CIA in a plot to assassinate Castro, (1976); George De Mohrenschildt, a CIA operative who befriended Lee and Marina Oswald in Dallas, (1977); Charlie Nicoletti, Chicago hitman working for Sam Giancana, (1977); and Carlos Prio, a Miami-based Cuban property developer involved in the planning of the Bay of Pigs invasion, (1977).

William Sullivan was one of the most senior agents in the FBI, involved in the investigation of the JFK assassination. On 9th November, 1977, a few days before he had been scheduled to testify before the House Select Committee on Assassinations, he was shot dead near his home in Sugar Hill, New Hampshire. Sullivan was one of six top-level FBI officials who died within a six-month period in 1977.

Others who were due to appear before the committee who died in highly suspicious circumstances, included; Louis Nicholas, special assistant to J. Edgar Hoover, and his liaison with the Warren Commission; Alan H. Belmont, special assistant to Hoover; James Cadigan, a document expert with access to documents that related to the death of John F. Kennedy; J.M. English, the former head of the FBI Forensic Sciences Laboratory, where Oswald's rifle and pistol were tested; and Donald Kaylor, an FBI fingerprint chemist who examined prints found at the assassination scene. In addition, there were several important figures in the CIA who died before they could give evidence to the House Select Committee on Assassinations. Sheffield Edwards, the CIA official who attempted to organise the assassination of Fidel Castro, died in July 1975. William Harvey, head of the covert ZR/RIFLE project set up by the CIA to assassinate Fidel Castro, died as a result of complications from heart surgery in June 1976. William Pawley, who took part in the covert Operation Tilt, involving two Soviet officers based in Cuba who wanted to defect to the U.S., died of gunshot wounds in January 1977. David Morales, who some believed was part of the rogue group that organised the assassination, died, aged 53, in May 1978.

Another important figure in CIA covert operations was Thomas Karamessines, who died of a heart attack in September 1978. An interesting case was that of John Paisley, who was the deputy director of the CIA's Office of Strategic Research. On 24th September, 1978, John Paisley took a trip in his motorised sailboat, on Chesapeake Bay. Two days later, his boat was found moored in Solomons, Maryland. Paisley's body was found in Maryland's Patuxent River. The body was fixed to diving weights. He had been shot in the head. Police investigators described it as "an execution-type" killing. However, Paisley's death was recorded as a suicide. According to the journalist, Victor Marchetti, Paisley was a close friend of Yuri Nosenko, the defector to the U.S. whom James Angleton accused of being a KGB agent. Marchetti also claimed that Paisley knew a great deal about the JFK assassination, and was murdered during the House Select Committee on Assassinations because he was "about to blow the whistle."

And then we have the case of Jack Ruby. Why did he shoot Lee Harvey Oswald? I believed he had no choice. When something went wrong at the Texas Theatre where Oswald was apprehended by Dallas Police, and wasn't killed by CIA operatives; Jack Ruby was instructed by Sam Giancana's Chicago mob, acting on behalf of Angleton and his rogue CIA conspirators, to finish the job in the basement of Dallas Police Headquarters. This, he duly did.

Ruby was well known to Dallas Police, many of whom would frequent his strip club, so gaining access to the basement was no problem. Ruby had close contact with the Dallas Mafia Don, Joe Civello, who himself had close ties to Sam Giancana and the Chicago Mafia. Ruby had been stalking Oswald on the weekend of the assassination. There are photos of him in Dealey Plaza, Parkland Hospital after the shooting, and at the Dallas Police Headquarters on the Friday night of the assassination, correcting the cops on the name of the "Fair Play for Cuba" movement, in which Oswald had been involved, in New Orleans. So Ruby had inside knowledge about Oswald.

After he shot Oswald on live television, Ruby became extremely agitated – asking if Oswald was still alive. When he finally found out Oswald was dead, Ruby immediately relaxed and appeared relieved. His mission had been accomplished. Justice Earl Warren, the head of the Warren Commission, investigating the assassination, and commission member, future president Gerald Ford, interviewed Jack Ruby in Dallas, during a break in his murder trial in 1964. This interview was video recorded, and in it, Ruby can be seen begging Warren to take him to Washington D.C., where he promised he would tell the "whole story" of his involvement, and knowledge of, the assassination of JFK.

Ruby consistently claimed he knew a lot more, but could not speak freely in Dallas, because of his fear of reprisals. When Warren asked him if the people he was afraid of were in high places, he emphatically answered, "YES." This was an absolute bombshell, yet Warren and Ford purposefully ignored him. Why? None of this made its way into the Warren Commission Report. When Dorothy Kilgallen, the well-known columnist, conducted a rare interview of Ruby in prison; she announced he had given her information that was going to blow the whole JFK assassination case, wide open.

She had a notebook full of details. As she was getting close to finishing her book, which would announce the Ruby bombshell, on 8th November, 1965, she was found dead in her Manhattan townhouse, in an "apparent suicide" deemed to have been caused by a combination of alcohol and barbiturates. She consistently refused to reveal what Ruby had told her, nor reveal the sources he had referred to her. In the last few months of her life, she fell in love with a much younger man – film journalist and suspected CIA operative, Ron Pataky. He denied an intimate relationship with Kilgallen, and any ties to the CIA, but others, including Kilgallen's daughter Jill, believed otherwise. Dorothy Kilgallen's "Ruby interview" notebook, and book manuscript, were never found.

The official Warren Commission Report of 1964 concluded that neither Oswald or Ruby were part of a larger conspiracy, either domestic or international, to assassinate President Kennedy. Despite its seemingly firm conclusions, the report failed to silence conspiracy theories surrounding the tragic killing in Dallas. Then, in 1978, the House Select Committee on Assassinations concluded that Kennedy was probably assassinated as a result of a conspiracy that may have involved multiple shooters and organised crime.

As the morning progressed, and I continued to numb my senses with a few more gin and tonics, the justification for my plan of action in Dallas, began to crystallise clearly in my mind. I was convinced James Angleton orchestrated the murder of JFK. He had numerous motives. His mentor and close friend, Allen Dulles, the former director of the CIA, was fired by JFK, for the 1961 Bay of Pigs fiasco; an aborted attempt to overthrow Fidel Castro, which had been conceived by Dulles and elements of the Pentagon.

Dulles had assured President Kennedy, that once the CIA-trained Cuban exiles landed on the beaches of the Bay of Pigs, an uprising of the people would be triggered, which would lead to the removal of Castro from power, thus paving the way for an "American-friendly" leader to be installed instead. Of course, this never happened. The Bay of Pigs was an unmitigated disaster for JFK's presidency. He blamed the CIA, and Dulles in particular. So he fired him, and a number of other high level CIA and Pentagon operatives. He vowed "to splinter the CIA into a thousand pieces and scatter it to the winds," and cut their budget significantly.

Being the height of the Cold War, the CIA was thriving on its fervent anti-communism, anti-Soviet, anti-Cuban, stance. Yet, here was a young president, who was reaching out to achieve peace with the Soviet Union, and not acting strongly enough against Cuba. JFK was perceived to be soft on communism by the extreme right wing elements of the CIA and military. James Angleton saw it as his patriotic duty to protect the interests of the CIA, and keep America strong, by eliminating JFK.

I was convinced the plan to assassinate JFK was first conceived by Dulles and Angleton. Dulles knew that Angleton was the best person within the bowels of the CIA, to plan and execute the killing. He had the power, relative anonymity, abundant resources, shrewd and bold intellect; and a close-knit network of no more than a handful of highly secretive covert rogue CIA operatives, working closely with the Chicago Mafia, to pull it off.

Piecing this assassination together, was like constructing an elaborate jigsaw puzzle. I certainly didn't have all the pieces, probably not even most of them, but I had enough to put together this scenario. Angleton recruited a number of U.S. marines into the CIA, in the late 1950s.

They were recruited as "covers." A cover is an agent who appears to support a particular anti-American ideology or national interest, but in reality, the agent is acting as a decoy, to distract from his real intentions.

So in the case of Lee Harvey Oswald, I believe he was recruited into the CIA by Angleton, in early-mid 1957, to act as a communist sympathiser. The Cold War was reaching its peak in the late 1950s. Political assassinations were being carried out all over the world with alarming frequency when the 18-year old U.S. Marine, Oswald, arrived at the Atsugi Naval Air Station in Japan, in September 1957, at the very apex of the worldwide standoff between American capitalism and Soviet communism.

Fidel Castro's Cuban Revolution was in full swing, having started in July 1953, and would culminate in Castro's takeover of Cuba in January 1959, creating a Soviet-backed communist state, right in the backyard of the United States, less than 90 miles off the coast of Florida. Although Joseph McCarthy, the architect of America's anti-communist hysteria, had died earlier in 1957, the United States was still paranoid about the possibility of the Soviet Union and China forming an alliance to foster monolithic communism on the Asian continent. The Korean War had only recently come to a stalemate, and there were ominous signs coming out of Vietnam.

As he checked in at the U.S. Navy base in Kanagawa Prefecture, southwest of Tokyo, nobody would have guessed that Lee Harvey Oswald would later leave the Marine Corps, defect to the Soviet Union, and only a few years later, become the accused assassin of an American President.

Private First Class Oswald must have found Atsugi more than he had hoped for or even imagined. Having been trained at military bases in Mississippi, California, and Florida, Oswald had never been outside the United States. And now he had stepped right into the middle of the Cold War that was raging in Asia. Radical leftist students throughout Japan were protesting the hawkish actions of Prime Minister Kishi Nobusuke, one of Japan's most unabashedly nationalist right-wing leaders. The anti-American movement was growing, and pro-American Kishi was intent upon extending the controversial treaty that gave the United States the right to station hundreds of thousands of troops in Japan. The students were just as intent on bringing Kishi down. The battle-lines had been drawn.

Later reports by The New York Times clearly illustrated, as the student activists suspected at the time, that Kishi's Liberal Democratic Party – formed in 1955 – was being supported by money flowing into its coffers from the Central Intelligence Agency, or CIA. "Japan had just come out of the post-war Occupation Period (1945-1952), and was trying to gain its balance as an independent country when I took command of Atsugi Naval Air Station in July 1958," said retired U.S. navy Captain Aram Y. Parunak.

He received the Third Order of the Sacred Treasure from the Japanese government in recognition of his contribution towards improving bilateral relations. "I was there when Francis Gary Powers' U-2 was shot down by the Russians in May 1960," he recalled. Oswald had access to key performance data on the CIA's U-2 high altitude spy plane, while serving as a Marine radar controller at the Atsugi station. Valuable covert information which provided perfect cover for a CIA agent defecting to the Soviet Union. And that's what he did. Oswald arrived in the Soviet Union just before he turned 20, in October 1959. He had taught himself Russian, and saved $1,500 of his Marine Corps salary. He didn't share any secrets about the U-2, or anything else, with the Russians. Why would he? He was a CIA operative.

The KGB came to the conclusion that he was of no use to them. Oswald ended up in the city of Minsk, where he met his future wife, Marina Prusakova. Marina worked as a pharmacy assistant in a local hospital, and in March 1961, met Lee Harvey Oswald at the city dance hall. At the time they met, she was living with her uncle, a colonel in the Soviet Ministry of Internal Affairs. Six weeks later, the couple got married. In the following year, they had a daughter.

Oswald soon became "disillusioned" with life in the Soviet Union, and in June 1962, he was given "fast-track" permission to take his wife and baby daughter to the United States. James Angleton had achieved the first phase of his plan for Oswald – to make him appear to be a Soviet defector, who still sympathised with communism – and that he had returned to the United States, for family reasons. By the time Oswald arrived in America, James Angleton had secured a new mission for him – to kill President John F. Kennedy. Almost certainly, at this stage, Oswald himself would not have been aware that he was being groomed for this monumental act of infamy.

The Oswald family settled in Fort Worth, Texas. Later, the family lived in New Orleans, and then Dallas. While in New Orleans, Oswald became active in left-wing politics, and joined the Fair Play for Cuba Committee. Again, this was a perfect CIA cover to show that even though he had returned to the United States, Lee Harvey Oswald was still a communist sympathiser, and a supporter of the Cuban communist leader, Fidel Castro.

Now, James Angleton needed to move to phase two – to demonstrate that Oswald was capable of carrying out a political assassination. The target was going to be the right-wing political leader, General Edwin Walker. Oswald's instruction was not to kill him, but to fire a shot in close proximity to him. So, on the night of 12th April, 1963, Oswald fired that shot, shattering the window of Walker's kitchen as he was standing nearby. Angleton now had to figure out how this attempted assassination could be attributed to Oswald, for the "future record," but not to make this deed public knowledge.

He came up with the perfect solution. He instructed Oswald to tell Marina about it. Angleton knew she would keep this secret, for fear of her family breaking up, and she being deported back to the Soviet Union. After he told her he had just tried to kill General Walker; Marina claimed she asked him who General Walker was, and then said: "How dare you to go and claim somebody's life." To which Oswald replied: "Well, what would you say if somebody got rid of Hitler at the right time? So if you don't know about General Walker, how can you speak up on his behalf? He is a fascist!"

James Angleton had the perfect minder for Lee and Marina – CIA operative, George de Mohrenschildt. In 1961, George de Mohrenschildt was invited to a lunch in Dallas, by CIA agent, J. Walton Moore. During this lunch Moore told de Mohrenschildt about Lee Harvey Oswald, who was living in Minsk at the time. According to de Mohrenschildt's autobiography though, he gives a different version of events: "Early in the summer of 1962 the rumours spread out among the Russian-speaking people of Dallas and Fort Worth, of an unusual couple – the Oswalds. He was supposedly an ex-marine, an unfriendly and eccentric character, who had gone to Russia, and brought back with him a Russian wife. He had lived in Minsk, where I had spent my early childhood. And so, I was curious to meet the couple and to find out what happened to Minsk. Someone gave me Lee's address, and one afternoon a friend of mine, Colonel Lawrence Orloff and I drove to Fort Worth, about 30 miles from Dallas."

Over the next few months, George de Mohrenschildt took Oswald to anti-Castro meetings in Dallas, at which General Walker spoke. Was this done, so witnesses could identify the future killer of JFK attending gatherings of his enemies? George was asked by J. Walton Moore to befriend Lee and Marina, and basically keep a regular watch on them; reporting back to Moore, regularly. George complied. In February 1963, George introduced Lee and Marina to Ruth Paine. A friend of Ruth Paine, Mary Bancroft, was alleged to be a mistress of former CIA director, Warren Commissioner, and Angleton's mentor – Allen Dulles.

Oswald was becoming increasingly violent, and displayed erratic behaviour towards Marina, often losing his temper and flying into a rage, for the most random and trivial of reasons. Marina had enough, and took her two daughters in April 1963, and moved in with Ruth Paine, who also taught her English. Oswald rented a room in Dallas, but stored some of his possessions in Ruth Paine's garage. Ruth also helped Oswald to get a job at the Texas School Book Depository building. In June 1963, George ceased contact with Lee and Marina, when he and his wife moved to Haiti, for business reasons.

After the JFK assassination, George de Mohrenschildt was recalled to America to testify before the Warren Commission. He was asked about the claim by Marina Oswald that he knew about Lee's attempt to kill General Edwin Walker. George denied this. But he was clearly being severely harassed and pressured about his knowledge and involvement in the killing of JFK; appearing close to a complete nervous breakdown. This must have concerned James Angleton.

On 5th September 1976, de Mohrenschildt sent this message to the then CIA director (and future president), George H.W. Bush: "Maybe you will be able to bring a solution to the hopeless situation I find myself in. My wife and I find ourselves surrounded by some vigilantes;

our phone bugged; and we are being followed everywhere. Either FBI is involved in this, or they do not want to accept my complaints. We are driven to insanity by the situation. I have been behaving like a damn fool ever since my daughter Nadya died from cystic fibrosis over three years ago. I tried to write, stupidly and unsuccessfully, about Lee H. Oswald and must have angered a lot of people I do not know. But to punish an elderly man like myself, and my highly nervous and sick wife, is really too much. Could you do something to remove the net around us? This will be my last request for help, and I will not annoy you anymore."

This letter would certainly have been passed on to James Angleton for his "action." Angleton needed to ensure George was permanently silenced. Well, two months later, George de Mohrenschildt was committed to a mental institution. According to his wife Jeanne, he was suffering from severe depression. He was taken to Parkland Hospital and underwent electroshock treatment. In February 1977, a friend of George, Willem Oltmans, met George at the library of Bishop College in Dallas, where he taught French. Oltmans later told the House Select Committee on Assassinations (HSCA): "I couldn't believe my eyes. The man had changed drastically, he was nervous, trembling. It was a scared, a very, very scared person I saw. I was absolutely shocked, because I knew de Mohrenschildt as a man who wins tennis matches, who is always suntanned, who jogs every morning, who is as healthy as a bull." According to Willem Oltmans, George confessed to being involved in the assassination of John F. Kennedy. He told him: "I am responsible. I feel responsible for the behaviour of Lee Harvey Oswald, because I guided him. I instructed him to set it up."

Oltmans also claimed that de Mohrenschildt had admitted serving as a middleman between Lee Harvey Oswald and H.L. Hunt, in an assassination plot involving other Texas oilmen, anti-Castro Cubans, and elements of the CIA. Oltmans testified to the HSCA: "He begged me to take him out of the country because they are after me." On 13th February 1977, Oltmans took de Mohrenschildt to his home in Amsterdam, where they worked on his memoirs. Over the next few weeks, de Mohrenschildt claimed he knew Jack Ruby, and argued that Texas oilmen joined with CIA intelligence operatives to arrange the assassination of John F. Kennedy.

Willem Oltmans arranged for George de Mohrenschildt to meet a Dutch publisher, and the head of Dutch national television. The two men then travelled to Brussels. When they arrived, Oltmans mentioned that an old friend of his, a Soviet diplomat, would be joining them a bit later for lunch. De Mohrenschildt said he wanted to take a short walk before lunch. Instead, he fled to a friend's house, and after a few days, he flew back to the United States. He later accused Oltmans of betraying him. Author Russell Baker suggests in his book, Family of Secrets: "Perhaps, and this would be strictly conjecture, de Mohrenschildt saw what it meant that he, like Oswald, was being placed in the company of Soviets. He was being made out to be a Soviet agent himself. And once that happened, his ultimate fate was clear."

The House Select Committee on Assassinations were informed of George de Mohrenschildt's return to the United States, and sent one of its investigators, Gaeton Fonzi, to find him. Fonzi discovered he was living with his daughter in Palm Beach, Florida. However, Fonzi was not the only person looking for George. On 15th March 1977, George had a meeting with investigative journalist Edward Jay Epstein, that had been arranged by the Reader's Digest magazine. Epstein offered him $4,000 for a four-day interview. On 27th March 1977, George de Mohrenschildt arrived at the Breakers Hotel in Palm Beach, and spent the day being interviewed by Epstein.

According to Epstein, they spent the first day talking about his life and career up until the late 1950s. Two days later, Edward Jay Epstein asked George about Lee Harvey Oswald. As he wrote in his diary: "Then, this morning, I asked him about why he, a socialite in Dallas, sought out Oswald, a defector. His explanation, if believed, put the assassination in a new and unnerving context. He said that although he had never been a paid employee of the CIA, he had "on occasion done favours" for CIA connected officials. In return, they had helped him in his overseas business contacts. By way of example, he pointed to the contract for a survey of the Yugoslavian coast, awarded to him in 1957. He assumed his 'CIA connections' had arranged it for him, and he provided them with reports on Yugoslav officials in whom they had expressed interest."

Epstein and de Mohrenschildt, broke for lunch and decided to meet again at 3pm. George de Mohrenschildt returned to his room where he found a card from HSCA investigator, Gaeton Fonzi. George de Mohrenschildt's body was found later that day. He had apparently committed suicide by shooting himself in the mouth. On 11th May 1978, Jeanne de Mohrenschildt gave an interview to the Fort Worth Star-Telegram, where she said that she did not accept that her husband had committed suicide. She also said that she believed Lee Harvey Oswald was an agent of the United States, possibly the CIA, and that she was convinced he did not kill John F. Kennedy. She then went on to say: "They may get me too, but I'm not afraid. It's about time somebody looked into this thing." James Angleton could rest easily, now that George de Mohrenschildt had been permanently silenced.

There was another CIA operative, who died in mysterious circumstances. His name was John Garrett Underhill Jr. Near the end of his life, Underhill became surrounded in controversy. Shortly after the assassination of JFK, Underhill told his friend, Charlene Fitsimmons, that he was convinced that Kennedy had been killed by "a small clique in the CIA." He knew the people involved, and what they knew. He also said: "Oswald is a patsy. They set him up. It's too much. The bastards have done something outrageous. They've killed the President! I've been listening and hearing things. I couldn't believe they'd got away with it, but they did!" Jim Garrison, the New Orleans based, Louisiana District Attorney, conducted an investigation into the assassination of Kennedy.

Garrison's investigation featured in the Oliver Stone movie, "JFK." Among the witnesses he sought out was John Garrett Underhill. In an interview that Garrison gave for Playboy magazine, Garrison mentioned a CIA agent with valuable information relating to his investigation. He was referring to Underhill, who was believed to have a connection with Harold Isaacs, who in turn, knew Lee Harvey Oswald's cousin, Marilyn Murret. Prior to Garrison being able to meet and interview Underhill, he was found in his bed with a bullet wound behind his left ear. Underhill died on 8th May, 1964, from this wound. This death was highly suspicious. I believe Angleton's rogue CIA operatives permanently silenced him too, for fear of him blowing the conspiracy open, to Jim Garrison.

Lee Harvey Oswald took a bus from Dallas to Mexico City. He arrived Friday morning, 27th September, 1963, and left very early on the following Wednesday, 2nd October. This was phase three of Angleton's plan for Oswald. Supposedly, Oswald had travelled to Mexico City to obtain a visa either from the Cuban, or Soviet, foreign embassies. In both cases, he failed. But this was not the point. Angleton wanted to leave a trail of evidence that showed Oswald was attempting to flee the United States for a safe-haven in a communist country, after he killed the President.

We have seen the deliberate confusion the CIA created in Mexico City, regarding the true identity of Oswald. I believe Ruth Paine was working with the CIA, when she secured the job for Oswald at the Texas School Book Depository Building. We have seen that it was George de Mohrenschildt who introduced her to Lee and Marina. Lee started working at the Texas School Book Depository, on the 15th October, 1963. At this time, the Mayor of Dallas was Earle Cabell. His brother, Charles Cabell, was appointed deputy director of the CIA in 1953. Charles was closely involved with Allen Dulles, in the planning of the 1961 disastrous Bay of Pigs invasion of Cuba, which crippled JFK's early presidency. I believe that in his capacity as the Mayor of Dallas, Earle Cabell had the final say regarding the route the Kennedy motorcade was going to take, in the streets of Dallas.

There is evidence to show that Earle Cabell requested that the motorcade make the left turn from Main Street, then Houston, and into Elm Street in Dealey Plaza; slowing the presidential motorcade right down, and placing it in the direct line of fire, from the sixth floor southeast corner window of the Texas School Book Depository building. Lee Harvey Oswald was set up. He was a patsy, as he claimed, when he was arrested. Lee was led to believe he was the only gunman. Angleton's CIA operatives had told Lee that after he fired the shots, he was to leave the rifle on the sixth floor, where it could be easily discovered, calmly make his way down the stairs, and exit the building. He was then instructed to briskly but unobtrusively walk from the depository building to the bus stop at the corner of Elm and Murphy.

He was told to board the bus (which he did at 12.40pm – the shots were fired at 12.30pm). The purpose of this very short bus trip was to get Oswald away from the immediate panic and commotion of the Dealey Plaza area. So, at 12.44pm, Oswald got off that bus, and started walking to the Greyhound bus terminal, three and a half blocks away. Oswald entered a taxi at the Greyhound bus terminal. After the two and a half mile ride, he told the taxi driver to drop him off at the corner of Beckley and Neely; a short walk to the boarding house he was staying in. This was all planned. When Oswald arrived home, the housekeeper, Earlene Roberts, had just learned that the president had been shot, when she saw the front door swing open, and Oswald come in. "Oh, you are in a hurry," she said. He ignored her comment, moved quickly past her, and into his small room to the left of the living area.

Although it was a warm day, Oswald pulled a white "Eisenhower" jacket from the rack, tucked a revolver into the waistband of his pants, and rushed out of the house. Back at the book depository, within minutes of the assassination, the supervisor told police that there was only one employee missing – his name was Lee Harvey Oswald. Oswald left the boarding house shortly after 1.00pm, zipping up his jacket to hide his pistol, as he walked out the door. Angleton's CIA operatives had arranged for Oswald to meet them at the Texas Theater, where he was to discreetly enter, and they would then whisk him away to a safe location. This is what they told him. In reality, they were planning to execute him in the darkness of the theater, and then make their escape, having permanently silenced Oswald in the process.

What thwarted this plan was how quickly the Dallas police figured out that Oswald was the only employee missing from the depository building, and immediately put out a notice to all police cars, and the media, to keep a look out for a man matching the height, build, and description of Lee Harvey Oswald. As a result of this quick police work, an employee at the ticket counter of the Texas Theater called the police when he saw a man enter the theater, who matched the description given for Oswald, over the radio. The Dallas police arrived moments before the CIA operatives did. It's as simple as that. The CIA operatives missed their opportunity to execute Lee, when the Dallas police escorted him out of the theater.

Did Oswald kill police officer, J.D. Tippit? J.D. Tippit was one of the few officers in the Dallas Police Force not to be called to Dealey Plaza to help control the crowd and investigate the assassination. Instead, at 12.45pm, he was sent to the Oak Cliff area of Dallas.

At 1.16pm, Tippit approached a man, later "identified" as Lee Harvey Oswald, walking along East 10th Street. A witness, Domingo Benavides, later testified that after a short conversation, a man resembling Oswald pulled out a hand gun, and fired four shots at Tippit.

However, another witness, Acquilla Clemons, was sitting on a porch of a house nearby, and claimed that she saw two men involved in the attack on Tippit. Another witness, Helen Markham, also saw the killing. However, she described the killer as being short and somewhat on the heavy side, with slightly bushy hair. Later, Markham identified Oswald in a police line-up, but this was after she had seen his photographs on television. Warren Reynolds did not see the shooting, but saw the gunman running from the scene of the crime. He claimed that the man was not Oswald. After he survived an attempt to kill him, Reynolds changed his story, and identified Oswald as the man he had seen.

I had no doubt it was not Oswald who killed police officer J.D. Tippit. Angleton arranged for professional hitmen to murder the police officer in close proximity to the theater, so it could be pinned on Oswald – to show he was capable of cold blooded murder. It was fortunate for them there was a police officer in the vicinity. If there hadn't been, somebody else would have been murdered, to make the same shocking point – somebody like the Texas Theater employee.

Of course, by the Friday night of 22nd December, 1963, James Angleton had a major problem on his hands. Lee Harvey Oswald was alive and well, and was being intensively questioned at the Dallas Police Headquarters by the police, and the FBI. He had already declared that he was "just a patsy" and that "he did not kill the president." What else would he disclose. Something drastic had to be done to shut him up. And something was done. Angleton asked Chicago Mafia Boss, Sam Giancana, to arrange for somebody to kill Oswald on the Sunday morning, when it was widely announced that Oswald would be transferred from Dallas Police Headquarters to a Remand Prison facility.

The Chicago and Dallas Mafia had the perfect person to carry out the hit – Jack Ruby. On that fateful Sunday morning, while most of America was riveted to the non-stop television coverage of the JFK assassination, a man darted out of the crowd in the basement of Dallas Police Headquarters, as Oswald was being escorted to an armoured car by two detectives, and he fired a single shot into Oswald's abdomen – to the horror of millions watching on live television. Oswald died later that day, in Parkland Hospital – the same hospital in which JFK had died.

When John F. Kennedy was shot on 22nd November, 1963, he was taken to Parkland Hospital, and was treated by Dr Malcolm Perry. He performed a tracheotomy over the small wound in Kennedy's throat, inadvertently destroying crucial evidence concerning the direction of the bullet that hit the president. At the press conference that followed the death of Kennedy, Perry stated he believed the throat hole looked like an entrance wound.

Dr Charles Crenshaw also treated Kennedy at Parkland Hospital. He later stated: "Two wounds were visible. There was a small, round opening in the front of the midline of the throat. This became the site of Dr Malcolm Perry's tracheostomy incision. In the occipito-parietal region at the right rear of the head, there was an avulsive wound nearly as large as a fist. I considered the throat wound to be an entrance wound, and the large head wound to be an exit wound. Along with many of my Parkland colleagues, I believed at the time that President Kennedy had been hit twice from the front." This conclusion reached by the team of trauma doctors at Parkland Hospital in Dallas, who first saw the president, clearly meant that Lee Harvey Oswald could not possibly have fired the shot that killed the president, because the sixth floor of the Texas School Book Depository building was behind the JFK motorcade, not in front.

So, if Oswald was involved in the shooting, there had to be at least two assassins. Oswald was set up by the CIA as a decoy, a patsy; so the assassination could be blamed on him – and him only. Angleton knew it was highly unlikely Oswald's shots would kill the president. At best, one shot might hit him, with no guarantee of it being fatal. So, meanwhile, literally within seconds of Oswald's shots being fired, two professional hitmen – organised jointly by Angleton's rogue CIA operatives, and Sam Giancana's Chicago Mafia, would actually finish the job. Well, as it turned out, only one was required to do the killing. He was on the grassy knoll, to the front-right of the motorcade, behind the picket fence. I believed the other assassin was standing directly in front of the motorcade, on the freeway overpass bridge. He was there as a backup. He wasn't required. The job had already been done. But now, Angleton had another headache to sort out urgently. He needed to ensure the official autopsy in Washington contradicted the Parkland doctors, and decisively showed the neck and head wounds resulted from shots fired from the rear – supposedly by the lone gunman, Oswald – and not from the front.

An autopsy on the body of Kennedy was performed during the evening of 22nd November, 1963, at Bethesda Naval Hospital in Maryland. This involved Commander Dr Joseph Humes, who was in charge of the autopsy, Lieutenant Colonel Pierre Finck, and Commander James Boswell. When interviewed by the Warren Commission, Humes insisted "that the bullet penetrated the rear of the President's head and exited through a large wound on the right side of his head." This directly contradicted the Parkland Dallas trauma surgeons. So, the official autopsy supported the argument that the shot that killed the president came from behind him – from Oswald.

William Bruce Pitzer, was a Lieutenant Commander who held a senior position at Bethesda Naval Hospital. A few days after the assassination, a colleague, Dennis David, found Pitzer working on a 16mm film, slides, and black and white photos, of the Kennedy autopsy. David noted that those materials showed what appeared to be an entry wound in the right frontal area, with a corresponding exit wound in the lower rear of the skull. This is not what the official autopsy declared. Jerrol F. Custer, an X-ray technician at the hospital, later stated that Pitzer had photographed the JFK autopsy proceedings, including the military men who attended the Kennedy autopsy. Pitzer also had copies of the autopsy photographs. According to Dr Joseph Humes, Pitzer was not present at the autopsy. However, he admitted that the Bethesda Naval Hospital was equipped with closed-circuit television. This was the responsibility of Pitzer, who, over the years, had used these facilities to make instructional movies.

It appears that Pitzer had secretly made a 16mm movie film of the autopsy on President Kennedy's body, without actually being present in the autopsy room when it was carried out. After 28 years in the US Navy, Pitzer decided to retire. He told friends he had been offered a good job working for a network television station. He intended to make a television program which would reveal the truth about the Kennedy assassination. His life was cut short, though. On 29th October, 1966, Lieutenant Commander William B. Pitzer was found dead at the Naval Medical School, at Bethesda Hospital.

Investigations by the Naval Investigative Service, and the FBI, later concluded that a gunshot wound to the head, had been self-inflicted. During the weekend on which Pitzer died, the Kennedy family transferred formal possession of the materials relating to the late president's autopsy, to the National Archives. An investigation carried out by Dr Cyril H. Wecht in 1993, revealed that some items from the autopsy were missing – including the remains of Kennedy's brain, that had been stored in a stainless-steel container. FBI files on the investigation, released in 1997 under the Freedom of Information Act, revealed that there was a strong possibility that Pitzer had been murdered.

FBI tests indicated "that the revolver must have been held at a distance of more than 3-feet when discharged." Pitzer's autopsy showed both an entry and exit wound to the head, and a third wound that was not related to the gunshot wound to the head. Pitzer had been busy writing notes to people, in the time just before he was killed. However, he did not leave a suicide note. One of these notes was found on the floor near Pitzer's body. It bore a partial heel print that was not from the shoes Pitzer was wearing. In May 1995, ex-Special Forces Colonel Daniel Marvin, claimed to have been solicited by an agent of the Central Intelligence Agency, to "terminate" William Pitzer. Was that CIA agent, James Angleton?

Finally, we have the farcical Warren Commission. After the death of John F. Kennedy, his deputy, Lyndon B. Johnson, was hurriedly sworn in as president, on board Air Force One, within hours of the assassination; with his wife Lady Bird, to his right, and Jacqueline Kennedy still wearing her pink blood-stained Versace dress, to his left; on the tarmac of Love Field airport, in Dallas. He immediately set up a commission to "ascertain, evaluate and report upon the facts relating to the assassination of the late President John F. Kennedy."

The seven-man commission was headed by Supreme Court Chief Justice, Earl Warren; and also included congressman and future president Gerald Ford; former head of the CIA and close friend of James Angleton, Allen W. Dulles; former Assistant Secretary of War and presidential advisor, John J. McCloy; former Governor of Georgia, Richard B. Russell; senator, John S. Cooper; and lawyer, Thomas H. Boggs. President Johnson also commissioned a report on the assassination from FBI Chief, J. Edgar Hoover. Two weeks later, the FBI produced a 500-page report claiming that Lee Harvey Oswald was the sole assassin, and that there was no evidence of a conspiracy. This report was then passed on to the Warren Commission. Rather than conduct its own independent investigation, the commission relied almost entirely on the rushed FBI report.

The Warren Commission report was published in October, 1964, and concluded that the shots which killed President Kennedy, and wounded Governor Connolly, were fired from the sixth floor window at the southeast corner of the Texas School Book Depository building, by Lee Harvey Oswald. The commission also concluded that three shots were fired; the first, missed, the second was the "magic bullet" that struck the president in the neck, and also hit Governor Connolly in the upper-back, and the third, was the fatal shot that hit the president in the head; and that Oswald acted alone. In other words, there was no conspiracy to kill the president. President Johnson personally picked each of the commission members. Why did he include Allen Dulles?

As we have seen, Dulles was removed by JFK, as director of the CIA, after the Bay of Pigs fiasco. Also, we have seen that James Angleton had the overall responsibility for controlling what CIA information on the assassination, was provided to the Warren Commission, and also to the FBI. The result? A lot of highly sensitive CIA documents and pieces of evidence were withheld. Disturbingly, the Warren Commission report only included witness statements and "evidence" which supported the conclusion it always wanted to reach – that Oswald killed the president, and acted alone.

I was due to travel down the wormhole to Dallas, Texas, in an hour. As I continued drinking, I collected my thoughts on the actual bullets that were fired in Dealey Plaza. I believe, Lee Harvey Oswald fired the first two shots from the southeast corner window on the sixth floor, of the Texas School Book Depository building. The first shot completely missed the presidential motorcade, hit the curb to the left of the vehicle, ricocheting and grazing the cheek of a bystander. The second Oswald shot struck Texas Governor John Connolly in the middle of his back. Connolly was seated in the same car, directly in front of the president. The Zapruder film clearly shows Connolly moving forward as he is struck in the back, and then turning around towards the president.

Then, almost instantaneously, a third shot was fired – but not from the Texas School Book Depository building. This third shot came from the front-right of the motorcade, and was fired by an assassin standing behind the picket fence, on the grassy knoll; and behind where Abraham Zapruder was filming the JFK motorcade, as it was passing. The third shot struck Kennedy in the throat. In the Zapruder film, he can be seen holding up his right hand and forearm, towards his throat. Finally, there was the fourth, and fatal shot. This one also came from the same assassin at the grassy knoll, and struck President Kennedy in the right-side of his head, shattering his skull, and blowing away a sizeable portion of his brain. The Zapruder film captured the president being struck in the head, and he is seen to be jolting violently backwards as he is hit. It would have been imperative to James Angleton and his rogue CIA operatives that the president did not survive Dealey Plaza. This is why I was convinced there was a third assassin, to make sure the hit was completed. I believe this assassin was standing on the freeway overpass bridge, dressed as a policeman, directly in front of the motorcade. He wasn't required. The gruesome job had been done. The president was dead.

Over 50 witnesses heard shots coming from the grassy knoll; some saw a suspicious man behind the picket fence; other witnesses saw another man, dressed in black, standing on the freeway overpass, and placing an object in a sports bag, before calmly walking away from the crime scene. None of these witness statements found their way into the rushed FBI investigation, nor the government sponsored Warren Commission Report.

It was a bright sunny day in Dallas, as I arrived at Dealey Plaza, 12 noon, on 22nd November, 1963. My contact was Dallas police officer, Adrian Thomas, an unassuming and loyal man, whom Otto had selected because he was not caught up in the original assassination events; instead he had been at his desk at police headquarters, a few blocks away, when the shots were fired. There were people everywhere. Excited. Happy. Joyful. In a celebratory mood. Clearly looking forward to seeing their beloved president, and elegant first lady Jackie.

The assassination was thirty minutes away. My gut felt empty, as I realised that within half an hour, this amazingly happy scene was going to quickly turn into the worst possible nightmare. A nightmare on Elm Street. It never made sense to me why the motorcade route included a sharp left turn from downtown Main Street, then Houston, and finally into Elm Street, where the cars had to slow right down, creating a security threat for the Secret Service agents protecting the president and first lady. Of course, if the route was changed, with the intention of providing assassins with a perfect opportunity to ambush and kill the president – it made absolute sense.

I was standing directly opposite the Texas School Book Depository building, on the other side of the road. At that moment, the southeast corner window on the sixth floor was firmly shut. I knew that in about twenty minutes, it would be opened, almost certainly by Lee Harvey Oswald. I looked to my left towards the grassy knoll and the picket fence. There were a lot of people gathered on the grass bank, giving them an elevated birds-eye view of the presidential motorcade. I couldn't make anybody out behind the picket fence. Again, too early.

I could see Abraham Zapruder and his female employee, getting ready to film the motorcade. He was going to stand on a concrete block and film the president with his Super-8 camera, while his companion held him firmly by the waist from behind, so he wouldn't lose his balance. Then, I instinctively looked up at the freeway overpass bridge. There were a group of people up there, probably excited with the excellent spot they had secured, soaking in the joyful atmosphere. I couldn't help thinking – how anxious and nervous would the assassins be at this point in time, knowing the infamous deed they were about to carry out? Or was it just a routine hit, for them? No empathy. No emotion. No sense of shattering a visionary dream that would change America, and the world forever.

I inconspicuously walked amongst the crowd, looking at all the faces – looking for anything suspicious. I was amazed at the number of men in black suits and dark sunglasses there were, scattered around the plaza. Were they FBI? Secret Service? CIA? Mafia? Or just businessmen and other ordinary citizens? I must have scoured every part of the plaza before making my way back to my original position.

There, waiting for me, was officer Adrian Thomas, chatting with a couple of young ladies. He saw me approaching, and walked towards me.

'Officer Thomas, it's my pleasure to meet you. I wish it was in more pleasant circumstances.'

'Mr Evangelista, it is my honour, sir. Please call me Adrian.'

'I will, if you call me, Luca.'

'It's a deal.'

'Just come over here, away from the crowd, so we can talk. Adrian, we have a big job on our hands. We are about to attempt to change the course of history. Your role is going to be critical, because I can't be in two places at the same time. Are you up to it?'

I could see Adrian was shaking. He was so young. Although 22 years of age, he looked like he was barely 15. He was the textbook all-American boy. Crew-cut cropped hair, square-jawed, blue-eyed, over 6 feet tall, built like a grid-iron pro, flashy teeth, and innocent, but very determined eyes. The kind of boy a mother would want her daughter to bring home.

'I love our president, sir. We are going to get him out of here, alive.'

'That's what I wanted to hear, Adrian. Now, we are going to swing into action, like lightening, and with absolute precision. I think there are two assassins out here. That's not including the one in the Texas School Book Depository building. We don't have to worry about him, because I believe his shots will not strike the president.'

I hoped I had figured it out, right. Suddenly, my heart began to pound heavily. I could hear a brass band playing "The Eyes of Texas" accompanied by cheerleaders. The sixth floor window was now open! I clearly saw the outline of a man – but couldn't make out if it was Oswald. Ten minutes to go. I looked up towards the overpass bridge. I knew it! There was a man dressed in black, easily passing for a police officer, standing right in the middle of the overpass, facing Elm Street, the glare reflecting from his dark sunglasses. I looked closer. My God!

It was Thero. What the hell was he doing there? I knew he couldn't possibly be one of the assassins, because he wasn't allowed to kill anybody. Hang on! A frightening thought came to me. What if he was one of the original assassins on that day? One of the three assassins? The spare assassin, who wasn't required? Or was he just there to distract me from the real assassins? A decoy? I was confused; but I knew where I needed to go. Not to the sixth floor. Not to the overpass. Instead, straight to the picket fence facing the grassy knoll. This is where I was confident I would encounter the killer of JFK. But, at the same time, Adrian needed to race to the overpass bridge, and confront Thero!

'Adrian, do you see that man on the bridge, dressed in black? I don't believe he's a police officer. I think he might be one of the assassins. You need to stop him from firing a shot, but you cannot kill him, do you understand?'

'Yes sir!'

'Okay, let's swing into action, we haven't got much time left! I'm going to stop the guy behind the picket fence, on the grassy knoll.'

Wanting not to attract any unnecessary attention, I calmly walked across the road, and up the grassy knoll, making my way behind the picket fence, about 50 metres away from where I believed the shooter to be. Just as I got into position, I saw the motorcade on Main Street. It was getting close to turning onto Houston, and then Elm. Five minutes to go!

Then, I saw him. He was totally in black, again, looking like a police officer, but without the badges; he was carrying a black sports bag. He had come from the carpark behind the picket fence. I hid behind a tree. There was nobody else between me and the gunman. On the other side of the fence, on the grassy knoll, it was full of people. He had a crate, which he positioned firmly, and then was going to stand on. This would give him the extra height to fire the shots over the crowd. The motorcade was now turning onto Elm. He opened the bag, took out the components of a rifle, and began to assemble it. Then he stood on the crate, ready to fire. I snuck around, behind him.

He didn't see me. He was intensely focused on firing the shots. Just as he was looking through the viewfinder of the rifle, I jumped him from behind, making sure I dislodged the rifle well away from him. He lost his balance and crashed to the ground. This gave me an advantage. I kicked and punched him furiously, while he lay on the ground. He didn't have a chance to get up. I had totally ambushed him. I looked into his empty-frenzied eyes. He was full of hatred. He looked inhuman, devoid of any emotions. He put up an enormous fight, but I had hit him so many times, my knuckles were bleeding. I had seen so many photos of potential assassins – mafia hitmen, CIA operatives, Cuban exiles, military sharpshooters, international assassins for hire – but I didn't recognise him at all. He looked French or German to me.

Anyhow, it didn't matter. I knew he wasn't going to talk. I had done the job. I let him flee into the carpark and towards the railway yard. Just then, I heard two shots. They definitely came from the Texas School Book Depository building. I saw the motorcade. Governor Connolly had been shot in the back, but Kennedy was unharmed. Then, there were two more shots, just as the car was accelerating. I could see JFK had been struck on his right shoulder. The other bullet appeared to have completely missed the motorcade, as it now raced under the overpass bridge, towards Parkland Memorial Hospital. Did Thero fire those last two shots? No! Officer Thomas had succeeded in distracting Thero. Later, he told me that Thero didn't even put up a fight, and didn't utter a word. Thero was also unarmed. He just vanished before Thomas's eyes.

So, there must have been a third assassin, exactly as I thought. Not on the overpass bridge, though. From what position, did he fire the two shots? I was baffled. All I could deduce was that he was in front of the motorcade, and clearly wasn't positioned behind the picket fence, nor on the overpass bridge. Nevertheless, even though he fired two shots, he didn't kill the president. My mission had been completed. President John Fitzgerald Kennedy was alive, suffering only a superficial wound to his right shoulder, which eventually fully healed. There was one more thing I needed to do, before leaving the world of 1963.

I needed to go to Washington. I couldn't get a flight out of Dallas. All flights in and out of the city had been cancelled until further notice. The only way to get there was to drive. It would take me nearly 24 hours, but that was fine. I had to go there. I hired a blue Chevrolet Corvair convertible, and off I went – leaving at 2pm. Every road leading out of Dallas was heavily secured by the police. After showing my ID, and answering a few questions about who I was, why I was in Dallas, and where I was heading – they let me through.

I felt a surreal sense of freedom as I accelerated away from the Dallas city limits on the Interstate 30, while the car radio was blaring "Be My Baby", the timeless Ronettes world-wide hit. During the drive, I was certain I was being followed. There was a car constantly behind me – when I slowed down, it slowed down – when I accelerated, it did – never overtaking me. I arrived at Little Rock, Arkansas, at around 9.30pm, and checked into a Howard Johnson motel, along the highway. There was no sign of the car that had been following me.

As I waited at the motel reception desk, a television was delivering the news of the day's tragic events. I was riveted to the small black and white flickering screen. The president and governor Connolly were rushed to Parkland Hospital. Both were out of danger, and recovering well. With a cigarette hanging off his lip, the news announcer went on to say that the alleged gunman, Lee Harvey Oswald, had been captured by Dallas police in the Texas Theater, and was now at police headquarters being questioned. Dallas chief of police, Jessy Curry, stated Oswald was believed to be the sole assassin. He was a lone gunman. It wasn't a conspiracy, according to Curry. Then, the police chief went on to say that Oswald had been charged with the murder of police officer J.D. Tippit. I couldn't believe what I was seeing and hearing! In spite of Kennedy being saved, Tippit had still been shot dead, and they were still pinning the whole thing on Oswald! I watched the screen as Oswald was being paraded in front of the news media, where he told them he did not shoot the president; nor did he murder the police officer. He claimed he was a patsy. Was Jack Ruby still going to kill Oswald in the basement of the Dallas police headquarters on Sunday morning? I couldn't wait to see.

As I lay on the bed, in a sparsely furnished room, with a tiny adjoining bathroom, and not much else, I collected my thoughts. Undoubtedly, Angleton would have planted undercover CIA operatives in Dealey Plaza, looking for any people behaving suspiciously. Even though I tried to blend into the crowd, and remained calm, I did move around the plaza quite a bit – and of course, then made my way up to the grassy knoll. Did they spot me? Were they following me? Suddenly, there was a knock on the door.

'Sir, sorry to bother you at such a late hour, but we need to talk to you; we are from the FBI. My name is agent Douglas, and this is agent Crawford.'

As they stood at the door, they both produced their ID badges. Amongst the items Otto had prepared for me, was an ID card, giving my name, and other personal details. I had used it to get out of Dallas. I presented it to them, when they asked me my name.

'What can I do for you, gentlemen?'

'Mr Evangelista, we need to ask you some questions, regarding the attempted assassination of the president. Were you in Dealey Plaza this afternoon, at the time of the shooting?'

'Yes, I was.'

'What were you doing there?'

'I am a history teacher, visiting America, from Australia. I was there to see the president and first lady, just like everybody else.'

'Did you see anything suspicious, before the shots were fired?'

'No. I was soaking up the happy atmosphere, when suddenly, I heard the shots being fired. It was so shocking.'

'Where exactly were you, when the shots were fired?'

'I was on the grass bank, in front of the picket fence, amongst the crowd. Not far from the man who was standing on a concrete block, filming the motorcade.'

'How many shots did you hear?'

'I can't be absolutely certain, because of the screaming and commotion after the first shots were fired; but I'm pretty sure I heard a total of four shots.'

'From which direction do you think the shots came from, Mr Evangelista?'

'I think the first two shots came from one of the buildings behind the president. The other two shots came from somewhere in front of the president. They sounded like they came from the freeway overpass bridge area. Thank God the president wasn't killed. He looked like he was struck by a bullet, though.'

'Yes. The president was struck in the right shoulder. It's not a serious wound, so he should be fine. Governor Connolly was also struck. In the back. It looks like he will also make a full recovery. This has all been reported in the media. Haven't you been watching it on television, like most of the country is?'

'No. I had planned to take a flight from Dallas to Washington, which is the next stop on my tour; but all of the flights leaving Dallas have been cancelled. So I rented a car, and am now on my way to Washington, sir.'

'Washington?'

Both agents looked at each other, and appeared intrigued. They had been recording every word I was saying, in their notebooks.

'What will you be doing in Washington?'

'Sight-seeing. I'm planning on spending a couple of days there, until I head to New York.'

'Are you meeting anybody there?'

'No.'

'What will you be doing for accommodation?'

'I'll be checking into a hotel.'

'Which hotel?'

'I haven't booked one yet. I'll sort that out, when I get there.'

'Do you know anybody in Washington?'

'No.'

'Nobody?'

'Yes, nobody.'

'Okay, Mr Evangelista, here is my card. If you have any further information, please call me. In the meantime, I would like you to call into our Washington bureau office, and ask to speak to this agent, just before you leave Washington for New York. He will have more questions to ask you. Will you do that, sir?'

'Yes. That's fine.'

Next morning, I got up late. It was just after 10am. I think I had only slept for five or six hours. I had stayed up well into the early hours, wondering why the FBI was following me; and what I was planning to do in Washington. I checked out of the motel. It was a bright sunny Saturday morning. I was dying for a strong coffee, and was famished – not having really eaten since I arrived in 1963. I made my way into downtown Little Rock, and pulled up outside a diner. I felt like I was in an episode of "Happy Days" or the classic movie, "American Graffiti." The jukebox was playing the Dion and the Belmonts smash hit, "The Wanderer"; the place appeared to be popular with teenagers – each booth occupied by young guys and girls. I sat on a stool at the main counter and ordered a big breakfast – two fried eggs, sausages, bacon, hash browns, pancakes laced with honey, and unlimited strong coffee – all for less than $5! As I enjoyed the delicious food, I caught a glimpse of a young man sitting in the back corner booth, alongside another guy, and opposite two girls. I rubbed my eyes to make sure I wasn't hallucinating, and then focused my attention on him again. He was looking straight at me. It was Bill Clinton.

Just 17 years old, Bill Clinton was in his senior year at Hot Springs High School. From a working-class family, Clinton's biological father had died three months before he was born, and he was raised by his mother and an alcoholic, abusive step-father. Clinton's life was a world away from that of the wealthy urbane president, but, like many other Americans, he deeply admired President John F. Kennedy and his family.

Clinton was a gifted and talented student but was still uncertain about his future, debating possible careers in music, medicine, law, or even the ministry. He was selected as one of Arkansas' two delegates to that year's Boys Nation. Organised by the American Legion and begun in 1946, the prestigious program brings some of the country's best and brightest students to Washington DC, for an intensive, week-long seminar, where students meet elected officials and government leaders. In 1963, that included meeting Secretary of State, Dean Rusk. The 98 students held a series of mock Senate legislative sessions, meant to provide them with an insight into the workings of the American government. Clinton participated in putting together a resolution on civil rights.

On 24th July, 1963, Bill Clinton and his fellow delegates gathered in the White House Rose Garden. Kennedy was fresh off a successful European tour that included his famous "Ich bin ein Berliner" speech in front of a crowd of 450,000 in West Berlin. He addressed a much smaller crowd that sunny summer day, speaking of the importance of public service. He also praised the students for their civil rights resolution, noting that earlier that week, the annual meeting of the National Governors Association had been unable to pass a similar resolution, and remained divided over the issue of civil rights. Kennedy then moved into the crowd to meet the students. Clinton later recalled the moment, saying, "I was about the third or fourth person in, and I sort of muscled my way up to the front." Their interaction was brief, a firm handshake before Kennedy moved on to the next student. But a video and photos capturing the event show Clinton's admiration and near disbelief that he was meeting his political idol.

The impact of that moment was obvious almost immediately. According to several of his fellow delegates, Clinton spent the bus ride back to the Boys Nation dorms talking about the event. As future Minnesota Congressman Jim Ramstad recalled, Clinton said to him, "Someday, I'm going to have that job." Just four months later, Kennedy was dead. Clinton was in his high school math class when he found out that Kennedy had been assassinated. "I remember it as if it were yesterday," Clinton said. "I was heartbroken. I was hoping he would live. We didn't know in the beginning whether he was dead. I just remember being totally bereft." Of the impact of that moment, he wrote: "He meant something to the country, and he symbolised the future. It was as if it was snuffed out."

I could overhear the teenagers discussing how shocked they were about the attempted assassination. Young Clinton in particular, looked visibly distraught. I could see tears welling in his eyes, as he spoke.

'My God, they could have killed him. One shot could have snuffed out all of our hopes and dreams for a better future. He is our president. He represents our future.'

Then I saw Bill take out a photo. I was close enough to see it was the photo of him shaking hands with JFK. He became emotional as he passed the photo around to his friends.

'I will treasure this photo for the rest of my life. You know, my life totally changed on that day in August earlier this year, when I met him. From that day onwards the doubts in my mind about my future, vanished – and instead a torch was lit for me. I want to serve the people. I want to go into politics. I want to make a difference. One day, I will be the president of the United States.'

It was amazing to see a young charismatic Bill Clinton, holding his audience spellbound; as if the other guy and two girls listening to him, and believing every word he spoke, were the most important people in the world to Bill. This was at the core of Clinton's success as a politician, and the ultimate fulfilment of his dream to become president – he could captivate an audience; and when he was talking to people in small groups, or one on one, they felt like he was listening exclusively to them, and that he really cared about what they said. He was the consummate empathiser.

Finishing my breakfast, I got up and walked towards the teenagers.

'Hi kids. You don't know me. My name is Luca Evangelista. I'm a history teacher visiting your great country from Australia. You are right, young man. We nearly lost a great president and word leader yesterday.'

Then, just as I was about to leave the diner, I looked into the eyes of the emotional teenager, and said: 'Don't ask me how or why I know, but you are destined for great things. You will serve the people in a spectacular way, Bill Clinton. Stick to your dream, no matter what the future holds.'

As I drove on to Washington, I was sure I was still being followed by the FBI. I arrived around 10pm on the Saturday evening, checked into a motel, and slept heavily; awakening at 9am on Sunday morning. I switched the television on. There was non-stop coverage of the attempted assassination. I went out for a coffee, and then sat in my room, waiting for the live coverage of Lee Harvey Oswald being taken out of Dallas police headquarters, to a remand centre. It was surreal. I had seen it so many times before. But this time it was live, and in an alternative Earth.

The elevator door swung open. Two detectives came out, on either side of Oswald. They walked towards the waiting prisoner-transfer van. A crowd of mainly media and police had gathered in the basement. It was exactly as I had seen it so many times before. Then suddenly, out of the crowd, jumped Jack Ruby, and bang, the shot was fired into Oswald's stomach, echoing throughout the basement. Oswald collapses. Everybody panics. He is groaning in pain. He is placed onto a stretcher, and rushed to hospital. Even though I changed the course of history by preventing the assassination of JFK, it didn't alter the shooting of Oswald! Angleton and his co-conspirators were absolutely determined to shut Oswald up. They were not going to allow him to be put on trial, and spill the beans, opening up the conspiracy for the world to see.

I made my way to a public phone box, across the road from the motel.

'Hello, is this James Jesus Angleton?'

'Yes. Who are you?'

'I am somebody you will really want to speak with. Meet me in the park near your place, in one hour. I will recognise you.'

I got there ten minutes early, and found a bench overlooking the lake. Otto had given me Angleton's home phone number. Just the fact that I rang him on his secure private number would have spurned his curiosity and unnerved him. There was no way he wasn't going to turn up. Then, I saw him walking in my direction. Heavy full length overcoat, gloves, and hat. I stood up and motioned him to come to me. He sat on the bench alongside me.

'Who are you? What do you want?'

'Now, now, Mr Angleton, you don't need to be so abrupt and anxious.'

'What do you want!!?'

'I am your worst nightmare, Mr Angleton. I stopped the assassination of the president. I am responsible for your conspiracy failing.'

'What the hell are you talking about? I had nothing whatsoever to do with that.'

'I know the truth. You will never know how I got to know the truth about you and your fellow conspirators.'

'Who are you? What is your name?'

'I represent a group that is much more powerful than you could ever imagine. We know your every move, James Angleton. We know how you planned to kill the president, and who your helpers were. You will not find any record of my existence on any public document, or government database. I represent the deep state within the deep state. Do you understand me?'

'I have no knowledge whatsoever about the attempted assassination of President Kennedy. In fact, we are actively working with the FBI to identify whether anybody else, other than Oswald, was involved. So far, it is definitely looking like he acted alone.'

'That's bullshit, and you know it!'

'Who the hell are you?'

'As I said, I am your worst nightmare. If you and your out of control rogue group so much as try to harm the president, or any of his supporters again, you will suffer the most severe consequences. We are watching your every move. We are always ten steps ahead of any of your diabolical schemes. Do you understand?'

'Are you threatening me?'

'Yes, I am.'

With that, I got up, walked away, and made my way back to the 21st century.

'My goodness Luca, you really shook Angleton to the core, when you threatened him.'

I had become very fond of Otto. Every time I saw him, he was becoming more human-like in his mannerisms. He was really enjoying his gin and tonic, and actually swaying from side to side, as the Billy Joel impersonator belted out a cool interpretation of *Tell Her About It.*

'Now, Luca, let me tell you what you achieved. In that version of the Earth, John F. Kennedy not only makes a full recovery, but he also goes on to win the 1964 presidential election by a landslide. The Vietnam War never happens. Kennedy negotiates a massive reduction in nuclear weapon stockpiles, with the Soviets. The Cold War ends with the collapse of the Soviet Union in 1980, over 10 years before it came crashing down in your Earth. Nixon and Watergate never happen, so the American people continue to have confidence in their government. Bobby Kennedy is elected president in 1968, and serves two terms. Then, in 1976, Teddy Kennedy is elected president, and serves another two terms. The Kennedy's dominate the American and global political landscape literally from 1960 to 1984 – a quarter of a century of liberal democratic socialism, which amongst other things, results in comprehensive universal health care coverage for all American people; significantly reduced tax rates for the lower and middle classes, funded by the rich; a strong America protecting and encouraging human rights, freedom and democracy, worldwide; and the suppression of the military-industrial right-wing nationalist forces, which people like Angleton and general Walker, tried to protect. The world sees America as a beacon of hope. China never rises to the level of an economic and military superpower. In fact, China ends up becoming a representative democracy, along with most of the rest of the world, by the end of the 20th century.'

'Phew! That's one hell of a better world, Otto.'

As I left the piano bar, I had an overwhelming urge to see Isabella. But I couldn't. I knew what the outcome would be. I didn't want to be hurt again. I didn't want to give her false hopes that we could have a future together. I vowed to remain single. Then, I would never have to expose my emotions to anybody. I looked at my phone. There were literally dozens of messages from Isabella. She was crying out to me. I was torn. It was a moonless night, creating an eerie darkness as I was walking home. I could hear footsteps behind me, getting closer and closer, louder and louder. As I turned around, literally metres from my home, two men jumped on me. One of them held me down, while the other frantically and brutally kicked me in the head, back, and stomach. I held my clenched hands and arms close to my face, to cushion the full impact of the blows. Nevertheless, blood was streaming down my face. This frenzied attack went on for what seemed like ages. Then they stopped. I lay motionless and barely conscious, gasping for breath, certain I had cracked some ribs.

'Let this be a warning to you. You are playing with fire, Evangelista. Very powerful people know what you're up to. They are watching your every move. You are not going to succeed. It will all amount to nothing. If you care about your loved ones, you will stop this now.'

Tell Her About It

Listen boy don't want to see you
Let a good thing slip away
You know I don't like
Watching anybody make
The same mistakes that I made

She's a real nice girl
And she's always there for you
But a nice girl wouldn't tell you
What you should do

Listen boy I'm sure that you think
You got it all under control
You don't want somebody telling you
The way to stay in someone's soul

You're a big boy now
And you'll never let her go
But that's just the kind of thing
She ought to know

Tell her about it
Tell her everything you feel
Give her every reason to accept
That you're for real
Tell her about it
Tell her all your crazy dreams
Let you know you need her
Let her know how much she means

Listen boy it's not automatically
A certain guarantee
To insure yourself you've got to provide
Communication constantly
When you love someone
You're always insecure
And there's only one
Good way to reassure

Tell her about it
Let her know how much you care
When she can't be with you
Tell her you wish you were there
Tell her about it
Every day before you leave
Pay her some attention
Give her something to believe

Cause now and then she'll get you worrying
Just because you haven't spoken for so long
Though you may not have done anything
Will that be a consolation when she's gone?

Listen boy it's good information
From a man who's made mistakes
Just a word or two that she gets from you
Could be the difference that it makes

She's a trusting soul
She's put her trust in you
But a girl like that won't tell you
What you should do

Tell her about it
Tell her everything you feel
Give her every reason to accept
That you're for real
Tell her about it
Tell her all your crazy dreams
Let her know you need her
Let her know how much she means

Tell her about it
Tell her how you feel right now
Just tell her about it
The girl don't want to wait too long
You got to tell her about it
Tell her now that you won't go wrong
You got to tell her about it
Before it gets too late
You've got to tell her about it
You know the girl don't want to wait
You got to tell her about it
You got to tell, tell, tell her about it
Now, tell her about it

Billy Joel (1983)

14

Osama Bin Laden

Boston, United States of America, September 2001 CE

September 11, 2001, 19 militants associated with the Islamic extremist group al-Qaeda hijacked four airplanes, and carried out suicide attacks against targets in the United States. Two of the planes were flown into the twin towers of the World Trade Center in New York City; a third plane hit the Pentagon in Arlington, Virginia, just outside Washington DC; and the fourth plane crashed in a field in Shanksville, Pennsylvania. Almost 3,000 people were killed during the 9/11 terrorist attacks, which triggered major US initiatives to combat terrorism, including the invasions of Afghanistan and Iraq; and defined the presidency of George W. Bush. The attacks were believed to be strategically planned to severely shake the three pillars of American power – the economy (Twin Towers); the military (Pentagon); and the government (the failed attack on the White House or Capitol Building). Well, this is the official historical account of what happened. The truth may be much murkier.

The tragic events of this day, shocked the people of the United States, and the world. Two planes, supposedly hijacked by Islamic jihadists vowing death to all Americans, slammed into both towers at the World Trade Center in New York. Another plane was flown into the Pentagon in Washington DC. A fourth plane, presumably headed for the White House or the US Capitol Building, was heroically diverted by passengers, and ended up crashing in an empty field in Pennsylvania. After reports of the first plane hitting the North Tower, hundreds of millions around the world watched the second plane hit the South Tower on live television. It was a terrifying, startling, and humbling event for the country.

The 9/11 attacks were the deadliest on American soil since the shock attack by Japan at Pearl Harbor in Hawaii, 60 years before, and the sense of outrage was reminiscent of that moment. The attacks in New

York occurred in the nation's busiest city on a working day, designed to inflict maximum carnage. And the staggered nature of the attacks meant that news footage captured almost everything as it happened, ensuring that millions of Americans in particular, saw the events on live television precisely as they unfolded. Although to many Americans 9/11 seemed like a random act of terror, it appeared the roots of this infamous event had been developing for years. If we believe the official history, a combination of factors that coalesced in the late 1990s led to this catastrophic event. These factors included regional conditions in the Middle East that motivated the perpetrators, as well as intelligence lapses and failures, particularly between the CIA and FBI, that left the United States vulnerable.

Osama Bin Laden was relatively unknown in the United States before 9/11, even as he was amassing popularity, followers, and fame, in the Middle East during the 1990s. In 1988, he was one of the founders of al-Qaeda, a militant Islamic terrorist organisation that was held responsible by the US government for planning and carrying out the 9/11 attacks. Bin Laden called for the indiscriminate killing of all Americans who, he claimed, were "the worst thieves in the world today." It was the perfect historical moment for that rallying cry. Throughout the latter 20th century, a wave of secular, nationalist revolutions swept through the Middle East, taking root in Egypt, Libya, Iraq, and Yemen, amongst other countries.

While these peaceful movements of the people were awash in promising ideology, including the hope of sowing the seeds of democracy; the new regimes quickly became autocratic in nature, and suppressed all dissent. Their critics turned to violent revolution to express widespread dissatisfaction with these autocratic secular governments. At the same time, social alienation, especially among young men who were struggling to find decent jobs, and start their own families in corrupt oil states, provided easy targets for radicalisation. Bin Laden's message that America was the "head of a snake" and the root of all society's problems, resonated well with this discontent.

By the mid-1990s, Bin Laden was the head of al-Qaeda, a multifaceted and highly developed terrorist network, carrying out attack after attack on Americans in the Middle East. It was a new type of terrorism to which the US intelligence agencies struggled to adapt to. Much of the intelligence community had not even imagined the specific type of hijacking and terrorism carried out on 9/11. They were instead preparing for threats such as the 1993 basement bombing of the Word Trade Center, and the bombing of the USS Cole in the Yemeni port of Aden. Much of the intelligence community's focus was on reactive law enforcement activity rather the proactive countering of terrorism.

A telling quote from the 9/11 Commission Report focuses on the lack of a proactive response: "The process was meant, by its nature, to mark for the public as the events finished – case solved, justice done. It was not designed to ask if the events might be harbingers of worse to come. Nor did it allow for aggregating and analysing facts to see if they could provide clues to terrorist tactics more generally – methods of entry and finance, and mode of operation inside the United States." Bin Laden had amassed substantial power due to conditions in the Middle East, as well as his charismatic leadership; and the US intelligence community was underprepared for a 9/11 style attack. In the aftermath of 9/11, these two factors continued to affect US policy in the Middle East, particularly in Iraq.

The immediate response to 9/11 was the George W. Bush administration's War on Terror, which began with an invasion of Afghanistan as a retaliation against al-Qaeda for carrying out the attack. The Bush administration soon expanded the War on Terror, by attacking Iraq; and the consequences of these wars continue to affect the Middle East to this day. There were domestic long-term effects of 9/11 as well. Thousands of people struggle with cancer and other chronic health problems relating to the toxicity of Ground Zero, the site where the Twin Towers used to stand. The September 11 attacks also changed American and global air travel as airlines began to require stringent security checks designed to prevent the types of weapons the hijackers used, from slipping through. Finally, the 9/11 attacks resulted in extensive changes to the US federal government, and an expansion of its executive power.

A new cabinet department, the Department of Homeland Security, was created; and the intelligence community was consolidated under the Director of National Intelligence, to improve the coordination between various government agencies and departments – particularly between the CIA and FBI. New legislation, such as the USA Patriot Act, dramatically expanded domestic security and surveillance, not only disrupting terrorist funding by cracking down on activities such as money laundering, but also severely restricting the freedom and movement of ordinary law-abiding citizens. The tragedy of September 11, 2001 will never be forgotten, and the aftermath is still continuing to unfold, well into the 21st century. The 9/11 Memorial and Museum opened on the site of the former World Trade Center, on September 11, 2011, and features reflecting pools in the footprints of where the Twin Towers once stood.

I was feeling the pressure intensely. This was going to be my last time-travel mission. If I didn't stop the 9/11 attacks, all the good work I had done on the eleven previous missions, would amount to nothing. The future catastrophic course of our Earth would not change. As with all of the other missions, I had thoroughly researched the events of 9/11. But I had a naggingly disturbing thought. Was this attack really carried out by al-Qaeda? Or was the US government somehow involved, as many widely circulating conspiracy theories claim? Why would the Bush administration have engineered it? Well, there could have been several motives. Firstly, to create the conditions to introduce draconian legislation to give the government the power to control the people. Tick that one – the USA Patriot Act, achieved that objective. Secondly, to create an excuse to invade Iraq, and take control of its oil fields. Tick that one – even though there was no evidence whatsoever that Saddam Hussein had anything to do with 9/11, and no evidence that Iraq possessed chemical weapons of mass destruction – the United States did invade Iraq in 2003, and took control of the oil fields.

I carefully reviewed the official timeline of events that occurred on that fateful day:

5.45am Mohammad Atta and Abdul Aziz al-Omari, two of the intended hijackers, pass through security at the Portland International Jetport in Maine. They board a commuter flight to Boston Logan International Airport. They then board American Airlines Flight 11.

7.59am American Airlines Flight 11 takes off from Boston, headed for Los Angeles, California. There are 76 passengers, 11 crew members, and 5 hijackers, on board.

8.15am United Airlines Flight 175 takes off from Boston, also headed for Los Angeles. There are 51 passengers, 9 crew members, and 5 hijackers, on board.

8.19am A flight attendant on Flight 11, Betty Ann Ong, alerts ground personnel that a hijacking is underway, and that the cockpit is unreachable. American Airlines notifies the FBI.

8.20am American Airlines Flight 77 takes off from Dulles Airport, outside of Washington DC, headed for Los Angeles. There are 53 passengers, 6 crew members, and 5 hijackers, on board.

8.24am Mohammad Atta, a hijacker on Flight 11, unintentionally alerts air controllers in Boston to the attack, when he presses the wrong button in the cockpit. He meant to press the button that allowed him to talk to the passengers on the flight.

8.37am After hearing the broadcast from Atta on Flight 11, Boston air traffic control alerts The Federal Aviation Administration.

8.40am Air traffic controllers at The Federal Aviation Administration (FAA) alert North American Aerospace Defence Command (NORAD)'s Northeast Air Defence Sector (NEADS) about the suspected hijacking of Flight 11. In response, NEADS scrambles two fighter jets located at Cape Cod's Otis Air National Guard Base to locate and tail Flight 11. They are not yet in the air when Flight 11 crashes into the North Tower.

8.41am United Airlines Flight 93 takes off from Newark International Airport, New Jersey, after a delay due to routine traffic.

It was scheduled to take off at 8.00am, around the time of the other hijacked flights. It was headed for San Francisco, California. There are 33 passengers, 7 crew members, and 4 hijackers, on board.

8.46am Mohammad Atta and the other hijackers aboard American Airlines Flight 11 crash the plane into floors 93-99 of the North Tower of the World Trade Center, killing everyone on board and hundreds inside the building.

8.47am Within seconds, NYPD and FDNY despatch units to the World Trade Center, while Port Authority Police Department officers on site, begin the immediate evacuation of the North Tower.

9.03am Hijackers crash United Airlines Flight 175 into floors 75-85 of the WTC's South Tower, killing everyone on board, and hundreds inside the building.

9.05am President George W. Bush, in an elementary school classroom in Florida, is informed about the hit on the second tower. His chief of staff, Andrew Card, whispers the chilling news into the president's ear. Bush later wrote about his response: "I made the decision not to jump up immediately and leave the classroom. I didn't want to rattle the kids. I wanted to project a sense of calm. I had been in enough crises to know that the first thing the leader has to do is project calm."

9.24am The FAA notifies NEADS of the suspected hijacking of flight 77 after some passengers and crew aboard are able to alert family members on the ground, using their phones.

9.31am Speaking from Florida, President Bush classifies the events in New York City an "apparent terrorist attack on our country."

9.37am	Flight 77 crashes into the Pentagon. All of the people on board are instantly killed, and so are 125 civilian and military personnel in the building.
9.42am	For the first time in history, the FAA grounds all flights over or bound for the continental United States. Over the next two and a half hours, some 3,300 commercial flights, and 1,200 private planes are guided to land at airports in Canada and the United States.
9.45am	Amid escalating rumours of other imminent attacks, the White House and US Capitol Building are evacuated (along with numerous other high-profile buildings, landmarks, and public spaces).
9.55am	Air Force One with President George W. Bush on board, takes off from Florida.
9.59am	the South Tower of the World Trade Center collapses.
10.07am	After passengers and crew members aboard the hijacked Flight 93 contact friends and family, and learn about the attacks in New York and Washington, they mount an attempt to retake control of the plane, by storming towards the cockpit. In response, the hijackers deliberately crash the plane into a field in Somerset County, Shanksville, Pennsylvania, killing all on board.
10.18am	President Bush authorises any non-grounded planes to be shot down. At that time, all four of the hijacked planes had already crashed, but the president's team was operating under the impression that Flight 93 was still in the air.
10.28am	The North Tower of the World Trade Center collapses.

10.53am Secretary of Defence Donald Rumsfeld orders the US military to move to a higher state of alert, going to DEFCON 3.

11.45am Air Force One lands at Barksdale Air Force Base, near Shreveport, Louisiana.

12.15pm Airspace in the United States is completely free of all commercial and private flights.

1.30pm Air Force One leaves Barksdale.

2.30pm Rudy Giuliani, the mayor of New York City, visits the fallen Twin Towers of the World Trade Center, at what becomes known as Ground Zero.

3.00pm Air Force One lands at Offutt Air Force base in Nebraska, and President Bush is immediately taken to a secure bunker that is capable of withstanding a nuclear attack.

4.30pm Air Force One leaves Offutt and heads back towards Andrews Air Force base near Washington DC.

5.27pm The 47-storey Seven World Trade Center collapses after burning for hours. The building had been evacuated in the morning, and there are no casualties; though the collapse forces rescue workers to flee for their lives. It is the last tower to fall.

8.30pm President Bush addresses the nation, calling the attacks "evil, despicable acts of terror", declaring that America, and its friends and allies would "stand together to win the war against terrorism."

I couldn't stop thinking about the astonishing heroism of the passengers on United Airlines Flight 93. The passengers ranged in age from 20 to 79. Among them was a federal wildlife biologist, a former bookkeeper, a toy-company executive, an arborist, a retired bartender, attorneys, college students, and an ironworker who had helped build the World Trade Center. Forty-five minutes into the flight, at around 9.30am, air traffic controllers received two radio transmissions – a frantic "Mayday!" and the sounds of a violent struggle, followed by "Get out of here!" United 93 plummeted seven hundred feet, over eastern Ohio.

A hijacker, one of four, was heard announcing that there was a bomb on board. Using autopilot, the hijackers directed the airliner toward Washington DC. Its transponder disabled, the flight became harder to track. The plane's cockpit voice recorder captured the sound of a woman struggling with a hijacker; she then went silent. The crew and passengers, herded into the back of the plane, used the on-board phones, and their personal cell phones, to call people on the ground.

Learning that other hijackers had just flown jetliners into both towers of the World Trade Center, they held a vote. Unarmed citizens, unbound by duty, they included a college judo champ, a former air-traffic controller, and a retired registered nurse. In an act that has become American folklore over the past twenty years, the passengers and crew members chose to attack the knife-wielding hijackers and "retake the plane." They rushed the first-class cabin, carrying out what the 9/11 Commission Report called a "sustained" assault. One of the plane's data recorders captured "loud thumps, crashes, shouts, and breaking glass and plates." The hijacker flying the plane, as if to throw the assaulters off balance, rocked the aircraft left and right. One hijacker asked: "Shall we finish it off?" Another said to wait. A passenger shouted: "In the cockpit. If we don't, we'll die!" The hijacker soon asked again: "Shall we put it down?" this time, the answer was: "Yes!" The 9/11 Commission concluded that the hijackers "judged that the passengers were only seconds from overcoming them." The plane roared low across a farming area of Somerset County, Pennsylvania, skimming the village of Lambertsville. The aircraft flipped, then crashed at nearly six hundred miles per hour near Shanksville. People miles away felt the ground shake.

Lieutenant Heather (Lucky) Penney, an F-16 fighter pilot who was ordered airborne that day, later said that she and fellow D.C. Air

National Guard pilot, Marc Sasseville, "fully expected to intercept Flight 93 and take it down." A fourth hijacked plane had already hit the Pentagon. Flight 93 crashed about twenty minutes away, by air, from Washington. Penney said: "The real heroes are the passengers on Flight 93 who were willing to sacrifice themselves." Sasseville said: "They made the decision we didn't have to make." One passenger's widow recalled that her husband had said, by phone: "We're waiting until we're over a rural area." The authors of the 9/11 Commission Report highlighted the passengers' selflessness: "Their actions saved the lives of countless others, and may have saved either the Capitol or the White House from destruction."

The report reached an astonishing conclusion: "The defence of U.S. airspace on 9/11" was "improvised by civilians." Flight 93 went down on the barren site of an old strip mine, where generations of labourers had extracted bituminous coal. All around it was beautiful scenery – Somerset County is known as the "Roof Garden of Pennsylvania" for its verdant, rolling hills. Locals arrived first at the scene of the crash, expecting to see a fuselage and perhaps even survivors. Instead, they found it "eerily" quiet. The plane's explosive impact, compounded by seven thousand gallons of jet fuel, had vaporized nearly everything. Those on board had not just died; they had all but disappeared. First responders found a crater marked by the ghostly imprint of airplane wings, at the edge of a smoking, sizzling forest of hemlock.

The County Coroner, Wally Miller, later said: "You could hear this melted plastic dripping out of the trees." Miller felt sorrow for the families of the passengers and crew, who would have envisaged "caskets that they could open up, and see somebody." Instead, he had to inform them that what they could expect to recover was no more than "a tooth, or a fragment of bone." FBI evidence-recovery teams walked the site shoulder to shoulder, or crawled on their hands and knees, looking for human remains. Much of the emotionally and physically demanding work fell to those who lived and worked in Somerset County – including, excavators, pastors, and hospital staff. The coroner deputized undertakers so that they could help process human remains at a temporary morgue. A local plumber ran cold-water lines to the facility, allowing for four extra wash sinks. A janitor's closet became a darkroom, for developing X-rays. Glenn Kashurba, a local psychiatrist and Red Cross volunteer, collected oral histories, writing that one first responder said: "The first night was bad. I closed my eyes, and I would see whatever I saw that day."

Several days after the crash, the families of Flight 93's passengers and crew started visiting the site. Mark Schweiker, then the Lieutenant Governor, said: "If anyone wanted to know the nature of overwhelming grief, then they only needed to spend a few days on that hillside." All forty passengers and crew were identified by DNA, dental records, or fingerprints. None of the hijackers' families reportedly provided genetic information, so, by a process of elimination, investigators designated certain biological evidence as Hijacker A, B, C, and D, keeping it separate from the rest. The FBI completed its investigation in around two weeks. The coroner ordered the crater backfilled, layered with topsoil, and seeded with a mixture of wildflowers and grass. Federal authorities and the Flight 93 families spent years planning a memorial that encompassed the crater, meadows, and forest.

The families and the Park Service envisioned a memorial "quiet in reverence, yet powerful in form." The planners asked themselves why the actions of Flight 93's passengers and crew were "important to the nation." Ultimately, they pointed out the value of creating a place where "all generations" could "find meaning and inspiration" from their sacrifice. The site of the Flight 93 National Memorial consists of twenty-two hundred acres, much of which is open to the public. The rebirth of the onetime strip mine provided a fitting metaphor for healing. Today, the overwhelming majority of the area is lush with wildflower meadows and native grasses. Ilse Homer, the mother of Flight 93's first officer, LeRoy Homer, observed: "It's peaceful," and added, "It's exactly as if you come home – you are home now, we are here, and we are holding you." The mother of another passenger once gazed out at the park with her arms around her grandsons and said: "Isn't this a beautiful place where your daddy is? Isn't this a beautiful place to be?"

One of the heroes of Flight 93 was undoubtedly, Todd Beamer. Todd and other passengers had been in communication with people on the ground, using the plane's phones, and their own cell phones.

This is how they found out that the World Trade Center had been attacked using hijacked airplanes. Beamer tried to place a credit card call using a phone located at the back of a plane seat, but was routed to a customer service representative instead, who passed him on to a telephone supervisor, Lisa Jefferson. This is a transcript of that conversation:

Todd Hello. Operator. Listen to me. I can't speak very loud. This is an emergency. I'm a passenger on a United flight to San Francisco. We have a situation here. Our plane has been hijacked. Can you understand me?

Lisa (exhaling a deep breath to herself) I understand. Can the hijackers see you talking on the phone?

Todd No.

Lisa Can you tell me how many hijackers are on the plane?

Todd There are three that we know of.

Lisa Can you see any weapons? What kind of weapons do they have?

Todd Yes. They don't have guns. They have knives. They took over the plane with knives.

Lisa Do you mean, like steak knives?

Todd No, these are razor knives, like box cutters.

Lisa Can you tell what country these people are from?

Todd No, I don't know. They sound like they're from the Mid-East.

Lisa Have they said what they want?

Todd Someone announced from the cockpit that there was a bomb on board. He said he was the captain, and to stay in our seats and stay quiet. He said that they were meeting these men's demands and returning to the airport. It was very broken English, and I'm telling you, it sounded fake!

Lisa Okay sir, please give me your name.

Todd My name is Todd Beamer.

Lisa Okay Todd, my name is Lisa. Do you know your flight number? If you can't remember, it's on your ticket.

Todd It's United Flight 93.

Lisa Now Todd, can you try to tell me exactly what happened?

Todd Two of the hijackers were sitting in first class near the cockpit. A third one was sitting near the back of the coach section. The two up front got into the cockpit somehow; there was shouting. The third hijacker said he had a bomb. It looks like a bomb. He's got it tied to his waist with a red belt of some kind.

Lisa So is the door of the cockpit open?

Todd No, the hijackers shut it behind them.

Lisa Has anyone been injured?

Todd Yes, they, they killed one passenger sitting in first class. There's been lots of shouting. We don't know if the pilots are dead or alive. A flight attendant told me that the pilot and co-pilot had been forced from the cockpit and may have been wounded.

Lisa Where is the third hijacker now Todd?

Todd He's near the back of the plane. They forced most of the passengers into first class. There are fourteen of us here in the back. Five are flight attendants. He hasn't noticed that I slipped into the pantry to get the phone. The guy with the bomb ordered us to sit on the floor in the rear of the plane. Oh Jesus. Help!

Lisa Todd, are you okay? Tell me what's happening!

Todd Hello. We're going down. I think we're going to crash. Wait. Wait a minute. No, we're levelling off. We're okay. I think we may be turning around. That's it – we changed directions. Do you hear me? We're flying east again.

Lisa Okay Todd. What's going on with the other passengers?

Todd Everyone is really scared. A few passengers with cell phones have made calls to relatives. A guy, Jeremy, was talking to his wife just before the hijacking started. She told him that hijackers had crashed two planes into the World Trade Center. Lisa, is that true?

Lisa Todd. I have to tell you the truth. It's very bad. The World Trade Center is gone. Both of the towers have been destroyed.

Todd Oh God! Help us!

Lisa A third plane was taken over by terrorists. It crashed into the Pentagon in Washington DC. Our country is under attack, and I'm afraid that your plane may be part of their plan.

Todd Oh dear God. Dear God, Lisa, will you do something for me?

Lisa I'll try. If I can. Yes.

Todd I want you to call my wife and my kids for me; and tell them what's happened. Promise me you'll call.

Lisa I promise, I'll call.

Todd Our home number is 201 353 1073. You have the same name as my wife, Lisa. We've been married for 10 years. She's pregnant with our third child. Tell her that I love her (choking up). I'll always love her (clearing throat). We have two boys. David, he's 3, and Andrew, he's 1. Tell them (choking), tell them that their daddy loves them, and that he is so proud of them (clearing throat again). Our baby is due January 12th. I saw an ultra sound. It was great. We still don't know if it's a girl or a boy. Lisa?

Lisa (barely able to speak) I'll tell them. I promise Todd.

Todd I'm going back to the group. If I can get back, I will.

Lisa Todd, leave this line open. Are you still there?

Lisa (dials the phone) Hello, FBI? My name is Lisa Jefferson. I'm a telephone supervisor for GTE. I need to report a terrorist hijacking of a United Airlines Flight 93. Yes, I'll hold.

Goodwin Hello, this is Agent Goodwin. I understand you have a hijacking situation?

Lisa Yes, sir, I've been talking with a passenger, a Todd Beamer, on Flight 93, who managed to get to an air phone unnoticed.

Goodwin Where did this flight originate, and what was its destination?

Lisa The flight left Newark New Jersey at 8am, departing for San Francisco. The hijackers took over the plane shortly after take-off, and several minutes later, the plane changed course. It is now flying east.

Goodwin Ms Jefferson, I need to talk to someone aboard that plane. Can you get me through to the plane's phone?

Lisa I still have the line open sir. I can patch you through on a conference call. Hold a moment.

Todd Hello Lisa. Lisa, are you there?

Lisa Yes, I'm here. Todd, I made a call to the FBI. Agent Goodwin is on the line and will be talking to you as well.

Todd The others all know that this isn't your normal hijacking. Jeremy called his wife again on his cell phone. She told him more about the World Trade Center, and all.

Goodwin Hello Todd. This is Agent Goodwin with the FBI. We have been monitoring your flight. Your plane is on course for Washington DC. These terrorists sent two planes into the World Trade Center, and one plane into the Pentagon. Our best guess is that they plan to fly your plane into either the White House or the United States Capitol Building.

Todd I understand. Hold on. I'll. I'll be back.

Lisa Mr Goodwin, how much time do they have before they get to Washington?

Goodwin Not long ma'am. They changed course over Cleveland. They're approaching Pittsburgh now. Washington may be twenty minutes away.

Todd (*breathing a little heavier*) The plane seems to be changing directions just a little. It's getting pretty rough up here. The plane is flying real erratic. We're not going to make it out of here.

Lisa Todd, what are you going to do?

Todd We've hatched a plan. Four of us are going to rush the hijacker with the bomb. After we take him out, we'll break into the cockpit. A stewardess is getting some boiling water to throw on the hijackers at the controls. We'll get them, and we'll take them out. Lisa, will you do one last thing for me?

Lisa Yes. What is it?

Todd Would you pray with me?

They pray:
Our Father which art in Heaven
Hallowed be thy name,
Thy kingdom come, thy will be done
On earth as it is in heaven.
Give us this day our daily bread,
And forgive us our trespasses
As we forgive our trespassers,
And lead us not into temptation
But deliver us from evil
For thine is the kingdom, and the power, and the glory
The Lord is my shepherd, I shall not want,
He makes me to lie down in green pastures
He leads me beside the still waters
He restores my soul
He leads me in paths of righteousness
for His name's sake
Yea, though I walk through the valley of the shadow of death
I will fear no evil, for thou art with me.

Todd (*softer*) God help me. Jesus help me. (*clears throat and louder*) Are you guys ready? Let's Roll!

Did one man really mastermind the 9-11 attacks? This question was troubling me. No actually, it was really disturbing me. I knew that Osama bin Laden had worked closely with the Americans, when he was fighting against the Russians in Afghanistan, after the invasion of 1979. My phone was lighting up with text messages from Isabella. She was really keen to see me. I couldn't reply to her at this stage. I was totally consumed by how I was going to stop the attack on America.

Bin Laden was one of more than 50 children of Muhammad bin Laden, a self-made billionaire who, after immigrating to Saudi Arabia from Yemen as a labourer, rose to undertake major construction projects for the Saudi royal family. By the time of Muhammad's death in an airplane accident in 1967, his corporation had become one of the largest construction firms in the Middle East, and the bin Laden family had developed a close relationship with the Saudi royal family. Osama bin Laden studied business administration at King Abdul Aziz University in Jeddah, where it is likely that he also received instruction in religious studies from Muhammad Qutb, brother of the Islamic revivalist Sayyid Qutb, and Abdullah Azzam, a militant leader. His time at the university was key to his future role as leader of al-Qaeda, not only in influencing his radical views, but also in providing him with the skill to market al-Qaeda.

Shortly after the Soviet Union invaded Afghanistan in 1979, bin Laden, who viewed the invasion as an act of aggression against Islam, began traveling to meet Afghan resistance leaders, and started raising funds for the cause. Funds which were used to buy military equipment from the United States. By 1984, his activities were centred mainly in Afghanistan and Pakistan, where he collaborated with Azzam to recruit and organise Arab volunteers to fight the Soviet occupation. Bin Laden's financial resources, along with his reputation for piety and bravery in combat, enhanced his stature as a militant leader. A computer database he created in 1988, listing the names of volunteers for the Afghan War, led to the formation that year of a new militant network named al-Qaeda (in Arabic: "the Base"), although, the group remained without clear objectives, or an operational agenda, for several years.

In 1989, following the Soviet withdrawal from Afghanistan, bin Laden returned to Saudi Arabia, where he was initially welcomed as a hero; but he soon came to be regarded by the government as a radical and potential threat to the stability of the kingdom. In 1990, the government denied his requests for permission to use his network of fighters to defend Saudi Arabia against the threat of invasion posed by Saddam Hussein in Iraq. Bin Laden was outraged when Saudi Arabia relied instead on US troops for protection during the Persian Gulf War; leading to a growing rift between bin Laden and the Saudi royal rulers; and in 1991 he left Saudi Arabia, settling in Sudan at the end of that year.

In the early 1990s, bin Laden and his al-Qaeda network began to formulate an agenda of violent struggle against the threat of US dominance in the Muslim world. Bin Laden publicly praised other groups' attacks on Americans, including the 1993 bombing of the World Trade Center in New York. In 1994, as bin Laden expanded his group's infrastructure in Sudan, and trained Islamic militants to participate in conflicts around the world, Saudi Arabia revoked his citizenship and froze his assets, forcing him to rely on outside sources of funding. In 1996, under heavy international pressure, Sudan expelled bin Laden, and he returned to Afghanistan, where he received protection from its ruling Taliban militia.

Later that year, bin Laden issued the first of two fatwas (Arabic: "religious opinions") declaring a holy war against the United States, which he accused, among other things, of looting the natural resources of the Muslim world, occupying the Arabian Peninsula, including the holy sites of Islam, and supporting governments servile to US interests in the Middle East. Bin Laden's apparent ultimate goal was to draw the United States into a large-scale war in the Muslim world that would overthrow the existing world order and establish a single Islamic state. To this end, al-Qaeda trained militants and funded terrorist attacks.

In 1998, bin Laden ordered an operation larger than any of al-Qaeda's previous operations – the simultaneous bombings of US embassies in Nairobi Kenya, and Dar es Salaam Tanzania, which killed a total of 224 people. The United States retaliated by launching cruise missiles at sites believed to be bin Laden's bases in Afghanistan. Another al-Qaeda bombing in 2000 targeted the USS Cole, an American warship harboured in Yemen, and killed 17 sailors.

The growth of the organisation was attributed in part to bin Laden's charisma. He was known to be a skilled orator, able to manipulate a variety of rhetorical strategies, and to make his messages easily accessible to the uneducated. By the end of the 20th century, bin Laden had thousands of militant followers worldwide, in places as diverse as Saudi Arabia, Yemen, Libya, Bosnia, Chechnya, Indonesia, and the Philippines. In 2001, after 19 militants allegedly associated with al-Qaeda staged the September 11 attacks, the United States led a coalition that overthrew the Taliban in Afghanistan. In December 2001, bin Laden went into hiding after evading capture by US forces in the Tora Bora cave complex. In the following years, US forces searched for him along the Afghanistan-Pakistan border, during which time bin Laden remained absent from the public eye.

Then, in October 2004, less than a week before that year's US presidential election, bin Laden emerged in a videotaped message in which he claimed responsibility for the September 11 attacks. After that, he periodically released audio messages, including in 2008, when he threatened retaliation for the deaths of Palestinians at the hands of Israeli forces, in the Gaza Strip. In 2009, he challenged the nerve of the newly-elected US President, Barack Obama, to continue the fight against al-Qaeda.

Meanwhile, US forces had continued to hunt for bin Laden, who was still thought to be hiding either in the mountains of Afghanistan, or in the tribal regions of Pakistan, near the border with Afghanistan. US intelligence eventually located him in Pakistan, living in a secure compound in Abbottabad, a medium-sized city near Islamabad. On May 2nd, 2011, bin Laden was apparently killed when a small group of US special forces, transported by helicopters, raided the compound in the middle of the night. His body, "identified visually" at the site of the raid, was taken out of Pakistan by the US forces, for examination and DNA identification, and soon after he was given a sea burial.

Why wasn't his body taken back to the United States? Hours after its confirmation, bin Laden's death was announced by Obama in a televised address. Several days after Obama's announcement, al-Qaeda supposedly released a statement publicly acknowledging bin Laden's death, and vowing revenge. Later that month, a final audio message, said to be from bin Laden, purportedly recorded by him shortly before he was killed, was circulated on the internet. In the message, bin Laden praised the Tunisian and Egyptian uprisings of early 2011, and called on al-Qaeda followers around the world to help people struggling against oppressive and unjust governments.

From the extensive research I had done, I discovered a number of unanswered questions and anomalies regarding the events of 9/11. What really caused the twin towers to collapse? Credible scientific and engineering voices believe that the impact of commercial planes, even those fully loaded with fuel, could not alone have caused both of the towers to collapse. Could it be that the towers fell because of explosives which were planted at strategic spots, in both buildings, and that the plane impacts covered up this fact? If that's the case, who placed the explosives in the buildings, and why?

In September 2021, US President Joe Biden ordered the release of previously classified files from the investigation into the 9/11 attacks; many of them detailing connections between the Saudi government and the hijackers. We already know that there were substantial contacts between Saudi spies and the 9/11 hijackers, 15 of whom were Saudis. One Saudi spy named Omar al-Bayoumi met two of the future hijackers, as they arrived off the plane at Los Angeles International Airport in January 2000, arranged for them to be put up in a flat for which he signed the lease and paid the rent, and regularly checked in on them. Why was a Saudi government official paying the rent of two 9/11 hijackers?

Exposing further links between the Saudi government and the hijackers strengthens already plausible claims that the Saudis were deeply implicated in the events of 9/11. We already know that there were extensive links between the Bush family, the Saudi royal family, and the bin Laden family. These connections were so strong that the bin Laden's had substantial investments in a corporation called the Carlyle

Group, on whose board sat former president George HW Bush, the elder. Incredibly, as the 9/11 attacks began, Osama bin Laden's brother, Shafiq bin Laden, was at a Carlyle sponsored business conference, that George HW Bush had attended the previous day. The families knew each other well, and had mutual business dealings in the oil and construction industries.

With regard the hijackers themselves, there were a number of odd inconsistencies. As we have seen, most of them were Saudis. Their spoken English was poor. Prior to the attacks, many of them behaved in ways which one would not expect from devout jihadists, prepared to give their lives for Islam; including snorting cocaine, drinking excessive alcohol, engaging in gambling, and visiting strip clubs. These were very unusual Muslim fundamentalists who somehow managed to pull off a daring raid, with military precision. The pilots themselves were woefully unqualified.

Hani Hanjour, who was said to have carried out a brilliant technical manoeuvre in piloting a commercial plane into the side of the Pentagon, was unable to control a single-engine Cessna 172, just a few months before 9/11. An Arizona flight school instructor who dealt with Hanjour said: "He could not fly at all." They had dreadful flying records. Many people don't realise that there was a fifth plane that was due to have been hijacked. On the morning of 9/11, United Flight 23 was delayed on the tarmac, so it missed the crucial airborne commencement of the attacks, and was returned to the terminal, instead of taking off. During the taxiing of the plane back, a number of Middle Eastern men in first class became extremely agitated, and fled the airport the moment they disembarked. The two pilots had already taken precautionary steps to protect the cockpit.

As Air Force One flew back to Washington from Florida, Vice President Dick Chaney told President George W Bush that a threat had been made to the president's plane; one that contained top-secret code words, and was therefore being assessed as highly credible. The pilot of Air Force One, Colonel Mark Tillman, was told of the threat, and an armed guard was posted at the door of the cockpit. This threat was instrumental in Bush being kept on an itinerant journey across America until nightfall on September 11; but it has never been fully explained how at the precise moment of the attacks, someone with access to top-secret codes made a credible threat to the life of the president. Was this threat made by a rogue group within the CIA or Pentagon?

The streets of New York City were swarming with television news crews on 9/11, many of them interviewing people about their terrifying experiences at the World Trade Center. There was an eerie consistency to the stories being told – firefighters, police officers, reporters, and civilians, repeatedly said that there had been "secondary explosions" going off throughout the towers, prior to their collapse. At least 118 eyewitness reports spoke of these explosions, yet the vast majority of this testimony was ignored.

A third building fell in New York on 9/11. Tower Seven of the World Trade Center was 47 stories high, and fell around seven hours after the horrific plane attacks. Strangely, the building's collapse was announced on several TV networks, minutes before it actually happened. The building fell suddenly, at a freefall speed, and in such a straight line downward that almost all of the rubble collected in the footprint of the building. This is what you would expect to see in a controlled demolition implosion. Officially, the reason given for the building collapsing was because of fires ignited by the earlier attacks; but this would make it the only steel-framed building in history to collapse because of fire.

In addition to these events, there were a bunch of other suspicious things going on that day. War games, including ones that normally took place at other times of the year, but in 2001 all centred around September 11, confused air traffic controllers, who responded to the hijackings by asking: "Is this real-world or an exercise?"

There was disturbing inaction by those at the highest level of government. When first told of the second plane hitting the tower, President Bush, who was attending a primary school in Florida, continued on with his story-reading activity with the students for a further 30 minutes, as if nothing of great importance had happened. When the two most senior defence officials in the American government – Donald Rumsfeld and Paul Wolfowitz – saw the second plane attack, they simply continued on with their scheduled meeting, and didn't take any immediate action.

Many have forgotten the spate of anthrax attacks that occurred in the immediate aftermath of 9/11, which took seven years to explain, and were finally blamed on a deceased man. Were the anthrax attacks designed to escalate the climate of fear after the attacks, in order to allow for the easy passage of the government's repressive Patriot Act? The Patriot Act was presented to Congress in the days after the tragedy, supposedly as a response to it; yet it clearly had been drafted long before the 9/11 attacks.

In Washington, Air Force pilots demanded to fly, but instead were ordered to stand down. Planes that lose contact with control towers, or believed to be hijacked, are usually intercepted by fighter jets within ten minutes, but this never happened on that day. The jetliners that struck the twin towers were allowed to proceed for more than half an hour; and the plane that supposedly crashed into the Pentagon was not intercepted for more than an hour and forty minutes, even though by the time it "struck", it was widely known that four planes had been hijacked. The twin towers could not have collapsed as a result of burning jet fuel. Most of that fuel was consumed on impact. In the south tower, most of the fuel was spilled outside the building. Heat caused by burning jet fuel does not reach temperatures required to melt steel. This is why I couldn't help thinking that explosives had been placed on the structural supports within the towers, enabling controlled implosions to topple the towers.

FBI Director, Robert Mueller, insisted that his officials had no idea this kind of attack could happen, when in fact, the FBI had been investigating the possibility of exactly this kind of attack, for almost ten years. Numerous previous attempts at using planes as weapons, intimate knowledge of terrorist plans called "Project Bojinka", and knowledge of suspicious characters attending flight schools who were being monitored by the FBI, make Mueller's comments difficult to believe. In the weeks before 9/11, the United States received warnings from all over the world that an event just like this was about to happen, but FBI investigations into suspected terrorist activities were suppressed, and those warnings appear to have been deliberately disregarded.

The names of the alleged hijackers, all supposedly Muslims, were released to the public only hours after the attacks, despite the FBI saying they had no knowledge this kind of attack would happen.

What about the attack on the Pentagon? It is difficult to believe that the hole in the Pentagon building was made by a jetliner. Damage to the building was simply not consistent with the size of the hole, nor the absence of debris. At the supposed point of impact, whole rows of windows remained unbroken, and there were no impact marks on the surrounding lawn.

Was the plane in Pennsylvania shot down in mid-air? The wreckage was spread out over a six-mile area, and many eyewitness accounts describe debris falling out of the sky. Also, at that time, cell-phone calls could not be made from airliners in flight, that were not close to the ground.

Then there were the people who made a killing from betting the share prices of American Airlines and United Airlines were going to collapse. Who benefited from the suspiciously high number of put-options in the shares of these companies, purchased just before September 11? What was the role of CIA executive director and former banker, Buzzy Krongard, who handled a significant number of these transactions?

Why was the debris from the collapsed Twin Towers removed from the site, before a comprehensive forensic examination could be carried out? Why was almost all of it sold to scrap merchants, and shipped abroad, where it would not be available for scientific examination? Why does the government refuse to release the transcripts of communications from the four hijacked jets? How and why did so many employees of companies in the World Trade Center who failed to come to work that day, know in advance that something bad was going to happen on September 11, 2001?

What was the connection between 9/11 and Iraq? Obsessed with Iraqi dictator, Saddam Hussein, the Bush administration misled the American public into believing that Iraq was connected to the September 11 attacks. Bruce Riedel is an American expert on US security and counter-terrorism. He is a former CIA analyst, who acted as a key adviser to the Bush administration, on counter-terrorism, particularly relating to the Middle East. He was in the White House immediately after 9/11 on the staff of the National Security Council. He kept a diary where he recorded brief notes on each day's activities.

He met with National Security Adviser Condoleezza Rice every day, and President George W Bush almost as frequently, during that time.

On September 14th, he was with Bush when he had his first phone call after 9/11 with British Prime Minister, Tony Blair. Bush immediately said he was planning to "hit" Iraq soon. Blair was audibly taken aback. He pressed Bush for evidence of Iraq's connection to the 9/11 attack, and to al-Qaida. Of course, there was none, which British intelligence already knew. On September 18th, a week after 9/11, the Saudi Arabian Ambassador, Prince Bandar bin Sultan, came to the White House to see Bush. The meeting took place on the Truman Balcony. Vice President Richard (Dick) Chaney and Rice were there as well.

According to Riedel, who was also present, Bush clearly believed Iraq was behind the 9/11 attack. His questions to Bandar showed his bias. Bandar was visibly perplexed. He told Bush that the Saudis had no evidence of any collaboration between Osama bin Laden and Iraq. Indeed, their history was one of being antagonists. Afterward, Bandar told Riedel privately that the Saudis were very worried about where Bush's obsession with Iraq was going. The Saudis were alarmed that attacking Iraq would only benefit Iran, and set in motion severe destabilising repercussions across the Middle East. The Saudis pressed Bush to come out publicly in support of a Palestinian state, as he had privately promised Crown Prince Abdullah Al Saud.

On September 28th, Bush was visited by King Abdullah of Jordan. The king pressured the president to take action to restart Israeli-Palestinian peace talks. He argued that the Palestinian conflict was the driving force behind al-Qaida's popularity and legitimacy in the Middle East and beyond. But the president remained obsessively focused on Iraq. Of course, the United States ultimately invaded Iraq. The Bush administration was eager to mobilise the anguish of the 9/11 attack to support the war. Despite the intelligence community's unequivocal conclusion that Iraq had nothing to do with either 9/11 or al-Qaida, the administration let Americans believe the contrary. As a result, the United States went to war in Iraq on a false pretence that it was somehow avenging those killed by al-Qaida. A *Washington Post* poll conducted two years after 9/11 dramatically illustrated the lie: 69% of Americans at the time believed Saddam Hussein was "personally" involved in the 9/11 attack.

Even more disturbing, 82% believed Saddam provided assistance to Osama bin Laden. Both statements were utterly false.

I arrived at the Caffe Vittoria in Boston at 10am local time, on 10th September, 2001. Caffe Vittoria was established in 1929 as the first Italian café in Boston. It is located in the North End, the centre of Boston's extensive Italian community. This café is renowned as having some of the best cappuccino and cannoli in the United States. Cannoli is a cylindrical tube-shaped Italian pastry delicacy, usually filled with either, custard, cream, or ricotta cheese. It was a bright sunny crisp Autumn day. I ordered a cappuccino and ricotta cannoli while I waited for my contacts to arrive. Neither the coffee or pastry was a disappointment.

As the morning sunlight was invigorating me, I savoured the aroma of the cappuccino, while closing my eyes, taking a deep breath, and contemplating the feat I was determined to pull off over the next 24 hours. As I was sitting there, a little girl with a doll walked up to me, and looked at me with her big brown eyes – the same eyes as Isabella. It was as if Isabella was there, pleading with me to forgive her.

'Louisa! Louisa! Come to nonna now', said an elderly Italian woman from another table.

I watched the little girl smile at me, and then run to her grandmother.

I had two contacts for this mission; both were highly trained ex-marines, selected by Otto for their reliability, combat-martial arts training (just in case), and the ability to hold their nerve under pressure.

Just as I was finishing my cappuccino, they arrived.

'Hey, you must be Luca Evangelista?'

'Sure am.'

'I'm Dave, and this is Pete.'

'Great to meet you both. Coffee? Would you like to try cannoli? They're delicious.'

'Just coffee for us.'

'Right guys. Let me explain to you what we're going to be doing tomorrow. I know Otto has briefed you both on the objective of the mission. This is how we're going to pull it off. I'm going to take care of the situation here at Boston's Logan International Airport. Dave, you are going to take care of Washington's Dulles Airport; and Pete, you are going to do the same at New Jersey's Newark International Airport. You'll both drive directly to your destinations this afternoon. Tomorrow morning at 5.50am, each of us will place a phone call to our respective airports. The messages will be exactly the same. We are going to let them know that bombs have been planted throughout the airport, and they will be detonated at set times during the day. To show them we are serious; we're going to throw a grenade into the airport carparks at exactly 6am, making absolutely sure that we don't harm anybody. Being early in the morning, there won't be a lot of cars, so we will be able to avoid harm. Also, the grenades we will be using are of a limited-damage nature. Do you understand?

'So, make the phone call first, then detonate a grenade?'

'Yes, Pete.'

'Now, as soon as you throw the grenades, you will need to get into your rental cars and flee the airport. Then you need to find a discrete bar well away from the airport to hide and lay low.'

'What if they don't evacuate the airports, Luca?'

'Dave, I can assure you, once a grenade goes off in the carpark, they'll start evacuating everybody and will shut down the airport. The purpose of the phone call is to escalate the emergency for them, to the point that they will take our threat very seriously.'

'What about the hijackers? What if they board planes at other airports later in the day, or on later days?

'That's unlikely to happen, Dave. Otto has arranged for a message to be sent to the highest level of the United States government in Washington, and to all US embassies around the world, alerting them of everything we know about the 9/11 –style of attacks, using the hijacking of airplanes as deadly missiles. So hopefully, they will take Otto's message very seriously, and take the necessary precautions in airports around the country, to prevent such an attack-scenario from happening in the future. In any event guys, our mission is only to prevent these particular attacks from happening tomorrow, not subsequent attacks.'

'Okay, lets swing into action then.'

'Right Dave. Good luck guys.'

It was a much needed calm before the storm. I had the afternoon and evening to myself. So I was going to explore the best of Boston, whilst remaining discrete. I set out to walk the streets of this great historic city, including visiting the Freedom Trail, where I saw Kings Chapel, the Old South Meeting House and State House, Paul Revere's House, the USS Constitution, and Boston Common. I then visited Bunker Hill, before spending a couple of leisurely hours walking the campuses of Harvard University and the Massachusetts Institute of Technology.

I have always loved university campuses. As a fourteen-year old, I developed a keen interest in astronomy, buying my first telescope with savings from my vacation work. Then, at that tender age, I joined my local astronomy club, which met on the first Tuesday of each month, at the physics department of the city's major university. I remembered I had to take two buses in the evening, to get there. I was by far the youngest member. But the others looked after me, and I gained valuable knowledge of this great hobby of mine. Eventually I progressed to buying a larger telescope and taking photographs of some spectacular astronomical phenomena, such as the craters of our Moon, the rings of Saturn, the great red storm of Jupiter, and the Andromeda galaxy.

Later that afternoon, before heading to my hotel, I took a train to the outer suburb of Brookline, to visit the birthplace and childhood home of JFK. The house is at 83 Beals Street in the Coolidge Corner neighbourhood of Brookline. The property is now owned by the National Park Service, after being designated a National Historical Landmark in 1964, and a National Historic Site in 1967. Having saved JFK's life, this visit was particularly poignant for me.

That night, I stayed at Omni Park House, the longest continuing operating hotel in the United States. Founded by Harvey D. Parker in 1855, it was here where the brightest lights of America's golden age of literature – writers like Emerson, Thoreau, Hawthorne, and Longfellow – regularly met for intellectually stimulating conversation in the legendary nineteenth-century Saturday Club. It was also at this hotel where great Americans like Babe Ruth, Ulysses S. Grant, Franklin Delano Roosevelt, John F. Kennedy, Colin Powell, and Bill Clinton, assembled for private meetings, press conferences, and power breakfasts.

After a steak and mashed potatoes dinner at the hotel restaurant, I made my way into the streets of Boston, dropping into a blues bar, and then later, a jazz club. Mesmerised by the beautiful voice of a young singer doing perfect renditions of Ella Fitzgerald numbers, I sat at the rear of the lounge, on a comfortable couch, gin and tonic in hand, thinking about Isabella. I knew I needed to see her when I got back. She had made a mistake. She was deeply in love with me. As I was, with her. As broken and fragile as she was, I needed her in my life. She was now almost certainly carrying my child. Anyhow, did it really matter who the father of the baby was? All that mattered was we loved each other. Isabella had tremendous talent, as an actress, and as a soul-jazz singer. It just needed to be nurtured. She needed to be nurtured. By me. Many times before Otto had come into my life, Isabella and I had discussed packing up everything and moving to Los Angeles, where I would take care of her, and manage her creative talent. Help her fulfil her dreams. That's how much I loved her. I was prepared to sacrifice my ambitions, for hers.

I woke up at sunrise the next morning – September 11, 2001. After a simple bacon and eggs breakfast, with coffee, I called Dave and Pete. Thankfully, they were both up, prepared, and ready to swing into action. The grenade was in the trunk of my car, carefully packaged in a small wooden box to ensure it wouldn't go off. I made my way towards Boston's Logan airport. After securing a secluded position in the airport carpark, I dialled the number of airport management, on my cell-phone.

'Hello? Is this airport management?'

'You are speaking to Bill McDonald. I am the operations manager of the airport. How can I help you, sir?'

'We have planted bombs throughout your airport. They are timed to go off during the day. This is not a hoax. I repeat, we have bombs which will go off. You have 45 minutes to clear the airport.'

I then promptly ended the conversation, opened the door of my rental car, exited the car, lifted up the trunk, carefully took the grenade components out of the wooden box, delicately assembled it into detonation mode, and then hurtled the grenade into an area of the car park that contained 6 vacant cars, and no sign of anybody nearby. As the grenade exploded, there was an extremely loud bang accompanied by a shaking of the ground. I jumped into my car and drove off, as far away from the airport as I could.

'Have you spoken to airport management and then detonated your grenade, Pete?'

'Yes sir. Job done.'

'Good.'

Then I called Dave, who also confirmed he had completed the job.

Now, all there was to do was lay very low, and watch the events of the day unfold. I found a sports bar in downtown Boston that was full of TV screens, and their gin and tonic wasn't bad either. Soon after I settled into a secluded booth at the rear of the bar, TV right in front of me, above; the news flashes started.

'We interrupt this program for a special announcement from our newsroom. Simultaneous explosions occurred at exactly 6am this morning, in the carparks at Logan International Airport here in Boston, Dulles International Airport just outside Washington DC, and Newark Liberty International Airport in New Jersey. The latest reports are no casualties, and only damage to vacant cars in each of the airports. The airports have been evacuated and temporarily closed, as the FBI investigates, and security personnel scour the three airports for any bombs. All flights in and out of the three airports have been cancelled until further notice.'

So far, so good. I had a few hours to kill. I couldn't leave the bar. I didn't know if anybody had seen me in and around the airport. So, I kept the rounds of gin and tonic coming. All of the televisions were now transmitting the events unfolding live, at the three airports. It was mainly talking heads, literally killing time, analysing every minute nook and cranny, constantly repeating what happened, while waiting for fresh news to emerge. Suddenly, I saw a familiar face enter the bar. A very familiar and unwelcome face. What did he want? It was Thero, and he was walking ominously straight towards me. He then sat opposite me in the booth.

'What the hell are you doing here, Thero? It's too late, man. I have stopped the hijackers from carrying out the attacks.'

'You may have stopped the hijackers, but not the attacks.'

'Are you crazy? What are you talking about?'

'Look up at the television, Luca Evangelista.'

He had this god-awful mischievous grin, I couldn't believe this guy. He was an evil villain straight out of central casting.

'We need to interrupt you, sir, something has happened in New York City. We are going live to our sister station in New York City, so viewers can see the situation down there.'

I was absolutely stunned. It was worse than a nightmare. Was it a nightmare? I wished it was, so I could snap out of it. But it wasn't. There, on the television screen, was one of the buildings of the World Trade Center, smouldering with fire and smoke, after being struck by a jet airplane.

'We don't know what happened. It seems like a plane has accidently struck the tower. Oh My God!! A second plane has just struck the other tower! This is not an accident. It is a deliberate attack. America is under attack!'

The horrific vision that was now unfolding in front of my eyes, was a precise duplication of what happened originally on 9-11, except it was happening at around 11am, not 9am.

'You have failed, Luca Evangelista. Not only have you failed in this mission. But you have also failed to change the future course of your planet.'

'How could this have happened, Thero? I stopped the hijackers. Who was behind this attack?

As the words came out of my mouth, a sickening thought struck me like a bolt of lightning.

'Was this attack carried out by a rogue group within the American government, or military-intelligence?'

'You are such a weak, feeble-minded, man. You failed! Do you understand? You failed miserably. There are very powerful forces on your planet. These people don't need wormhole technology to change history. They control 90% of the world's wealth. These families have been at the apex of global power, for centuries. Starting wars. Making peace. Manipulating the global economy and stock markets. Controlling media. Creating pandemics. Culling the world's population. Enslaving people with distractions such as home mortgages, celebrity worship, social media, and big sporting events. Anointing kings, presidents, and prime ministers. Fabricating existential crises such as global warming. And all the time, these people are the real winners. Accumulating incomprehensibly vast wealth. They are the Elite 300. The 300 most powerful families in the world, Luca Evangelista.'

'Jesus Christ! Are you kidding me!? Are you telling me the world is controlled by 300 families? That this is not a far-fetched conspiracy theory?'

Thero quietly got up, and just walked out, without saying another word.

Back in the 21st century, and at the bar, I needed answers from Otto.

'What the hell happened, Otto!!?'

'Believe me, Luca, I had no idea of the existence and power of this Elite 300. But, I have done some research and have some information for you. I have found out that Thero sowed the seeds for the creation of this highly secretive and very influential group, by initiating meetings with the Rothschild family, back in the 18th century. They are the most famous European banking dynasty, and have had a major influence in Europe and beyond, during the 19th, 20th, and into the 21st century, Luca. I also know they developed very strong and close ties with the Rockefeller family of the United States, who also have accumulated enormous wealth, power, and influence. It is here, that the foundations of the Elite 300 were laid, and it is now clear that Thero played an instrumental role in the creation of this group.'

I was stunned. My head was spinning. I felt gutted. I failed to stop the dreadful future of planet Earth. I was about to go into a tailspin of emotional turmoil. I knew it then and there. I could feel it more than anything else I had ever felt in my life. I couldn't possibly get back with Isabella. I had to hunt down the Elite 300, and stop them from taking complete control of the world.

Against All Odds
(Take A Look At Me Now)

How can I just let you walk away, just let you leave without a trace
When I stand here taking every breath with you, ooh
You're the only one who really knew me at all

How can you just walk away from me,
When all I can do is watch you leave
Cause we've shared the laughter and the pain and even shared the tears
You're the only one who really knew me at all

So take a look at me now, oh there's just an empty space
And there's nothing left here to remind me,
Just the memory of your face
Ooh take a look at me now, well there's just an empty space
And you coming back to me is against the odds and that's what
I've got to face

I wish I could just make you turn around,
Turn around and see me cry
There's so much I need to say to you,
So many reasons why
You're the only one who really knew me at all

So take a look at me now, well there's just an empty space
And there's nothing left here to remind me, just the memory
of your face
Now take a look at me now, cause there's just an empty space

But to wait for you, is all I can do and that's what I've got to face
Take a good look at me now, cause I'll be standing here
And you coming back to me is against all odds
It's the chance I've gotta take

Take a look at me now

Phillip David Charles Collins (1981)

Printed in Great Britain
by Amazon

79924719R00278